Blizzard Lights
The Dominion Falls Series 9

Sarah Cass

Historical Romance
Romantic Suspense
Historical Western Romance

A Divine Roses Ink Book
Historical Romance
Romantic Suspense
Historical Western Romance

Copyright © 2023 Sarah Cass
First publication: February 2024

Cover design by Sarah Cass
Edited by Annie Farrell
Proofread by Mary Terrani
All cover art and logo copyright © 2013 by Sarah Cass

PUBLISHER
Divine Roses Ink
http://www.divinerosesink.com

Other Books in
The Dominion Falls Series

Independent Brake
Changing Tracks
Derailed
Dark Territory
Green Eye
Runaway Train
Home Signal
Red Zone
Dust Raiser
Chasing the Red

Coming Soon in
The Dominion Falls Series

Dead Man's Switch
Bird Cage
A Highball Arrangement
Douse the Glim
Blood
Grave Digger
Bad Order

Books by Sarah Cass
The Tribe Series
The Tribe
The Wolf
The Chief
The Raven
The Lake Point Series
Santa, Maybe
Deep-Fried Sweethearts
Stalled Independence
Witch Way
A Thorough Thanksgiving
Eve's New Year
Heartstrings & Hockey Pucks
Luck of the Cowgirl
Stars, Stripes & Motorbikes
Free Falling
Love for Hire
Haunted Hearts
Stand Alone Novels
Masked Hearts
Leap

Dedication

Loss is never easy,
Loss is often unexpected,
To those who have lost ones close to them,
Who feel the sting days, and years after,
I wish you peace and love.

Table of Contents

Cease to ask what the morrow will bring forth. And set down as gain each day that Fortune grants.
—Horace

Jane closed the ledger with a firm snap. Lucky for her, Cole was exceedingly careful in his running of their money. Nothing was out of order, and everything easy enough to follow that she felt certain she could manage them for the few weeks, at most, he'd be gone.

After the news of his father's passing, they'd discussed for some time what to do. In the end, they agreed he'd go to find out what the lawyer was talking about, and so he could see for himself that the man had died.

He'd gone to tell Leanne afterwards. Even though she'd had less interaction with their shared father, she had a right to know. She'd gone to the depot to purchase his ticket because she knew he'd waver on whether or not to leave. He had plenty of arguments to stay, but she knew this was something he'd have to do.

However, he'd been gone for nearly two hours, and she wasn't sure what was taking so long. She locked the ledger in the drawer and rose. The train would be arriving soon, with the Youngs on it. At the moment she wasn't feeling much like a Young. The woman she'd once been, Clara Young, had at times seemed very close to the surface of her memory indeed, at others she was nowhere to be found.

At the moment, what with the recent miscarriage, Michael's arrest, and the imminent departure of Cole, she was too busy mourning her own life to worry about the past she'd long since forgotten. Cole's past was far too present for her own to bring much turmoil to her mind.

The door flew open, two hounds bounding in ahead of the man she'd just been thinking of. Cole's rich voice called after the beasts, "Whiskey. Bourbon. Sit."

Surprisingly, the pair of pups sat on command. They still seemed too young for such obedience, but Cole had proven as adept at training them as he was with horses. Seeing as he hadn't spotted her yet, Jane remained silent to watch the interaction.

"To the stove to dry off, you beasts." He pointed to the stove in the corner. That's when he spotted her. Instead of the customary sly grin he normally granted her, he only managed a grimace.

She eyed the dogs as they went to the stove as commanded. Rather than lie down, they started wrestling. When she turned back, Cole still hadn't managed to find his smile. "Hello to you, too. What is it now?"

"I'm not going."

"Of course you are. You said as much, we agreed to it together." Jane pulled open a draw in the desk.

"I can't. Your brother, the casino, the saloon." He moved closer. "We just lost a baby."

"I'm well aware of all of those factors, seeing as I live, work, and love with you." Rather than pull the ticket from the drawer, she turned to face him dead on. "We will not continue to go in circles ad nauseum."

"It ain't right to be leaving. He weren't worth nothing, there's nothing to be done."

She frowned as she thought of the telegram from the lawyer in California informing Cole of his long-despised pa's passing. Why a lawyer would reach out about the estate of a man that was, by all accounts, a worthless bastard, was confusing. Still, there was one small possibility to be considered. "You've changed a lot in the years since you left California. Perhaps he changed, too. There may be something to deal with. Possibly another family."

Cole's entire visage turned fierce at that suggestion. "Then I'm definitely not going."

She pulled the ticket from the drawer she'd opened and handed it to him. "You are. One week from today. If all is as expected, and there's nothing to deal with, you will return home well before Christmas. If there is something there, then you should still return before Christmas."

He stared at the ticket, his features pale. "When did you do this?"

"While you were talking to Leanne, I assume." She slid her arms around his waist and pressed her body to his. Since before they'd been together this action had always served to distract him thoroughly. Thankfully even in his current state it still proved true. His features softened. "You were struggling with the choice, even after our discussion. I bought the ticket because you'd never be settled unless you went to see for yourself. I only wish it was possible for me to go with you, but one of us should remain here to see to the businesses and children."

"I can't leave you. Not now."

Tears burned her eyes at the mere thought of his leaving. She refused to let them fall and give him more excuse to remain. "I wish you didn't have to. Or that I could go with you. I will miss you with everything that I am, but you must confront this. Much as I ever had to confront what Clara did."

His forehead pressed to hers. Voice thick with emotion, his words emerged rough, "I can't. I wanted to forget, and I done a good job of it."

"You must face the ghosts of your past or they'll haunt you forever."

"I ain't the man I was."

"You aren't," she agreed quietly. "You're all the better for it, too. None of that means you can ignore this."

"We're still…we just…the baby."

"We are mourning, and yet we're still living. I will not be alone, and I wish to God you didn't have to be for this. If anyone could go with you—"

"There ain't no one I would trust to but you."

"Leanne."

"No," the vehement anger in his tone nearly pushed her away from him. "She's free."

"I'm guessing she offered anyway."

"I said no. He weren't ever a pa to her anyhow."

"No, he wasn't. You took that role for her." Jane rubbed her hands along his back in a vain attempt to soothe away the tension. "And for Alma. What of Tom?"

"Your brother's gotta stay here for Mikey."

"Then Mr. Hamm."

He chuckled low, as she'd hoped he would. "Don't think that old coot would make the trip. He's only got a few miles left on him."

"Fair enough." She did her best to smile up at him, folding her hands in his.

"I gotta go."

"I know."

"I don't like leaving you alone."

"You are the one that will be alone. I will have far too many people around. The children, my friends, and every single one of the Young's who will not let me suffer one moment on my own, even if I wish it." She frowned. "Clara's parents are going to fuss over me."

"That's what parents do. You fuss over the kids."

"I do not."

"Do too."

She pursed her lips rather than argue further. "Either way, there will be fussing. I'm only beginning to feel like myself again. Fussing will bring me back to it."

"You haven't stopped feeling it." He searched her gaze quietly. "They might help make it better. You know your ma lost a few kids herself."

"Misery does not require company. You and I might share in it on late nights, but I have children and businesses to tend to. I don't wish to discuss it ad nauseum."

"Your ma is a smart woman, and she knows you. Doubt it'll be like that."

"Your lips to God's ears."

He smirked. "You know he doesn't have much to do with me."

"Oh, I tend to disagree. Look at all we have. None of that is without a fair dose of God's grace in our lives." The reality of his departure cut through her again so quick, she dropped her head to his chest rather than let him see the turmoil. "And we must continue to request his grace seeing as we're about to be parted again."

"Leastwise this time it isn't your past doing it."

"That is a turn of circumstance to be sure." She chuckled softly, able to lift her head without tears again. "One I don't mind, although the fact it's yours is burning you up inside."

"I left my ghosts behind."

"No, you didn't. They're in a trunk in the closet right now. You never erased them, and you wouldn't ever. It's not who you are."

"They're a distant memory now." He pressed his forehead to hers. "The life I got now is enough. I don't like going back there, although it'd be good to see that he is dead and gone."

She let him draw her close without argument. "It will be a short trip, and then you'll be home. With all of us eagerly awaiting your return."

"That's the best part. You, eager."

Warmth spread across her cheeks. "I didn't just mean me, Mr. Mitchell."

"I did, Mrs. Mitchell."

She laughed softly. "Well, I won't let you miss me too much. I'll write you every day. Letters and telegrams so you won't be bored or in want of something to read."

"Don't you go sending Leaves of Grass. That'll make it more lonely."

"We could read at the same time very night, it would be like we were together."

"You get grumpy when you're unsatisfied."

"Quite true." She popped onto tiptoe to kiss him gently. "When you return, we will discuss trying again for another baby."

"Sure you want to risk it again?"

"Once more. Success or failure, we'll not try again."

"I almost lost you this time."

"You'll never lose me. So long as you are mine, I will never be lost."

"I'm gonna be lost without you knocking sense into me."

She smiled softly at his attempt at humor. "I wouldn't worry too much. You'll have my nagging in your head."

"Damn straight."

"Now." She stepped back, but kept her hands in his. "There's still over an hour before we must meet the Young's at the train."

"Is that so?"

"It is." She released his hands to step close again. She let her hands slink down his back until they ran over his firm ass. "Perhaps we should use it to relax you."

"You don't play fair."

"I know."

It is best to love wisely, no doubt;
but to love foolishly is better
than not to be able to love at all.
-William Makepeace Thackery

Cole didn't move from the bed while Jane bustled about the room gathering clothes. He still had it in mind to convince her to stay right where they were. The second she drew close he snatched her wrist to pull her back to the bed. "We still got time."

Pink flooded her cheeks in a sexy little acknowledgment of how much she'd like it. She laughed softly. "No, we don't. You greedy man."

"Always greedy when it comes to you." He tugged her flush on top of him. "You're just as greedy. Don't you dare deny it."

"Never." The word emerged breathless, her lips mere centimeters from his. Her kiss came moments after, laced with fire and need he wasn't about to deny. When he reached for her she grabbed his hands to pin above his head.

Her lips left a trail of fire along his neck, then his chest. The delicate hands that had pinned him slipped along his flesh. Scratching, teasing, pleasing.

Moments before her mouth would have sent him into new waves of pleasure, she disappeared. Cole groaned at her absence. By the time his head wrapped around the loss enough for him to open his eyes she had on her chemise and a wicked grin. "Evil woman."

"I'll make it up to you later. That's a promise."

"Evil."

"You didn't think so an hour ago." Her swollen pink lips curved into a sexy smirk. She wrapped her corset around her still swollen waistline. When she tightened the strings, she winced.

He sat at the sight. Once again his concern bubbled forth over her state. Though as a whole she was much improved from only a couple days ago, sometimes the small things would set her off. Heaven knew they had enough big things going on that she didn't need the small moments messing things up. "You good?"

Her brow furrowed in frustration as she tied off the strings. Her fingers danced along the surprisingly wide strip between her laces. "I cannot seem to make this damnable thing comfortable. Last time I was able to get back into my corset within a week."

"Last time you were shedding weight because of all you were going through." He grimaced at the look she tossed him. She was going through plenty this time around, he knew. Still, there were things that were different. "You were thin as anything when you went to see if it was Starbird that shot you.

This time you got me, and Kathy and Leanne and Cora. Didn't have much but Kathy the first time."

She dropped her hands, offering him a sweet, if watery, smile. "It's of no matter. This time I'm rather happily involved with the man I love rather than pining for him and our child both at once. You're right. Still…"

"It'll be back in no time."

"I suppose it will. Now."

At the flick of her hand, he glanced at the clothes she'd tossed on the end of the bed. His clothes for meeting the train. "Don't wanna. We've only got a week."

"I told you I would make it up to you tonight. For now, we must go meet Clara's parents."

"We're Clara's parents, so come here and meet me."

"I don't mean our daughter, and you know it."

He grabbed his trousers, mulling over what she'd said. "They're not your parents today?"

"Apparently not. It goes without saying that I will greet them as such, but right now Clara is quite far away, nearly nonexistent. It leaves me feeling a mite disconnected."

"That so?" He'd been around Jane long enough to know that she usually felt most disconnected from her kin when she was at her most stressed. For the most part she was happy to call Clara's family her own, but when she didn't that was a sign of trouble. Maybe it wasn't a good idea to leave. Hell, he knew it wasn't. Jane needed him too much right then.

"Don't even think about it." She buttoned her bodice, a frown firmly in place.

"What?" He didn't like being accused of something he hadn't done, or said. The look she gave him told him she had a good idea. Hell, she knew him well as he knew her. She probably did.

"You're leaving in a week. End of story." Two sentences, and she confirmed she'd guessed right. She turned away to fix her hair, only to give up and pin a hat over the stray curls. "My not feeling much like a Young makes no difference in the matter."

"You need me."

"I always need you. That will never change whether you are here, or you're away. I have more than enough people around me annoyingly ready to give support when it's needed."

"Should be me."

"You have more important things to do."

"Nothing is more important than you!" Cole shoved his arms in his sleeves so rough he heard a seam rip. With his back to her, he buttoned it up quick as he could.

"I know." Her arms slipped around his waist. She squeezed him in a gentle hug, her cheek resting on his back. "And I love you for believing it. Even more for living it every day. It still changes nothing."

Every time he thought about returning to Holle Creek, he thought he'd get ill. Anger coursed through his veins with a vengeance until he wanted to hit something. Too many bad memories lingered in those streets to his way of thinking.

The pa that went and married someone else behind his ma's back. The same man that had wanted to kill Alma for being different, forcing Cole to rescue the whole family with what little savings he had, and then again when their ma died.

Then there was Ella, and Lydia. When he closed his eyes he could still see their crosses side by side in the cemetery the night he left. Too much pain had happened there. Pain he didn't want to revisit. Going back would be a fool's errand.

"My ghosts are all gone, but yours remain." Her hands laced with his. The gentle touch, along with the tender note in her voice served to help calm him some. "You'll never be rid of them if you don't face them."

"I was doing fine before that telegram."

"I know, but we both know it was always there. To this day you don't claim either of your sisters, though you treat them like they are."

"Too much bad back there."

"You faced down a literal maniac when it was time to deal with my past. All of yours are dead and buried. Do you not see the disparity?"

Anyone else he could tell that the past was best forgotten. Jane was living proof of the opposite, and would call him on it in a heartbeat. "How often are we going to have this argument?"

"Several times a day, most likely." She brushed her hands long his back as though smoothing wrinkles in his shirt. "Get your vest and tie on, we need to head to the station."

Only because of her nerves did he comply immediately. By the time she was ready, she had the door to their room open. He rushed to her side, setting a hand on her waist even as he closed the door behind them. They paused to throw on coats against the biting wind. He let out a sharp whistle to call the dogs, who followed him back to their run. Soon as he'd locked them in, he and Jane rushed toward the depot.

Already the train whistle bellowed its closeness to town, so they would be cutting it fine indeed. When they hopped onto the platform, the three brothers not in jail were gathered near a bench to await the train, along with Sally. Jane had mentioned that due to the winds she'd requested Alma keep the children warm in the kitchens with Cora.

Jane didn't rush toward her brothers as she normally would have, instead she hovered closer to Cole. He gave her hand a quick, reassuring squeeze before stepping toward Tom's greeting. He spoke low under the next whistle. "She's not feeling much like a Young today."

Tom spared Jane a quick glance before nodding. "I can see that. Always gets nervous when Ma and Pa visit. Easier to think of them in the abstract and in letters than in reality."

"It's when she feels most like she's stuck in between," Cole agreed.

Charlie shook his head. "Should be when she feels least like it."

"You can't tell her when and how she's supposed to feel things." Nick's stoic expression broke with a glare. "She's got a right."

"Tell me when, exactly, you became Clara's biggest defender?" Charlie smirked at Nick. "You're usually the first to string her up."

"Not funny." Cole tensed at the turn of phrase. His worst memory until Jane might have been Ella's death, but Jane's death now gave him the most nightmares. For that matter, it gave Jane even more than it gave him. Just the memory had him reaching for the woman herself.

Thankfully she didn't leave him disappointed. Her fingers laced into his easily. She allowed him to tug her close to his side. With a nod to her brothers and Sally, her gaze fell on the approaching engine. "I imagine they'll want to see him straight away."

"Knowing Ma, she'll want to give her former son-in-law a piece of her mind as well," muttered Tom. Her former son-in-law, of course, being David Schaffer, the town's Sheriff. The man had been the one to put Mike behind bars. For that matter, Jane still wasn't talking to the man she'd once considered among her dearest friends, even if he was her ex-husband.

"As well she should. Heaven knows he isn't listening to me. Or you." Her hand clutched Cole's as the passengers disembarked. "I shall reassure them we'll get their things to the Inn and let them take care of matters."

"Jane." Nick extended a hand toward her. When she took it, he guided her away from the group. With the ensuing chaos of disembarking passengers and hissing brakes, Cole hadn't the slightest idea what Nick was saying to her.

Charlie hadn't been wrong. Nick's relationship with Jane had been the rockiest of all of her siblings. For years he'd carried a deep wound from the way his sister had left their lives and pushed his anger and mistrust onto Jane. Only in the past year had they made real headway in closeness.

Then the Young's approached, with their oldest child James in tow. He'd been in Dominion Falls only a few months before with his wife for the statehood celebration. This time his wife hadn't accompanied him. It appeared the Young's were planning to make an entirely united front for Mike.

Hugs were exchanged all around him, and before he knew it Jane was in the group as well. Though her smile wasn't as bright as he knew it could be, it seemed genuine enough. When Jane's ma turned to him, he extended his hand. "Eunice. Good to see you again."

"Oh, please." Eunice Young swept him into a brisk, strong hug. "Why do you keep forgetting we're family? No matter if it's Jane now, she's still our daughter. You may not have married her, but you're still family."

Cole chuckled softly, because he and Jane were actually married, not that any but a handful of others knew that fact. Rather than let her delve too deep into the reason for his laughter, he turned it into her repeated words. "I'm gonna make ya say that to me every time."

"Don't you worry, I will say it until it sticks." Eunice turned toward Nick, scolding him about something or other.

Jane's pa extended his hand in Eunice's departure. "Cole."

"John. Good to see you again. Sorry it's under these circumstances."

"No more than we are." John released his grip as Jane drew near. "We were sorry to hear your news as well, Jane."

Jane's head lowered at the reminder of the baby. "Thank you. Now, I assume you wish to see Michael immediately."

"Of course we do." Eunice gathered her boys close. The woman had been raised in the society of Buffalo, and carried herself with the grace of any elite on the hill of Dominion Falls. Marriage had made her a farmer's wife, though, and she was boisterous and fun when the call came for it. Smart as a whip, and hilarious to boot. Jane resembled her ma closely, even if she sometimes didn't want to admit it. "Lead the way."

Jane laced her arm through Cole's, then her other arm through her father's as they headed for the jailhouse. Cole leaned close, glad he was on her left side instead of her right where her ear was nearly completely deaf. "What did Nick say?"

"Reminded me they love me, too. Not just her." She gave him a soft smile.

"Who wouldn't?"

We bear the world and we make it.
There was never a great man
who had not a great mother –
it is hardly an exaggeration.
–Olive Schreiner

Jane leaned on the doorframe of the jail. On a normal day she enjoyed being around people, that day had been rough. Most of the days lately had been like that. Aches in her bones had her leaning toward sleep, but the day was far from over.

The cell door stood open for the family. David had made a respectful departure up the stairs after an impressive scolding from Eunice. She now sat in the cell with her son and husband. Sally remained just inside the cell doors, perhaps listening to see if Mike had remembered anything new to aid the investigation. James, who it turned out was a lawyer as well, and Nicholas huddled in discussion at the desk.

Cole and Tom were off to the side enmeshed in their own quiet conversation she suspected had nothing to do with Mike. Especially with the glances they each kept tossing her way. When Cole's eyes met with hers again, she offered a small smile and nod.

She ducked away from the scene inside to stand on the porch. The position of the building behind her blessedly protected her from the worst of the biting wind as it whipped through town. Clouds on the horizon hinted at a fresh snowfall if the wind didn't send them right off over the mountains again.

"Ma?"

Jane turned to find Sally creeping toward her position at the porch railing. "I thought you were listening for any clues."

"They've moved past what happened, mostly. It's words of comfort and some reminiscing of good times now." Sally's gaze swept over Jane. "How are you?"

"Tired. It's been a long couple of weeks." Jane smiled bright as she could before turning back to the street. "I should return soon and relieve Ada of her duties. Our apartment will be quite full tonight, I believe."

"Seems like it. I think I heard Jesse say Cindy and Lizzie were coming over, too." Sally leaned on the railing beside her. "What's got you and Pa upset?"

"Your powers of observation are growing."

"They were already pretty good being around you."

"Flattery so late in the day?"

"No. Honesty."

Jane chuckled quietly at that. "Fair enough."

"Are you going to answer?"

"Cole has to leave town for a couple of weeks. We don't expect him gone long, but the timing isn't ideal. Not that it ever is for such matters."

"He's leaving? But Uncle Mike, the baby, and…well, you."

"Unfortunately something has come up that he must attend to. He leaves in a week. I expect him back before Christmas." Jane patted Sally's hand. "I have support, he's the one that will be alone for the trip. Don't worry for us, worry for him."

"Why's he going by himself?"

"With Michael in the situation he's in, there's hardly a soul that could go with him. Cole is capable of handling himself most times."

"Doesn't mean you aren't worried."

"I always worry when we part. Even if he only has to go to Cripple Creek, or Pueblo, or Denver. This is only a slightly longer excursion." She didn't mention the reason he was going was the largest cause of her distress. She worried over what he'd find, or how he'd handle what he found. By all accounts his pa was pretty despicable.

Sally wrapped an arm around Jane's shoulders. Her cheek rested on Jane's shoulder. "Seems to be worrying you more than you say."

"I'll miss him deeply. There's little to be done about the matter, though. He will go, and be home before we know it with how busy the Young's will be keeping us." Jane did her best to put as much cheer in her tone as she could. "Thank you for worrying, though."

"Of course I worry. You're my ma."

"I most certainly am." Jane smiled warmly as they moved a step apart. She noticed Eunice framed in the doorway, a peculiar look on her features. "Ma?"

Eunice shook off whatever had left her in some sort of mood Jane couldn't place. She smiled warmly. "There's two of my girls."

"Hey, Mams." Sally met Eunice's hug. "I'm going to save Ada from the children so you don't have to, Ma. We'll meet you back in the apartment soon as I can pries them from Cora's cookies."

"Thank you for doing that for me. Good luck." Jane waved at her parting ward before meeting Eunice's oncoming hug. "I didn't expect you out so soon."

"I've said my piece to your brother, and the Sheriff. Now I need to see how my child is doing in all of this."

"I don't think—"

"It wasn't a question or a request." Eunice cupped Jane's face in her hands. "We will sit and talk a while. Just the two of us."

Jane knew better than to argue. The woman in front of her had a very determined look in her eye. There'd be no legitimate excuse to be made. "Then let's go to the library. At the apartment we'd be likely to be interrupted by children or the men."

"To the library, then."

They both bent against the wind on the short walk down and across the street to the library. She'd not found anyone to mind the library yet, so she'd had to leave it closed that day. Jane unlocked it quickly and led her mother inside.

While Jane lit a lamp, Eunice was already bustling about near the stove to prepare some tea.

"Ma, you don't have to do that."

"Sit. Rest. Your body went through a lot, even if your stubborn head won't let you continue to rest."

"I laid in bed for three days."

"Three days is nothing. You can't tell me you aren't still feeling it bodily as well as emotionally."

"I…" Jane hesitated to admit the way her body was ignoring the fact of the child no longer being there. She simplified it rather than go into detail. "My body is playing tricks on me."

"That does happen." Eunice sat beside her in the comfy chairs near the stove. The fire now stoked made the corner cozier. "You longed for this child; you were already making plans. Grief plays tricks on us and crops up in the strangest ways and at the strangest times."

Jane didn't think she could bear to speak on it any longer. She grasped for a subject change. "The fact Cole is leaving doesn't help."

"What's this?" Eunice's brows furrowed. "Why is he leaving?"

"He has business to attend to, and it isn't of the sort that can be delayed."

"I doubt that."

"No, it really can't." Jane gazed out the window at the darkening town. "It's something he must do. I'll be fine. I have our family here. He's the one that will be all alone."

Eunice rose to finish preparing their tea. She didn't say anything for several long minutes. When she did speak, her tone was kind. "The timing of his departure—"

"Can't be helped. This isn't something he chose. He received news that must be dealt with." Jane closed her eyes to avoid whatever look her mother cast her way. "Believe me, he wants to avoid this trip, with all his soul. That doesn't mean he is able to."

Eunice remained silent for a few minutes. The clink of spoons in cups and the pouring of the water was the only sound until a warm cup pressed in Jane's hand. "I'm not doubting his commitment, child."

"You wouldn't be the first too, if you were." Jane took a sip of her tea. Thanks partially to their own behavior, the rumors were often tossed around. No matter that they'd been together for years, living together and raising children. Their recent dive into causing a stir with the brothel as well as Patrick's presence would exacerbate such things. "Mostly by our own hand we've certainly inspired much talk."

"Which you do because such rumor annoys you."

"I'd rather the gossip were about me, as I'm secure in where I am, than for it to turn to much darker talk about those undeserving of it."

"You aren't deserving of it, either."

"My track record isn't spotless, but I agree." She turned to face her mother. "Unfortunately in all the years Cole and I have been together, timing is rarely on our side. We almost lost every investment penny before we could rebuild the Inn. It was only a stroke of fortune after the misfortune that brought us another investor. I can only take comfort in his leaving by remembering that as often as bad luck strikes, good fortune does as well."

"I wish he didn't need to."

"As do I, as he does."

"This is a torment one should go through with their partner."

"We didn't the first time. This time, we are. Both of us. In the privacy of our home we deal with the matter and our grief. We have another week before he leaves. Then we shall continue to grieve together, though apart."

"If only it was so easy."

"It never is." Jane sipped her tea. "The added struggle of Michael's troubles have made things quite trying."

"Not to mention your child studying with your brother. I know how nerve-wracking knowing what your child does can be."

"I've long wished for Sally to come into her own, to find the joy and stimulation in life that I have." Jane couldn't stop her grimace. "I'd be lying if the danger of her choice doesn't worry me greatly, though."

"As it always did with me. A gut-wrenching mix of pride and fear is what I existed on when he left to protect the president. When all of my children left. To fight wars, to cross the country." A little twitch of a smile crossed Eunice's lips. "Especially when I set that child up with a good family that she abandoned soon as she could pay her own rent."

Jane blinked, staring at Eunice. "What? I thought Clara went to Utah on her own volition alone. No one has told me of this."

"I imagine you've never asked. It's a detail most of the children don't know or remember because they were off fighting a war. I took you to Utah. I found a good family for you to reside with. You only stayed with them for a month. Soon as you got your first pay, you got a home of your own. It was almost enough to make me come back across the country to get you."

Jane studied her mother quietly. Was it possible the woman knew the secret Tommy had kept for years? That she was aware of the student that had taken advantage of Clara, the reason Clara wanted to go far away? "But you didn't?"

"No. Tommy went to check on her for me. She wasn't happy about that. Threatened to find somewhere else and not tell me." Eunice shook her head. "That child lived to break my heart sometimes. Most of my children did, to be fair. You've all grown into fine people, though."

Jane bit her tongue to avoid pointing out Clara became a different person completely to grow into a fine person. She suspected that would have the effect of breaking the woman's heart with the reminder.

"You'll see as your children continue to grow. They have a unique capability of worrying you and strengthening you."

"I already see it. Almost daily. Even the ones that don't consider me their ma."

"One year is not enough to erase a decade."

"I don't want to erase it. I want to embrace it."

"And that will make all the difference in the end."

"I hope you're right."

Grief can take care of itself,
but to get the full value of joy
you must have someone to divide it with.
—Mark Twain

The apartment was overflowing with people on a normal day. At that moment with all eight of their children, as well as all of the Young's, Cole could hardly breathe for the chaos. At least Jane's nerves seemed to have dissipated in the midst of their kids.

Cole took advantage of a moment of distraction and laughter to slip into the cold night. Over the course of the afternoon snow had fallen thick and deep in the town. The paddock behind the Inn was a thick field of white as deep as the first fence post.

Outside of the peals of laughter coming from inside the apartment, the night sat silent as could be. Cole had a thought to get Alma and bring her out away from the chaos. Then again, the warmest place out here would be the barn, and they still hadn't eased her fear of horses.

He couldn't keep his mind still. The thought that this was how Jane lived all the time crossed his thoughts, and he couldn't help his smile. With the exception of her darkest moments, she was never still for one second. The moment things got quiet, her mind would take off again.

There had to be a way out of leaving. Jane would fight every one of them, but he had a week to convince her that the place he needed to be was here.

He closed his eyes. No, she was right. In order to lay his past to rest for good, he had to go tie up this last loose end. Even if it was the last thing he wanted to do. The timing wouldn't have mattered. Things could have been great without any turmoil and he still wouldn't want to go.

His biggest worry now wasn't going, but Jane's concern over him going alone. No matter what way he searched his mind for a solution to this problem, there wasn't one that would work. The few he would trust to join him couldn't leave. Anyone else, it was too great a risk. It was bad enough that Norman had received the telegram. He took a little comfort knowing it had been Norman at the telegraph when it arrived instead of Kathy. That woman would be full of questions over the content, even if she was supposed to keep mum over private matters.

The laughter from the apartment grew louder for a brief moment, a splash of light from the door crossed over the fresh snow. A figure slipped into the night, closing the door behind them.

If Cole hadn't been intimately familiar with every bit of Jane, he might have mistaken the approaching individual as her. Their height was the same, her coloring, everything but the eyes were so similar to Jane. In the past couple years as their ward, Sally had certainly grown into being every bit Jane's child. The resemblance between the girl approaching him and his wife had become startling, especially knowing they were of no blood relation.

Cole nodded to her when she drew close. "Sally. What are you doing out here?"

"Checking on you." Sally drew her muffler tighter around her neck.

"Sure you weren't trying to escape the noise? It's loud out here, and worse inside."

She laughed softly. "I don't mind that so much. It's nice to be around family."

It didn't take Jane's keen eye to spot the grimace that crossed Sally's features. "You sure about that? You don't look too happy."

"No. It's not that. I just…well, I never thought I'd say something like that."

"Is that so?"

"Yeah. My ma didn't really want me. We had no family nowhere near. If Ma had any, she didn't talk about them." She leaned on the fence, staring into the snow. "Didn't really know what it was like to have a family. Hard to imagine thinking it was nice to be around one."

Sally so rarely spoke of her life before she came to Dominion Falls, Cole didn't quite know how to proceed. Afraid he'd scare the girl off, he held his tongue a moment to consider. When he spoke, he kept his tone low, "Sometimes even when you grew up with a family things happen and ya don't think you want it no more."

"Arthur never understood. He loved his family, his pa and ma. He used to wonder why I'd leave mine."

"Sometimes ya got no choice but to leave. Ain't nothing good about staying. Or…" His mind finished the sentence he didn't dare utter, *or you ruin it yourself.* Before she could question, he shook the thoughts off. "Or bad things happen. Like Jane and what happened to her."

"I suppose."

"Sometimes ya find your family when you're not looking." That's what had happened to him, after all.

"I guess so." She took a deep breath. "I've been thinking."

"Quite a bit from what I can see. You and Tom have been busy."

"Not about that. I mean, yeah, about that too. I mean…I could go with you Pa. Then you wouldn't have to go alone. Ma seems real worried that you're going on this trip by yourself."

"It's good of you to offer."

"It makes sense. I can help with whatever it is."

"It's something I gotta do on my own. If it wasn't, I'd take you up on it, I swear." He draped his arm across her shoulders. "Besides, you and Tom gotta save that fool in jail."

"I can give Tommy my notes."

"Even if ya did, he ain't got your guile." He grinned at her embarrassed flush. "Wanna know a secret?"

"Always."

"Come on." He led her into the stables. "Your ma ain't seen them yet."

"Why are you talking like that?"

"What?"

"You're talking like the miners. Or like you did when I first came to town."

Cole straightened at the accusation. He hadn't even noticed he'd slipped back into it. Without a doubt, Jane likely had. Could be the reason for her frequent sly smiles that day when she talked to him. He put some thought into his next words. "Before your ma, I talked like that all the time. Even growing up. Sometimes it comes right on back without me realizing it."

"Like when you're at the saloon."

"Yeah." He lit a lamp and removed it from its hook. "Come on, back here."

"Is Ma going to be mad?"

"Maybe. Probably. It's the kids Christmas presents." He led her to the backmost stall where two tiny ponies stood. On the left, a small black horse with a white mane and tail. On the right, a deep brown with black mane and tail. "The black is for Clara, the brown for Colton."

"Oh, yeah. Ma is going to kill you." Sally chuckled softly. She bent over to pet the noses of the ponies. "She's still mad about the dogs."

"Not so much. They're training up good." He wished he'd had more time to train them up, leaving meant he'd be breaking her rule that he'd be responsible. Still, they listened pretty damn well if he said so himself. He gestured to the next two stalls. "I didn't forget Willow and Jay, neither. Hope you don't mind I didn't get you one. I gave ya Agatha last year."

"And I wouldn't want another, she's perfect." Sally admired the two pintos he'd picked for their newest wards. "Did you get these at the auction of Indian ponies up in Cheyenne?"

"How'd you know about that?"

"Um, I read." Her sarcasm was so blatant, he swore he could hear her eyes roll.

He chuckled. "Fair enough."

Sally stepped out of the barn into the paddock. She took a deep breath of cold air and sighed it out in a little cloud of air. "My goodness."

"What?"

"It's pristine."

"Well, I ain't—"

Sally took off at a hopping run into the thick white snow. In moments she dropped onto her back right in the middle of the corral.

A warm hand to his back surprised Cole out of his humor. When Jane leaned against him, he grinned down at her. "I believe Sally's enjoying the quiet."

"I think it's you that's enjoying the quiet." She lifted her chin until she met his gaze. Her lips pursed in what he imagined she thought to be a stern expression. "Ponies, Cole? Really?"

"We gotta have good riders."

"Because you train horses does not mean we must have good riders."

"Out here you gotta know how to ride a horse. Look at that doc. He can't go see some of the people in the farther edges of the valley without a wagon. Even that he's no great shakes at. Seems only able to handle a carriage, and that's if someone hooks the horse up for him."

"I suppose you're right."

"You know I am. You just wanna be mad about the ponies."

"Perhaps." She allowed a warm smile, accepting the kiss he offered.

"How long have you been out here anyway?"

"Since you lit the lamp." She turned her attention back to Sally. "At least you remembered Willow and Jay when you decided to spoil the children."

"I'd do the same for Jesse and Cindy, but Kathy said no, and you ain't talking to Davie."

"Why on earth did Katherine say no?"

"Lizzie."

"We would have done the same for her. That's a ridiculous reason."

He grinned, raising an eyebrow. "Knew you weren't too mad if you wanna do the same for Lizzie, too."

"Are you saying you wouldn't have?"

"I would have. I'm not always an idiot."

"Well, I suppose not always." She sighed softly. "Then again, you didn't ask me my thoughts on these four."

"I like to beg forgiveness after I do things."

"Beg, hm?"

He pulled her in front of him. The moment he had her full attention, he got on his knees before her. "I think you like my begging."

"Do I ever." She leaned down to kiss him gently. "You will have to teach the young ones to ride. I have other things to do."

"Yes ma'am."

She straightened, looking back over the paddock. "It is beautiful out here tonight."

"Sure is. Ya know, Sally offered to come with me."

"She did, did she?" She set her hand on his shoulder. "Too bad you don't need her knowing why you're making the trip."

"She's gotta help your brother anyhow." He rose again to his feet. "Maybe we should head back in."

"Perhaps. Sally?"

The girl sat straight, waving at Jane. "Hey, ma!"

"You're going to catch your death." Jane laughed softly. "What are you doing?"

"What does it look like?" Sally flopped back into the snow.

Jane bent down, gathering some snow in her hands. When she had it formed into a ball, she threw it toward where Sally lay. The ball landed with a thump right on Sally.

Sally screeched her surprise, launching to her feet. Within moments a snowball came back their way. Before Cole knew what happened, the snowball fight had begun in earnest. He had no choice but to join in.

In no time, the entire group from inside had joined them. Snowballs flew fast and furious until everyone was soaked, laughing, and exhausted.

Jane leaned against a fencepost. "That was not the smartest thing for me to do."

Cole dropped beside her as the rest of the group began to settle down. "Sure it was."

"I hurt."

"You laughed."

"I suppose I did."

"Keep laughing when I'm gone."

"I'll do my best."

Friendship is the union of spirits,
a marriage of hearts,
and the bond of virtue.
–William Penn

Jane lined the bottles along the shelf one at a time. Footsteps pounded down the stairs in a quickstep that pulled her out of her task. She smiled at the saloon manager. "Good morning, Wil."

"Morning, Janey." He slipped behind the bar. When he passed behind her, he smacked her on the ass. Soon as he had, he stopped short. Slow and steady he turned to face her. The man didn't blush, but his eyes widened marginally. "Sorry 'bout that."

The shock of what had just happened kept her still in place. She stared at him via the mirror behind the bar. Though many men that didn't know their place, or hers, had groped her—Wil was the first to take such a casual action in the matter.

Wil cleared his throat, apparently concerned over her delayed reaction. "Uh. Um. I mean, really sorry, Janey."

The shock faded into amusement at his boldness, and ensuing embarrassment. The man looked worried she was about to retaliate. He went so far as to take several steps backward. She busted out laughing, punching him on the arm. "You're quite lucky Cole wasn't present for that little display."

"Hey, if there's a woman behind the bar, she's getting attention." He chuckled low. The tightness in his shoulders eased, his bright smile returning. He poured himself a whiskey. "Leastwise the saloon is still empty."

"You'd have heard quite the protest from Mr. Hamm if it hadn't been. He's quite protective of me and who's allowed to play fast and loose with my virtues."

Wil leaned close. "What virtues would those be?"

"You are in quite the mood today. Feeling your oats in a way I haven't seen in a while." Jane had grown accustomed to the dichotomy that Wil had proven to be. Without the usual crowd, he was rather funny and personable. The moment a customer crossed the threshold, or a whore made and appearance, he could be gruff, brusque, and downright cold. A real son of a bitch. Hell, the same could have been said of Cole when she'd first met him.

Still, even for Wil, his mood could be called downright chipper. She wondered over its meaning. He poured another drink and offered her one as well. "What of it?"

"Not a thing." Jane took the drink he offered. Though she usually restricted herself to coffee when working, the saloon wasn't open so she saw no harm. She tossed back the whiskey. "Does this have anything to do with your new bartender arriving on the train? Cole said you were good friends, but it had ended badly when you last parted."

"We had a fight." He scrunched his nose at his glass. "He said he'd come. I take that to mean it's forgiven."

"You take it to mean as such?" Last thing she needed with Cole leaving was a potential problem. "I need to know it's forgiven. I'd like to not have a fight break out between the pair of you. With Cole leaving I'm going to need to be in too many places to have time to worry that you're going to be working out your issues with fisticuffs."

"I mean what I said. If it weren't forgiven, he wouldn't come."

"Good." She returned to stocking bottles on the shelf. "How long have you known Mr. Schmidt?"

"Garit and I grew up near each other in Pennsylvania. Kept running into each other after we left home. Back in Abilene we ran a saloon together for a while until the fight."

"That's quite a long friendship."

"Yeah."

Jane glanced at the man sipping on whiskey. Something about the abbreviated story begged her to ask more. Then again, it wasn't much her business no matter how piqued her curiosity might be. "I guess you'll be glad to see him then, again."

"Sure will."

"How long has it been since you parted company?"

"Near about a year."

She opened her mouth to say more, but the transformation that took over the manager's face caused her pause. A smile that could only be described as pure joy, and something more indescribable, crossed his features. In an instant he caught her looking and schooled them back to a more stoic expression.

"Jane." Cole's voice pulled her attention away from the man beside her. Next to Cole stood a man that in all appearances was Wil's opposite. Pale to Wil's dark hair and olive skin. He had a thin, wiry build that opposed Wil's stocky form. "Meet Garit Schmidt."

"Mr. Schmidt." Jane stepped from behind the bar to extend her hand. "It's good to meet you. Welcome to The Golden Touch."

"Thank you. I appreciate the job offer." Garit's soft voice held the faintest hint of a Germanic accent that Wil's lacked.

"Thank Wil. He's the one that suggested you might join us." Jane smiled at the man's surprisingly strong handshake. "We're glad to have the extra hand. We're going to need it."

"Garit." Wil approached the group. Rather than extend his hand, he rubbed it along his thigh. "It's good to see you again."

"Wil." Garit eyed him almost coolly. "I was surprised at your telegram."

"Let me show you where you'll be staying. I'll explain things." Wil gestured toward the stairs. When Garit began to move, Wil took the lead.

By the middle of the steps, Garit was almost directly behind Wil. Wil spoke low to his friend, she could only tell by the movement of his lips. The two got closer as they conversed, a familiar aching intensity to Wil's features.

Jane remained close to Cole, intrigued by the interaction between the two. Something about the two nagged at the back of her mind. "Interesting."

"What is?"

"Life." She didn't dare suggest that the two men seemed quite close. They were lifelong friends, and so long as no one else got wind of her suspicions, she imagined they'd be safe enough. She turned to face Cole, leaning into him. His instant distraction toward her breasts pleased her to no end. "What?"

"I know you're mad that your corset still don't fit proper, but there's some things I don't mind still being swollen."

"Boor."

"All the time." Cole jumped when a door slammed upstairs. "What the hell? I thought they weren't still fighting."

"Oh, I don't believe they are."

"What's that supposed to mean?"

"It means they're old friends seeing each other for the first time in a year." She slipped her hands over his chest. "Now remind me again why I think you're such a boor?"

"That's easy enough." He captured her lips with his, tugging her tight against him.

"Lady Jane." As always, Hammy timing was impeccable.

Cole groaned, his head dropping back at the old man's voice. He didn't utter a word of complaint, though. Not that he ever did with the old man. "Hammy. Here for your beer?"

"If it ain't too early." Hammy grinned hopefully toward Jane. "I'm a few minutes early today."

"You're never early at the casino, but ever early at the saloon." Jane gestured to the bar. "Step right on up, Mr. Hamm. I'm always happy to serve."

Cole begrudgingly released his hold on her. He followed her to the bar. "You're probably early because the snow is keeping you from working too much."

"That it is." Hammy slurped his beer soon as Jane handed it to him. "Once we got the lodge built for them tornado victims, we didn't have much else to do."

With so many dispersed by the freak storm several months before, Jane had suggested that they once again build a lodge so everyone could have a roof over their heads before the worst of winter hit. There were too many homes to rebuild to get them all done before it got cold, and a lodge for them all made more sense.

"Soon as it starts to lighten you'll be busy as all get out replacing all of those homes, Mr. Hamm. I wouldn't fret too much." She poured Cole a drink, as well as another for herself."

"Oh, I ain't frettin'." Hammy beamed at the fresh beer she set before him. "I always get good business come spring. Besides, we gotta finish that sweet shop."

"Jesse is very much looking forward to the confectionary, what with all the stories my brothers have told him about the deliciousness they provide." Jane didn't complain when Cole moved behind her, his body pressed into hers. "We'll have to remember to tell the new bartender of our rules for Mr. Hamm."

Cole chuckled low, his body trembling against hers. "What rules? Free beer all the time?"

"Precisely."

"Hammy, you gotta tell me how you got Janey wrapped around your finger s good. She ain't ever given me as much special treatment as she does you."

"Oh, I give you special treatment, just in a very different way." Jane set her hand on Hammy's. "Besides, Mr. Hamm was so very kind to me and defended me when a rather vile man would not release my hand."

"It weren't nothing." Hammy's cheeks darkened under her praise. "Just told him to let ya be."

"And I am ever grateful."

The door upstairs slammed again. A moment later, Will hopped down the stairs. His grin had returned, his features a little flush. He nodded to Jane and Cole. "Garit's getting settled in."

"Good." Jane smiled in relief. "You worked things out, then?"

"We did." Wil nodded to Hammy. "You're early today."

"Hammy ain't ever early. We just don't open soon enough for him." Cole's rich voice rumbled near her ear. "Isn't that right?"

"It most certainly is. Speaking of which," Jane glanced toward Wil. "Can I trust that you'll let Mr. Schmidt know that Gilbert Hamm always drinks free?"

"Sure will. Plan on introducing him to the locals tonight."

"Wonderful. Now." Jane spun on the spot to face Cole. "I need to head to the library."

"I'll come with ya."

"That's what I was hoping you'd say."

I awoke this morning with devout
thanksgiving for my friends,
the old and the new.
-Ralph Waldo Emerson

Sally knocked sharply on Alma's door. "Are you ready, Alma?"

The door opened to reveal Alma grinning broadly. Though her gaze focused on a point over Sally's shoulder, she wasn't looking down. That meant a good mood, one Sally hoped wouldn't be interrupted by the chaos of the day. Alma tapped her head several times. "Hat. No hat. Hat. No hat."

"Hold on." Sally laughed brightly, clasping Alma's free hand. "Are you saying you do want a hat, but have none on? Or are you asking if you should have a hat on?"

"Want a hat. No hat." She fanned out her skirt.

"Ah, you're wearing your new dress. You're right. I don't think any that you have will match. Let's see." Sally scanned the hats set in neat rows in the closet. "You could wear this straw piece. A few of the feathers could be called the same color."

"Not the same." Alma skipped out of the room without another word.

"Alma? Where are you going?" Sally darted from the room to find Alma standing inside her own room. "You think I have a hat that matches?"

"Yes." The young woman disappeared behind the door to where Sally's own clothes hung in her small closet.

"Don't you think you should ask permission first?" By the time Sally made it in the room, Alma was already placing a hat on her head. It was a hat she'd gotten weeks ago that Alma kept admiring every time Sally wore it. Sally narrowed her eyes. "You've been wanting that hat since I bought it."

"It's pretty." Alma put her hands on top of it as if afraid Sally would swipe it from her head. "Matches my dress."

"You have a point." Sally couldn't deny that the pink flowers along the brim matched the accent details of Alma's new dress perfectly. She sighed. "Fine. You can wear it today. I want it back in my closet by the end of the day."

Alma tied the ribbon with a flourish, her smile now unstoppable. "Train time."

"Not quite yet. We have about half an hour. We'll start walking, though. Maybe we'll see some friends on the way. Come on." Sally took Alma's hand as they hopped down the stairs. No one was in the living room, but she could hear discussions going on in the twins and Jay and Willow's rooms.

So they didn't bother whatever discussions were going on, she led Alma right on out of the apartment and through the empty casino toward the restaurant. Eunice was setting cutlery around a group of tables that had been pushed together.

Eunice smiled at them both. "Good morning, ladies. Don't you both look smart?"

Alma released Sally's hand to affect a little twirl at the compliment.

Sally chuckled softly. "The thief has absconded with my hat for the day. She claimed none of hers matched. It does compliment the dress well, though."

"That it does." Eunice nodded to Alma. "What are the pair of you up to?"

"We're going to meet the train. We can help when we come back, Mams. If you'd like."

"No need. Cora and I have everything under control, and I believe Lillian will be along in short order. Plenty of hands." She winked at Sally. "Besides, we haven't figured out if you are any hand at cooking yet. You should include such lessons in with your others. If for no other reason to keep yourself fed in the future."

"Perhaps I will." Sally grinned at Alma. "Maybe Alma will learn, too. She's so good at gardening and with her chickens, maybe she should learn to do something with the fruits of her labors."

"No fruit. Carrots," Alma objected. "Potatoes."

"Sorry. The vegetables of her labor, then." Sally chuckled softly. "Let's make our way to the train station, Alma."

The sun shone brightly with none of the wind they'd had recently. Early in the day the streets had been cleared, and it appeared most of the shop owners had cleared the walk in front of their stores. Despite the holiday, a few people milled about the streets exchanging greetings and good wishes.

Across the way, Sally spotted a familiar face. She stuck her hand in the air to wave. "Andrew!"

Andrew returned the wave from his vantage point on the porch of the clinic.

"Would you like to say hello to Andrew before we head to the depot, Alma?" Sally descended the steps with Alma, avoiding an icy patch clinging in the shadows.

"Doctor Cross is nice," Alma said in a way of agreement.

"I agree." Sally made her way across the street, Alma clinging to her arm. "Hello, Andrew."

"Hello to you as well. Good morning, Alma. How are you?"

"It's Thanksgiving!" Alma beamed at the doctor. "We're having a big dinner. Lots of people. Cora is using my potatoes."

"If Cora is cooking, I have no doubt it's going to be delicious." Andrew grinned in return. "And your potatoes are probably the best in town."

"They're huge. Alma has a magical touch when it comes to growing." Sally kept her own laughter at bay even as Alma giggled wildly. "Will you be joining us for supper?"

"I offered to remain at the clinic today along with Lydia so Dr. Young could enjoy the holiday with his family. I know your grandparents just arrived, and it's George's first holiday. I don't mind. Lydia and I are both here without family."

Sally frowned. "That's not very festive. I'll bring you both some plates of food and dine with you. I'd hate for you to go without."

"That's not necessary." Andrew shrugged. "I don't mind."

"It is necessary. You might not have family, but you have friends, and this friend doesn't want you alone." Sally kept an eye on Alma as she wandered over to the clinic window, her gaze locked on something in the pane. "What about Bonnie?"

"She's cooking for her family. Matthew and Stephen, possibly all of their hands as well. I imagine she's very busy today."

"Makes sense. All the more reason for me to join you later." The faint echoes of the train whistle carried through town. "I'll be by later, then. Alma, I heard the train."

"Ten minutes away." Alma tilted her head to the side, her finger slipping along the swirls in the pane. "Ten minutes, fifteen seconds."

Andrew glanced at Sally, his eyes alight with curiosity.

"You can set your watch by that," Sally acknowledged the curiosity. "That means the train is a bit early today. The engineer is probably in a hurry to get home."

"I came here on a train. Swoop!" Alma swooped her arm through the air in accompaniment to her statement. She walked away without a goodbye. "Telegraph swoops."

"I remember." Sally waved farewell to Andrew in her rush to catch up with Alma. Along the way she exchanged greetings with those they passed. She didn't dare stop again for any conversation, for Alma seemed determined to make it to the depot quite quickly.

They climbed the steps to the depot, and were immediately intercepted by Lizzie. The girl took Alma's hand, walking with her to the bench. Her free hand moved rapidly in sign language. Alma returned the gestures, a bit more halting and hesitant.

Sally left the pair to their conversation, grinning when Cindy skipped toward her. "Good morning, Cindy. Your sister already absconded with mine."

"I see. She's mad at me. Can I stand with you?"

"She's mad at you?" Sally knelt in front of Cole's daughter, meeting her gaze. "What ever could she be mad at you for?"

"I told her I didn't want her to sit with Jesse at supper. Told Ma, too. She ignores me when she does that." Cindy glared toward the train. "They're gross."

"Who's gross?"

"Boys."

Sally dipped her head to hide her chuckle. "Jesse's been your friend for a long time."

"He's still gross."

"Understood." She imagined it bothered the girl that she wasn't quite the same age as Jesse and Lizzie, and therefore hadn't reached the age where she actually liked boys. A couple years down the line, and she imagined Cindy's tune would change. "Well, you can always sit with Willow or Alma."

"Can I sit with you?"

"I'm going to the clinic so Dr. Cross and Lydia aren't by themselves."

"Can I go?"

"If your ma says yes, I don't see why not." Sally rose at the next train whistle. She doubted there would be anyone on the train she could see to getting to the Inn. Still, she'd try.

When she glanced around the platform, she noticed the Sage Brush's manager, Rueben standing under the sign for the hotel. The man fidgeted restlessly, his gaze flickering to Sally with unusual frequency. He tugged his collar, then clasped his hands in front of him.

Confused, Sally turned her attention to the train. To be honest, she didn't know the man all that well. Perhaps he was always fidgety. However, when she glanced back, he'd gone from the platform. Rather than wait for the trains occupants to depart, he'd walked away. Odd.

"Arthur!" Alma squealed, clapping heartily from her seat.

Sure enough, Arthur had been among the first off the train. He approached Alma, so Sally watched the disembarking passengers for anyone that appeared to be looking for lodging. Only a few paid attention to the signs, each of them turning away in the end. Until one couple actually paused.

Sally stepped forward to greet them. After a few minutes discussion, she got their names to have their luggage sent on, and gave them directions to the Inn. By the time she finished that, and passed on the information to Norman, Alma was approaching on Arthur's arm.

Sally nodded to her former beau. "Arthur. Welcome home. I expected you a few days ago."

"A few friends and myself decided to stay on for some parties." Arthur smiled, though it didn't quite reach his eyes when he met her gaze. Unlike when he turned to Alma, when his eyes softened in kindness and warmth. Still mad at her, it seemed. "Ma said long as I made it home for Thanksgiving, she didn't mind."

"Well, Denver agrees with you." Indeed it did. Arthur was carrying himself differently, and was dressed smarter than he usually was in Dominion Falls.

"Thank you." He turned his attention to the girl at Sally's side. "Hey, Cindy. How are you?"

Before Sally could say more, one more figure disembarked from the train. Another familiar face. Sally's smile broke wide before she could help herself. "Molly!"

Molly's gaze lifted, widening in surprise. She audibly oofed at the hug Sally swept her into. "Goodness. I was gone not even a week."

"Well, I missed you." She guided Molly over to where Arthur, Alma, and Lizzie stood. "Arthur, this is Molly. She's been helping train me along with Tommy. Also, she's a good friend. Molly, this is Arthur. A good friend."

Arther's harsh look faded when she called him friend. He extended a hand. "Good to meet you, Miss."

"Malone, but call me Molly. I'm rarely a miss." Molly shook his hand. "Sally speaks kindly of you. It's nice to finally meet you."

"I didn't know she spoke of me at all." Arthur grimaced at his own words. "I mean, I'd say the same, but I haven't been home in a while."

Alma danced in place, her grip firm on Arthurs' arm.

Lizzie waved at Sally, then her hands moved almost too fast for Sally to keep up. Sally chuckled softly. She replied verbally as well as with sign, "If your Ma says you may, you may come along. You too, Cindy."

The two girls scampered off. Arthur set his free hand on Alma's. "Do you want to start moving now? Would you like to get home?"

Sally had been about to suggest such a thing, for Alma's nerves had kicked up to the point where she was plucking her skirt along with her swaying steps. She smiled at Arthur gratefully. "That's a wonderful idea."

Arthur nodded to them both, guiding Alma toward the street.

Molly leaned closer. "That's your former beau, then. Handsome."

"Kind. Good man. Too good."

"Shame. Although, that can be fun, too."

"How's that?"

"A little corruption can be fun when done the right way."

Sally chuckled softly. "You're terrible."

"Who's more terrible? The one that says it, or the one that agrees?"

"A circle has no end."

"Precisely."

*The direction in which education starts a man
will determine his future life.
-Plato*

Jane took several books out of the box Cole had delivered the hour before. Sally, who had supposedly come to aide her in putting the books away, leaned against a shelf, her nose deep in a newspaper. Jane shook her head, scanning the spines of the newest purchases.

One by one she wrote them into catalog in their appropriate genre.

Jane glanced at her ward. "How is Arthur doing? I hardly had a moment to speak to him during supper yesterday."

Sally turned a page, seemingly oblivious to Jane's question.

"Sally."

"Hm? What? Oh." Pink dotted the young woman's cheeks. "Sorry."

"What are you reading that has you so enraptured?" Jane grabbed another book from the box.

"The New York Herald." Sally folded the page to focus on Jane. "I see why you read the papers from all around. The news is different."

"Different than our small town? Yes, it certainly is." Jane pushed away the pang in her heart at Sally's exploration of other places. She knew it was something she'd one day leave home to do. At least for now it was merely newspapers. Besides, she read those papers herself. When she had time. "Your welcome to read any of mine. I get a stack with relative frequency. There's a few on my desk at home. Boston, Chicago, St. Louis, and San Francisco."

"Thanks, Ma." Sally reopened her paper. "It's interesting to read about other places in the paper. It helps remind you that books often make them more perfect than they are."

"Quite true. Books are for escape. News is reality." Jane wrote the final books' title in the catalog. "You still haven't answered my initial question, though."

"There was a question?"

"Yes."

"What was it?"

"I asked how Arthur was doing. I didn't have much of an opportunity to speak with him at supper yesterday."

"I haven't really had much of a chance to speak to him, either. Molly arrived at the same time, and he walked back with Alma. Then Molly and I took supper to the clinic for Andrew and Lydia. By the time I returned home, I went straight to the apartment. I did tell him Denver agreed with him. He was looking quite dapper."

"That he was."

"I wonder if he might have his eye on a new young lady the way he gussied up."

"Or perhaps wanted to impress you." Jane smirked when Sally's head lifted sharply at her words. The young woman's brows twisted in consternation. "You didn't think of that?"

"Honestly, no. It would be cruel to say to him directly, but I fear I haven't had much time to think on him lately. What with lessons and the deaths and all."

"And, perchance, other countenances catching your attention?"

Sally turned her attention back to the newspaper, pointedly ignoring Jane's assessment. "I probably should find some time to speak with him. I do miss his friendship."

"If you wish to maintain a friendship, speaking to each other is critical." Jane pushed to her feet, stretching out some discomfort below her right breast. The pain had started to come and go since Thanksgiving. As though she'd eaten too much, and it wasn't sitting right. "I'm curious about how college is going for him. It must be lovely to keep learning like that."

"I suppose. I never had proper learning except for you tutoring me. I don't know that I'd like it. Not that women have as many opportunities as men for such things."

"The movement is slow, but it is growing. After all, there are even women doctors and lawyers. We had one here, and Charles is hiring at least one more."

"I suppose. It's still an unnecessary fight for us to get an education."

"Too true." Jane reached for her personal notebook. The idea of a college seemed a brilliant one. Something the valley could use one day. She jotted down her note, then paused when the letters seemed fuzzy. Could her eyes be failing already? Shaking her head against the thought, she continued to write and spoke aloud as she did, "A college. One that teaches women and men."

"What?"

"Making a note for myself. I think having a college here would be lovely when the town grows a little more. A good way to keep the town alive."

"How do you mean? You think the town could die?"

"Towns do it all the time. There are empty businesses and homes all over parts of California where the rush was so big. On the prairies when resources dried up from drought or Indian attack."

"I can't imagine Dominion Falls dying. Do you really think it could?"

"Anywhere could, even here. The mines give us much of our population. While the ranches are helping, they don't draw in near as many workers. Mines dry up. No mines, no money. No money, no town."

"I hadn't thought that far ahead. The mines could dry up?"

"It's far less likely here seeing as the majority mine-owner happens to be Henry Daugherty. He and Lillian are quite business-minded. Many places with mines that have died were plundered. Night and day in unsafe conditions to strip every ounce of gold and silver thread to be found."

Sally tucked her paper under her arm as she listened. "Our mines close at seven."

"And no miner works over 6 hours, with very fair wages. They have weekends off, as well as holidays. Henry gave them all the day off for the statehood. The Daugherty's don't want our town to bleed dry before it becomes something on its own. Maybe not even then. They mined hard to get their fortune, then backed off. You know how many miners come here to work because they've heard of the fair conditions?"

"I've heard mention of it here and there."

"I'll see if I can't find a copy of the newspaper article out of Colorado Springs about the strike they had there. The conditions they were working under were frightening. They didn't keep up with inspections for structure and a collapse killed quite a few men. The Daugherty's are rather the opposite. It's how we remained flush here through the silver crash."

A low grunt of surprise was Sally's response. She seemed deep in thought as she fiddled with the edge of the paper under her am. "Interesting. You think a college could really help?"

"I do. It would bring folks in for learning and teaching. It's something I'd wait to really suggest until after the hospital is built, if Charles ever gets around to it."

"You'd start a college?"

"Oh, no. I have more than enough on my plate. It's a suggestion I'll level to the ladies, and the town, when the time seems right."

Sally laughed softly. "You do have a full life."

"Between the library, casino, and brothel, I wouldn't dare think of such an undertaking. Besides, I wouldn't know where to begin."

"You always seem to figure it out."

"When I want to." Jane lifted her finger. "That is a key aspect. While I might think a college would be good here, I don't care to do it myself."

"But you'll push for it."

"Perhaps." Jane allowed a smile to Sally's outright laughter. "What are your plans today? Do you have lessons with Molly?"

"We already did. She's teaching me to read tarot cards, of all things. She says with as many spiritualists as there are, it might come in handy." Sally shrugged. "I'm having trouble remembering all of the meanings. I can't keep them straight in my head."

"I've never paid them much mind myself. We don't even have a book on such matters in the library. I suppose I can try to find one if you think it'll help."

"Reading will only confuse the matter."

"Is there anything on the cards you can use for association as we did with your history lessons? One thing that on each card that you can tie to a clue in your own mind?"

"Molly says there is. I'm not seeing it." A frown tugged Sally's lips down. "There are more important matters at hand, anyhow. I don't feel like I'm getting anywhere with Mike."

"You will. Your brain is working on the puzzle any time you get a chance. I've seen your concentration to the matter." Jane crossed to Sally's side. "I trust you and Thomas will figure it out. I know these matters don't move quickly."

"I'd like it to move more quickly. I feel terrible that Uncle Mike is still sitting in that jail. If only he could remember one detail."

"Our minds are powerful things. They hide a great many secrets. I should know, mine hides more than its fair share. Michael must work through his own guilt for his behavior these past months, and it's hard to do behind those bars."

Sally opened her mouth, likely to complain more based on the consternation set in her features. The clock on the wall chimed, pulling her attention away. "Speaking of, I need to meet Tommy. We're going over everything. Again."

"That's fine. Remember, and remind my brother, that repetition is not always our friend. We can get too focused on what we know, and forget to remember the smaller details."

"I will. Thanks, Ma." Sally hugged her quickly before departing the library. On her way out, she passed Cora coming inside.

Jane smiled at her friend. "Cora. You're a little early. I hadn't even started setting up for the tea yet."

"I thought I'd take advantage of the respite to leave early. Tonight will be Colleen's first time running the kitchen on her own." Cora sank into a chair, a heavy sigh slipping free. "I won't say I'm not a bundle of nerves. I don't like leaving my kitchen in another's hands."

"Colleen has been working hard to get to this point. I find her cooking quite accomplished, though she could never replace you."

"But she will, one day. Young as she is." Cora shook her head. "She's such a hard worker. I worry that she's working too much and will lose time with her mother."

"Yes, but that's why she's working hard. To see her mother get the care she needs." Jane set a hand on Cora's. "You hired her so you might have some time to yourself as well. You cannot work all day every day and be complete."

"It's all I've known since Kelly opened the store all those years ago. I don't know what I'll do with myself if I'm not working."

"Oh, I imagine you'll find ways to fill your time. My mother keeps trying to get me to learn knitting so we might sit together in the evening and knit. As though my life affords me such luxury."

"See? I'm not the only one working all day, every day."

"Yes, but I'm not doing it alone. And I have my pleasures as well. You have work and your ever obstreporous son."

"I thought Isaac might calm down as he grew up. Arthur was a bit of a handful when he was younger, but grew into such a calm, kind man. Isaac is nearly thirteen and shows no sign of slowing down. I am quite unsure what to do with him."

"Thankfully he isn't approaching age alone. He and Jesse are still fast friends."

Cora lifted a brow. "Not as much now that Jesse and Lizzie are practically courting. Isaac finds his antics annoying."

"Yes, but they still play and go fishing. I know Stephen Coleman has joined them a few times. Although, based on what I've heard, he might be quite as rambunctious as Isaac."

"Their teachers have a time of it, that's for certain."

Jane carried the tea pot to the table along with enough cups for everyone as they arrived. She set it on the table, setting Cora's full cup in front of her. "I should ask Mr. Coleman if he'd like Stephen to come along when the rest of the children do for their work. I'd hate for him to fall behind his friends."

"You might as well turn this library into a school the rate you're going, Jane."

"Oh no, I don't wish to be a teacher."

"You already are."

"Of a few select children. I've no wish to lead as many as attend that school."

Cora grinned over her cup. "Of course not."

"You hush."

A woman is always a mystery:
one must not be fooled
by her face and her hearts inspiration.
-Edmondo De Amicis

Sally stared at the card in her hand without really seeing it. No matter how hard she tried, her mind wouldn't focus on the task at hand. All her mind tended toward any longer was letting her thoughts race in circles. Worst part was that it didn't help provide any answers. It only went over things time and again until she fell asleep exhausted.

"Sally." Molly perched on the couch beside her. Her hand rested gently on Sally's arm. "You should know this one. You knew it yesterday. Tell me again, as you did then. What does The Star signify?"

"I don't know." Sally dropped the card to the table. The exercise frustrated her. Learning tarot cards for a mission she'd likely never get didn't seem a priority when Mike remained in jail. Add in the fact that Cole was leaving in a few days. Though she'd been acting the part, Sally could tell

Jane was distraught over his departure. Then there was everything else.

How could her training matter any longer with all that was going on? She had no idea. She was beyond discontented with how long everything was taking. Why in heavens with both of them, and Molly, working on the matter had she and Tommy had no luck figuring out how it all connected together? Even more, who had done each of the murders?

Sure, Tommy was plenty distracted with his family in town, and he'd been making time with Leanne again. However they were still working on it. Only the day before they'd spent a couple hours going over every detail again. It didn't help their case that nothing had happened since Daisy's murder. How horrible she must be to wish for something awful to happen in hopes she'd get more clues.

Sally practically growled out her frustration. "This is pointless. I should be focused on Mike."

"When you are investigating there will always be distractions." Molly's hand settled on hers, warm and comforting. "Plus intense focus on one matter detracts from it. Minds work better with some distraction. That's why you must continue on with your training. You have to learn to keep thinking when your mind requires its focus elsewhere."

"I barely figured out how to make my mind work to get through school. I can't do this."

"You can, and you have been. You're trying to rush something that can only come with time and practice. This is preparing you for whatever you might face."

Sally blew out a gust of air rather than her complaint.

"Tell me about when you were a whore."

Caught off guard by the question, Sally stilled. She assumed it was another distraction, another way to prove the point of the matter. Previously Molly had been dismissive and uncaring of what Sally what had been. The woman hadn't thought it mattered much at all.

"Sally?"

"I'm not used to anyone asking." Sally turned to face Molly. "Most people would prefer to pretend I never was one. You yourself have acted as though it wasn't anything important."

"I never meant to give that impression. You were a whore. It helped you learn things you wouldn't otherwise. Such as how to read men, and women." Molly moved closer, her gaze fixed on Sally. Her arm draped over the back of the couch. "You were taught how to pleasure others."

"The women before me were taught by the owners, and some were still taught by Graham. Tales tell he wasn't nearly as…accommodating as Cole was. Based on what Ma says, those tales were likely true."

A sly grin crossed Molly's features. "Based on what I've seen of those two together, I've no doubt that's accurate."

"Even though I missed that training, which I'm now grateful for, seeing as he's my Pa."

"In name only, but I see your point."

"The others did teach me a lot. I knew how to avoid certain men, and which to entice—even those I hadn't seen before."

"The women taught you, you mean. They taught you how to perform all of your duties, I imagine." Molly's fingers danced along Sally's shoulder.

A tingle coursed down her back, teasing and pleasant. Heat rose to her cheeks at the intimation. She couldn't deny it, the quarters they'd been in were small and no privacy was afforded. "Yes. They also indulged in each other's company after a frustrating night."

"Did men ask to see such a show?"

"Some. Either they'd pay to watch or to participate." Sally cleared her throat against the lump that formed when Molly scooted even closer. If she were smart, she'd get up and leave the room. Sally was familiar with the hunger in her friends gaze, though she usually saw it in men. The glimmer of excitement in her belly, and the sudden ache between her legs kept her firmly in her seat.

Molly drew her other hand up Sally's arm to her neck. Her thumb ran along Sally's jawline before she leaned even closer. Sally's breath hitched a moment before Molly's warm, soft lips closed over her own.

Within a heartbeat Sally opened to the woman, moaning as their tongues met in a passionate dance. Her trembling hand found purchase on Molly's knee as she leaned closer. Molly's hands coursed over Sally's aching breasts, squeezing as they passed. The throbbing need at her core burgeoned stronger.

Sally's thoughts raced forward to fill her with panic. She pulled out of the kiss with a sharp gasp.

Heat coursed under her flesh to match the lust in Molly's hooded eyes. Doubt over the sanity of her actions rushed forward. She'd just kissed a woman. Worse, it had excited her.

Sally flew to her feet. "I have to—I must—oh, dear."

"Sally. Wait."

"I'll see you tomorrow." Sally raced out of the room too fast to hear anything Molly had to say. Her hands shook as she paced the hall to the front steps and back. What was she doing? Hadn't she said all along she wanted stimulation?

Oh, how she'd felt it right then. So much so part of her longed to go back. The heat cooled, settling into utter confusion over what had just happened.

Groaning, she leaned into the wall.

"Sally? Are you all right?" A strong hand grasped her elbow.

Her eyes flew open to find Patrick Warner's concerned gaze on her. His eyes were kind and soft, the strong cut of his jaw twitched into a beguiling smirk. She took a deep breath, unsure what to do now. "Oh. Dear."

"Sally?" His lips curved into a sexy smile that succeeded in setting her bits ablaze once again. "What's happened? You're all aflush?"

"I'm all…I suppose I am." She set a hand to her chest. It would have been impossible to miss that his gaze lowered toward where her hand had settled. The unsatisfied excitement from her kiss with Molly flared back to life from his attentions. There was one way to settle the matter, she hoped. "Mr. Warner."

"Hm?"

The second he'd lifted his gaze from her bosom, she moved. Her arms slid around his neck as she pressed her lips to his.

He didn't disappoint as his hands slid around her waist. His body pressed hers into the wall, fingers dancing along her waist, up to the breasts he'd just been enjoying. Every nerve sparked to life as it had moments ago, and the burning need grew into a straight up fire.

Sally pulled herself gently from the heat of his lips. Her body remain flush against the wall as he hovered several inches away now, at the tip of her fingers, in fact. When had she pushed him away? And why?

"Well," she whispered. "That didn't help."

"Help what?" He touched her swollen lip. "Nothing can be helped with an unsatisfied libido but to finish the task."

"But how?"

"I believe you know how."

"Of course, but how?" Her gaze drifted down the hall toward where Molly's room sat around the corner. "With whom?"

"There is another?" Patrick followed her gaze. "Well, fair Sally."

Sally blinked back to him as he pressed a warm kiss to the back of her hand. The simple gesture was enough to warm her through again. "Yes?"

"If you require assistance, or even more than that, you know where I might be found."

Sally closed her eyes as he excused himself and disappeared down the steps. "Damn."

She spun on her heel and rushed to the back stairs. In the apartment she found most of her family there. Jane was lounging with Cole on the settee, though she'd looked up when Sally had entered. Her voice emerged in an undignified squeak. "Ma."

Jane didn't need further encouragement and extricated herself from Cole's arms in a heartbeat. Sally raced up the stairs toward her room. Though she sat on her bed at first, the stillness pushed against her riled nerves. Instead, she paced the room until Jane entered, and even after her ma had sat.

To her credit, Jane remained calm. That helped ease Sally's nerves enough that her pacing slowed. In the lingering silence, Jane kept her hands folded on her lap, eyes never leaving Sally's progress for a moment.

Sally had no idea where to begin, or what to say. Would Jane be ashamed of what she'd done? What she'd felt? "Oh dear."

"I suppose that's a start. You are rather aflutter, Sally. Would you like some water?"

"No. Yes. Maybe. Oh dear."

"Sally." Jane rose to put an arm around Sally's shoulders, effectively ending the ceaseless pacing. "Why don't you tell me what's happened, and then I can let you know how I feel about the situation. Unless you have no desire for my opinion, in which case I'll simply listen."

"I do, I think. I'm so confused. Worried. Was I wrong?"

"I cannot know until I know what happened. Please, sit."

Sally sank to the bed beside her. "In the brothel, you know how the women can be with each other…and what some men asked us to do—with each other."

Jane's eyes widened, but her smile never wavered. "Of course, Sally. One cannot run a brothel without being aware of such things. Especially seeing as men, despite their disgust at men sharing love, really enjoy when women do just that."

"Right." Sally cleared her throat, her hands clenched tight in her lap. "Molly kissed me. Just now. It was—I found I liked it. It was…"

"Stimulating?"

"Oh yes."

"I see." Jane set her hands on Sally's. "That's what you—"

"Then I kissed Patrick." Sally couldn't let Jane finish her sentence, not until she'd said everything. "Rather thoroughly. I really enjoyed that as well. I am feeling awful—flustered."

"Flustered might be putting it mildly." Jane chuckled softly. "You found yourself stimulated by a man, and a woman, then."

"What you must think of me."

"What I *must* think? No, Sally. I mustn't think anything." Jane brushed a lock of hair over Sally's ear. "What brings us joy, brings us joy. I learned long ago that I was not about to deny myself, or anyone else, pleasure where I could get it. There is so little in this life."

"But—a woman. Isn't that wrong?"

"By all accounts Cole and I are wrong. Do we look wrong to you?"

"No. You look happy. When you aren't pining over his departure."

"I am pining over his departure because we are happy. That's all I wish for you, Sally. That you find what makes you happy, content as you can be in the sort of life you choose." Jane pulled her into a half-hug. "I cannot see how love, or happiness, can be wrong."

"How can I be interested in both?"

"They are both very attractive, and kind, with a hell of a wicked streak. I could see how anyone could be intrigued by either of them. One's heart cannot be controlled. For that matter, neither can our desires in many cases."

"What do I do?"

"You do what gives you everything you've ever wanted. Whether it's one, or the other, or both. I doubt either of them will be the first, or last, person you're attracted to."

Sally took Jane's hand in hers. "I don't know if I can."

"You can. If you dare."

"Should I?"

"What do you want to do?"

"I can only imagine."

"That's an excellent start."

Family connexions
were always worth preserving,
good company always worth seeking.
—Jane Austen

Cole hopped up the steps to the saloon. He'd much rather have been spending his day with Jane, but she'd shooed him away. Never mind that they only had a few days before he left, she kept insisting they work. All he wanted to do the remaining days was spend every minute he could with Jane and the kids.

The thought made him pause, staring into the brothel that they'd set up nearly identical to his original saloon. How he'd changed in the five years Jane had been in his life had never been so clear as at that moment. Entering a brothel where he no longer paid much mind to the girls, wishing he was home with his kids?

He chuckled softly to himself, entering the business with his humor growing. A familiar figure sat hunched at the end of the bar nursing a beer. Behind the bar was the new bartender, Garit. Cole still didn't know much about the man. He didn't like leaving such an unknown entity in charge when he was about to leave.

Tom and Jane would be around, but he knew the saloon was more his than Jane's. She might have her rules for the girls and the business, which she definitely enforced, but she wasn't in the brothel every day as she'd once been. In fact, he was surprised if she went in there more than once every week. All of her focus went to the casino, the library, and their family.

Cole nodded to Garit before he approached Hammy. He clapped a hand on the old man's shoulder. "Hey there, Hammy."

"Hey Cole." Hammy offered a goofy grin. The man seemed to be several beers in already. Unusual for a weekday. "How's Lady Jane?"

"Same spitfire she always is." Cole took the seat beside Hammy. "I got a favor to ask you."

"Name it."

"You know I'm going out of town for a couple of weeks. Got some business to attend to."

"Yeah, I heard." After a few blinks, Hammy focused on Cole much clearer than moments before. "Lady Jane seems right sad about it."

"She is." Cole leaned toward the old man. "Will you keep an eye on her for me? Make sure she doesn't get too sad. She's got a sweet spot for you, after all. If anyone can make her smile, I know you can."

"Aw, I don't know about that."

"Don't be modest." Cole nudged him. "You know she likes you. In some rough times I've seen ya make her smile like the sun."

The man's sun-darkened cheeks grew ruddy under the compliments. "I'll do my best, Cole. Ya got my word."

"That's good enough for me." He nodded to Garit when the man set a whiskey in front of him. "Thanks. How are ya settling in?"

"Well enough. Your woman gave me a talking to about how to handle the business." His gaze was hard, unforgiving. "I know how to."

"Jane's the boss. May seem like I am, but Jane's got a good mind for handling the business. She's the last one you want to piss off, right Hammy?" Cole grinned at Hammy's immediate agreement. "We might mostly leave this place in Wil's capable hands, but Jane likes to make sure the rules are well known and followed."

"You let a woman run your business?"

"That ain't all she runs." Cole tossed back his whiskey. "For me, it's worth the reward. For you, it'll be worth keeping your job."

"Not used to having a woman boss me around."

Cole did his best to hide a grin. "Sometimes, it's well worth it. In my case, it sure is."

Garit hmphed before he moved down the bar to get a drink for Jake.

Cole glanced around the saloon to see who was there. He paused when he spotted Rueben in the corner, eying the whores. Far as he could remember, he didn't recall seeing the manager of the Sage Brush in the saloon.

Granted, he wasn't here all the time, so he could have easily missed the man's appearance. Cole shrugged it off to return to his drink.

Light footsteps approached. A delicate finger tapped his shoulder. One quick glance in the mirror told him it wasn't one of the saloon's whores.

He turned to face his half-sister. "Leanne."

"Could we talk?"

"Don't really need to, far as I can tell."

"Yes. We do." She stepped closer, closer than most women would be allowed if Jane saw them. "In private."

"Jane wouldn't like it." In truth, Cole knew she wouldn't mind, but they did have some curious onlookers to their exchange.

"Jane will get over it. Now."

He quirked a brow at the near-order. No woman but Jane ordered him around, and Leanne knew it. Her realization came in the form of a blush.

"Please."

"Fine." He slid off the stool, gesturing for her to follow. Instead of going to the storeroom, he led her to one of the rooms across from the bar. He closed the door on the curious glances.

"I should go—"

"Nope."

"Cole."

Cole sat on the edge of the bed. He had a feeling this was coming. Whether of her own volition, or with the added worry of his wife, he knew she'd suggest, ask, perhaps demand. "This ain't something you need to worry yourself about."

"He was my pa, too."

"You didn't know him, not really, and you can thank God for that."

"So what?" She sat beside him, her hand came to rest on his. "You've been in an ugly mood since that telegram. You hate going back. Why go by yourself?"

"It's better I do. You don't need to worry about whatever mess he left behind. What other kids and families he's destroyed." He glared at the floor. "You got a business to run."

"And you've got two businesses, three if you count mine. I've got whores that can take over in my absence."

"No."

"Why are you being so stubborn?"

He thought for a long minute about the question.

"I'm a grown woman now. You don't need to protect me anymore."

Yeah, he did. There was plenty Leanne didn't know. Like the fact that their pa may not have managed to kill Alma, but Cole and Tom both suspected he was the reason Cole's ma and siblings were dead. "It's better I go alone. I can make quick work of it not having to deal with your emotional nonsense."

She sat in silence at that.

"It's going to be right quick. I'll be home in no time. I don't hate going by myself." He glanced sideways at her. "That's not what I'm worried about."

"She's going to be fine. This is Jane we're talking about."

"I know. We also just lost a kid. Mike's in jail. She's beset with Young's when she doesn't feel like one right now. She needs ya more than I do."

"That isn't fair."

"You and Kathy are closest to her. It's best you stay. I'll be fine. Angry, cleaning up a mess that ain't mine, but I'll be fine."

"He was a bastard. Didn't want anything to do with me when he came to see Ma. I had to go play elsewhere. Ate dinner with the chickens." Leanne sighed softly. "If you're absolutely sure, I won't argue again."

"I'm positive."

"Fine. Fine. I hate you a little."

"I always woulda preferred you hated me a lot."

She snorted. "Too bad you're too good for that. Not nice. But good."

"Not nice, good. I guess I can take that." He chuckled low. "I got Tom sending me updates on Jane, but he's got other work to do."

"I will, too. You don't have to ask." She rested her head on his shoulder.

He sighed softly, wondering if it was time to reveal the truth about who she was to him. It wasn't fair to her how he'd denied her for so long. Maybe when he got back to town, it was time for secrets to come out. He didn't know about Jane, but he was getting tired of them.

"Think we've been in here long enough to have some tongues wagging?"

He laughed outright. "We only had to be in here a minute for that to be true."

"Fair point. Although it would be disgusting for it to be true. After all, you're my brother."

For the first time, he didn't correct her with the *half* part of it. "They don't know that."

"True." She stood. "Well, I tried. That's all I can do. If you change your mind, I can be ready to go very quickly."

"I won't, but I appreciate it." He let her leave, not following for several minutes. It was good of her to offer, but really he didn't want company. He hadn't been lying. His big concern about his departure isn't so much what he'd find in Holle Creek, but at Jane being here. The past few years they'd done nearly everything together. Love, loss, and everything in between. They hadn't been apart for a long time. To do so after everything they'd been through recently was going to be rough on her. Her emotions still seemed close to the surface like they were when she was with child.

A knock on the door drew his thoughts back to the present. He nodded to the man that poked his head in the room. "Tom."

"What're you hiding for?" Tom grinned as he pushed open the door. "Moping again?"

"I don't mope, ya brute." Cole got to his feet to grab another whiskey. "You need to keep your woman in line. She's in here harassing me."

"You're a fine one to talk. Keep yours in line."

"Like that would happen."

"Exactly."

He laughed along with Tom, circling the bar to pour them both a whiskey. A quick check of the bar told him Garit was handing drinks to a table across the room. "Keep an eye on that one. He doesn't seem to happy to have a woman boss. Might give Jane some trouble."

"I'd love to see him try. She'll give him what-for quicker than I will." Tom tossed back his drink. "She's felled bigger men than him."

Cole grinned in response. Immediately, he pictured the night she broke Graham's nose. A terrible night all around, but that was a shining moment. "I hope she's learned better how to punch. Don't need her breaking her hand again."

"I've taught her proper. She'll be fine should the need arise."

"Good to know."

"She's going to be fine, you know."

"Keep saying it. One of these times I'll believe it."

We have enough religion to make us hate,
but not enough to make us love one another.
—Jonathan Swift

Jane strolled arm in arm with Leanne away from the jail. Her visit with Michael had afforded her the opportunity to hug him, and talk to him freely as Leanne served to distract David. Unfortunately, the only productive part of the meeting had been the hug. It had helped her, and she believed him as well, to offer some small measure of comfort.

Mike still couldn't remember much about the days after he'd left the saloon. Definitely nothing about what had pushed him to start drinking in excess again. Certainly nothing about Daisy's murder, which didn't surprise her since she knew he hadn't done it.

With little progress on retrieving his memory, he'd instead begged her for talk of all that was happening in the town. He'd longed to discuss anything but his current state.

Having been in his situation herself once, she'd obliged his request. She'd told him all about the presents Cole had gotten for the children, about his imminent departure, and any other bits of news and gossip she could share.

Leanne sighed softly beside her. "I'm so glad you're speaking to me again, and that Tom is. I know it was mere days, but they were torture."

"They were hardly torture." Jane squeezed her friend's hand. "I couldn't be getting through all I am without my friends. My upset was genuine, though."

"I can tell by the way you continue to ignore the sheriff."

"Him, I'm not certain I can forgive."

"Jane."

"I'm sorry Cole refused your offer to join him in California."

Leanne frowned at the change of subject. She followed suit despite her objection. "His arguments were valid, I can't deny. I hardly knew the bastard myself. I still feel like I should go. I don't feel right about him going by himself. I don't care if he thinks it'll only be a day."

"I admit I'm feeling much the same. He needs to go alone to face the ghosts he left behind, but he also shouldn't be alone because of them."

"Damned if we do, damned if we don't."

"Pretty much." She climbed the steps to the Inn, still clinging to Leanne's arm. "However, with him leaving, I admit that I'm glad you're here. Alma will need someone close to her nearby. I fear what Cole's departure is going to do for her temperament."

"I've already made plans to spend some extra time at your apartment the next few weeks."

"Thank you." Jane hugged her tight. "For everything."

"What are sisters for," Leanne whispered. They both laughed at the secret joke.

Jane was relieved when Tom hollered out from the Inn at Leanne, for she'd been about to cry yet again. At this point she was honestly surprised she had any measure of tears left to shed. When Leanne made a quick goodbye to head inside after Tom, Jane remained on the porch. The train would arrive soon, and she'd need to be at the platform to greet some guests anyway. There was little point in heading inside for a bit of warmth first.

Besides, this was her favorite time of year in the town. Near constant snowfall kept everything hushed and crisp even as the bustle of activity tried to erase all the cleanliness and silence the snow left behind.

Preparations for Christmas were in full swing. Lillian had blessedly made the arrangements for decorations around town this year. Though Jane and Kat usually did all they could to decorate the town for its festivals and dances, Jane hadn't much been in the mood of late. To her credit, and of little surprise to Jane, the decorations were beautiful while also understated. Strands of garland draped on every railing, every balcony, and even the windows of folks that had neither. The lamps were even wrapped in bits of garland and holly.

"Miss Spencer."

Jane turned from her admiration of the town to find the source of the vaguely familiar voice. When she realized who it was, she was unable to stop the frown tugging her lips down. "Hello Pastor Eckles. To what do we owe the visit to town?"

"I'm making the townspeople aware of the service I'm hosting on Christmas Eve. I do hope you and your family will be able to make it. We would love to see you at Glorious Valley."

"You would? That's news to me, Pastor."

"I can't imagine why it would be." After a mere sentence from her, his nose had already wrinkled in annoyance—or perhaps disgust.

"Because you hardly have any desire to have a soul such as mine at your church. You've made it abundantly clear through your sermons what you thought should happen to a person like myself." Jane descended one step closer to the man. He'd arrived in Dominion Falls to learn under Reverend Greene, much as Reverend Lyons had.

Unfortunately, he'd proven overzealous in his damnation of many souls in town. While Reverend Greene often took a forgiving stance filled with love, Eckles would rather have damned them all to hell and left a sparkling blankness behind. Between his own convictions, and the request of many townspeople, Reverend Greene had dismissed Eckles. To the dismay of many, Eckles remained in Dominion Falls and had started his own church.

Eckles smiled a bit too broad for Jane's comfort. "There is always time for a soul to be saved. We could still save yours."

"My soul is fine. Whether or not I am saved is between myself and God."

"If you would come to our service, think of how many would follow and also be saved."

"You wish us to come so you might fill us with hate instead of love and forgiveness?" Jane finished her descent down the stairs so she stood right in front of the man. "And why do you wish me to come? You find me beyond help. You've said as much to my face."

"No soul is beyond help."

"I will remain where I have attended church all along. The Reverends Greene and Lyons live by First John, chapter four, verse eight. 'He that loveth not, knoweth not God; for God is love'." Jane turned away. "If you'll excuse me, Pastor. I must meet the train."

She high tailed it to the depot. There was to be one couple arriving on the train with plans to stay at the Inn. She'd greet them, see they made it to the Inn, and go find her husband to enjoy their last day together before he left.

As she climbed the steps to the platform, she was delighted to see Lee under the sign for the Sage Brush. "Lee."

Lee's brow furrowed, but she accepted Jane's hug. "Jane. I thought…what with David."

"Is that why you weren't at tea this week? Nonsense. You didn't arrest my brother." Jane clutched Lee's hands in her own. "How are you holding up without Michael at the hotel? Not to mention your beautiful baby that you must attend to."

"We're getting by. It's been difficult. Nick said he's bringing in another manager to help until he can get Mike out of jail."

"Good. I'd hate to see you overworked."

"Jane, about David."

"I'm sorry, but we can't discuss that matter. Please, join us for tea on Thursday if you have time. You can bring Marjorie. We'd love to see you." Jane scooted away before Lee could bring up David again.

Certainly she was being stubborn, but she wasn't ready to let go of her anger yet. Fortunately the train arrived and she was distracted by seeking out her guests. The couple decided to walk the short distance to the Inn, and after assurance she'd see to their bags, they departed.

When Jane turned back to the train, she noticed many people were glancing toward a couple on the platform. Worse, they were whispering as they walked passed them. Jane frowned at the treatment of the pair who were exceptionally well dressed, and also happened to be black. The judgement of the others on the platform worked on Jane's nerves.

She didn't agree with Pastor Eckles on much, but she hoped that he was correct that where she went others would follow. Jane smiled warm as she could, extending her hand as she approached the pair. "Good afternoon, folks. Welcome to Dominion Falls. I'm Jane Spencer, part-owner of The Hangman's Inn. Were you perhaps looking for a place to stay?"

"Oh. No ma'am. We have a place. We'll be taking over the mercantile in town." The man smiled in return, his joy at his declaration infectious.

"You're the folks that bought the place sight unseen. Well, goodness. I'm very glad to meet you both at last." Jane nodded to the woman, who seemed much more cautious about returning any warmth. "Will you be keeping it as a mercantile, then?"

"That's why we bought it all, ma'am." He drew the woman closer. "My name's Abraham Jones. Most folks call me Abe. This is my wife, Faith."

"It's wonderful to meet you." Jane extended her hand to Faith. "And please, call me Jane. Mrs. Jones, I'd like to extend an offer for you to join my friends and I for tea on Thursday at my Inn. I'm certain they'd be delighted to meet another woman of business."

"We shall see." Faith offered a perfunctory smile with her handshake. Not cold, but definitely cautious. "If you'll excuse us, we should locate our business."

"It's easy enough to find. Follow Main Street into town. Soon as you step off the platform here you'll be able to see my Inn. Head toward it, and turn right on First Street. The mercantile is at the end of First Street on Miner's Row. You can't miss it. Mrs. Jones, Abe." Jane shook their hands once again before they left.

Though she could tell several pairs of eyes stared hard at her for the interaction, she ignored them all. Certainly a couple of color purchasing the mercantile lock, stock, and barrel was unusual, but if they were to do any business in this town they'd best have some tough skin. It would take some work, even so many years after the war fought for their freedom. One thing in their favor was that the new general store hadn't nearly the amount of supplies that could be found at the mercantile.

"Jane Doe Spencer." Katherine's bark of Jane's full name pulled her attention from the departing couple. As she approached, Kat took notice of Jane's wandering attention. "Who was that you were talking to?"

"New owners of the mercantile. Abe and Faith Jones. Now what has you upset enough to use my full name?"

"It wasn't your full name," Kat carried on in a half teasing tone that assured Jane she wasn't as angry as she was putting on. As Jane's best friend, she was one of the few people that knew she and Cole were actually married. Luckily she'd kept her silence. "And I was just looking over the manifest of today's train. What are you and Cole playing at?"

"What?" Jane's full attention turned to her friend for that. "What are you talking about?"

"Three more horses are on this train to be delivered to your barn?"

"Three more—oh, that man." Jane laughed. "That means one for Jesse, one for Cindy, and one for Lizzie."

"You can't give them horses. We haven't anything so grand."

"Horses are a necessity in this town, not a luxury. We don't mind." Jane squeezed Kat's hands. "You can pay us back if you wish. Cole didn't want them to be left out when four of our other children are getting them. Neither did I for that matter."

"Lizzie—"

"I promised to care for her just as you did. You may have adopted her, but we share her as much as we share Cindy, or I share Jesse. It's the way of things, and I thought you were used to such things by now."

"You're a horrible friend."

"I know. I love you too."

"Tell Cole he's in terrible trouble."

Jane backed away. "I'll go punish him myself."

"That's not punishment, Jane."

Daring ideas are like chessmen moved forward. They may be beaten, but they may start a winning game.
-Johann Wolfgang von Goethe

Sally couldn't focus on the task at hand. She had finally figured out how to put her notebook back together how she wanted. Unfortunately, in the process she'd realized she found it easier to look over everything when it was all spread out in a bigger layout.

Nothing like that was feasible to carry around, so that was a problem she'd deal with later. For now, she was stitching the pages back together, with some extra blank pages in between to add notes as she thought of them.

Her mind sat firmly elsewhere, entranced by Cole and Jane. With Cole leaving tomorrow they were fascinating to watch. He wasn't even sitting with Jane. For the moment he was with Alma at the piano, carrying on a quiet conversation while she played.

Jane sat on the couch with a book in her hand. She hardly looked at it, she only had eyes for Cole. The adoration shone out of her like a beacon, and was equally met when Cole cast his gaze her way.

Sally would give anything for something like that in her life. She'd never get it if she kept scurrying away from every opportunity.

Molly had left town again on another mission the very same day she'd kissed Sally. Likely it was because of Sally's reaction. It was probably for the best, Sally didn't think she was quite brave enough to face that yet.

There was one other opportunity she could grab at. Should she? Yes. A tingle of excitement fluttered through her belly at the idea.

She flew to her feet so fast, she startled Jane.

Jane's brow pursed. "Sally? Is something wrong?"

"No. Nothing. I just—I have something I need to do."

"All right. It's Cole's last night in town, I hope you'll be joining us all for supper. We're going to have it here in the apartment so we aren't interrupted."

"I'll be back." Sally set her things aside on the desk, then rushed from the room.

She wasn't sure where she might find Patrick, but as it was still mid-day, she hoped he wouldn't be difficult to find. Or at Kat's. She didn't think she'd have the gumption to ask him while he was in the presence of others.

The first place to look was easy enough, the casino. She paused at the railing around the pit to scan the patrons already present. With no sign of him, she continued to the restaurant.

Patrick sat quite alone at a table near the reception desk. Reading a paper and sipping tea, pretending to be oblivious to the giggling table of young women goggling at him.

Seeing the girls sent a niggle of a doubt through the previously excited flutter. Still, Patrick caught sight of her and offered a warm smile.

Sally straightened her shoulders in hopes it would add to her bravery as she approached. "Mr. Warner."

"Miss Spencer. Would you join me?"

"I was hoping we might chat." Sally didn't take the seat he'd indicated. "On the private matter we discussed recently."

His eyes lit with a wicked gleam. "How delightful. I would be honored."

She ignored the glares from the women at the next table, slipping her hand through his offered arm. "Where to?"

"We'll take a walk, shall we? I'd suggest my room, but as we haven't set any boundaries, such a thing would be too soon."

A shiver of excitement trickled down her spine at his mildly seductive tone. "You are experienced at such matters. Ma wasn't wrong."

"She wasn't. Tales of my rakish behavior often precede me. Most women are too scandalized to approach me first, rather than the other way around. You're only the second to do so."

Though she suspected who might have been the first, Sally didn't dare ask. She wasn't sure it was something she wanted to know as fact. She walked with him through the cleared streets, pondering how best to make her request without seeming too eager, or an idiot.

"Before I make assumptions, I want to be certain we're discussing the same thing."

"Which would be?"

"Your virtues."

A gentle heat tickled under her cheekbones, but not the burning heat of embarrassment. "Virtues might be stretching the matter. I was once a whore."

"Fair enough point. Seeing as you are knowledgeable of certain skills, might I ask what you are seeking as far as a dalliance with me?"

"Excitement," Sally blurted the word without thinking. Now that it was out there, more spilled forward. "Stimulation. Ma once said one day I'd know what it was like to demand what I wanted."

"Then you demand it." Patrick paused their progress to face her dead on.

"I find that my past has left me less inclined to do so. I fear…"

"The one you demand it of will think you no more than what you were?" He stepped back and scanned her top to bottom. "Only a fool would think so."

"Most here know of my past. Those that don't would be told."

"The right person will not care." He offered his arm again. "What else?"

"I've only known sex as business." Somehow with the line crossed, she found it much easier to talk about it. Patrick's open attitude certainly helped her push away the shyness. "I'd like to know it as pleasure. I'd like to know what I do like, and what I don't."

"Those are easy enough things to learn. Unfortunately, most women equate finding pleasure with love. There are lines I don't cross as well."

"I don't know what love is, honestly."

"A confession I could make myself. I believe I've come close once or twice, but none have truly left me besotted."

"I courted Arthur for a while, then realized that while I care for him, I didn't love him the way Ma loves Cole. I don't know that I'll ever find love like theirs, but I do know I won't ever find it hiding away from my own desires."

"Speaking of, why have you not asked your friend for such favors? I imagine she would be as willing as myself to enjoy your pleasures."

"She's not here right now." Sally met his gaze. "Perhaps when she returns, I will. However, if I were to ask only her, how would I know if I desired a man's touch, or a woman's?"

"Or both?"

This time the heat of embarrassment blazed forth. She ducked her head away from his intense gaze.

"No point hiding away now, young Sally. You think I haven't been with multiple women at once? I've explored much of the pleasures of sex. There is no judgment here."

"It's often frowned on."

"Perhaps, but again with the right people, it matters not. I don't mind sharing, or joining if your friend so desires. Your desires are safe in my hands. However."

Sally lifted her gaze again.

"If there is a hint of anything beyond desire, I must ask you to tell me. As we've discussed, love is not something I desire or know."

"Then we're on the same page. I'm not looking for love. I'm looking for experience."

"And excitement."

"Quite."

Patrick lifted her hand to his lips. His warm kiss sparked her nerves to life. The hunger in his eyes sparked even more alive. "Then I look forward to our next meeting. When would you like to start?"

"Oh, well that's a good question." Sally frowned. Cole was leaving the next day, so it would do her no good to start then. Although, Jane would have plenty trying to placate her and keep her happy. "How about tomorrow around one?"

"Splendid." He offered her his arm again. "Allow me to return you safely home. I have some errands to run after."

"How kind of you, sir." She couldn't help but add teasing to her tone. "No wonder you fear women falling head over heels with such manners and thoughtfulness."

"I do attract more bees with honey than vinegar, tis true. Not many women are like your ma and more attracted to the rake before the gentleman hidden beneath."

"The more is their loss. Pa is a wonderful man."

"A diamond in the rough, honed to perfection by a strong woman."

"How poetic." She laughed softly. "He'd hate it, especially because it was true."

"Hence, why I would never say it to his face." He paused at the steps to the Inn. Once again he placed a warm kiss to her hand. "I'll leave you here. I look forward to seeing you next."

"As will I." Sally tipped her head to him, grinning as he headed down the street. The excited spark kicked up stronger again.

"Dare I ask?" Tommy spoke from the porch. He leaned on the railing. The shadows from the porch and his hat brim hid his expression.

"Do you really want to know why I was making time with Patrick?"

"Patrick now, is it? Then I definitely don't want to know." He grinned as she climbed the steps. "Just like I don't want to hear your Ma bragging, I don't want to hear you do it, either."

"We aren't related by blood." Humor flooded forward at his grimace.

"We're as good as, and I don't want to hear it."

She let her laughter free, glad he joined along with her. "Oh, it's good to laugh. The mood has been increasingly difficult as it gets closer to Pa leaving."

"The last couple of times Jane and Cole parted company it was in dire situations where they weren't sure they'd see each other again."

"But it isn't like that this time."

"No, but it brings it to mind. Plus, they're going to miss each other. It's called love."

She turned her attention to the town at the word. Though she'd just admitted to Patrick she wasn't sure she knew what love was, she'd meant for herself. She'd certainly seen evidence of it with Jane and Cole. Plenty of other relationships around town reflected it as well. Tommy and Leanne, Charlie and Millie, even Kat and Norman though he was so much older than her.

"You good?"

"Hm? Yes. I'm fine. Just thinking about the happy couples around town."

"You'll find someone. Maybe even—"

"No. Don't say Patrick. I will not be falling in love with him."

He snorted. "You sound sure of yourself."

"I am. I won't. I'm not even sure I want to find someone. I'm a little busy at the moment."

"Oh yeah? With what?" He glanced her way. "Don't say with learning. I learned the hard way there's more to life than learning and detective work."

"I wasn't going to."

"Than what?"

"Finding myself."

Every heart sings a song, incomplete,
until another heart whispers back.
Those who wish to sing always find a song.
At the touch of a lover,
everyone becomes a poet.
—Plato

Jane leaned on the doorframe to the twin's room. Cole knelt beside Clara's bed, carrying on a hushed conversation with the young girl. In a rare moment for their boisterous daughter, she looked terribly serious in what she was saying to her pa.

Colton sat nearby on the floor, his ever-serious expression fixed on Cole. For all she knew they could have been discussing all the woes of the world. Whatever it was, she was content to keep her near-deaf ear on them and allow them their moment.

Another rush of grief rose through to her chest where her heart ached even more. Sometimes she swore she could feel it ripping apart when the grief hit. That she'd lost the chance to see him with another child as he was with the twins. The idea that they would lose these moments for even a few scant weeks.

She ducked from the room before she began to cry in earnest. Last thing she wanted to do was disrupt Cole's moment with the twins. Willow sat at Jane's desk, staring hard at a paper before her. Her brows furrowed as she gripped the pencil so hard Jane thought it might break.

"Willow?" Jane moved closer, noting the lines of basic text on the page. "What is it?"

"I don't want to." Willow shoved the paper away. "Why?"

For the past year Jane had been working with the two to learn to read and write. Never before had Willow put up such a fight in the matter. "Learning to read and write can be beneficial in life. Certainly there are people that never learn, but there is much joy to be found in reading, and writing allows you to communicate with others while they're away."

"Like Cole."

"Exactly." Jane knelt beside the girl. "Miss Ada says you've been unwilling to listen to her instructions."

"I don't like her."

"You don't?"

"No. She should go away." Willow turned her face away, but not before Jane took note of the whisper of a tear in her eyes.

"What is it you don't like about her? We can't face a problem until we know what it is."

"We were fine without her."

"Yes, you were. I was terribly busy, though. I've found it increasingly difficult to be at all places at all times. Ada is here to help. She's an excellent teacher, Jesse adores her."

Willow kept her head turned away. A sniffle reached Jane's ears, but the girl kept her gaze fixed hard on the window.

Behind Jane, in his still-halting English, Jay ratted out his sister's woes. "She says…the lady…looks like Ma."

"What?" Jane turned to face Jay in surprise. "She looks like your Ma?"

"No." Jay's brow furrowed. "No. Not my ma."

Jane turned back to Willow. With the gentlest touch of her finger to the girl's chin, she drew Willow's shimmering gaze back to her. The realization struck as she saw the depth of true grief in her eyes. "Oh, Willow. You remember the ma that birthed you?"

Willow shook her head fiercely. With the heels of her hands, she swiped at her tears.

Despite the negative response, Jane suspected that was the cause. "Oh, you dear child. How confusing it must be for you. Did meeting Ada make you remember?"

"Not my ma," Willow insisted.

"Not the ma that raised you, no. The one you knew before her when you were a small child no older than Clara. You were so young. I imagine it's hard to remember such things. More surprising that you actually do." Jane handed her the kerchief she'd had tucked in her belt. "I understand your grief, and we will try to work around it. However, I won't dismiss Ada."

Willow glared at her. "I don't like her."

"It isn't her you don't like. It's that she made you remember something other than the life you loved and always knew before this." Jane tucked the girl's long, dark hair behind her shoulders. "However, now that we know the problem we can work on it. Together. We'll also work on your letters together."

"No."

Jane took Willow's hands in hers. She fixed the girl with a firm gaze. "I've promised since you came to be with us that I will never make you forget the life you led. That will never change. It doesn't mean that you can forgo learning. I'm sorry this memory saddens you, and that it makes you angry, but it's one memory when you have many more of the ma and pa that raised you all of those years in Utah."

Jay moved to Jane's side, staring at his sister. Then he turned his gaze on Jane. "You want us to be white."

"I want you to be you. No more, no less." Jane tapped his nose. "That's why you go with Black Moon. Why your sister works on her beading. Why I let you wear what you like at home. It's also why I don't make your sister wear a corset and fancy gown despite being of age. You will be you. You are my wards, and I will treat you as I would any of my children, though I never expect you to call me Ma. You have a ma and pa that you love."

"She's worried if she remembers…"

Jane pondered over his trailing words. The only logical conclusion was that she'd forget what she'd been if those old memories returned. Jane sighed softly, squeezing Willow's hands. "It changes nothing if you remember or if you don't. I remember nothing from my first twenty-seven years of life.

If I were to start to remember, it wouldn't change who I am now."

Willow glared at her brother for telling her secrets. As Jane stopped speaking, she focused on her. "It is confusing."

"I imagine so. It would be confusing for me to start remembering as well. We'll work through it. I'm sorry that bringing in Ada as governess led you to such confusion." Jane offered her a smile, then drew Jay into a half hug. "You two are very unique, and I really like that about you. I won't be asking you to change anything, only that you learn."

Willow nodded weakly.

"Why don't you both take the rest of the evening off from learning? Sally should return soon with some cocoa from Cora's. You can play your games before bed. We'll start fresh tomorrow."

Jay moved like a shot to their room, likely to get the dice. Willow moved slower. Before she passed Jane, she leaned down to give her a brutal hug before taking off after her brother.

Jane stayed kneeling on the floor, the suddenness and fierceness of the first true hug from the girl keeping her in place. It wasn't until a warm hand settled on her shoulder that she moved. She tilted her head back, smiling at the man towering over her. "Did you have a nice conversation with the twins?"

"Always." He held out his hand without returning her smile. "I..."

"Hush. You're leaving. Tomorrow." She accepted his hand and assistance to her feet. "No more doubts, no more second guessing. Do not ruin our final hours together with such foolishness."

"I'm gonna miss ya so damn much."

"The feeling is mutual." She guided him to their room. For the rest of the night, nothing short of a disaster would get her out of their room.

Soon as they'd entered, he closed the door behind him. The lock clicked into place. He wrapped his arms around her, holding her close. His breath brushed along her hair.

She leaned into his embrace with a heavy sigh. "We'll be fine here. We'll miss you, but we'll be fine. It's you I'm worried about."

"It's you I'm worried about."

"I know."

"Write me every day. Tell me what's happening. It'll make it easier. And harder."

"Of course. Letters, telegrams. You'll never be for want of a reminder of home."

With regret, she pulled free of his embrace. In the closet she bent to get the box under her vanity. When she emerged from the closet, Cole had removed his tie and vest, but sat at the edge of the bed quietly. He eyed the box with a frown. "What's this?"

"Well, I contemplated several gifts for you to remember me by. The coat Graham and I got for you several years ago is still quite good. Men have no need for rings, though I wouldn't mind you having the reminder on your finger every day as I do. I could have got you a new cigar cutter, but in the end I thought this more necessary. Plus, you'll wear it every day because you're never without."

"You didn't have to get me anything."

"I'm well aware of that, but I wanted to. This was to be for Christmas, you're getting it a little early instead."

Through his continued frown, Cole opened the box. He withdrew the carefully crafted holster. She'd asked Mr. Kilmurry to make the belt from worn leather so it wouldn't be stiff on first wearing. The actual holster had been made to fit his Walker like a glove. Strap details wrapped around the holster, with images of horses pressed into the leather of the belt.

"Damn."

"It should fit your Walker just right."

"Damn."

She laughed softly and ran her fingers through his hair. "I'll take that as a thank you."

He it aside to place his hands on her hips. "At least this time I won't be coming back to you about to be hanged. Or worried that maniac's gonna kill ya before I can save ya."

"Thank heavens for small favors, I guess." She brushed her lips across his. "You'll be back in no time. A quick trip is all this is."

"Still too long."

"Don't I know it?" At his small tug, she straddled his lap. "I love you."

"Love you too, Mrs. Mitchell."

"Oh, say it again."

"Mrs. Mitchell."

"I do like that. Perhaps it's time to end the subterfuge." She kissed him deeply until he sank back to the bed. "When you return, perhaps we should let it slip to Mr. Hamm that we are actually legally married."

"The whole camp'll know in an hour."

"It's a town now, not a camp—and that's precisely my point."

"You want everyone to know?"

"That I'm yours in every sense of the word?"

"Ya have been for a long time." His hands danced along the buttons of her bodice, popping them free one by one. "Thought you liked the game."

"I like being yours more."

"That so?"

"Yes."

"Then prove it, Mrs. Mitchell."

The minute I heard my first love story
I started looking for you, not knowing
how blind that was. Lovers don't finally
meet someone. They're in each other all along.
—Jal ad-Din Rumi

Cole's memory was admittedly nothing like Jane's, but he could remember the last time they'd parted at the train station with crystal clarity. It had been pouring down rain and she'd been struggling so hard to keep those three words unsaid. He'd wanted her to say it, told her to say it, but she'd refused. Instead, she'd let the rain hide her tears. Her hands had fluttered about fussing with his coat.

At the moment she fussed over him much the same way. Delicate hands flattened the lapel of his coat every time the wind whipped around the corner to lift it again, which was often. Her eyes were dry this time, though that might have been attributed to the brutal wind. Or perhaps the lack of rain to disguise them.

"I don't expect you to write every day, that isn't who you are. A telegram once a week will suffice. I'm certain the children will be happy to hear from you." Her words were whispered low enough he barely heard them over the wind.

He set his hands on hers to still them. "You're fussing."

"Would you rather I stamp and scream and tell you not to go?"

"Actually…" It didn't sound half bad—a good reason to not leave, for sure.

"I won't do it, stop looking so hopeful." She leaned closer against him when the train whistled. The thick woolen layers weren't nearly enough to deter him from his usual distraction at her presence. "We'll see you at Christmas."

"Sooner."

"We'll plan for Christmas, and hope for much sooner."

"Of course." He pulled her into a slow, sweet kiss. If he dared apply any of the heat or need that coursed through his veins, he knew she'd pull away. Instead, he let his lips dance along hers, soft and subtle. Tenderness nearly always reserved for their apartment lingered in the kiss. "I'll send a telegram when I get there, or sooner if we get delayed."

"That'll be fine." She smiled softly at him, her eyes still dry. "Be safe for me. Don't be gone too long."

"Be quick as I can." The next whistle sounded to announce the train's looming departure. He dug into his pocket to remove a small box. "You gave me a present early, it's your turn."

"You romantic sod. You're determined to make me weep."

"Really not." He couldn't bear to watch her weep. It would make it near impossible to leave. "Open it after I go, then."

"Not a chance. We have five minutes still." She tugged the string free. The box popped open to reveal a silver dip pen, inscribed with her married name. "Oh, goodness. How lovely."

"Thought you could use it for your journaling."

"I will." She leaned up to give him another soft kiss. "I might have protested if it were another piece of jewelry. You've bestowed me with far too much already."

"No such thing."

"I can only wear one necklace at a time. At last count you'd given me five, plus ear bobs for at least three of them."

"Don't mean that's enough."

She pursed her lips, wagging the box at him. "There'd better be none on the tree, sir."

"Won't make no promises I can't keep."

She laughed softly, and he was grateful for the teasing laughter. Somehow it made it easier as the train whistle blasted again. Her laughter faded into another frown, but at least it wasn't tears. "I suppose that means it's time for you to board."

"I could wait until last call."

"If you wish my eyes to remain dry you will do no such thing."

When she leaned in for another kiss, he happily obliged. This time when she moved to step back, he laced his arm around her waist to pull her closer. One quick brush of his tongue along her lips and she opened to him.

As if it were the last time they'd parted, she clung tight to him. Warmth and desires ebbed off her, and he drank them in like a sweet wine. The blistering wind barely touched him through her heat.

Too soon it cooled and when he allowed her release, a single tear trembled on her cheek. With his thumb, he brushed it aside. "Take care of them yahoos."

"I'll make certain they are absolutely undisciplined for your return, after which I will stay at Katherin's for a week and see how you feel about it."

"Maybe we need to talk about a divorce."

"Don't you dare." She shoved him playfully. "We're just getting ready to tell the world. I'm not letting you get away that easily, you're stuck with me. Besides, my lawyer is better than yours."

"We have the same lawyer."

"Ah, but whose side do you think my brother will choose?"

"Damn, woman."

She nabbed a quick kiss when the conductor yelled the last call. "Go. I'll see you before Christmas."

"In two weeks if I can get it sorted quick enough."

"Then I'll pray for a quick sorting."

He paused soon as he hopped on the train to keep her in sight. As she waved, Kathy walked up behind her. It eased his mind to know she'd not be alone when he pulled away. He'd made his goodbyes to the kids at the apartment, because Jane thought it too cold for them to linger in farewell. Plus, he'd really wanted a private goodbye from her anyhow.

Cole offered a final wave as the door shut on him. He strode through the car to find a seat near the window. As expected, Jane remained there waving though she didn't likely know where he was. With one final whistle the brakes hissed, and the train moved. The moment he could no longer see Jane, he turned to face the front.

Now that he was moving the nerves subsided somewhat. An underlying thread of anger lingered underneath it all as it had since he'd received the telegram. The interruption to his life thanks to the no-good bastard couldn't have come at a worse time.

Then again, that's how his pa had always worked. For as long as Cole could remember. Paul had done nothing but make life worse whenever he could, and really bad when it was already trouble.

Cole leaned back in his seat, but when he went to set down his bag, he noticed something that hadn't been there before. A hard lump in the front pocket suspiciously shaped like a book. When he opened the flap, there sat Jane's favorite book, *Leaves of Grass*. The book he'd intentionally used to learn to read so he could join her in her pleasure at the poems. Because it was the book she'd left in his room, the book that turned his room into theirs.

The well-worn copy had to have come from her nightstand, where it had sat for years. The original copy she'd left in his room years before she'd even lived there had burned in the fire. This one was newer, but no less softened with use and time. The cover faded, pages aged in a few short years of use.

He opened it, unsurprised at the note he found in the front from her.

I know you say it makes it lonelier, but perhaps that what I wish. I want you home soon. I love you. Remember our favorite and read it often. I will be. Every evening after we close I will read Pent Up Aching Rivers *and think of you.*

"Evil woman," he muttered under his breath.

With that, he opened the book to the poem she'd mentioned. He leaned back, reading every line carefully as he thought of Jane, and how soon he could get home to her.

One swallow does not make a summer,
neither does one fine day;
similarly one day or brief time of happiness
does not make a person entirely happy.
—Aristotle

Jane looked over the slate Willow showed her. The letters were a little wonky, but mostly correct. "Very good, Willow. Do you remember how to do your name like we did yesterday?"

Willow nodded. "Yes."

"Wonderful. Can you show me?" Jane straightened, rubbing her ribs again. The discomfort so like indigestion had been rearing up every couple of days. It always went away quick enough, but was becoming quite annoying.

Willow held up the slate again. Her name spelled clear and in a straight line.

"Very good. You're doing very well."

"Not my name," Willow mumbled.

"What?" Jane studied the girls face as she wiped the slate clean. The familiar defiance darkened Willow's features. Realization dawned. "Oh, dear. That's right. That isn't your full name. I'm sorry, Willow. We are so used to one word names, I didn't think. Here."

Willow let Jane take the slate, her gaze fixed on the letters Jane wrote.

"There. Shivering. Willow. You're familiar with Willow. Now try Shivering." Jane brushed her hand along the girls hair while she wrote. The past few days Jane had worked with Willow to give her some time without Ada's teaching. The timing was good as it helped keep her distracted.

Cole had already sent one telegram for an update, but she didn't expect another until he arrived in Holle Creek. Footsteps descending the stairs pulled her attention. Jane smiled at the young woman that appeared. "Sally. You're looking in good spirits this morning."

"I am. The weather's fair, so Tommy and I are going out to practice tracking." Sally grabbed a cloak from near the door. "And this afternoon I have a meeting with Patrick."

"A full day, then. Do you have all you need for your meeting with Patrick?"

"I do. I plan to head to the clinic today for more as well. I don't want to deplete your stores."

"Cole is out of town for several weeks, and we aren't actively trying to stop a pregnancy. We don't need protection against it." Jane couldn't help but smile at the young woman. "I must say, I'm proud of the progess you've been making this past week."

Sally looked up from clasping her cloak. "What? What for?"

"A week ago my asking if you needed protection, or the thought of going to the clinic to ask for more would have sent you blushing. Not normal for a former whore, but then again because of it, you were a bit fearful of being forthright with it."

This time Sally's cheeks got the faintest hint of pink. "Patrick's a good teacher."

"I'd heard as much in rumor, but with this evidence before me, I must agree." Jane glanced back down at Willow's slate. "Nicely done. Would you like some free time now? Ma is going to be along shortly to take the twins on an adventure if you'd like to join them."

Sally tilted her head. "What about Ada?"

"She is working on numbers with Jaybird and Jesse this morning. This afternoon everyone will come together for some more learning." Jane met Willow's gaze. "Everyone. Yes?"

Willow didn't appear too thrilled with it, but still nodded her agreement.

"I have an idea." Jane crouched before Willow to meet her gaze. "Your people had stories that told their history, didn't they?"

"Yes. Lots."

"I thought so. Since Miss Ada is working on history this afternoon, and it's the history of our people. Maybe after supper you'd like to share one of the stories of yours for us?"

Willow's eyes lit at the idea, but she withheld a smile. "Really?"

"Really. I think it would do us all some good to learn more about the world you and Jay came from. I'll even write it down to share with Cole on his return. Would you like that?"

"I'd like that."

"Good. If you want to go with Ma and the twins, you'd best get ready. Dress warm, please." Jane nodded to Sally. "Have a good day. We'll see you at supper, I suppose."

"Yes. I'm working the casino tonight, anyway."

Jane waved Sally off and sank onto the couch with a heavy sigh. It was only eleven and she felt as though she could crawl right back into bed. That was a luxury she couldn't afford with her partner out of town, though. She'd have to muster the energy to get to work very soon.

More footsteps on the stairs got Jane to force forward another bright smile. The enthusiasm behind it increased at the sight of Eunice. "Good morning, Ma."

"Pshaw. I've been up for hours. I had to return upstairs to get dressed for my adventure with the twins."

"And Willow."

"Oh, she's going to join us? Wonderful." Eunice eyed her with sharp gaze. "What's wrong?"

"I'm tired. That's all. I'm not sleeping so well with Cole gone." Jane pushed to her feet. "Since there's no rest for the wicked, I'll be heading to work soon."

"Fine, but if you need more help, you let us know."

"You came to be here for Michael, not me."

"And your brothers are helping Michael. John and I go and visit often and offer support how we can. It's fortuitous that we came in a time of need for you as well." Eunice gripped her chin. "You need our help, and you'll take it."

"Yes, ma'am." Jane grinned at her mother's scowl. "If you don't wish to be called ma'am, don't bark orders like a general."

"I'll bark whatever orders I like. Now get on out of here and let me deal with my grandchildren, thank you."

Jane scooted all the way to the door before she called back to the room, "Yes, ma'am."

She shut the door on her mother's scolding, her mood once again lighter.

The casino already had a decent patronage, so she got right to work. Between passing drinks and running a few rounds of twenty-one until their afternoon dealer arrived several hours had passed.

In all of the rush of working a headache had bloomed between her eyes. Pressing until her vision blurred slightly. Imagining she was hungry due to the afternoon hour she made her way to the front to get some food from the kitchens.

She found Charlie in the restaurant having some coffee and reading a book. Without asking, she took the seat beside him. "Good afternoon, Charles."

"Same to you." Charles slid a paper between the pages to mark his place. When he turned his full attention on her, his brow furrowed. "Are you well?"

"I must look terrible for all the people asking me today."

"Not terrible, but not up to snuff."

"I'm tired from not sleeping well. I now have a headache because I was too busy for a noonday meal. It started a while ago, but Peter only now arrived for his shift so I've been stuck dealing the past hour."

"Headache, hm?" Charlie grabbed his bag from the chair beside him. He rummaged through it for a moment. "I believe your assessment might be right. However, if food doesn't ease it, this should help."

She took the bit of folded paper he procured from the case. "Thank you. I may take it anyhow to speed up the process. It's disturbing my vision. The cards were a little blurry. Such a thing makes it difficult to deal properly."

Like their mother so recently had, he took her chin in hand. After he'd turned her head side to side, he released her. "Sounds almost like a megrim. If this medicine doesn't ease it, please come to the clinic and I'll give you something stronger."

"I appreciate your concern. I have no doubt this powder and some delicious food will ease all of my pains."

"Even if they don't, you'll avoid the clinic at all costs."

"I'm not nearly as bad as I once was. I promise to come if it doesn't ease."

"Good." He patted her hand before returning to his coffee. "How is Cole doing on his journey west?"

"Bored, I believe. He dislikes travel when there's so little to do." Jane paused to request her food from the waitress. She dropped the powder in her mouth, following it with a swig of water. "Boredom has always been Cole's worst enemy. While I can often find plenty to do, he usually only can when there's a business to run, or me to do."

Charlie snorted out the sip of coffee he'd just taken. Cursing, he dabbed at his own face and the table with his napkin. "Jane."

She chuckled softly. "You act as though I've never said such a thing."

"You've been well behaved of late. That comment blindsided me." His face scrunched around a few times. "Well, thank you for that."

"Anytime." Jane was distracted by movement at the door. The twins raced into, and right through the restaurant, but they weren't what caught her eye.

Eunice was all but supporting Willow into the building. The girl had her medicine bag pressed to her face, but her wheezes carried over the quiet hum in the room.

Jane flew to her feet. "Charles."

"Already on it. Give her here, Ma." He scooped her into his arms.

Jane glanced toward where the twins had disappeared.

"Go on with Willow. I've got the twins." Eunice set a hand on her arm. "I don't know what happened. She was mostly sitting quiet while the twins raced about. With all the snow I didn't think there'd be anything to set her off."

"It's fine, Ma. I'll go to her. Make certain the twins haven't gotten themselves into any trouble." Jane darted from the Inn. Already Charlie was out of sight. She raced across the street to the clinic.

It didn't take any searching to find them, Willow's wheezing led Jane down a few doors to one of the exam rooms. Charlie worked at her side preparing herbs while speaking low reassurance to her.

Jane moved to Willow's other side. "I know it's scary, but Charles will take care of you. Keep with your pouch until he's done."

Willow's wide green eyes focused on Jane over the pouch covering her mouth and nose. Her hand found Jane's, squeezing it tight.

"I know. It hasn't been this bad in some time. We'll get you fixed up right." Jane brushed a stray lock of hair from her forehead. "Breathe, sweetheart. Slow as you can."

Charlie poured a few drops of chloroform onto a cloth. With a gentle hand, he pulled the bag from Willow's nose. "A few breaths of this will help everything relax, and then I'll finish with your mudge inhaler."

Willow shook her head away from the cloth. She hated it as much as Jane ever had. No matter if it helped.

"Please, Willow. I know it's awful, but a few breaths and we'll get your bag back until Charles finishes. It'll help you breathe, and that will help you be less afraid." Jane gently urged the girl back toward Charlie.

Willow allowed the cloth for two large wheezes before pushing it away.

"That's better than nothing." Charles poured boiling water into the mudger. He dropped the leaves in before carrying it over to hold under Willow's nose. "Would you like to sit at a chair in the kitchen to do this rather than try to hold it?"

Willow took a few breaths over the steam. Though she still wheezed, the panicked gasping for breath had eased. After a moment, she nodded.

"Then we will. Jane, please carry the pot, I'll get Willow there."

Jane followed them both back to the kitchen. While Willow got settled, Jane grabbed a towel to drape over her head to direct the steam.

Once everything was in place with Willow taking her treatment, Jane turned to her brother. "What could have happened? Ma said she wasn't playing wild like the twins."

"The cold air. I've seen it in others with her condition. It can trigger an event like this." Charlie frowned down at the child.

"She survived all last winter without an attack like this." Jane couldn't keep her hand from resting on Willow's shoulder. Whether the reassurance was for herself or the child, she no longer knew. She only knew she couldn't stop.

"Last winter was relatively mild, and Willow wasn't much for socializing last year, neither was her brother."

"True. She and Jaybird remained angry for a very long time. Only in the past six months have we begun to see true progress." Jane took a deep breath. "No biting cold, then. Is that the only way to prevent this from happening again?"

"It's your best defense. Stay inside where it's warmer. If there's a milder day, she should be safe to go outside." Charlie set a hand on Jane's shoulder "This isn't something that simply goes away. It's going to take you both time to figure out how to handle things. Every time there's something new to learn, you'll learn."

"I know. It's just frightening for us all." Jane couldn't help but smile a little when Willow's hand rested on hers. "Do I need to be worried about anything now?"

"This might have weakened her, so be on the watch for illness. I have another mudge pot you can take home, and I'll prepare some herbs for you to use. She might need to use the mudger more now for a few days until she feels back to strength."

"Will do." Jane let out a long breath, swiping at a tear that fell.

"She's going to be fine," Charlie reassured quietly.

"I know. Thank you."

Anger, if not restrained,
is frequently more hurtful to us
than the injury the provokes it.
—Seneca

Sally's body hummed with energy and pleasure. A smile formed as fingers danced along her arm. She opened her eyes to focus on the man lying beside her. "I daresay that was an afternoon well spent."

Patrick's handsome features creased into a smile. "I'm pleased you think so."

"The past few days have taught me quite a bit."

"Is that so?"

"Yes. Back when I was a whore the days and nights were not for my pleasure. My life was about the pleasures of men. You've taught me well in a few short days how to ask for what I want."

"I believe this afternoon you rather demanded."

"I did, didn't I?" She flopped onto her back, reveling in the happiness of the idea. The idea she'd done as she hadn't thought she could hummed along her flesh with the remaining tingles of passion satisfied. "I rather enjoyed that."

"I could tell. Now tell me." He propped himself on his elbow. "You have been spending your afternoon reposes with me. What about the lovely lady that got you flustered in the first place?"

"She hasn't returned to town yet." She turned to face him again. "I don't know if she'll even care to continue my lessons if she returns."

"I hardly doubt as much. She's probably more worried she scared the little colt right out of the stable."

"She definitely did, but it was more surprise at myself than at her."

The clock chimed on the wall. His brow rose. "You'll speak to her when she returns."

"Of course." When the clock's chime finished, Sally's brain wrapped around how many chimes had come. Eyes wide, she sat straight up. "Oh dear."

"What is it?"

"It is really five o'clock? Goodness, I'm going to be late. So are you. If you expect to be in the Gold Room by six, you must get downstairs and eat." She flew from the bed without further ado. Locating her chemise, she scooted into it fast as she could.

When it came to her corset however, the darn thing was nowhere to be seen. She dropped to her knees to check under the bed.

"Sally?"

"Where is my blasted corset?" She hopped to her feet. "Do you have any idea?"

Already mostly dressed, he began to scour the room with her. With a chuckle, he leaned over the back of the sofa. "Here it is."

She caught it when he tossed it her way. "Thank you."

Soon as she'd bound herself within it, he caught her about the waist. "I must be off."

"Yes, you must." She grinned up at him. "Shall we meet again, two days hence?"

"Again? Oh, the delights we will have. I only need your reassurance."

"Reassurance of what?"

"That you aren't falling hopelessly in love with me."

She snorted her attempt to cover her laughter. Laughing wouldn't be kind, but she couldn't help herself. Thankfully he chuckled right along with her. Sally met his gaze and tried to seriously ponder the question. Love still wasn't something she was sure she'd ever felt.

There was plenty of something there with Patrick. Excitement, fun, laughter. Not the emotion he certainly didn't want. Neither did she, for that matter. She'd only just begun to explore. She offered a firm shake of her head with no laughter in sight. "No. Definitely not love."

"Definitely not? Stronger women than you have caved to my charms."

"There aren't stronger women, and still no. I assure you. I told you I'm not even certain what love is. I know this isn't it, though. This is a much baser emotion, sir. Lust. I admire your not seeing less of me with my scars—"

"Ah-ah. What did I say?"

"You can tell me not to hide them al you wish, but they still concern me." She set her hand on his chest to push him back. "Rest assured, I am not falling in love with you."

"Good. I have many more hearts to break before I rest…and I'd hate for yours to be one of them. Your wonderful mother would have my balls for dinner if I did."

"You're not wrong. Now go. Eat something or you'll be starving while you gamble. You know Ma allows no food in the Gold or Silver rooms."

"Will you lock the door as you leave?"

"Of course. Go." Now free of his entanglement, Sally dressed in her multitude of layers in short order. She locked his door with the master key and headed to the stairs. Not even halfway down the first flight she spotted someone on the landing. "Molly?"

Molly lifted her gaze, paling slightly. "Oh. Sally."

"I'm so glad you're back." Sally moved down the steps quickly.

"You are?" Molly eyed her in suspicion. "Really?"

"I am. I'm terribly sorry for taking off as I did." Sally paused on the landing right beside Molly. After a moment's hesitation, she took Molly's hand in hers. "I do wish we could talk right now, but I've got an important appointment to keep."

"Then when? I wanted to tell you I was sorry—"

"Don't, please. You have nothing to be sorry for. Can we meet tomorrow? At…" Sally had to think over her plans for the next day.

As Sally's silence lingered, Molly withdrew her hand.

"Sorry. With Pa gone, I have a lot more responsibilities to consider. Ma needs all the help she can get. Would ten tomorrow at the library do for a chat?"

"At the library?"

"Yes, unfortunately. Ma's focus is on the casino and brothel so I took some of her time at the library. We should have relative solitude at that time of day, though." Sally clasped her hands. "I have much to tell you, I would love it if you came."

"All right, then. Ten."

"Yes, ten." With one final squeeze to Molly's hands, she descended the rest of the stairs. She passed through the restaurant right into the bustling kitchen. "Evening, Miss Cora. Looks busy out there tonight."

"It is. Your tray is on the table. I put on a plate for Arthur." Cora moved through her workers with ease to season and plate. "Alma invited him."

"Oh. Well." Sally picked up the tray, uncertain how to feel about that. Still, she wasn't about to argue with Alma's invitation. Her mood was already on edge since Cole had been gone. Sally wondered how she'd managed all those years living at the school away from Cole.

Sally skirted through the crowded restaurant, and nearly as crowded saloon with the tray held over her head in the tightest spaces. The tray balanced precariously on one hand when she moved to open the door. As she closed it she called out to Alma, believing her upstairs. "Alma. I've got our dinner."

"Sally," came Alma's reply from the living room where she sat with Arthur. "L-look. Arthur."

Sally eyed the excited rocking of her fellow ward, and couldn't help but smile. "I'd heard a rumor he was joining us from none other than his ma."

Arthur rose as she approached the couch and set the tray on the low table in front of it. "Hope you don't mind. Alma saw me when walking with Tommy and asked me to come."

"I don't mind at all, so long as you don't." Sally offered him a smile. "We haven't had much time to talk since you arrived home."

"You've been busy." A note of bitterness made his words a bit harsher than perhaps he'd intended. Red seeped into his cheeks as he seemed to think better of it. "What with your family and all."

"With Pa gone it's even worse now. I'm trying to do all I can to help Ma." Sally laid a napkin across her lap. "How is life in Denver treating you?"

"D-Denver. My school." Alma's fingers jerked and contorted as her rocking stopped.

"Damn," Sally muttered. She glanced at Arthur with a grimace. "I should have said college. Alma's been having a rough time with pa not here."

"Where'd he go?" Arthur kindly set Alma's food in front of her. Careful not to touch her directly, he set everything out where it needed to be. "There you go, Alma. When you're ready."

Sally couldn't help but smile at his kindness to Alma's needs. "California. No idea why. Neither of them would talk about it. It seemed as though he didn't want to go, but then he did, and then he didn't. Seemed like a necessary thing that he didn't want to do."

He wore an expression she'd seen before when writing stories for Rusty's paper. "Interesting."

She pursed her lips. "What are you wanting?"

"The whole story."

"Well, good luck with that. I don't have it and Ma won't tell you. Besides, it's not story. It's someone's life. Someone that likes his privacy and always has."

"I didn't mean for an article or anything."

Sally harumphed into her bowl of soup.

"You look good too, Sally. You look—happy."

"I am. I've been learning a lot. There's so much more to it than learning how to fight. I've also been doing a lot more around here the past few days. It's been busy, but mostly in a good way." She sipped the soup, pausing as the flavors of the carrot soup washed over her tongue. Creamy and sweet with a pop of spice that made her crave more. After a few more spoonful's she spoke again, "Are you glad to be home?"

"I really am. It's been really good. My classes are interesting, but there's nothing like being home."

Sally was relieved to see Alma sip at her own soup. She'd been worried Alma would refuse to eat again. With a shake of her head she returned to the conversation she'd been having. "Home is a good place to be."

"There's no place like this."

"Without a doubt there isn't. Dominion Falls is very special." Sally lifted her gaze from her soup to find the hopeful doe-like eyes watching her. She frowned. "Arthur."

"What?"

"I'm not staying in Dominion Falls. Not forever. I'll finish my training and then I'm going to explore. Dominion

Falls may be home but there's much more out there to be seen."

"You just said how special it is."

"A home is a place you can always return to, and that's what Dominion Falls is for me." Sally slapped her spoon on the tray. "But to return to it, I must leave. I have to find out what I want in life. I have to figure out what love is and maybe find it."

Arthur's features crumpled.

"Don't do that." Sally flew to her feet. A high-pitched keening made her stop. Alma had begun to rock again. "Oh, Alma. I'm so sorry. What do you need? Do you need a hug, or to play?"

Alma rose and moved to the piano where she began to pound out a loud tune.

Sally sighed and circled the table to sit beside Arthur where Alma had been moments before. When Alma's harsh notes softened, Sally drooped. "I'm sorry. I need you to stop hoping I will change. I am changing, but not how you want me to. I will never be happy living quietly as a wife here. I'm sure in time I'll return and live the rest of my days here, but until then I want to go and see what's outside of this valley. I've only ever known it and the nowhere place I lived before I came here."

"I thought…"

"What?"

"You said you loved me."

"I care about you a great deal. I just told someone else, I'm not certain I even know what love is. I do know that I see it with Ma and Pa, and Kat and Norman, Leanne and Tommy.

The way they see each other and everything seems…I can't even describe it. I want that. I want you to have that."

"Doesn't seem possible." Arthur sighed deeply. "My ma and pa were like that. Ma hasn't seemed happy since he's been gone. I mean, not like she was."

Before Sally could reply, a howl rented the air, accompanied by a second one. "Oh, those hounds."

"Hounds." The playing halted and Alma clapped before hitting discordant notes that matched the howling pair outside.

"Oh, Alma. Will you stop if I bring them in?"

"Whiskey. Bourbon. Whiskey. Bourbon."

"I'll take that as a yes. Excuse me, Arthur." Sally scooted past him to head outside and let the pups in. Before she got to the run, something caught her eye. In the shadows behind the street lamps she could have sworn she saw a shadow creeping along.

Curiosity got the better of her. She crept along the back of the building toward the street to try to catch a better look. Once again a shadow moved in view before the figure disappeared into the alley. The hair on the back of her neck rose, warning her of danger she had no idea of what it could be.

She clung to the shadows herself, searching across the street for any sign of the shadow again. Nerves jangled her to full alert for anything on the street. Instead, something happened much closer as a hand touched her arm.

Without a second thought she spun and swung at what her tense body told her was an attacker. She landed a solid hit, then spun again to repeat the hit with her elbow. The moment she made the second contact she realized it wasn't an attacker.

It was Arthur.

"Oh my goodness! Arthur. I'm so sorry." She bent to help him back to his feet. "I didn't know you were behind me. I thought I saw—oh, dear. You're bleeding."

Arthur groaned when she pressed a handkerchief to his eye. "Blast, Sally."

"I'm so very sorry." Sally spotted Jane approaching the apartment door, keys in hand. Her gaze fell on the two of them, and Sally grimaced. "Sorry, Ma. Alma's in a mood, but I just felled Arthur on accident. I'm gonna run him to the clinic."

Jane's mouth twitched as if she was fighting laughter. After a moment of that, she nodded. "Very well. I'll see to Alma. I'll expect you back in short order."

"Of course, Ma." Sally guided Arthur around the Inn, then down the street to the clinic. Fortunately Charlie was there and dismissed them rather fast, saying Arthur had a mild concussion and to make sure he stayed awake for a while.

When Sally dropped him off at his house next door to the clinic, Isaac proved eager to help his brother stay wide awake. Sally grimaced at the helpless expression Arthur trained on her over Isaac's enthusiasm. "I'm really sorry. I have to go back and work some hours on the floor. I'll come check on you soon as I'm done at the casino."

"You don't gotta."

"I know. But your ma stays late to clean up every night, and I'm certain Isaac has something of a bedtime. Besides, I want to make sure you're all right."

Arthur touched his eye. "I don't need your pity for punching me."

"I know. I am truly sorry, though. Plus, you are above all else, and despite what's happened, my friend. I'm going to worry about you unless you let me come check on you."

"Fine," he grumbled, but Sally detected a hint of a smile. "If you must."

"I must." She waved as she backed into the street. Over Isaac's cheers, she called, "See you in about four hours, then."

"See you then."

These times of ours are serious and full of
calamity, but all times are essentially alike.
As soon as there is life there is danger.
                -Ralph Waldo Emerson

Jane wiped down the tables in the restaurant. At nearly nine in the evening the casino bustled with people, but Cora's restaurant was shut down. Despite her long day, she'd sent home the staff so she could clean the tables herself.

The first treatment on Willow hadn't eased her symptoms as much as they'd hoped. Charlie had opted to keep Willow overnight at the clinic to be certain she improved. Leanne had offered to stay with her, and Willow had seemed pleased at the idea.

Thus Jane had been allowed to get to work. She was glad for the busy work of cleaning the tables. Cole had been gone for three days. The telegram she'd received that morning had revealed a delay due to a storm in Utah, but he still expected to be in Holle Creek before the end of the week. He'd also thanked her for the book she'd left in his bag.

Jane tried to explain away her raw nerves since his departure as everything else going on. It couldn't be because of his departure, that would be silly. Unlike the previous times they'd parted company, there was no immediate threat to her. Granted, there'd been far too many deaths in town to make her happy, but at least this time her past was finally in order.

Her parents and children were doing a splendid job of keeping her quite busy and preoccupied. She was definitely grateful for the arrival of the Young's, even if the reason they'd come was because of Mike. Michael's issues were likely the cause of her great unease.

It wasn't Cole leaving. Painful as that was, it wasn't the end of the world. After all, he'd be home soon enough.

No. There was no soon enough for her.

Sally'd been beyond exceptional the past few days, despite her own bevy of distractions. The young woman had stepped in to help anywhere she could within the casino to ease the loss of Cole's assistance. If the girl weren't so determined to run with this detective idea, she'd have made an exceptional woman of business. Then again, being a detective didn't mean she couldn't still be if she started her own business.

A movement near the door caught her eye. Nick entered, removing his bowler hat. He crossed to accept Jane's hug. "How are you doing? Ma told me about Willow."

"I'm doing as to be expected. Leanne is with her now. Charles expects she'll come home in the morning, thank heavens." She sighed softly. "That girl gave me quite a scare. I've not seen her that bad in some time."

"As long as she's recovering, and next time you know."

"That we do. Now, what brings you by?"

"I came to get a drink. James is right behind me."

"That's a late night." She hated the hopeful note that entered her voice. Perhaps a late night meant some sort of progress.

"We're going in circles at this point. Without more information we are stuck. Lewis will be along in a few weeks, and the judge a day or two after."

"Sally and Tom will find something. They have to."

Nick squeezed her hand but offered no reassurances.

James entered before Jane could ask for them. He smiled, giving her a quick hug. "I thought you'd be tucked in with your children after the scare you had today."

"The little ones are already in bed, and I still have a business to run. Luxuries such as a night off are few and far between with only myself in charge."

"Fair point." James nodded to her. "Don't overwork yourself. Nick and I are going to enjoy some of the brandy he says you have hidden away."

"It's quite divine. Enjoy." Jane waved them off, returning to her cleaning immediately.

Cora emerged from the kitchen, frowning at Jane. "What do you think you're doing?"

"I dismissed the staff. I don't mind cleaning."

"You do realize it's their job." Cora's stern expression dissolved into soft laughter.

"Idle hands, Cora."

"Your hands are never idle."

"Neither are yours." Jane peeked at the clock over the reservation desk, then toward Cora's kitchen. "You know what? Why don't you leave early as well? I know you'd like to check on how Arthur's doing."

"Oh, no. I don't mind. It's only a few more pots to scrub."

"Then let me scrub them." Jane wiped some sweat from her brow. Her back smarted, and once again her corset seemed to squeeze tighter. She winced, letting out a shaky breath. "I'll have to have Miss Bee check my measurements again. I'm certain she made this new corset wrong. I cannot get it to sit right for the life of me."

"I don't trust her for nothing. I swear the woman is blind and can't read the measuring tape she uses. Vanity will be her death if she doesn't put on those spectacles she wears around her neck."

Jane laughed. "We finally get a dressmaker in town and she's useless. I believe I need to send a telegram to Leanne's in Denver to get a dress for the dance Lillian is insisting we have again for St. Valentine's."

"I'm looking forward to it. It was so lovely to see all the young couples at that one."

"Cora Turner, you are hardly an elderly woman. Go with someone. I'm certain Nick would accompany you as a friend again." She held up her hands at the side eye Cora gave her. "I said as a friend. Goodness. I promise I'm not playing matchmaker, especially with that brother. I wouldn't have the faintest idea what a good match for him would be."

"He is a good man, but definitely a little…"

"Particular," they said in unison.

Cora chuckled. "I would consider it if he asked, if anyone asked."

"Good to know."

"No matchmaking."

"I said I wouldn't matchmake my brother. I said nothing about you."

Cora bumped her shoulder. "You're terrible. I think I will let you scrub my pots if you're going to be so wicked a friend."

"That's no punishment. I need the busy work. Now go on, check on your boy." Jane pushed her friend toward the coat rack where her cloak hung. "I'll take care of your kitchen. I may not be able to cook, but I can scrub a few pans."

"Thank you." Cora hugged her tight before throwing her cloak over her shoulders.

Jane headed back through the restaurant. Tom and Sally entered the room laughing loudly. Jane eyed them both. "Are you sharing what happened with Arthur?"

A blush brightened Sally's features. "Yes. I was on my way to see him. I told him I'd stop by since his Ma worked later."

"I just sent Cora—"

The crack of gunfire cut through town. Jane and Tom stared at each other for a long moment. She couldn't release the breath she was holding for what seemed forever. When the echo dissipated, she moved.

Racing to the doors, she threw them open. In the middle of the street lay a prone form, not moving. "Cora!!"

Jane moved to rush toward her, but Tom grabbed her arm. He hissed, "What if they fire again?"

"Charles is going for her!" Jane wrenched free of his hold as Charlie tore into the street from the clinic. She followed suit, racing toward Cora's still body. She fell to her knees beside the woman at the same time as Charlie. "Cora. Oh please, Cora."

When Charles rolled her friend over, a small groan drifted through the air. Jane released a gust of air. "She's alive."

Charlie pulled aside her cape to look her over. A spot of red bloomed over her right side. "Let's get her to the clinic immediately. Someone run to get Andrew, and then Bonnie. Lydia is inside, but we may need the extra hands."

Everyone that had filtered into the street sprang to life at the doctor's orders. Jane didn't know who went after the other doctor and nurse, but she didn't care at the moment. She rushed behind the men that carried Cora into the clinic. Sally called out that she'd go for Cora's boys, and that was the last Jane heard before she made it into the clinic.

Kat was at her side a moment later, hand at her elbow. "What in blazes happened?"

"I don't know. I sent Cora home to check on Arthur and after she left a shot rang out. She's been shot."

"What?" Kat gasped, moving aside when Graham bustled through to the exam room.

"Graham. She's not—"

"They might need extra hands." Graham paused at Jane's touch to his arm. "Until the other doc gets here I'll do what I can."

"Thank you." Jane put her hand to her side where again her corset pressed too hard into her. The room swam before her. With every breath she struggled to regain her senses. There was another pain on her other side now.

"Jane?"

"Yes?" With as deep a breath as she could take, Jane managed to focus on Kat. "I was just talking to her. I'm the one that sent her home early."

"It isn't your fault. That's a ridiculous notion." Kat ran her hand along Jane's back. "You know it as well as I do."

"I do. I…oh." A flash of pain caused Jane to double over. Her heart pounded in her chest, the air thinning. "Oh…dear…ow. Oh."

The last thing she heard was Kat' cry as she fell into darkness.

Where there's life, there's hope.
-Cicero

Kat called out for assistance when Jane collapsed, but there was no one nearby. The doctor and nurse were in the room with Cora, as they should be; and Graham was in there, too. She had no idea what had happened to spark this. Jane had had some fits of hysteria in the past, like when the saloon burned down, but it had been years. Even with all that was happening it didn't make sense.

Nick entered the clinic, took one look at Kat bent over Jane and rushed to her side. He scooped her into his arms easily. "What happened? I heard someone was shot."

"Cora was. Jane just collapsed. Acted like she couldn't catch her breath. I can't believe this would be a fit of hysteria?"

"While there's plenty going on to cause one, I don't think so. I saw her a short while ago and she was bearing up well under the strain. Knowing that Willow would be home in the morning was a comfort for her."

Andrew burst into the room, skidding to a stop. The man's hat was askew, his eyes wide. "Is this where—oh, Jane. What happened to her? I was told Mrs. Turner was in trouble."

"She is. They have her in surgery. I believe Jane had a fit of hysteria. Go ahead and help with Cora. Bonnie will be here soon and can check her over. I've got no doubt once I get the corset off, Jane'll be right as rain." Kat shooed the doctor off. A gunshot wound was certainly a more precarious ailment than Jane's, who was already stirring.

"Jane." Nick set his hand on her forehead. "Jane, wake up. Tell us what's wrong."

Jane's hand wrapped around Nick's. A low groan was her best attempt at speaking at first.

"That doesn't help, Jane." Kat tried to unfasten Jane's bodice. The fabric strained against the clasps until it was difficult to undo. "Goodness this is tight."

Nick frowned. "That makes no sense. Jane is quite particular about making certain her dresses are cut to fit perfect."

"Miss Bee," Jane murmured. "Wrong."

Kat chuckled softly, continuing to work the fastenings. "Miss Bee is a terrible dressmaker. I have no idea where mother found her."

Nick straightened when Kat managed to pop the last fastening free to get the to corset. "I'm going to watch for Bonnie. Though she's further out, I imagine she'll come quickly given the direness of the situation."

"Thank you, Nick." Kat undid Jane's skirts and petticoats for better access to Jane's laces. She didn't miss

Jane's wince as Kat had to turn her this way and that to free the laces she'd untied.

Noises in the hall drew her attention. Nick didn't lead anyone in, but leaned into the hall to speak to someone.

Since it clearly wasn't Bonnie yet, Kat returned to her task. With the last lace free, she peeled off the corset. Jane gasped in a deep breath, stirring a little more.

Kat didn't even look to see if her friend woke, she was too distracted by what she'd found in removing the corset. Despite the miscarriage weeks ago, Jane's stomach still swelled in a similar way to Kat's own pregnant self.

Kat sighed softly. "Oh, Jane. What have you done?"

"What?" Nick spun on the spot. Two more heads poked into the room behind him.

Eunice pushed her son aside to rush to Jane. "What is it?"

Jane blinked several times, her brow pursed as she looked from her mother to Kat. "What happened? What's going on?"

"You passed out, you silly thing." Kat set her hand on Jane's stomach. "You've been lacing yourself up tight trying to rid yourself of the reminder of the child lost, haven't you?"

"Last time," Jane's eyes closed as her words choked off. "Last time it was mere days before I was back in form."

Kat lifted her gaze to Jane's mother. They both lowered their gaze to where Kat's hand still rested. "This can't be, can it?"

"What can't be?" Jane tried to lift her head, and get on her elbows. Eunice kept her in place despite her weak attempts. "Mother. Let me up. I'm fine."

"You might be, but you should stay where you are for a few minutes." Eunice nodded at Kat quietly, tears in her eyes.

Kat wasn't sure what to do next, or how to broach the news with Jane.

"Would someone tell me what's going on?" Jane's usual strength was creeping back into her tone. She wouldn't lie still for long. "Wait, Cora. How is she?"

"Still in surgery. You were only out for a few minutes." Kat held her in place. "Andrew has arrived, we're still waiting on Bonnie. I imagine she'll be along any minute and we'll have her look you over before going to help with Cora."

"I don't need an exam. I'm fine. Miss Bee's poor craftsmanship is all. I should have put on one of my old corsets today." Jane pushed herself up so fast neither of the hovering women could stop her. "Ma? Why are you here? What about the children? Thomas and Sally are busy, and Leanne's upstairs. Ada—"

"Hush, child. Breathe. Do you think I'd be so careless? James is with them."

"Bonnie," Nick all but yelled. "Come here, quick."

Bonnie bustled into the room, stopping short at the group gathered around Jane. "I thought—I was told Cora—what's going on here?"

"I thought Jane had a fit of hysteria, but perhaps not." Kat noticed Jane's mother was still crying. "Eunice?"

"Jane, darling. My sweet child." Eunice cupped Jane's cheeks. "You poor dear."

Jane shook her head, her brow pursing. "Ma. What is it? Why is Bonnie here? I'm fine. It was an ill-fitting corset and the shock of Cora's accident."

"I must say I'm not quite sure why I was called in here instead of going to help with Cora. Would someone tell me why?" Bonnie smiled reassuringly at Jane as she approached. "I think we're both at a loss."

"Jane." Kat set her hand on her friend's. "I think your ma and I would like Bonnie to confirm for us before we go too far."

"Confirm what?" Jane searched Kat's face. "Would someone tell me what's going on?"

"I believe you're pregnant."

Jane shook her head, pulling her hand from Kat's. "Again? But I just lost…"

"Not again, my darling child." Eunice pulled Jane's hand to her chest. "Still."

"No. I lost the baby. We saw it, we buried him by the barn. I…I…what?" Jane pulled her hand free. She went so far as to scoot away from them, nearly off the table. "Why would you be so cruel?"

"I'm not trying to be." Kat drew close to her friend again. "Have you felt movement?"

"Phantom ones, as I did the first time."

Kat took Jane's hand and set it on her stomach. "There's a reason your corset pains you so much, and it isn't poor tailoring. You should not be wearing it."

Once again Jane's gaze swept the room only to land on Bonnie. Tears slipped down her cheeks. "Tell them they're ridiculous. Hurtful. To toy with me this way."

"I'm afraid I can't do that until I've looked for myself." Bonnie shooed them all away from the table. "Before any of you continue, let me do an examination. We'll go from there."

Kat gave a reassuring squeeze to Jane's shoulder before she followed the others to the door. Once outside the room she turned to Eunice. "But, how? It seems impossible."

"I'll explain when we know. I don't think I can share it twice." She leaned into her husband, who kissed the top of her head.

Nick cleared his throat. A swipe to his moustache was the only sign of emotion. He turned his attention down the hall where the sounds of surgery leaked out of the partially open door.

Kat turned back to the room with Jane, unable to think about what might happen with Cora. That was too painful an idea. Jane's predicament, while not ideal, had a more hopeful air about it. Whether or not Jane agreed remained to be seen.

How would Jane take the news? What about Cole so far away? How would he be told? The whole thing seemed utterly impossible. Incredibly happy, and yet so deeply sad with one fetus in the ground.

The door opened slowly to reveal Bonnie. The young midwife met all the faces focused on her, then stopped at Kat. "She is still with child."

Jane sat on the table, immobile. Her features were pale and slack, her gaze fixed on the wall. Not a word was spoken as this time all of them filed into the room.

Eunice immediately went to Jane's side. She perched on the table beside her daughter and took her hands in her own. "Jane, my love."

After a long moment of quiet, Jane face her mother. Through trembling lips, she attempted to speak without success. Her head dropped and she took a shuddering breath. "I don't understand."

"It's not something that commonly happens for most people. With the exception, it seems, of our family. It's happened to me twice. Once with James, and once with Nick." Eunice hardly moved at Kat's surprised gasp.

"Twice?" Kat shook her head, unable to fully understand. "What happened?"

"One child dies, another lives. My other two failed twin pregnancies ended with a stillborn child."

Jane turned her gaze on Nick, then her father, and Kat. Distress lined her features. "But I…we…by the barn."

Nick moved closer to Jane. "When you had Colton and Clara healthy as can be near term, we thought you'd broke the curse Ma and Aunt Effie suffered through."

Kat struggled to wrap her brain around what they were saying, even though they'd said it plain as day. "Jane miscarried a twin, but the other survives?"

"Yes." Eunice turned her attention to Bonnie. "I'm assuming, of course, that this isn't a new pregnancy."

"No. The child is well along and growing." Bonnie took a step back. "I'll give you folks some time to come to terms with this. I'll go see if I can help with Cora."

"Thank you," Jane murmured. When the door shut quietly, she shook her head again. "I don't understand this."

"Effie and I were twins ourselves, you knew that, didn't you?" Eunice didn't move one inch from her daughter's side. Their hands remained twined together. "Our ma, she had five sets of twins. She was a breeder, that one."

The bit of humor helped weave a little more life into the room. Jane even snorted.

Kat grinned, encouraged by Jane's reaction. "You sound like Cole talking about horses."

"It's not much different, and my ma was a breeder. Effie and I, we weren't quite so lucky. I had plenty of children, but no twins. Neither of us could make a twin pregnancy stick. I lost four, all in a similar way where one was lost, but the other survived. Effie lost three, but all of hers were complete. She finally gave up and started adopting."

Nick perched on Jane's other side. "You are aware this is good news, Jane."

"I know…I mean, I believe I do." Jane gasped, her hands flying to her mouth. Wide eyes welled with tears. "Cole! Oh, no. I can't tell him something like this through a letter. I can't keep it from him, but that's—I mean, I barely understand— no letter could explain. Oh, my goodness. A baby."

Kat smiled when Jane's hands fluttered to her belly. "Yes. A baby that you've been shoving in that corset the past couple of weeks, the poor thing."

Jane lifted her gaze to her ma. "This really happened to you?"

"Twice." Eunice reached around Jane to set her hand on Nick's shoulder. "Each time it made me so grateful I had another baby right after. First James, and immediately after came George. Then Nick, and right after him came my first girl. A most precocious child that lives to be contrary."

Jane pursed her lips at her mother, before turning a glare on Kat. No matter the glare, Kat couldn't stop laughing.

Jane sighed. "Stop it, Katherine."

"What? She's not wrong." Kat leapt to her feet to run to her friend. "Oh, this is truly wonderful. You're still pregnant. We'll still have our children together. Cole is going to be so surprised to find you in such a state. A fitting Christmas surprise."

Eunice chuckled. "I believe he'll be more than surprised. Thrilled."

"As he should be. So should you, Jane."

Jane offered a wan smile. "I am, I think. I'm just so surprised."

John spoke for the first time in the chaos. "You should be. No greater miracle than your children."

"Even in the face of tragedy. Yes, they truly are."

So many men, so many questions.
–Terence

Sally parted company with Arthur and Isaac at the door to the clinic. There appeared to be quite the crowd gathered, so she didn't go inside. She jogged over to where Tom stood. Blood stained the cobblestone under him. His gaze wandered the rooftops.

She followed the path of his gaze with her own. "What are we doing?"

"Trying to figure out where the shot came from."

"Where did the bullet hit?"

"Her right side." Tom poked her around her waist, but on the back. "Based on what little Charlie let me see before he had to start surgery. Looks like it went clean through."

Sally moved around him to face Cora's small home. She glanced over her shoulder at the Inn and moved to the right a little. "She was heading home from the Inn. If it hit her around there, it would have had to come from behind."

"Exactly what I was thinking. There's no room between her place, Kat's on the one side, and the laundry on the other for someone to hide."

Sally turned a hundred and eighty degrees to study the scene behind her. Best location would have been the dressmaker shop beside the saloon. The building sat dark and quiet now. "But where? Oh!"

"What?"

"The shadow I saw earlier. Then again, that was hours ago."

"Where'd you see the person?" Tom turned the same direction as her, studying the scene.

"Near the saloon." Sally walked that way. She moved at a quick pace to get to the saloon itself. After all, she hadn't seen the shadow near the dressmakers. "There. Between the saloon and Nick's new building."

Tom moved closer toward the alley.

Sally turned her attention to the saloon itself. In the time it had taken for them to get started, the crowd had long dispersed. The gunman would be long gone from wherever he'd hidden. The most logical place for them to go would be, "The saloon."

"Hm?" A match scratched along the ground before flaring to life in Tom's hand. He crouched low, studying the dirt. "What's that, Sally?"

"He would have gone to the saloon after. It makes the most sense. Everyone gathered in the street for the panic and then dispersed. They could blend in real easy at the saloon unless they were a woman."

Tom moved back to her side. "You want to check it out while I get a lamp and look to see if he left anything behind?"

She couldn't stop the frown that formed. Despite her growing confidence, she still hadn't stepped foot into the saloon since it opened for business.

"Sally?"

"Yes." She straightened her shoulders. No time like the present. "I think I will."

Without another word, she strode up the stairs to the saloon. One last deep breath to tamp down her nerves, she entered the saloon. Wil wasn't behind the bar tonight, which was unfortunate. Sally was at least familiar with him. This new man, Garit, was an unknown element.

"Well, well, well. Pansy came back to the garden." Zeb, who'd always had a penchant for her talents, swaggered toward her. "Care to dazzle us with a song? Or perhaps—"

Sally reacted quickly. The sucker punch to his nose wasn't hard enough to break it, but it was enough to—yes, he was bleeding well enough. "Don't even suggest it, Zeb. I'm no whore anymore."

"What the hell?" He gripped his nose, glaring at her.

"You don't think Ma or Cole would do worse to you if they'd heard what you were about to say? Be glad I didn't break it." Sally turned her back on him rather than wait for a reply.

Some of the faces that greeted her were laughing, others turned away quickly. She ignored them to approach the bar. "I had a question."

"May or may not have an answer."

"I really hope you do. I'd hate to force it out of you."

"I'd like to see you try."

"No. You really wouldn't." She didn't balk from the staring contest he kept her in. Until he relaxed the slightest bit, she held her place. The moment he did, she leaned forward to speak quiet under the hum of activity. "Anyone new come in after the gunfire out there?"

"Could be." Garit wiped down a glass. He didn't bother to look over the saloon full of men. "People come and go all the time. I don't got time to know who's in and out."

Rather than argue that if he were half the manager Wil was, or either of her parents, he'd know every soul and when they entered or left, she settled back on her heels. "Fine. If you insist on being difficult, I'll make my own inquiries."

"Stop disrupting business." Garit leaned on the bar. "No one'll want to come back if we go prattling on about their business."

Sally smirked at the false implication. "You'd be surprised what men will tolerate for booze and a whore."

"I really wouldn't."

She spun away from the bartender to scan the room. In the corner several whores lounged about lazily. Garit might not be willing to be forthcoming, or observant, but a whore knew. Sally abandoned the bar to head toward the women. The first woman to pay her any mind had a head full of chaotic brown curls. Sally beckoned her.

The whores' brow furrowed, but she rose slowly. As she sauntered over, she set a hand on her hip. "Don't get much call for women here."

"Doesn't stop you playing in the back room, does it?" Sally guided her back around the stairs where they'd mostly be concealed. A few men that noticed whistled their appreciation. She ignored them to focus on the woman. "What do they call you?"

"Peony."

"Nice to meet you, Peony. I'm Sally. They used to call me Pansy."

Deep brown eyes widened. A grin breached her features making her almost pretty. "That means you're the reason we can't use that name, eh? Wait until I tell the girls. Look at you, all gussied up like that."

"I got lucky."

"If you can call it that."

"Probably not. It took surviving a fire that left me with some scars to get out. Well, that and Jane and Cole." Sally perused the floor through an opening between stairs. "I know you girls keep track of all the men that come and go here. If you know what's good for you, anyway."

"What of it?"

"Tell me. Who didn't get here until after the gun went off?"

Peony frowned. She fidgeted with the edge of her top, her gaze drifted to the bar.

"Don't you worry about him. Ma will set him straight if he argues."

Peony hesitated, but then looked through the stairs as well. "Zeb was one, but ya took care of him. That one in the corner. He's new, but we don't go near him unless told. He's got that…"

"Air about him." Sally had clocked him soon as she'd entered. He was the sort that gave you a look to make your skin crawl. "I see it, too. Looks like he might hit women. I'll warn Garit about him on my way out. Who else?"

"Bert, Collin, Jake, and Hank. Ya know who they are?"

"They've been customers longer than I've been in town. I know them." Sally couldn't fathom that any of the men she'd known so long could have shot Cora. Even Zeb, idiot that he was, couldn't have. Could he? Such a thing seemed impossible. "Thanks, Peony. You'd better get back to work."

"Sure thing."

"Oh, here." Sally pressed a quarter in her hand. "For your time. Also, I have a tip."

"What's that?"

"Danny."

"Danny?" Peony cast a wary glance toward the stove where a man sat slightly hunched in his seat. "Him, by the stove?"

"Yes, him. He likes to watch, and pays more for the privilege to join. If you've got a good friend to help you out, you both could get a good percentage tonight."

Peony tilted her head. "We all pegged him as just that, a watcher. Never went for nothing."

"Make the offer. It'll be worth it. He can be generous in action and coin." Sally slipped out from behind the stairs to head back to the bar. This time she didn't bother to stand on politeness. She moved behind the bar as she'd seen Jane do often enough.

While she poured the whiskey, Garit eyed her suspiciously. The man wisely didn't make a move to stop her.

She tossed back her whiskey before focusing on the man across the bar. "Caleb. Good to see you. I expected you at the casino tonight."

"Wife said if I gamble again this week I'm sleepin' in the barn." Caleb took the beer she passed him with a grateful smile. "I really don't like the smell out there. Horses would be fine, but since she got it in her head to get a couple pigs, it's nothing I'd enjoy sleepin' in."

"Can't say I blame you one bit." Sally patted his hand. She sidled down the bar, greeting every man she passed. Fortunately all of them seemed to get the hint to behave with the help of Zeb's bloody nose.

Garit tossed back a whiskey when she leaned back against the counter beside him. "What?"

"Is this an act or are you really an idiotic ass?"

"You'll never know."

"Oh, but I will." She leaned in close. A half turn toward him got her close enough that the patrons would likely think she was making a pass. She murmured, "Keep an eye on the mudsill in the corner. I think he'll hit if you let him play, and Ma and Pa won't stand for that."

Surprisingly, Garit took her lead and tugged her closer. He leaned close enough that his quiet tone reached her ear. "What makes you think that?"

"A woman that's been a whore knows." She set her hand on his shoulder. "Now, how much of a show must we continue with?"

"I think that's enough."

"Do you really?" She bumped him hard enough with her hip to make him stumble. A few whistles of approval carried her on her way out from around the bar.

Sally left the saloon, but lingered on the porch. From there she could observe the five men Peony had mentioned without drawing further attention. Not a one of them acted entirely suspicious, though both Collin and Jake kept stealing glances toward the door.

Of course the man in the corner seemed suspicious, but that might have nothing to do with Cora. More like it likely had everything to do with her presumption he hit women.

The other men, though.

Could it truly be someone she'd known for so long? How could she suspect them?

How could she not?

*This is the true nature of home—
it is the place of peace;
the shelter, not only from injury,
but from all terror, doubt, and division.
—John Ruskin*

A wet tongue lapped Jane's cheek. She groaned her way to wakefulness. "Ugh. Whiskey. Knock it off."

A squeal beside her was quickly followed by laughter. Leanne twisted so fast she fell right off the bed. "Oh. Ow. Damn it, Bourbon. Jane, why did you let these beasts join us in bed last night?"

"I really have no idea." Jane pushed away the next attack by the hound at her side. At some point after the revelation of her continuing pregnancy the night before, Eunice had insisted watching Willow so Leanne could join in Jane's happy news. Somehow they'd both ended up in her bed with the hounds. "That's enough, you two. I'm guessing you both need to go outside."

Leanne remained leaning against the wall. Bourbon had settled at Jane's words, but his tail kept whacking Leanne on the hip. She reached above her head to tug the cord on the wall.

The door cracked open a minute later. No sooner had it done so than the puppies launched themselves out the door. Their barks at the back door shot through the apartment and Jane's open door. Sally entered the room, her brow raised. "You let them sleep in here?"

"Don't ask why. I can't remember. It was late, I was missing your pa, and Leanne isn't near warm enough to make up for him being gone."

"I would be if you'd let me." Leanne chuckled low. She ducked the pillow Jane tossed at her, her laughter growing.

"You hush." Jane stretched out the kinks from the awkward sleeping position she'd been in.

"What's the latest, Sally?" Leanne didn't get up from her position yet. A yawn stretched her mouth wide.

"Cora made it through the night. If she wakes up today, Charlie says it looks real good for her." Sally hopped onto the end of the bed. "Sorry I kept Tommy out with me."

"No worries. Jane and I made quite joyous over her news." Leanne climbed back into the bed. Without hesitation, she buried herself back under the blankets. "That was enough to keep us awake for some time."

"News?" Sally turned toward Jane. "What news? What did I miss?"

Jane didn't bother to stop her grin. "I'm surprised Charles didn't tell you if you've gone by the clinic. Then again, he was likely rather exhausted himself."

"He was pretty tired when I saw him early this morning," Sally concurred. "Then tell me what this happy news is."

"I'm pregnant, Sally."

"What? Again? So soon?" Sally bounced in place, setting Leanne growing. "Really?"

"Not again. Still. According to Ma, it's happened to her. I was carrying twins again. I lost one child, but another still survives." Jane yawned against the daylight. "I should go visit Cora after I've made it to the mercantile."

"It's too early. Both of you go away." Leanne threw the blankets over her head.

"Lazy lie-a-bed." Jane slipped from under the covers. The chill in the air sent a shiver running through her. "I'll stoke the fire for you, Leanne. It'll keep you warm until you're ready to be a human being."

"Never happen," came a groaning mumble from under the layers of blankets.

Sally turned in her spot to follow Jane's progress. "Have you told Cole?"

"No. If I do he'll never finish his trip. He'll know when he gets home." Jane went into the closet to select some clothes for the day. When she emerged, Sally lay across the foot of the bed staring at the ceiling. Jane frowned slightly. "Is something bothering you?"

"Only six people entered the saloon after the shooting, Ma. Only one of them was a stranger. I can't imagine a soul in this town doing such a thing to Cora of all people." Sally rose to sit again. "Nor what happened to Daisy. Or any of the others. Could this really be people we know?"

"I'm afraid it could be, though I also hate to imagine such a thing." For nearly six years now she'd lived in

Dominion Falls had gotten to know everyone fairly well. Though things constantly changed, people moved in or on, it would be difficult to face someone she'd known for years committing such atrocious crimes.

"I was wondering…"

"Yes?"

"I haven't said as much to Tommy yet, because I don't want to seem as though I'm overreacting. Or that I'm making too much of something that may have no connection."

"Out with it."

"Before Cora was shot—when I punched Arthur—I was on edge because I thought I saw someone in the shadows. It was hours before, admittedly, but then…"

Now that she was dressed, Jane stood before Sally and took her hands in hers. "I can't decide what I think if you don't finish a thought."

"After I felled Arthur I took him to the clinic. As we parted ways I told him I'd stop by in a few hours since his ma always worked later. We were out in the street where anyone could have heard. Could they have meant to shoot me?"

The very idea sent a chill right down Jane's spine. She swallowed against the lump in her throat. "What would make you think that?"

"My attack. Whomever it was didn't succeed in killing me then—perhaps they wanted to try again."

Jane studied the young woman. Fear had hedged her words, but a stubborn determination lingered in the set of her jaw. "Do you wish to stop investigating?"

"No!" Sally flew to sit.

"I guess not, then."

"Sorry." Sally lifted her gaze. "I can't stop because I'm scared."

"You are scared."

"Of course." Sally sighed. "I need to tell Tommy."

"Most definitely. You two are a team in this. Just like I will, Tom will tell you if he thinks you're being dramatic. You're not prone to such things, and I believe the concern might be a valid one. I certainly go nowhere without my gun since Mack attacked me, and that's hardly related to this mess."

Sally's brow furrowed at that.

"What?"

"I'm just not so sure it isn't. The names he was calling you."

"Are nothing he hadn't ever called me before."

"Still."

Jane pulled Sally to her feet. "Let's leave Leanne to her rest. You go talk to Tom before you head to the library. I'll be there around one myself."

Sally nodded, following Jane without argument. She paused at the stairs, turning back to Jane. "I'm talking to Molly today."

"It's about time." Jane patted Sally on the hand. "Be honest with her and yourself. I know Patrick has appreciated your honesty."

A blush lit Sally's cheeks before she darted up the stairs. Jane chuckled softly at the young woman's lingering embarrassment. Soon enough the discomfiture wouldn't be there, it had already shown a marked decrease since her dalliances with Patrick had started. Jane herself rarely felt it over her own desires. If she ever truly had, it had been at the expense of others. Then again, Cole had always been so all consuming she hadn't had room for embarrassment.

The thought of Cole brought another sting of melancholy to her heart. She longed to have him there to share in their happy news. The company of Leanne had been nice enough, and it had been wonderful to not have an empty bed reminding her of her loneliness, but nothing compared to having Cole there.

Rather than bask in such depressing thoughts, Jane rushed out of the apartment toward the kitchen. Inside she found Colleen, Cora's newest cook, already starting her day. Jane took some time to go over what supplies the kitchen needed from the mercantile so she might ensure the kitchen was well supplied even through Cora's absence.

Colleen had proven to be a rather good cook and stayed true to Cora's recipes. She'd even added a few of her own delicious dishes into the mix. Jane couldn't have been happier with the addition to their staff, especially seeing as she herself didn't cook.

Jane bundled up on her way out into the snowy streets. Rather than compete with the crowd on the boardwalks, she took to the street to get through town as quickly as possible. The list of things she had to do that day was rather large, and she hadn't time for too much idleness.

Once inside the store, she folded back her hood. The mercantile didn't bustle with people like it had for so long, and disappointment welled. Unfortunately, in the short time they'd been there the Jones' had already met so strong resistance to their ownership of the business.

Jane's continued patronage hadn't had too much effect yet. She thought she might speak to the reverend's about a sermon that might touch on the subject in a non-direct enough way to wake folks up without pointing fingers.

"Miss Jane." Abe extended his hand as she approached. A bright smile lit his eyes. The man had a sense of humor she appreciated. "It's good to see you again so soon."

"Good morning, Abe. You ought to get used to me as a regular customer. I tend to enjoy spending my hard-earned money on quality products."

"You're too kind, ma'am."

"Yesterdays trip was personal. Today is all about business. I need to place my weekly order for supplies for the Inn." Jane nodded to Faith as she approached the counter, some supplies in her hands. "Mrs. Jones. It's good to see you again. I'm sorry you missed our tea last week. I do hope you can join us this afternoon. I'll be hosting it at the library."

"I'm not sure I can get away." Faith fussed with the products she'd carried over. "I'm quite busy around here."

Jane made herself hold still to avoid glancing around the nearly empty store. "Of course. I understand you're very busy. I'd really love the extra company. We're going to be another woman short this week due to Cora's unfortunate incident. It will be myself, Kat, Lillian Daugherty, and Leanne DuBois."

Abe's eyes widened. "Mrs. Daugherty? And Kat Daugherty?"

"Yes, Abe. They're dear friends, and rather influential in this town." Jane turned her attention back to Faith. "I'm certain they'd be delighted to meet a new woman of business about town. We promise only the best, most enlightened conversation."

Abe leaned closer in a loud aside, "And gossip?"

"Goodness, Abe. We wouldn't dare." Jane winked at the man, then approached the end of the counter Faith stood behind. "I truly want to help you both. I can only imagine how such a thing would be hard to believe, but there is no ill will here."

Faith glanced at her husband, then back at Jane. After a moment she allowed a nod. "I'll consider your invitation."

"Wonderful. Two o'clock if you can get away. Do you know where the library is?"

"I do."

"Good." Rather than pressure the woman further, Jane turned back to Abe. "Now, about my supplies."

"Yes. Right this way."

*Those who restrain desire, do so because
theirs is weak enough to be restrained.
-William Blake*

Sally burst into the library on a gust of wind that sent a dusting of snow across the floor. After slamming the door behind her, she set about cleaning up the mess. Jane wouldn't be too happy if any snow melted on any books.

After her brief talk with Jane, she'd met with Tommy. As suggested, she'd explained to him her concerns. Every time she said it she wondered if she was becoming too suspicious of everything and everyone. She'd nearly convinced herself she was overreacting.

However, much like Jane, Tommy hadn't immediately dismissed the idea. He'd even suggested that because of hiding away after her first attack she'd learned to fight. He'd wondered if maybe that would be the reason behind the use of a gun instead of fists. The thought worried her somewhere in the back of her mind.

After all, if that were true she was in quite a bit of danger. Yet, she couldn't quite call it fear. Perhaps the distraction of everything she had to do, and the mysteries around all of the attacks took precedence over such a thing as fear. It wasn't as if she could do much about not being attacked without knowing who was behind it.

She scooped the books to be returned out of the bin and began to mark them in Jane's ledger while she continued to ponder. If all of the odd deaths and attacks were connected, there was only a slim possibility it was one person doing it all.

The pen slipped from Sally's hand, hitting the paper hard enough to leave a large blot of ink behind. If it were more than one person, that was the scariest thought of all. How could more than one get away with such things? Worse, how could more than one go about their lives as if they hadn't done a thing?

People talked. Quite a lot around these parts. All of the time.

Ma always said gossip like currency through the town. It was part of why her and Cole happily obliged scandal so much, or so she said. If they were talking about her, they weren't saying worse falsehoods against others.

No, it was ridiculous to think it could be more than one person. Gossip moved faster than a train through town. You could whisper a secret on Main and have the whole town know before you reached the mercantile.

What would ma say about secrets? Sally'd heard her on several occasions on such a subject. The words of Benjamin Franklin were the first to come to mind.

"'Three may keep a secret, if two of them are dead'." Sally slammed the ledger shut so hard the sound echoed through the library. "What if the men are dying to cover a secret? No, that doesn't make sense."

She gathered some books in hand and climbed the stairs to shelve them. "Not every one of the men, at least. No, I can't see any of them hiding something. Besides, that would be too obvious."

She slid a book into place, pondering everything over. "Emily and Daisy were murdered to be sure. Lucy, Cora, Ma, and I didn't see fit to do the same. We know who attacked Ma, and who attacked Lucy, but not who was with him."

Once again Sally thought over the broader picture. She really needed a way to write her circling thoughts more effectively than the notebook.

"Hello?" Molly's voice started Sally from her thoughts. "Sally?"

"Up here." Sally walked to the railing to peer down toward the desk. "I've got two more books to put away. I'll be right there."

With Molly's arrival, Sally rushed to put the final two books in their place. By the time she got downstairs, Molly sat perched on the chair in front of the desk.

Sally sped right past her to the stove. She added more coal and stoked the dying flames until they caught well enough to leave her satisfied. "It's a cold one today. Would you like some tea? Or perhaps something stronger? Ma always keeps a couple flasks of whiskey in the desk in case Pa comes by for a visit."

"Whiskey. No, I'd better not. Tea will be fine."

Sally ignored the correction. Instead, she pulled a flask from behind the stack of Poe books Jane kept in the bottom drawer. The grim reminder of Jane's past kept so close at hand struck her. Without thinking she muttered, "Odd."

"What's that?" Molly eyed the flask in Sally's hand. "I thought I said tea."

"Tea takes yime. Take a bracing sip. As to what I said, it was a passing thought on a much different subject. Nothing important in the grand scheme." Sally held out her hand for the flask once Molly took a swig. She took a bracing draught herself before setting the whiskey on the edge of the desk. "Thank you for coming by today. I'm sorry it has to be here. At this point I'm wondering how we'll fit in lessons if you agree to continue them."

"You want to continue?" Molly's brow furrowed. "I didn't think you would."

"I imagine so. I did take off on you with nary a word of explanation."

"And then kissed that gentleman."

"Ah. Yes. Saw that did you?" Heat warmed Sally's cheeks at Molly's askance look.

"You were in the hallway, not secreted away."

"True. Quite true." Sally sighed heavily and settled against the desk. "You confused me. When I kissed Patrick I was trying to see how confused I was. Unfortunately, that made matters worse because it turned out you both were able to leave me rather flustered."

"Flustered."

Sally straightened to pace the short length of the desk. "I'm attracted to you both. I did rather enjoy our kiss, and that's what startled me. I wasn't upset with you, I was confused with myself because I knew I was already attracted to Patrick. Then you went and kissed me and I wanted to take it further. I didn't know what to do with that information."

"Do you now?"

After another moment of pacing, Sally sank into the chair next to Molly. She lifted her gaze to meet the woman's dead on. "I do."

"All right." Molly turned in the chair and held out her hands. "What will it be?"

"In full disclosure, I've already been enjoying time with Patrick while you've been away." Sally took Molly's hands before she could pull away. "I spent near two years as a whore helping men with their pleasure, without knowing what it was like to find my own. Patrick has helped that endeavor."

"I see."

"I don't think you do." Sally rose, pulling Molly to her feet. On the off chance that someone were to walk in, she led Molly behind some stacks near the corner of the building. Once there, she pulled Molly closer. "I still wish to explore whatever it is I felt when I was with you. It turns out that Ma was right again. I had no idea the sort of pleasures I could find on my own."

Molly stepped even closer until they were as close as could be with their skirts and petticoats in the way. "You wish to be with both of us?"

"I suppose that's what I'm saying. I don't want to explore this if you'll be jealous of me spending time with another. I enjoy Patrick's company."

Molly's lips curved into a sexy smirk. "I can imagine why."

Sally's stomach jumped when Molly leaned closer. "I guess you don't mind, then."

"If I get to kiss you again? No."

*To the soul is hardly anything more healing
than friendship.
-Thomas Moore*

Jane set the second kettle on the stove. Sally had been kind enough to refill the first one before she left, but Jane knew she'd have to have plenty of tea ready. Even if there was only to be four of them there that day. She'd hoped Lee could come, but she had to work.

The door burst open to a swirl of snow before shutting firmly. A few stamps of feet and a shivering *brr* later, Kat approached the stove.

"My goodness. It's likely to be a blizzard if this nonsense continues." Kat held her hands in front of the warm stove. "You've got it nice and cozy in here, but it will take ages to warm that chill away."

"The tea will help."

"Definitely. We're all going to need some warming up from the inside."

"We wouldn't need it if we weren't having tea," Jane pointed out.

"True, but without regular communion, how would anything get accomplished? More so, how would we keep sane?"

"I can't argue your logic." Jane chuckled softly. The wind blew fierce outside the window and snow blustered past. It was all surface snow, though. Nothing fell from the clear blue sky quite yet. "I hope this doesn't keep anyone else from coming. We're already two shy what with Cora in the clinic and Lee far too busy between the hotel and little Marjorie."

"When is the new manager arriving? I swear that poor woman hardly had any time to enjoy her new child before she went back to work." Kat opened the basket Jane had sitting by the stove. "Candy as well as cakes? What a rare treat."

"A celebration that Cora has woken, and Charles believes she's going to recover well." Jane poured the boiling water into the teapots to warm them. She refilled the kettles to make the tea with. "To answer your question, Nicholas says they should arrive next week. Barring poor weather, of course."

"Of course." Kat busied herself at the table. "Who are you expecting today? I see six cups set out. Is Sally joining us?"

"No. Sally is—having some lessons this afternoon."

"She is? I thought Patrick was going to be at the depot with the girls and Jesse." Kat set a vanity cake and a piece of ribbon candy at every spot. Though Jane didn't cook and had no need for a kitchen at the library, shed seen to it that a table had been set near the window for the occasions they'd have tea there instead of the Inn.

The set up made it convenient for her to have her regular teas with her friends as well as devote some time to the library in her busy schedule.

Jane turned from the stove to face her friend. "It isn't Patrick. It's Molly."

"Oh." Kat stopped her fussing over a place setting to meet Jane's eye. "For detective work or…"

"Or, I believe. Perhaps both. Which remains between us, it goes without saying." Jane knew her friend would never spill such intimate secrets, but she always added the caveat. She dumped the steaming water from the teapots into the bucket and poured the fresh kettles into them. When they were full she sprinkled in the tea leaves.

"Undoubtedly. Well, then. Did you warn her Patrick would be interested in a trio?" Kat helped Jane carry the pots to the table. "He asked me several times when we were making nice."

"I imagine he'll tell her himself, if he hasn't already."

"I don't doubt it. I see mother coming now. Who else are we expecting?"

"Leanne, if she ever managed to climb out of my bed. My ma. The sixth is in hopes that Mrs. Jones joins us this time. I impressed upon her and her husband that your mother would be here. Abe might push the issue, he seemed properly impressed."

"I do hope she comes. It would be nice to get to know her."

"We really need to find a way to make people see sense. There was hardly a soul in the place when I went in there today." Jane's smile brightened when Lillian entered bundled in a thick woolen coat and muffler wrapped up to her eyes. "Lillian."

Lillian peeled off her layers, shrugging out of the coat last. "I'm deeply regretting not allowing Henry bring me in the sleigh."

"I imagine so." Jane hugged the woman after Kat finished her own embrace. "I may have to see if I can get our stable hand Leon to hook up the sleigh to take you and Leanne back to the hill after we're done."

"Nonsense. I can handle the cold. It's the wind that's atrocious, which would be made worse racing through the snow on runners." Lillian settled into a chair. "Ribbon candies. Lovely."

"A special treat to celebrate Cora's recovery." Jane carried the sugar and cream to the table. "Charles believes she'll make a full recovery."

"I'm pleased to hear it. Has there been any word on who did it?"

"Sally and Thomas appear to have some leads, but they aren't giving me any details. Not that I would ask for any, of course."

"Of course. We aren't gossips." Lillian winked.

The door opened again to allow Leanne into the library. She tossed her cape over the coat rack before proceeding to kiss every woman on the cheek. "My darlings. Sorry I'm late."

"You're five minutes early." Jane gestured to a chair. "I'm honestly surprised you're here at all. You were rather enjoying my bed."

"That quilt your mother made is deliciously warm." Leanne settled into a chair and immediately poured tea. "I declare it's warmer than the down blanket on my own bed."

"I don't know her secret, only that she grew up in Buffalo and knows how to deal with rather brutal winters around there as well." Jane was about to sit when the door opened again.

"No, not at all. Please, come in." Eunice held open the door. "I'm Eunice Young. It's good to meet you."

"Thank you." Faith entered hesitantly. Her gaze scanned every face at the table before her eyes dropped. "Afternoon, folks."

"Mrs. Jones. I'm so glad you decided to join us. I see you've met my mother." Jane stepped down from the alcove to collect Faith's coat.

"Only at the door, child." Eunice took the coat Jane had collected and set it on the second coat rack with her own.

Jane led Faith toward the table. "How about some introductions?"

"That would be nice." A slight lilt to Faith's voice reminded Jane of Al Webb. The hint of southern hinted that Chicago was not where she began life.

"This here is Leanne DuBois, owner of La Maison de Minuit. I believe you've met Kat Daugherty. My mother, Eunice. She doesn't live here, she's from Buffalo, but she always joins us when she visits. And this is Lillian Daugherty."

Faith made her greetings around the table. She finished with Leanne. "The House of Midnight?"

Leane burst into laughter. "Precisely. My place in Denver was La Bonne Nuit. I preferred it to the house of midnight, but it's all the same so long as the men come to play."

"A house of ill repute with a fancy name always brings in the big money." Jane settled into her seat with a sigh. "Of course, so does the women Leanne keeps on staff."

"Yours aren't so bad," Leanne hedged. "Only not quite up to snuff for my high standards."

"Gee thank you."

Lillian wasn't chuckling aloud, but her smile belied her amusement. She turned her attention to Faith. "It's good to meet you. I'd heard word that our new mercantile owners had arrived. I haven't had a chance to make it down to meet you yet. I'm afraid the Christmas decorations took all my time for a few weeks."

"It's of no matter." Faith fidgeted in her seat. "But thank you."

"Why don't we tell you a little about ourselves, and then you can do the same. We'll start so you don't feel like we're all being nosey. We'll get to know each other. I know it must be odd coming into a group that already know each other so well." Jane poured some tea in her cup and grabbed a vanity cake. "Someone go first, I need to eat this."

Laughter filtered around the table. Lillian dove in first with a small story. In turns they told Faith something about themselves. When it got to her turn Faith appeared to have relaxed some. She sipped her tea. "I don't rightly know where to start."

"How long have you been married?" Kat broke off a piece of her ribbon candy.

"Abe and I been married about ten years now. We worked hard in Chicago to raise money. Always talked about owning our own place, you see. Abe's real good with people. Could sell just about anything. Used all of our savings to get the mercantile." Faith's smile faltered. "Thought it'd be different out here."

"People will come around. They always do. Despite all the changes in the past few years around here, they are surprisingly resistant to change." Jane refreshed her tea. "You have the best products. Also far more variety than Bobo's."

"Jane," Leanne chided through her chuckle. "It's Beau Brown's."

"I'm aware what it is. I also know he's inept. Then again, Callahan wasn't much better, that's how that pitiful little general store opened." Jane nodded to Faith. "In such a short amount of time the store is already far less messy than Callahan kept it. He didn't seem a strong man of business."

"I think that's why he sold it. His brother's widow was a convenient excuse." Lillian shook her head. "I don't think the mercantile would have survived much longer if the Jones hadn't come along to purchase it."

"Truth be told," Faith hedged a moment. "The books were a bit off-kilter. I've been working on seeing where the worst problems are so we might fix them if we ever get business."

"I'd think the Inn alone would be enough to keep that place afloat." Kat glanced Jane's way. "You're always buying something or another."

"We do need food and whiskey to survive. Our patrons wouldn't like to starve or go sober." Jane pointed her candy at her friend. "You're the one always buying dresses for your girls."

"So do you. I've hardly seen children with more clothes than yours."

"Girls." Eunice held up her hands. "Why are you arguing? You both spoil your children. There's no contest here. You're both equally terrible."

They looked at each other, then said in unison, "True."

This time even Faith joined in the hearty laughter around the table.

Lillian stood to refresh the teapots. "Well, ladies. What shall be our first topic for discussion today? The confectionary again? The dance I'm proposing for St. Valentine's? How we'll raise the money to pave Fourth Street now that homes are being built? Or perhaps the dressmaker you all despise."

"The dressmaker," Leanne, Jane, and Kat all cried in unison.

Truth is beautiful, without a doubt;
but so are lies.
-Ralph Waldo Emerson

Tom sipped a cup of warm coffee on the Inn's porch. The blizzard had raged for two days before stilling into silence and blue skies. The temperature sat at a tolerable thirty-five with no hint of wind. In no time after the winds had died down the town had sprung to life.

Much to his chagrin Leanne had found her way home before the storm had hit. That had left him without company the past couple of nights. A situation he expected to see righted by the night's end.

One good thing about the blizzard had been the lack of anything akin to an attack on the citizens of the town. Sally'd used the time to go over every single inch of her notes and thoughts on the matter with him. She seemed to want to vent her own frustrations at the wall she'd hit in the investigation on him.

Then there was Jane. She'd spent most of the storm pacing the apartment like a caged tiger. The inability to tell her husband about the child was wearing on her. Add in the fact she couldn't get to the depot to see if any telegrams had arrived and it was near-impossible to keep her still.

At least Cole was expected to arrive at his destination within the next day or two. Perhaps when she heard from him she'd manage to find something akin to calm. Then again, perhaps not. For some reason he couldn't pinpoint she'd been edgier than he'd expected. Certainly the pregnancy could be the reason, but it hardly seemed the case.

She wasn't in any danger, and far as he could tell, neither was Cole. Still, Jane's nerves were heightened. Not helping matters was the fact that Alma's were, too. Cole's sister was at times nearly inconsolable since he'd left.

A figure stepped to the railing beside him. He braced to tell Sally to go back to her lessons. He thought better without her constant speculation in his ear. The girl was brilliant, and even better at learning than he'd anticipated, but he worked better solo. At least when it came to the sitting and thinking part of his job.

Instead of Sally beside him, he found Jane. She sipped her own coffee, a heavy cape buttoned around her. Thick hand-knit mittens on her hands courtesy of Lillian of all people. Her gaze seemed focused on the clinic for the moment.

"Saw Charlie first thing," he supplied before she could inquire. "He said Cora's doing well. She's eating and trying to move about already. Should be on her feet in no time."

"I didn't ask but thank you. I was wondering." The mug hovered just below her chin so the steam rose in her face. "I need to ask you something."

It would have been an innocuous question if not for her tone. Often Jane asked him questions or for advice. Today there was an edge to her words that belied the possibility of questions he couldn't answer. There were too damn many of those. Secrets were his currency, and he was wealthy in them. "What?"

She paused, her gaze darting around them to be certain they were alone on the porch. "You looked into his past, I know."

"We are talking about Cole?"

"Yes. I know you know about Leanne and Alma." Despite their privacy, her voice dropped to nearly unintelligible. "As well as Ella and Lyia."

"I do." Tom matched her volume. He'd looked into Cole's past long ago. "Once I knew about the girls, I didn't worry too much about going further."

"Is there anything I need to be worried about?" Her gaze remained on the street, following the progress of people and horses passing. The mug hadn't moved from its spot near her mouth, though she didn't drink from it. "I can't shake this feeling."

There it was. Her nerves. He honestly wished he had more than he did for her. Once he'd learned not about the wife and child, but Cole's sisters, he'd stopped looking. The way Cole had cared for Leanne and Alma had told him all he needed to know about the man. He hadn't even gone to California himself to dig, he'd trusted a friend to do it for him. "I can only tell you what I know, and it's not much more than you already know."

"Which is?"

"Wife and kid dead, buried in the town cemetery. His pa was a real bastard, maybe more than Cole realizes. Based on what I saw, he probably set that fire himself."

For that her mug dropped to the railing. "The fire that killed Cole's family? His ma? Brothers and sisters?"

"That's the one. Guess he took out fire insurance on the place."

She stared at him wide-eyed. "It wasn't much more than a cabin. Smaller than the house I used to own. Why take out insurance on such a place?"

"Like I said, he probably set it himself for the money." Tom frowned. "My guess is so long as his pa is really dead, he hasn't got much to worry about there but his own memories."

"That's all? Nothing else?" She fixed him with such an intense gaze, he knew she was gauging his honesty in the matter. He was too skilled for many tells, but she'd pick up on it if he allowed even the slightest twitch. The woman was damn good in this new personage.

Lucky for him, he didn't need to lie for this. "That's it. I told you I didn't dig deep. I just wanted to make sure my sister wasn't getting in with a bad element. The girls settled that worry for me."

"Good. I know you'd never lie to me."

That time he couldn't keep his damn brow still, the tic was one he'd worked hard to eliminate. It only crept up in the worst of his guilt. Of all the secrets he kept from Jane, there was one she'd likely never forgive him for. One meant to be nothing but kindness.

Jane didn't miss the tic, and after a miniscule step back, her relief dropped into a frown. "What? What are you hiding from me?"

"To be honest, a lot. You know I have all the secrets."

"No. That was about more than the world's secrets. I know you well enough by now, Tom. I let most of your secrets, and those of others you harbor, breeze on by with nary a word. This was about me, wasn't it?"

"Are you sure you shouldn't be a detective like your ward?"

"Don't change the subject."

He'd have to reveal something. Something that he'd not been sworn to keep until there was no other choice. Something that would explain his guilt. It wasn't too hard to find, either. The secret Charlie had once touched on when they'd had Alan Bingham in prison, dying. "Fine."

"Yes? Go on."

"Before I tell you, there's something you need to understand."

She had her full attention on him now. The mug of coffee forgotten on the railing as she faced him dead on. "What's that?"

"Clara and I didn't get along. Really, much all. Our whole lives we were oil and water. Loved each other as siblings, certainly, but there was no friendship."

"Really? I thought all of the Young's got along swimmingly when they weren't arguing, debating, or accidentally shooting each other."

He chuckled low at her jest. "Not entirely. George and Nick weren't very close, either. Shame, really. Both of them were the worst at memorizing verse."

"George was bad at it as well?"

"He was." Tom sighed. "Clara always pegged me as I was. A snoop and a bully. She didn't like it one bit. It all came to a head when I caught her student taking advantage."

She shuddered at the mention of the long-ago incident that wasn't even her.

"My visits to her in Utah weren't much welcomed. By Ma's rules she tolerated civility to allow me as a guest in her home. It was always begrudging. I suppose Joe accompanying me on a trip didn't help matters there."

"Probably not." She studied him when he left the story hanging unfinished. "Why are you telling me this?"

"I saw Clara after she disappeared."

Her features slackened, cheeks paled. Her mouth hung open for several long moments before it moved. Once or twice she tried to form a word, but no sound escaped.

"Three times, in fact."

"What? How? When? Why didn't you take her away?"

"I tried."

"I thought you were the best."

"I told you, she didn't like me much. Besides, this was all before she came to her senses." Tom thought back to the letters Clara had written while with the man who'd nearly killed her several times over. "Based on Clara's letters, I think I might have been the one that sparked her to think of the child. Never saw her again after that."

"Wait, the letters." Her eyes shifted back and forth fast as though she was reading every single letter again in front of her. She likely was reading them again in her mind. "She never mentioned seeing you. Not once. Why not?"

"She didn't want saved. Not yet, anyway. Definitely not by me. I doubt she'd waste the ink or time to mention me. Didn't want to see me. Like I said, didn't like me. I really did my best to get her out of whatever she was in. Unfortunately, I was the last person she'd listen to."

Jane remained silent for several long minutes. Then her arm laced through his and she pillowed her head on against his shoulder. "I always knew she was an idiot. How on earth could she not like you?"

"I'm a meddling spy."

"Ah, yes. Still. You're one of my favorite people."

"You're one of mine. Never could say that about her."

"Thank you."

"What for?"

"You've always seen me as someone separate. The others have gotten better, but you've always seen me as Jane."

"Well, you are." He thought back to when he'd first come to town, hidden as a stranger from Jane. It had been easy to see how different she was from Clara. His brothers were fools for not seeing it. "First night I saw you I knew, and not just because you're left handed when Clara was right handed."

"I'm glad you were a meddling spy for a few months before you bothered to tell me who you were."

"Me too." He patted her hand. "I didn't care if Clara was mad at me. I'd hate it if you were."

"Never."

"I'm going to hold you to that."

"Go right ahead. What is that?"

Tom straightened with her. He turned his attention to where she pointed off in the distance. A dark blob tore through the snow some miles away. The continuing absence of two buildings across the street was the only reason they could see it. "I'm not sure—is that a sleigh?"

"It must be. They're moving awful fast for a casual ride."

"Looks like maybe they're heading in from the Keenan ranch. That's the general direction."

She made for the steps. Her hand raised to shield her eyes against the glaring sun. It wouldn't help much with the amount of reflection off the snow.

Then Tom heard shouts. Whomever it was, was in a panic. He moved to Jane's side as the shouts became clearer shouts for help. Simultaneously, he and Jane stuck their fingers in their mouths and blew a hard whistle. The dual whistle carried through the clear, still air easy as pie.

As he'd hoped, Charlie emerged onto the porch of the clinic. Nick came darting around the corner seconds later. Right after, Sally emerged from the Inn still tying her cape in place.

"*It's Mort*," Marvin Keenan shouted across the narrowing distance. "Help! The ladder broke. He fell."

Sally turned a side-eye on Tom. "I'll saddle some horses."

"I'll check what's going on, and we'll head out."

Be silent in that solitude,
which is not loneliness-
for then the spirits of the dead who stood
in life before thee are again.
-Edgar Allan Poe

Cole sat in the otherwise empty stage on its way up the mountain to Holle Creek. It wasn't a surprise the stage was empty. The real surprise was that there was any stage run at all. The town had gone bust years before. It was a wonder it wasn't a ghost town.

He didn't bother to peek out the window to watch his approach. There was no excitement to find his way back to the place his old life had both begun and ended. Until he'd met Ella he'd been little more than a kid. He hadn't really been alive until he'd met her.

Colton Spencer, the man he once had been, had died the same time she had. Her pa, Richard, had given him money to get out of town. After lingering long enough to see her cross erected beside their daughters, he'd fled. Not once had he looked back, nor ever wanted to.

For years the past had clung to him in nightmares. He'd done all he could to forget, but the damn past never let him go. It had been his drive to keep everyone and everything at a distance. Without connection your world couldn't crumble.

Then he'd met Jane. She'd entered his life like a stampede. Under her guidance he'd finally managed to make some sort of peace with what had happened.

Since Jane, though, he'd truly left the past where it belonged. These days the box he'd kept the remnants of his past in sat buried in the bottom of a trunk in the closet. His life as Cole Mitchell had become so much more than Colton Spencer's ever had.

A bump in the road jolted the carriage enough that the curtain swung away from the window before it drifted back down. A glimpse of the graveyard had him straighten. He thumped on the roof to slow the driver. He'd grabbed his bag to hop out before they'd stopped moving.

The drivers continued on toward town with little more than a few packages and mail left to deliver. Cole made his way into the cemetery. He wove through the graves like he'd been there only yesterday. In the back near the iron fence two crosses sat worn by time. The names were boldly painted, as though refreshed by a loving, but shaky hand, only days before.

Cole crouched in front of the crosses, staring hard at the names. *Ella Spencer, Lydia Spencer.*

There were stones lining both graves in neat circles. Only a few branches marred the blank stretch of ground before each cross. The upkeep told him Richard still lingered to care for the graves regularly.

Being there staring at their names made him want to run again. He wanted nothing more than to swing right back onto the stagecoach when it creaked and groaned its way back out of town.

He turned his attention to Ella's grave first. Guilt made his lips twitch against the possibility of any tears. He plucked the branches from her grave. "Don't think I did right by you. I tried is all I can say."

He dropped one knee to the dirt and pulled off his hat. "Got married again. She ain't nothing like ya. Guess that's best, seeing as I ain't been the kid that married you in a long time. She knows all about ya. Makes me remember when I don't want to. I'm sorry things went so bad for us. I loved ya much as any kid can love someone."

With a low sigh, he turned to Lydia's smaller grave. Once again, he plucked the fallen branches from the dirt. "Got too many of ya in the ground now. Two more babies that ain't never had the chance to live even for how long you did. That's three too many. Still, I got three kids growing strong and healthy, and all them wards we took in. After ya died, I didn't think I would ever be a pa again. Didn't think I'd want to."

He rose, twisting his Stetson in his hands. "I don't ever forget, but I'm not Colton Spencer anymore. Got a new life. It's pretty damn good, too. Don't mean I don't ever miss ya, though."

After another few minutes that might have been called a prayer by a man that thought God had anything to do with him, Cole turned on his heel to head into town.

Not much had changed in the eighteen years since he'd left, except the town sat much emptier. Some buildings were clearly abandoned and falling to ruin. The never-ending bustling craze of the gold rush now long gone as pans had run dry, and so had the creek.

Cole wanted the first thing he did to be letting Jane know he'd arrived. He made his way to the small telegraph office. The damn stagecoach lingered, taunting him with the ease of departure. Hell, if he needed to he could buy a horse to ride down. He didn't have to wait for the timetable of the coach. Especially since they'd told him in Fresno it only ran every few weeks at best.

He stopped in the office to send the telegram. Quick as he could, he wrote a brief note telling Jane he'd arrived and would be leaving soon as possible. He paid the operator and headed outside.

The boarding house was conveniently located next door to the telegraph. Across the street sat a saloon, one of the only businesses that seemed to have any activity going on. A drink sounded better than anything except getting on that stage. Instead, he checked into the boarding house.

Something told him to keep his bag with him until he'd made his hellos to Richard. When he could settle in his room and find a good place to hide his cash he'd feel better about leaving anything in the room. This whole town seemed too desperate to risk leaving his things unguarded.

He knew his first stop wouldn't be a saloon, no matter how good a drink sounded. Maybe before he headed back to his room he'd make a stop. Or maybe he'd just buy some whiskey at Richard's store and not have to step foot in one of the two saloons lining the main street.

For all that he could tell of the town, much of it had been abandoned. He guessed that a few desperate souls still scraped the creek beds for flakes of gold. Whores still lingered outside the saloons. Hell, the only thriving businesses appeared to be the brothels. Even Richard's seemed quiet where it stood at the end of the street.

He wondered why his pa would have stuck around Holle Creek so long. What schemes could he have found to run, what women to settle down with? There couldn't have been any with money like his ma had had once. Only thing he might've managed to survive on would be gambling and a completely submissive spouse.

None of that mattered, he supposed. After all, the man was dead. Thankfully.

Cole passed right by the saloons to the general store. He stopped in the middle of the street to stare at the sign. Unlike the crosses in the cemetery, the building was worn down. When he'd worked there the store had been strong and solid. Now it bore great gaps in the smooth wood, thin layers of tar paper barely enough to cover any cold air when it hit, and up here in the mountains it did.

He wondered at Richard's lack of care over the business he'd been so proud of. Then again, he was getting older. Perhaps he couldn't tend to it as he once had.

Cole climbed the three steps and paused inside the open door. Like the outside the store had taken a turn for the worse. The once crowded shelves were sparse, bare in many spots. A few sacks of flour and sugar, tinned goods, some mining tools, and plenty of alcohol were the most prominent bits of merchandise in the room.

Richard wasn't behind the counter. An unfamiliar figure stood counting the rows of tinned goods with his back to the room. Rather than disturb the kid, Cole went to grab a couple bottles of whiskey for his room. He'd need it to sleep without Jane there with him. Why hadn't he made her come with him?

He shook off the thoughts and carried the bottles back to the counter.

The young man turned around at the sound of the bottles hitting the counter. Cole had an odd sense of familiarity looking at him. The kid didn't bother looking at him while he checked the bottles. "That'll be two dollars, Pa."

Cole extracted the money, then paused with it half extended. "What did you say?"

"I said that'll be two dollars." The kid took the money and put it in the register.

"I thought—I heard—where's Richard?" Cole could have sworn he'd heard the kid call him pa. That was impoosible, though. Then again, the eyes that met his were eerily familiar. His dark chestnut hair was familiar in a different way. Ella's hair had been that color, and wavy like this kid's.

"Been dead near about a month now." The kid wiped the counter.

"What's your name, kid?"

"James."

"Colton?" The weak feminine voice stopped Cole's heart dead on the spot.

Slow as molasses, he turned toward the voice. A woman emerged from the shadows like the ghost she could only be.

Flesh hung on bones where they'd once been strong, capable muscles. The rounded cheeks of youth had sunken into hollows in the cheeks. Once thick locks of hair responsibly tied into an efficient bun now hung limp and loose, thin, and breaking.

But the eyes. Light hazel with golden flecks sparkling in the lamplight. Same color he'd seen in his dreams for years.

It couldn't be real. None of this was real. He had to wake up.

"What's the matter, Pa?"

Thin, cold fingers touched his cheeks. Air rushed back into Cole's lungs as he gripped the hands to pull them from his face. She was real. Solid. Alive.

"Ella?"

And this maiden she lived with no other thought than to love and be loved by me.
-Edgar Allan Poe

Jane stared at the half-finished letter in front of her. She'd promised to write every day, and had kept the promise the entire time Cole had been gone. For some reason she couldn't think of anything else to say. Nothing had changed from her letter the day before, but that shouldn't matter. She'd written letters with less.

Though she longed to tell him of the baby still growing inside her, she was firm in the truth that she shouldn't put such a thing in a letter. None of that was affecting her ability to write.

Perhaps it was the state of the young woman sitting pressed against her. Though they sat in the restaurant in separate chairs, Alma had pulled her seat close to Jane. She rocked back and forth mumbling, her fingers dancing in jerky motions. Alma had been struggling since Cole's departure, it was true. For some reason that day had Alma completely out of sorts.

Sitting in the middle of the restaurant on a normal day would be cause enough, but at the moment things were relatively quiet. A handful of tables had customers, but the restaurant was hardly full. Only quiet conversations carried through the room.

In the corner James and Nick had their heads together working on Michael's case. She'd been surprised to learn on his arrival to town that before he'd taken over George's farm, James had been a lawyer. His wife Ida, raised in society like Eunice, had taken to the new life with aplomb. She now ran both farms in the absence of the Young's.

A low grunt emerged from Alma as she continued to rock. Her hands flapped against her legs before she pulled them close to her chest again. For the first time in the two days since Jane had received the telegram from Cole saying he'd arrived in Holle Creek safe, Alma spoke, "Cole."

"I know, Alma. I miss him, too. Terribly so."

"No." Alma rocked harder. "Cole."

"He should be getting on a train home in the next couple of days at most. He'll be home by Christmas." Jane eyed the door for any sign of Norman or Kat bringing her the telegram she longed to see. Even though she'd told Cole there was no cause for frequent word, the entire way there he'd sent her something every other day. Yet she'd heard nothing since the telegram telling her of his arrival. By all accounts, two days would be all he needed. "By Christmas."

Alma screeched, "No, no, no, no, no."

"Oh, dear." Jane flew to her feet but couldn't see a way to get the now-flailing young woman to privacy.

"I got her," said a surprising voice. Arthur drew close quickly. He must have just entered at the noise for he hadn't been there a minute before. He approached Alma's side opposite Jane. Though touching Alma in this state could make it worse, he wrapped his arms around her in a bear hug the moment he got a chance.

Jane stood there helpless to assist, though she wanted to badly. Alma's worst fits could usually only be helped by Cole himself. Alma fought against Arthur brutally, hitting her own head through her shrieks.

"Where?" Arthur didn't let go of Alma, and managed to keep her on her feet for the moment.

"Office." Jane rushed behind the reception desk to push open the door for him. Before she'd closed the door, both of her brothers were right behind her.

"What can we do?" James, who'd not seen such an event seemed deeply concerned.

"There isn't much. Let her go, Arthur." Jane cringed when moments after he'd released her, Alma threw herself to the ground hard.

Legs tucked under her, Alma curled into a ball. Her hand banged against the floor several times.

Nick stepped around her, hands on her shoulders. "Go. Arthur and I will handle this."

"No. I mean, there's too many people in here. You should—"

"You don't want to risk her hitting you with the baby." Nick pushed her gently. "Will getting her to the piano help?"

"No, I think she's beyond that now." Jane stood helpless, wanting nothing more than to get to Alma's side.

Right then Alma let out another loud cry. Rising to sit, her hands hitting her legs before she resumed hitting herself in the head. "No. No. No."

"I shouldn't leave," Jane hedged.

"Jane, it's going to be fine." Arthur remained close to Alma. "I've been with Sally when this has happened. We'll manage."

"We've got this, Jane." Nick pushed her from the room, closing the door in her face.

James pulled her against him in a one-armed hug. "They'll get her sorted."

Jane couldn't tear her gaze from the door. "I don't know what to do for her. Without Cole, she's worse than I've ever seen her. He's the one that knows what to do."

"Bull."

"What?" She startled from her thoughts.

He turned her to face him fully. Hands planted on her shoulders, he gave her a hard look. "Cole isn't the one that brought her here, you are. You've helped her often enough when Cole was working. You know that young woman as well as any of your children."

"I..."

"Don't deny it. Did you ever think she's having a hard time because you are?" The stern lines of his face melted into a warm smile. "Yes, Cole is important to her, but so are you. Ever since you found out you were still with child, your nerves have grown immeasurably. You're anxious for your man's return."

"I very much am," she admitted.

"You'll calm. Alma will calm. Then you'll know what to do. You'll remember she's your family and you know as well as Cole does."

"Thank you." She stepped toward him to wrap him in a hug. "I needed that."

"I could tell. You were panicking."

"You know, I know you mentioned you and Ida were thinking of adopting. Soon as you get back to New York, you should. You're going to make a great Pa for some lucky children."

He chuckled low. "We probably were anyway, but I appreciate the support."

"Good." She let out a sigh with the last of her tension. "I should get back to it. I'll have to head into the casino soon, and I'd like to finish this letter."

"Then you'd best do so." He clapped her on the shoulder once more before returning to his seat and the piles of papers on it.

Jane resumed her own seat, finding it much easier to complete the letter now. She signed her name and sealed it shut. Next she had to figure out where to send it. If she sent it on to California, he'd miss it, especially if he left today.

A throat cleared beside her. "Ma'am?"

Jane turned to find Garit staring at her. "Oh, Mr. Schmidt. Would you care to join me?"

"Nah. That Sally girl around?"

"I'm afraid she isn't. She's gone off with Patrick, or Molly? One of them anyway. Would you like me to pass on a message?"

"Just wanted to let her know she was right."

"She'll be delighted to hear it." Jane rose with half a mind to head to the depot to mail her letter. She was also put off by having to crane her neck to look at the man. "A woman does always like to have their wisdom acknowledged. What, pray tell, was she correct about?"

"That man she said would hit women. Just caught him at it." Garit's hands tightened around the back of the chair. "Kicked him right out, so's you know."

"Good. That's all we ask."

"Girl's got an eye."

"She most certainly does. Women are far more observant than we're given credit for." Jane laced her arm through his when he released his death grip on the chair. She led him onto the porch without asking. "Has your reunion with Wil gone well?"

"Gone just fine, ma'am."

"I've told you, it's Jane." She glanced sideways at him. It hadn't gone beyond her notice the friendship between the pair had been quite close. More so than would be acceptable for some. The pair shared a silent language. "A year is quite a long time to be apart from such a very good friend."

"It is." A tightness settled in his startling eyes.

"Mr. Schmidt."

"Garit."

"Garit, then. I dare say Wil was quite excited about your revived friendship after such a parting. I do hope you share the same excitement. I'd hate to lose good managers for our brothel."

Garit's nostrils flared. His pupils dilated so much she could hardly see the blue iris around them. The entire length of his arm tensed under her casual grasp. "Jane."

"My child is not the only observant one, Garit. Rest assured, your secret is safe with me."

"Don't know what you mean."

"Of course you don't. I wouldn't worry too much about it, people will never see what they loathe to see. I don't care what occurs when the brothel closes so long as my brothel and its whores are well cared for, and their managers keep lusty gazes and actions trained on said whores in public."

"Wil's good at that." A darkness to his tone drew her full attention.

"If another argument such as the one that caused your friendship to splinter should occur again, I ask that one of you remain until we can find appropriate replacements."

"Would like to say that won't happen."

"I understand. Friendships can be difficult at times." She squeezed his arm. "Go on, then. I'll be by tonight for some interaction with my patrons. Or perhaps I'll send Sally."

"Sally plays the game."

"She learned well." Jane nodded him on his way. After he'd made his way up the steps to the brothel, she turned to find Charlie climbing the steps. "Charles."

Charlie hugged her tight. "Jane."

"Where's Millie?"

"She and George are at Lee's."

"I see. You do realize that Millie and Lee are going to have those poor children married before puberty."

"Don't need to tell me that." Charlie led her inside.

"How is Cora?"

"She's doing very well. I expect she'll be able to go home soon if she promises to take it easy."

"And Mort Keenan?"

"He's in terrible pain. A femur fracture is no joke. He won't be riding for a long time."

Jane sat back at the table she'd abandoned minutes before. When Charlie joined her, she sighed. "Did you hear what Tom and Sally said about that ladder?"

"I don't see how it's possible. The ranch is crawling with people all of the time. Besides, how could they tell a rung had been partially sawed through? It broke, and then again as Mort fell."

"Still."

"Don't you start as well." Charlie wagged his finger at her. "I will not have my entire family being suspicious about every accident that happens in town. Accidents do happen."

"I'm well aware. However, Tom knows what he's doing. He's been doing it a long time. Sally's proven to be quite adept as well."

"It makes no sense if it were true. What would be the purpose?"

"I suppose you're right." Jane glanced toward James in the corner, finding Nick back with him. She wondered what had happened with Alma. "I need to go see Michael tomorrow. I know what he's doing, and it won't help him."

"What's he doing?"

"Alone in the jail for hours on end without distraction? He's focusing on nothing else but the black hole in his memory." Jane shuddered. "Something I'm all too familiar with myself."

"I'd rather you didn't remind me of that."

"I'd rather not be reminded of it." Jane frowned. "My handful of memories came when I wasn't digging for them. Trying to mine the darkness only gave me headaches."

"You never told me that. You get headaches when you try to remember?"

"I did. I've no idea if I still do. I don't go mining any longer."

"Ever?"

"No. We both seem to prefer it that way."

As men, we are equal in th presence of death.
-Publilious Syrus

Jane stood on the porch while Arthur walked with Alma toward the meadow. She'd returned to the apartment to find it full. The children were getting their lessons, which made it too busy for Alma just then. Arthur had still been with her, and already guiding her out the back door for a walk someplace quieter. Jane was infinitely grateful for the kindness.

Alma still hadn't given voice to what had set off her latest fit. Cole's absence certainly could be enough. So could Jane's own nerves over the same thing, for that matter. James had a point that Alma leaned on her as much as Cole. She'd have to do better at containing the underlying nerves that hadn't left since Cole's last telegram.

Charles had been called away from their conversation quite abruptly. Bonnie had rushed in to tell him there was an emergency with Mort.

Jane didn't want to ponder what the emergency could be. She had no desire to chase any further panics or terrors to their lives. All she wanted was for everything to settle like the snow in the meadow. Clean and smooth. Crisp and fresh. Nothing to break its muffled silence.

Nick took position at her side. He said nothing, his features as stoic as ever. Still, he set a comforting hand on hers. Thankfully he was more comfortable with silence than some nosy others would be and offered nothing more than his presence.

Jane soaked in the silence happily. The warmth of his hand helped keep the pesky nerves at bay in a way she couldn't explain.

Alma and Arthur made their way through the crisp snow to the church. Soon as they arrived they disappeared inside. Jane imagined Arthur was going to let Alma play her way calm.

For nearly fifteen minutes they remained standing there quiet. It was a lovely peace, but for her soul, it only covered the barest of nerves. Within that silence came the urge to talk it out with her level-headed brother.

"I know I told him he didn't have to write often. It isn't like him."

"No, it's not. Cole is a man of few words."

"I'd only expected to hear he was on his way back by now. That's all."

"Of course." Speaking of men of few words. Nick was proving one with his support now.

"My nerves can be explained away by the last couple of times he left. They were times of great stress and pain. Fear of death for either of us. This is all an echo of such things."

"It's perfectly natural."

"Stop agreeing with me."

"You have many children, several businesses, and quite a few other activities going on."

She glanced his way when he continued her excuses for her. "I do."

"You are used to doing all things in a partnership."

"Every day for several years now, yes."

"I've not seen a match like yours and Cole's since Ma and Pa."

"What about Charles and Millie? James and Ida?"

Nick turned to face her. "They are good matches as well, but they do not share nearly every minute of every day as you and Cole."

"Not nearly every minute."

"Don't be coy. It doesn't suit you."

"I have the library and my teas. He now has the brothel. It's not every minute." At his stern look, she acquiesced. "However, it is a great deal of every day."

"Each and every one of your daily activities echo with the missing piece. You're allowed to be melancholy even when not facing fear of death."

"And the certainty deep inside that something is terribly wrong?"

"Echoes of the past, such as you said. He sent a telegram when he arrived. He'll send another when he departs. Perhaps there was another family to contend with, as you suggested." Like Tom, Nick knew more about Cole's past than just about anyone else. Thanks to his status as a lawyer and having to help with certain legal matters around Leanne's brothel, which Cole still had a small interest in.

"His father had done so in the past, it isn't a stretch to imagine he would do so again. Perhaps even more times over." Jane released a long breath. "Thank you. I needed to sort that out in my head, but out loud with another saner brain than mine."

"Saner might be a stretch, except in this matter."

"I'm too close. You're more detached."

"When it comes to Cole, perhaps. Not to you."

She leaned her head against his shoulder in gratitude. "You're a good man, Nicholas."

"I get by."

She laughed softly. "More than, I'd say."

"Less than, most others would say."

"Which is a shame." She released a soft sigh, knowing if she delved too far he'd run faster than a jackrabbit to get away from the conversation. "Did you and James figure anything out?"

"We have a good defense prepared I believe. Our best hope is that by the time Marshal Lewis arrives after Christmas, Michael will remember what happened."

"We're pressuring him too much. He's pressuring himself too much."

"I had the same thoughts." Nick's gaze drifted toward the depot. "Distraction is difficult to come by within a jail cell. However, we can cease pestering him."

"I never have pestered. When I go, he begs distraction and I offer it as best as I can. I do not know how to help him. I couldn't even help myself with my own memory. His cause is different, but the consequences are near as drastic." She couldn't help herself, concern for one brother often bled into another. "Speaking of distraction."

"Why do I feel I will not care for this conversation?"

"It's nothing." She offered him a smile, for in truth she wasn't about to pester him over what she truly wanted to. Instead, she was going to help two people close to her at once. "I was only hoping you would do a kindness for me."

"Depends on the kindness."

"The dance Lillian is plotting for St. Valentine's."

"No."

"You haven't even heard me out." Jane clasped his hands. She stepped closer, hoping her earnestness came across. "If I swear I'm not playing matchmaker, will you listen?"

"You can't help yourself. You'll play matchmaker no matter."

"Not for you, though I do wish you would find happiness with a woman."

"Jane."

"You know. Have you considered a mail order bride? You can find someone to suit your particular nature. Especially as it appears no woman in town is of your taste."

"Clara Louise."

"Oooh, I have upset you." Jane laughed, holding his hands tight when he tried to pull them away. "Now, now. I wasn't serious. You know it."

"Tell me what it is you're asking me, or I'll doubt you."

"I'd like you to accompany Cora again, as a friend and nothing more. The poor woman still mourns Kelly, but she misses a good dance partner."

"Cora?" Nick's tension drained from his shoulders. "If that's all you wanted, then yes. I am happy to be Cora's companion for the evening."

"You truly are a good man." She squeezed his hands in a fashion that mimicked her hearts contraction in her worry for him. "You do know that I only wish happiness for you. Don't you?"

"I do."

"Good. Everyone deserves happiness, even you."

"It's difficult to come by. There are things that most wives wouldn't tolerate."

"If they truly love you, they will tolerate it all. Even the darkness you wish I couldn't see."

"Only those that have lived in the darkness could see it."

"Very true." After several years of solid hard work, Jane couldn't be happier that she and Nick had managed to reach such a place. He'd even shared some darker moments from the war with her. Even still, there was much he kept hidden deep down.

Before she could say more, movement caught her eye. Charles stepped out of the clinic, shoulders drooped.

"Oh dear. I don't think things went well with Mort." Jane took Nick's arm to head across the street. "Charles? What's wrong?"

"Mort's gone. He was doing well, but he threw a clot. Had a heart attack while I was trying to save him. He's gone." Charles rubbed his hand over his face. "I'm going to have to head to the ranch to tell Marvin."

"I'll go with you," Nick offered. "I handle the legal affairs of the ranch. Marvin might have some questions."

"Thank you. Jane, you all right?" Charlie turned toward her. "Did you need anything?"

"No. Go. I'm fine." She pushed them both toward the clinic. "Send my regrets to Marvin."

Rather than return to the Inn, she headed to the jail to see her brother. David stood on the porch, eying her approach. The brim of his hat hid his expression. Before she could pass him to enter the jail, he stepped right into her path. "Jane."

"Let me by, David."

"Your pa is in there now anyway. Please talk to me." Now that he was close enough, she could see the lines of regret creasing his features. The man appeared to have aged twenty years since he'd put her brother in jail. His usually vibrant hazel eyes were dull. "I hate that you won't talk to me."

"I'm no longer your wife. Haven't been in some time. You don't need me to talk to you."

"You are my friend. One of the best I've ever had. Mike's even talking to me now, but you won't."

"You put him in jail for a crime he didn't commit."

"All evidence—"

"All evidence my foot. You had none but a wounded man lashing out at the world. Now you've let that world chew him up and spit him out. He'll never be the same after this, David. Not ever. I should know."

"Jane."

"Let me pass, please." Damn her betraying tear ducts for unleashing tears she didn't care for him to see.

"I want you to know, I've talked to the others. The others I knew about anyhow. Some of her favorites. I've gotten nowhere. I'm letting Sally and Tom do most of it because they've uncovered more by digging. I don't know if Mike did it."

"He didn't!"

"But I'm doing all I can to help him. I want him to be innocent."

Jane closed her eyes when he brushed a tear from her cheek. "I need my anger."

"Then be angry at the one that did it. Not me." He tugged her close, wrapping her in a warm hug. "You need your friends right now, don't you?"

"I have plenty of those without you."

"Ah, but none of them are like me. Remember? I'm wonderful?"

Against every restraint against it, a laugh bubbled free. "That didn't work before the divorce, and it won't work now."

"I think it's working a little."

"You're the worst."

"Right back at you."

*A woman's whole life
is a history of the affections.
—Washington Irving*

Sally strolled arm in arm with Molly down Second Street. The unseasonably warm weather had come out of nowhere, and everyone in town was enjoying the day. The streets bustled with folks dead set on getting business done before the next storm hit.

Though they'd originally planned a stroll through the meadow, it had proven a soggy mess with the thick snow still melting. This was much better, though. Sally loved when the town came to life and people mingled and chatted.

There was something about the life and activity that made her feel content, despite everything going on. She'd meant what she'd told Arthur, there was no place like home.

She'd spent much of recent days with Tom going over the accident Mort had suffered, which might not have been an accident at all. That morning he'd insisted she enjoy the afternoon of nice weather. The past several days she'd not only spent in mystery with Tom, and occasionally Molly, but also with her Ma. The continuing lack of communication was proving difficult for her. It worried Sally to see her Ma so stressed.

Molly, however, was seeing to it that her studies in areas beyond the bedroom were not neglected. Their peaceful walk was more a review session of the tarot cards.

Sally truly wondered if she'd ever have a need for such an odd bit of knowledge. Then again, she imagined stranger things had happened.

"Four of cups," Molly offered into the small lull in conversation.

"Apathy. Disconnected."

"The Magician."

"Willpower." Sally cast Molly a sideways glance. "Desire."

"Knight of Wands."

"The big picture. Overcoming challenges."

"Very good. I believe that's all seventy-eight cards. You learned them plenty fast once you put your mind to it." Molly nudged her with her shoulder. "And you learned to relax a little."

"In more ways than one." Sally sidestepped with Molly as a horse and wagon came toward them. She waved to Hammy as he passed with a load of lumber. "Everyone certainly is enjoying the weather. Perhaps when we get back we should look at the schedule for the hot springs. It would be nice to soak in the warmth as the weather cools."

"We could invite Patrick as well." Molly and Patrick had finally met and gotten along swimmingly. She leaned closer to Sally. "We'd need to be certain things were private. How nosy is that caretaker?"

"Landon keeps to himself if told to do so by Ma. I've never had reason to ask though. Why?" Sally eyed Molly. "Are you truly suggesting we take Patrick up on his offer?"

"Why not?"

A niggling of embarrassment tangled with excitement at the idea. "All three of us?"

"Imagine it, or rather live it." Molly nodded down the street. "Speak of the devil and he appears."

A small carriage pulled to a stop beside them. Patrick beamed at them both. "Good morning, ladies. It's a lovely day, isn't it?"

"It certainly is." Sally eyed the carriage. It was familiar, bought a while ago right before the weather turned so it could see proper use. "Is this Ma's new addition?"

"Yes. I rented it for the morning. I'm taking Kat, Lizzie, and my darling little CC on a ride. I didn't figure we needed a larger carriage. The girls are small enough." He eyed the size of the seat he sat on. "I hope."

Sally laughed. "I'm certain it won't be a problem. Cindy will happily sit on your lap if it's too crowded for all four of you."

"Fair point." Patrick nodded to Molly. "You are in high spirits."

"Perhaps it is high spirits." Molly grinned broadly, drawing Sally closer to the carriage along with her. "Or perhaps I simply had a wicked idea."

"Wicked ideas are a favorite of mine." Patrick leaned closer. "Does it have something to do with the fetching Sally sitting on my lap later?"

"Most certainly."

"Even better." He pushed the brake in place. When he hopped from the carriage, he came indecently close to them both. "What's on your mind?"

Sally cleared her throat against the momentary shyness that blocked her words. "I had suggested seeing if we can't make it to the hot springs at dusk. We thought you might join us."

"I would be delighted." Patrick took each of their hands in turn to kiss the back of them. "If you secure a time, leave a note in my room. I'll make certain to clear my evening."

"We'll see you then." Molly offered a dainty wave as he hopped back in the carriage and rode off. Her voice rose in pitch, a sweet note of southern twang filtering through her words. "I do declare I may swoon from the excitement."

Sally shook her head. "You and your accents."

"Oh, but my darling. That is vat ees next in your training." Molly dipped back into the exotic voice she'd used at their first meeting. The rich notes sent a shiver down Sally spine. "Ve have only been dabbling. Ve shall get you trained to speak in such tones and languages your own mama vould not recognize you."

"I highly doubt that." Sally couldn't imagine adopting as many accents as Molly could. The idea of learning more languages as well? French had been easy enough with Ma teaching her, but that was the only language Jane knew outside of English. Much more with a different might tax her brain to its fullest. "You have too much faith in me."

"You, my dear, are far more talented than you give yourself credit for. It took you a while to learn the cards, but you've slipped into every accent I've thrown at you with little encouragement."

"It's been two accents, and one language that Ma taught me."

"I told you that dulcet singing voice would aide you in your endeavors. I meant it. We'll teach your lovely throat to do more than croon." Laughter added a tremor to Molly's words. "Don't look so terrified. We'll certainly get you ready for anything. If I must remain here for another year."

"It may take five if you want me to learn accents. Ten if you're adding languages."

"Nonsense. You're a quick study. Your ma didn't lie about that."

"My ma is biased, and so are you anymore."

"Who can blame me?" Molly winked, pulling her toward the brothel. "Let's get a drink."

"You only want to flirt with Wil." Sally wasn't jealous, far from it. Molly was a good friend, and one that liked to play. Their dalliance was just like the one she shared with Patrick. A good friendship with some fun mixed in.

"Who wouldn't?"

Sally laughed as she followed Molly inside the brothel. There was no doubt the brothel manager had a dark attractiveness about him. Garit, as his opposite, wasn't bad to look at either. Inside, she was pleased to find Wil behind the counter. Though Garit was starting to loosen up since their last interaction, she preferred the dark look of Wil, not to mention his humor. "Wil."

"Sally. Molly. Am I to guess you've been up to no good?"

"My reputation precedes me." Molly slid into the stool across from him.

"I've heard tales of Dublin's fair city, where girls are so pretty, of a woman fishmonter." Wil set down two glasses. "Or was it your mother and father before?"

"Cock…cles and muscles, alive, alive, oh." Molly grined at him. "Could we have a couple whiskeys to wet our whistles, unless you'd like to help the task."

"Sally could use boldness like you got." Wil poured the whiskeys, winking at Sally. "For a former whore, you're not too cocksure."

"Spent too long being good," Sally admitted. "Didn't realize I could be both until recently."

"Both is better. Much better." He leaned on the bar. "What are ya both doing in here? Isn't this blasted weather keeping everyone out in it?"

Sally glanced around the fairly empty bar. "Good weather bad for business?"

"No worries. When the sun goes down the cold will settle and everyone'll be looking for a warm body to curl up with." Molly tossed back her drink. "My bet's on four o'clock and this place is full."

"I'd say three." Sally pulled her own drink close. "Knowing night's coming, they'll cut out early to get a head start on the heat."

"You would know." Wil pulled a cigar box from under the counter. He held it out to them. Sally waved him off, but Molly grabbed one of the selection. He tossed a small box of matches her way. "I'm guessing it happened when you were working."

"Several times. Especially during that really mild winter we had. Usually around three we'd get the first big boom of customers." Sally plopped onto the stool next to Molly.

"Did you say the place looked like this before?" Molly turned in her seat to take in the saloon. The lit cigar dangled in her dainty fingers. "It was nice. Better than some of the places I've seen. Barely two rooms for whores, bar so overcrowded you couldn't breathe for nothing."

"You been in Fayette?" Will chuckled. "Sounds like my place there before I went to Abilene."

"Actually, I have." Molly spun back toward him. "I would've remembered you, though."

"When were ya there?"

Shouts from outside pulled Sally's attention from the conversation. A scream carried on the clear air. Sally shot out of her seat. She strode to the door to try to figure out what was going on. Near the porch of the Inn, Fanny Thompson held a hand to her mouth, the other pointing south. A moment later she clean fainted to the cobblestone.

Sally rushed to the railing to see what had caused her such turmoil.

A figure raced through the streets, darting between all of the people crowding them. The woman was buck naked, and filthy to boot. Gray hair hung limp down to her knees and flew behind her when she took off running again. She screamed and tore at Archie, her hands raised in claws. The man backed up a step, but when she tried to pass him, he tried to grab her around the waist.

The woman gave him the slip and tore down Main Street toward the saloon. By then the crowd had gathered and she heard cries of a name.

Opal.

Opal Chauncey, who hadn't been seen since her hsuband's death.

"My God. *Opal.*" Sally's cry was enough to make the woman pause in front of her. Opal tilted her head and studied her, eyes wide. Red stained her chin, and bubbled from her lips. The second a hand grabbed her arm, she tore off in another frenzy, right down the alley beside the saloon. "Opal!"

Several men took off down the alley toward the wayward woman. Molly and Wil appeared on the porch to see what the ruckus was. At that moment Opal tore back onto Main Street through the alley on the opposite side of the dressmakers.

Opal screamed again, tearing through town along First Street before disappearing into an alley again. Sally stood transfixed on the porch as a growing group chased after the wild woman. Several minutes later several of them poured back onto First Street, searching in bewilderment.

Sally frowned at their confusion. Opal had clearly been out of her mind, she couldn't have hid that well, could she? Then Molly shouted beside her and pointed to Kat's where Opal climbed the stairs to the balcony on all fours like an animal.

Before one person could start up the steps after her, Opal stood on the railing of the balcony, cackling like mad.

Opal flung herself forward.

Sally didn't see the end because Wil had tucked her into his chest. "Fuck me."

Sally pushed against him and found herself face to face with Molly, who'd suffered the same fate of Wil's gallantry. "What the hell was that about?"

"Don't know," Wil answered. "But I'm betting she's dead now."

"Gee. Ya think?"

In the middle of the journey of our life
I came to myself within a dark wood
where the straight way was lost.
—Dante Alighieri

Cole sat on the front stoop of the general store. In one hand his cigar smoked nearly untouched. In the other, a whiskey he'd been nursing for a good hour. That morning he'd gone to the telegraph office once again. Every single day that week he'd gone twice a day in hopes of a response to the missive he'd sent days before.

Once again the operator had told him nothing had come. Not even the supply wagon that had arrived that morning had any letters for him, or at all. It made no sense. He'd heard nothing from Jane since Fresno. Not a telegraph, not even a letter. She'd said she'd write every day.

Jane wouldn't ignore him. Not the message he'd sent telling her, almost begging her, to come to California. He hadn't told her about Ella, of course. That wasn't something you said in a telegram from hundreds of miles away.

What could have happened that she wouldn't have written him back? The past several days he'd sent multiple telegrams asking her to come immediately—with Nick if at all possible. He didn't expect that to happen, what with Mike's issues, but he'd asked anyway.

Maybe she'd already left Dominion Falls without bothering to reply. If she'd sensed his urgency it was a possibility. Maybe she'd be on the next stage or supply wagon.

He had no idea what to do to fix the situation. He needed Jane as much as he'd known he would before he'd left. No, more.

The whole situation with Ella was a mess. He doubted he could get her to leave the town without the baby she kept searching for. Then there was the boy claiming to be his son. He'd never in his life dreamed he'd find a fully grown son in Holle Creek.

He'd been so busy with the pair of them, mostly Ella, that he hadn't had a chance to look into what had happened to his Pa.

The supposed lawyer that had sent the telegram wasn't a lawyer at all. The telegram had been signed James Decker. That was the kid himself. According to Jim, Ella's pa Richard had given him his late wife's maiden name rather than Spencer.

Richard had removed Ella from the asylum when James was twelve, and Richard had switched to giving Ella the same surname of Decker. His intent was likely to separate Ella Decker from the supposedly dead and buried Ella Spencer.

Not that any of that mattered. Ella was hardly of sound mind to do a damn thing about anything. The strong young woman he'd once known had been lost to her madness. So often in the past few days she'd mistaken Jim for Cole, not even acknowledging that Jim was her child at all. Instead, she searched for Lydia everywhere. In the night she wandered back to the long-abandoned house she'd shared with Colton. He wasn't Colton anymore, hadn't been for a long time. Much as Jane was no longer Clara, and Ella was no longer herself.

Cole had tried to keep his room at the boarding house and had managed for five days before giving up to sleep on a cot in the nearly empty storeroom of the general store. Ella wandered often, and James couldn't be bothered to care one bit about his own mother.

Cole stared at the trail leading into town. It continued to sit empty as it had all week, save for the supply wagon that morning. The supply wagon that was long gone. He'd spent a couple hours putting away the measly supplies James had ordered to stock the handful of men, whores, and families still lingering around town for whatever reason.

"Jane, where in blazes are ya?" He'd nearly purchased a horse at least a dozen times during the week to head down the mountain toward Fresno. Part of him wanted to escape, but mostly he really needed to get in contact with Jane.

Something had to get through to her. What could he do to get her attention? What would snap her sharp mind into focus to make her understand he needed a word? Hell, he just needed her.

He glanced back into the store. For the time being Ella searched again for the long-dead child. It wasn't a frantic search yet, but would be eventually. She rifled through empty baskets, dug into old salt pork barrels, then searched the drawers under the register. Eventually she'd go upstairs and start searching those rooms as well.

Cole eyed the desk on the back wall for a long minute. All week he'd tried to get into the locked drawers. He wanted to figure out how much he could unload the store for. Or, in the worst case, find out how far in the hole the place was. It would be easier to cut losses and run, but he had to do right by Richard. Despite his faults, and not telling Cole what was really happening, his former father-in-law had saved his life by giving him a new one. The least Cole could do was take care of the shop, and Richard's daughter and grandson.

He'd not really explored the town or talked to others about what had happened to Paul, and Jim was of no help at all. He acted as though he had no idea who Cole was talking about, despite being the name on the telegram telling him of Paul's death.

Speak of the devil, Jim bellowed to his ma to knock it off, the only kid she had was him. James never did a thing for Ella, and most often only made her worse.

As to Jim's opinion of Cole, it wasn't any better. Cole couldn't blame the kid, it's not like he'd been involved in Jim's life at all. To be fair, Richard hadn't ever bothered to tell Cole that Ella was still alive, much less that she'd borne him another child. If he'd known, what would he have done? It was so long ago, when Cole had been no more than an angry, scared young man.

First instinct told him he would've ignored any such news of a kid. He'd left Holle Creek to forget everything. He'd have been all too happy to continue to do so.

Then again, there was Leanne and Alma. He'd done everything he could for them, even going so far as to adopt Alma to help save her.

What would his life be now if he'd known Ella had lived? If he'd known he had a son?

Would he still be here? Jim was miserable here. Hell, after the boom had gone, who wasn't? He imagined Jim was even more miserable after years of dealing with Ella's disturbed mind. Would Cole had left her in the hell of an asylum?

So many questions he couldn't answer. His mind raced with them until he couldn't think straight.

Jane. He needed to reach out to her again. Impress on her the urgency of his situation. He had to try again. If it were at all possible to leave that second, he would. Hell, as it was he didn't think he'd make it back in time for Christmas. He needed a lawyer, and information on a decent place to put Ella.

Information and advice. Two things he was in short supply of right then.

He needed to get Ella out, but he couldn't just wander into Dominion Falls with her. For that matter, how could he travel safely with a woman they couldn't even contain in the store? She'd never make it out of town, or in a rail car.

Cole rose to head to the desk. He might not have been able to get in the locked drawers, but there was paper and pencil available. He'd compose his next telegram to Jane carefully. Something that would for sure get her attention.

Three steps in, Ella all but tackled him. "Where is she?"

"Sleeping. She's sleeping, Ella. Come on, have a seat." Cole guided her to the rocker where she spent most of her time. "Rest. Lydia will be awake after a time."

He felt guilty for lying, but saying such things were all that calmed the woman sometimes. Soon as Ella got settled enough to satisfy him, he dropped into the chair at the desk. After a few minutes contemplation, he set to writing a short missive he hoped would have the right impact.

Annabel. The ghosts are real. Bring your most haunted with you, quickly. Best, C.

The way her mind worked, Jane would understand. It wasn't enough, though. He needed to reach out to another that might get the message. While he thought over what to say, Ella's chair creaked under her steady rocking. The rapid pace she'd begun with had slowed to something more soothing. Ella sang a soft song, a lullaby she'd sung to Lydia every night before she'd died.

For a moment it drew him back to the days when they'd been happy. Ella's pure joy over their daughter every time the child would do so much as coo or squeeze a finger. The familiar ache of losing all of it coursed through his heart until he had to shake it off.

He turned his attention back to the matter at hand. The next telegram.

Tom. Dig deeper. There's more than even you knew. Tell Lou. There's much more. C.

One of them would respond. They had to. If they didn't, he didn't know what his next course of action would be. The best thing would be to get Ella out of there. Jim too, if he could manage.

He collected a couple of bills from his pocket to cover the cost of the telegrams. One more trip to the telegraph office today and he'd pack it in. If only they had laudanum in the store, or a doctor in town to purchase it from, he could possibly get a decent nights' sleep by forcing Ella to get rest.

Then again, he didn't know that laudanum would even work on her. Perhaps he should wire Fresno to have some sent. If nothing else, he could use it for the trip home.

He'd have to arrange that at the telegraph office himself since he didn't know the doctor's name. He gathered the notes to head out to sent them. It would be a quick trip, and he'd be back.

Jim stomped his way down the back stairs. He glanced at the notes in Cole's hand and a frown darkened his features. "Where the hell are you going now?"

"Back to the telegraph office. I have a couple to send. I'll be right back."

"Ya just went. I was going the saloon. Getting the hell away from her."

"Give me fifteen minutes and you're free to go."

"No. I'm going now. Just leave her. Maybe she'll do us a favor and wander off a cliff."

Anger bubbled forward. He was doing all he could to help out, and to make things right, but the kid was nothing but anger and abuse. It was hard to believe Richard had raised him. "That's your ma you're talking about."

"She ain't no Ma to me. I ain't Lydia."

The mere mention of the name sent Ella back to a rapid rocking. "Lydia. Where is she?"

Jim's lip curled. "Dead, you idiot."

"*No.*" Ella launched at her son, shrieking like a banshee.

Before Cole could move to grab Ella, Jim punched her hard enough to knock the woman to the floor. Ella groaned low, clearly dazed, and bleeding near her eye.

"Damn it, Jimmy." Cole knelt beside Ella. James ignored him completely and stormed from the building without another word.

Thankfully the cut beside Ella's eye wasn't bad, but she was definitely stunned. Cole scooped her up to set her back in the rocker. "Rest, Ella. Lydia is napping. Rest."

Cole flopped back into the chair at the desk. He supposed tomorrow was as good a time as any to send the telegrams. He'd rather sooner than later, though. A glance at Ella told him she'd fallen asleep, but he couldn't risk leaving her there.

Could he?

If he locked the store from the outside, perhaps he could. Sure, locking the store at night hadn't helped, but that had been from the inside. If he did it from the outside, and was only gone maybe fifteen minutes, he might be able to do it.

Making up his mind that the risk was worth the reward if Jane finally got her ass on a train heading west, he rose to do just that.

A tall figure climbed the steps, then paused at the threshold to darken the doorway. The man hovered in the shadows in total silence. Made no difference, Cole knew instantly who it was.

He tucked his missives in his pocket and strode toward the man. "You son of a bitch. I knew you were still alive. It ain't a coincidence that it was James that sent me the telegram, is it?"

A cold smile crossed his pa's face. "Good to see you, son."

"Bullshit."

There is something fascinating aobut science. One gets such wholesale returns of conjecture out of such a trifling investment of fact.
—Mark Twain

Jane drew her cape tight about her shoulders, then turned to be certain Willow's coat and muffler were secure. Since the night she'd spent in the clinic, her condition hadn't improved much at all. In the past few days it had worsened further. Jane wanted Charlie to look her over again.

Of course, she was also curious about what had happened to Opal. She also wanted to check on Kat who had, upon finding the dead body on her stoop and the crowd around it, passed out. Charlie had kept her in the clinic overnight to be certain it was a passing trauma.

Jane crouched before Willow to be certain all buttons were fastened. The poor child had dark circles under her eyes, and her skin had a pallor. "Are you ready?"

Willow nodded, coughing into her muffler. She didn't fight when Jane guided her into the cold air.

The beautiful sunshine of the previous day lingered, though the warm weather had faded into the night and remained gone. Jane took care to walk them slow enough to not exacerbate Willow's condition. The slightest exertion seemed to tire the child anymore, which deepened Janes concern. When Willow turned away chances to play over doing schoolwork, Jane knew without a doubt there was a problem.

Inside the clinic she found no one in the reception area. Murmurs from the large back room drew her attention. She hesitated to go back for a moment as she knew Andrew had taken over the room as a sort of coroners office. He performed his autopsies there, but also had it set up as a laboratory of sorts.

The door stood open, so she doubted they were doing anything so unseemly as an autopsy. She drew closer. "Charles?"

Inside the room she found not only Charles, but Dr. Cross. While Andrew fiddled with some glass tubes, Sally leaned on the table watching him work with rapt attention. Tom leaned against a nearby cabinet, studying the work with no less attention.

Charlie turned his attention to Jane, stepping closer. "What can I do for you today?"

"I'd hoped you could examine Willow. She's still not feeling well at all. After she was in here overnight, her asthma much improved. In the past few days she's felt more weak." Jane nodded to Sally when the girl glanced there way in concern. "What's all this?"

"Come with me, I'll explain while I'm examining Willow. How are you doing, Shivering Willow?" Charlie didn't balk at Willow's weak, noncommittal grunt of reply. He led them into the first exam room. "Dr. Cross's years working as a medical examiner while in school served him well. He's trying to determine if Opal had any sort of drugs in her system when she was in her final hours."

Jane removed Willow's coat for her before helping her onto the exam table. "Do you believe she did?"

"Not particularly. Based on accounts of the matter, and what I've found on the body, I think a much simpler explanation is at hand. Willow, breathe deep as you can for me."

Jane remained silent while Charlie listened to Willow's breathing. The girl made barely two breaths before she began coughing heavily again. Jane clutched Willow's hand, all other thoughts flying away in concern for Willow's health. "You poor thing."

Charlie moved to the stove where he set a kettle to boil. "I'm concerned that this is more than asthma now."

Jane's heart stuttered to a stop. She recognized Charlie's tone, the warm concern used when he delivered difficult news. She'd heard it during her bout of scarlet fever, and too often to count during the epidemic of the grippe. "Charles."

"I believe she's developed pneumonia."

"Oh no." Jane folded Willow into a close hug. Pneumonia. So often she'd heard such a thing had been fatal. "I—what can we do?"

"I'd like to keep her for a few days."

Without a doubt she knew he wouldn't say it if he didn't mean it. She'd do anything to be sure the child was one of the few that made it. Her mind stumbled over the idea of having one of her children in here with so many others to care for as well. A weak protest erupted in a quiet whisper. "She doesn't like to be away from her brother that long. Plus, I can't remain here for days."

"She wouldn't be here alone any more than Sally was when she was ill."

"Sally's an adult." Jane rubbed Willow's back when she dissolved into another fit of coughing. "I should have brought her in sooner. I curse my distraction for not realizing how badly she was feeling sooner."

"You've been watching her like a hawk since the cold induced that severe attack." Charlie set a hand on hers. "People with asthma tend to get sicker much faster because their lungs are already compromised. This isn't your fault."

"I've been too focused on other things." Jane kissed the top of Willow's head. "I should have been more focused on the children."

"You're always focused on your children. Stop blaming yourself." Charlie left her side to pour the hot water into a mudge pot along with several herbs and a chunk of silver. He set it on a stool near the window, then dragged a chair up to it. "Come over here, Willow. I want you to do a treatment now while Jane's here. After that we'll make you comfortable in a room. Miss Bonnie has added some peg boards and dominoes to the rooms to join the jacks we already had. We can let your brother come and keep you company for a while, but you're going to need lots of rest."

Jane moved closer to the door. To stem their shaking, she folded her hands in front of her. Charlie spoke to Willow quietly as he got her set up at the mudge pot. When he left her and came to Jane's side, she inhaled sharply. "Pneumonia is deadly."

"In many cases, yes." Charie put a hand around her waist to guide her to a nearby chair. He pushed her down into it before she could protest. "I promise you that we'll do whatever we can to make certain that isn't the case for Willow."

"But you can't guarantee she'll survive," Jane said quietly to keep Willow from hearing. Not that the girls current bout of wheezing made it easy to hear. Jane forced herself to take several deep breaths in search of calm. "I'm not faulting you. I know you'll do all you can."

"Have faith."

"I'm doing my best."

"How is Cole's trip to Hell?"

"What?" Distracted from her concerned, Jane stared at her brother. "Did you mean Holle?"

"Holle is German. If you add an umlaut above that 'o', you get Hölle. It means Hell." Charles rubbed her cold hands. "Jane?"

"Hell Creek. Goodness, that does little to ease my worries."

"I've no doubt Cole is fine. Though not as sharp as you, he's a clever man."

"Charles, I haven't heard one thing from him since he got there. He should be on a train now, due to arrive any day, but I've heard nothing."

"Maybe he wants to surprise you."

"He wouldn't worry me like this. He knew I was worried before he left, so was he. We were worried over nothing, just past experiences of being separated."

"Then maybe he's in a hurry to get back to you."

"Perhaps." Jane glanced toward Willow. "I'll continue to write him. I'll send him a telegram to let him know Willow is ill. He'd want to know about it. Maybe it'll hurry him along."

"He would want to know, without a doubt. Have you told him of the baby yet?"

"No. There still being a baby is too big, too shocking. You don't put something like that in a letter or a telegram, even if it is startlingly good news." Jane set her hand on the increasing swell. Now that she'd released it from the corset, her stomach was growing quicker. She put a hand to her temple to try to stem the rising headache that seemed present all the time lately. "Christmas is in a week. He's supposed to be back for it. He was so excited for the presents he got for the children. He got them for all of the younger ones, even Jesse, Lizzie, Cindy, and Willow and Jay."

"He'll be back."

"I know." Jane had to stop talking about it or she'd be in a panic again. She closed her eyes against the headache. When she opened them again, she felt calmer. The headache was still present and a few spots swam through her vision. That meant the headache would get worse soon, or so she'd noticed in the past week.

"Are you well?"

"I think it's all the stress. I have a headache I can't seem to get rid of."

"I'll get you something for it."

"No. The baby." Jane smoothed her hand along the swell.

"If you aren't well, how do you think the baby is feeling?"

"Fine." She sighed her acquiescence. Then her mind hooked on the fact Charles knew German. She should have thought to ask sooner, but she hadn't had real reason. "Can you translate something for me?"

"Hm?" His brow rose. "You have something in German?"

"What does Armermann mean?"

"Nothing special." Charles busied himself quickly. He laid out small papers and proceeded to scoop some powder into them.

"Charles."

"It means poor man."

"Odd name for an investment group." Jane chuckled at the play of words. "The paradox is amusing. Seems our investors are clever."

"I suppose so." He focused his gaze on her again. "We're all here to help you. You know that. We'll all take turns with Willow and the other children."

"There's more than enough for all of you to worry about. Michael, these deaths, not to mention you have a new baby, Tom is training Sally. There are so many things to be tended to."

"Then abuse Ma and Pa. They'll be happy for anything to take their minds off of Michael's current predicament."

"They've been helping quite a lot. I wouldn't be here if not for them. Ada only helps on weekdays, so Ma and Pa came by after church." Jane sagged into the counter, resting her cheek against the cool wood. Another sigh slipped free as she thought about the church. "Months ago we would have struggled to find seating for them at church. Now the pews are lightening with all that's happened."

"The reverend's had been talking of building a bigger church over the summer. Lately it hardly seems as necessary. Then again, the town continues to grow." Charles kissed her temple before going to check on Willow. "Very good, Willow. We're going to do this four times a day instead of the once a day you've been doing recently."

Jane rose as he helped Willow to her feet. "I do hate that she has to stay."

"I'll feel better knowing there was always someone with medical expertise here to keep an eye on her. Our new doctor is arriving on tomorrow's train, so that will be another extra hand." He paused in front of Jane. "Why don't you go home to get some of Willow's things so she'll be more comfortable. Take that medicine home with you for your headaches."

Jane gathered the medicine he'd prepared while they talked. "How often am I to take these?"

"When you feel a headache coming, take one. Let me know if it doesn't help. I'll want to examine you further."

"I will." Jane glanced down at Willow. Tears shimmered on the girls' cheeks.

"Bonnie and I will get her settled in room four."

"Thank you." Jane tucked a finger under Willow's chin. "Would you like me to bring your beads over?"

Willows eyes shimmered with tears. She nodded. "Please."

Jane pulled her into a hug. "I'll bring Jaybird with me and we'll spend the afternoon together."

Willow nodded against Jane's chest.

"I'm going to send a telegram to Cole, get your things and Jay, and we'll be back."

Charlie squeezed her arm. "Stop blaming yourself, too."

"Just make her better. Please."

"I'll do everything I can." Charlie ushered Willow from the room.

Jane lingered in the room, staring out the window at the building across the alley. Her hands shook so much she tucked the medicine away lest she spill it. "Damn you, Cole. Where are you?"

"Lou?" Tom edged into the room. "What's wrong?"

"Willow has pneumonia. She's sick and I didn't get her here soon enough. Thena gain, is there a soon enough when it comes to pneumonia? Tom, I can't lose her."

"Easy." Tom wrapped her in a breath-stealing hug. "Breathe, Lou. She's a hell of a girl, and a fighter to boot. She'll be fine."

"Charlie can't even promise me that, and he's a doctor." Jane didn't fight his hug, even tried to tug him impossibly tighter. "Tell me again anyway. Lie to me if you have to."

"She's going to be just fine."

"Thank you." Jane extricated herself from his arms. She wiped at the tears she hadn't been able to stop. "I need to go send a telegram to Cole. I have to tell him Willow is sick. Maybe he'll respond to that for a change."

"He hasn't answered my telegrams either."

"Yours?" She eyed her brother in surprise. "You've sent him missives?"

"Yeah. Don't worry, I didn't tell him about the baby. He wanted me to keep an eye on you, and I've been filling him in best I can without telling him why you're doing well."

"He hasn't answered you, either? Tom."

"I know."

"Something's wrong."

"Maybe not." He took her hands in his. "If it'll ease your mind I'll look into getting someone out there this close to Christmas."

"I thought Christmas doesn't matter to Pink's."

"True, but those that aren't on cases may think it does. I'll send out some telegrams to try to get a bite."

"Thank you. If nothing else it would ease my mind. Not as much as Cole arriving on a train in the next few days. At the very least, your idea would help."

"We'll get it figured. I'd go myself if that would help."

"I'd go myself if it were possible." Jane straightened her shoulders. "No, that would be panic mongering for us to do right now. It's only been a week that he's been there. For all we know his bastard pa left behind multiple families to contend with."

"It's a good possibility, and Cole likes to do right by his family, even if they're ill-gotten." Tom frowned. "But that begs another question. If that's the case, why not reach out to Nick?"

"Don't add to my worry."

"Sorry. Pinkerton brain."

"Life of terror and turmoil brain."

"We're a sad mix."

"You're telling me."

*It is not enough to help the feeble up,
but to support him after.
-William Shakespeare*

Faith dropped the box of flour into the back of the wagon. She wiped her brow. "You folks have been here every week getting this many supplies. What is it you're doing with all of this?"

"We're taking it out to the settlement. These are donations for the families displaced by the tornado." Jane checked her list against the supplies in the wagon. "We started making such runs years ago during the Renegade attacks, and have continued wherever help is needed. Isn't that right, Reverend?"

"It certainly is. Jane and Katherine help organize every week, and we all go out together." Reverend Greene walked around some boxes toward the front of the wagon. "Reverend Lyons now helps, which is good since Kat is still resting today."

"What a shock that poor woman had." Faith rested her hands on her hips. "It's a good thing you're doing."

"Sure is." Abe dropped the last crate into the back of the wagon. "Next week, let us know what you need. We'd be happy to help how we can."

"That's very kind, Able." Jane turned to Faith. "Would you like to join us today? I'm certain the Reverend's would appreciate the extra hand, and it would be a chance for you to meet some new faces."

"I'm not sure." Faith glanced toward the store where still only a handful of people shopped.

"Being charitable and kind can only help business." Jane stepped closer to Faith. "My word only works so far if folks don't get to meet you."

"They might take offense to me being there." Faith brushed back an unruly curl that seemed to always drop to her brow.

"You never know unless you try. Besides, you'll be with me. I've been told I can be terribly charming company."

Faith laughed softly. "Fine, then. If Abe doesn't mind watching the store alone for a bit."

"I'll manage for a few hours." Abe kissed her cheek. At that moment none other than Graham climbed the steps toward the store. "Excuse me. Mayor Cooke. Welcome."

Jane gave an appreciative nod to Graham when he turned to greet Abe with a hearty handshake. She'd suggested to him that it would be quite the gesture for the mayor to shop in the store. Though begrudging in his agreement, it seemed her reminders of how his own wife was greeted had hit their mark. She leaned toward Faith. "Another good sign. You two will be drowning in business in no time."

"You've been too kind, Jane."

"I've not. I simply am me. Right, Reverend?"

Reverend Greene extended his hand to help her into the wagon. "Every day since I've know you, save for one, you've been Jane Doe Spencer."

"We don't discuss that one day." Jane knew he meant the day of her hanging. For that one day she'd allowed herself to be the woman she didn't know, Clara Young, to greet death. "Come along, Faith. It's going to be some work getting this wagon out that far. We really need a sleigh for winter runs, but I don't know that one would be large enough."

"Back in Chicago a vendor put sleigh runs on a wagon bed." Faith settled in beside Jane. "If you think you know someone that could do that."

"Genius. I can't believe no one out here has thought of such a thing, what with our winters." Jane pulled the thick blanket over her hands. "I'll have to ask Archie. I have no idea where we'd keep such a thing during the warm season. The Inn's stable is full to bursting with the new carriage I just purchased for clients to rent."

Reverend Lyons spoke from the other side of Reverend Greene. "What about the brothel's stable?"

"That's definitely an idea, Eli. That one isn't nearly as full." Jane thought she might go see Archie after she'd stopped to visit with Willow. If more storms were expected, they'd need something other than a wagon to get out to the settlement.

"How is your child, Jane?" Faith glanced her way. "I heard she was ailing."

"Charles is hopeful. He told me there are signs of improvement. The poor thing is too weak right now for me to feel secure enough to agree with him, even if he is the doctor." Two full days of Charlie's treatment regimen hadn't made any marked improvement in Willow's appearance. She'd been sleeping most of the time she wasn't getting treatments.

"Well, I've been praying for her."

"Thank you. I appreciate all the prayers we can get. It seems like things are going wrong everywhere. It's been a difficult year." Jane lifted her gaze to find the settlement appearing in the distance. "For everyone."

"There are blessings to be had in the darkness," Reverend Greene spoke quiet beside her. "The child you carry is an example."

"And all the babies being born," agreed Faith. "I swear this town is overrun with babies."

"Marjorie, and George. I'm expecting, as is Katherine, and Graham and Linh are anticipating a new child soon as well." Jane couldn't help but smile at the talk of the babies. "You're both right, they are beautiful blessings. Much better to focus on them."

"You and Kat will be welcoming your new little ones in the spring," Reverend Lyons joined in. "Near around the same time."

"And Abe and I a few months after," Faith added quietly.

"What?" Jane turned toward her newest friend. "Are you serious?"

"I am. Don't know how. We've been trying all along with no luck. I thought I was ailing and went to the clinic. Dr. Cross just told us last week. We couldn't be more surprised."

"That is the most wonderful news!" Jane pulled her into a tight hug. "I'm thrilled for you."

Faith broke into a huge smile when they separate "I simply can't believe it still."

"You'll believe it soon enough once your body tells you without question. Believe me."

"I look forward to it, though I may be cursing such a thing when it happens." Faith's chuckle faded as the wagon came to a sloshy stop in front of the lodge. "My goodness. How many families you got squeezed in there?"

"Too many. We wanted to build a second shelter, but the first storm hit before we got the supplies." Jane pushed off the lovely warm blanket. "Let's get to work."

Their arrival spurred the lodge to life. Women and children poured out to assist in unloading the wagon. Jane and Faith worked alongside the reverends to get every bit of food and clothing dispersed to families as evenly as possible. At least with the food it had become mostly communal, with only a few families insisting on doing their own thing.

Within two hours the whole lot was dispersed and they took the wagon back to town. Jane laced her arm with Faith's as the drew close to the store. "I saw you having several good conversations while we were there. It's a small step, but every one of them gets you closer."

"I do hope you're right. I really like it here, and we sank everything into that store. I don't want to have to leave. Especially not now with the little one coming."

"You'll always have my business, and therefore the business of the Inn and brothel. Not to mention Kat, Lillian, Graham, Lee, and the donations for the settlement. I'm certain that will keep you afloat for a good long while. Soon enough you'll be overrun with business. The mercantile has always done well."

"I still don't know why you ever helped me."

"It's just who I am." Jane nudged her gently. "Then once I got to know you I truly liked you. You're a good soul. Your husband is a good man. Good people deserve good things."

Abe descended the steps to meet the wagon. "How'd it go?"

"Well. I believe you're right, Abe." Faith allowed her husband to help her from the wagon. "We need to add to the donations ourselves next time. Our blessings need to be passed on."

Abe shook Jane's extended hand. "Count us in."

"Glad to." Jane nodded to them both.

"I do hope you'll come to one of our services some time." Reverend Greene leaned forward. "I know you folks have your own church, but you are welcome any time."

"Thank you, Reverend." Faith's features brightened at his welcome. "We'd be honored to attend one of your services."

They made their goodbyes and Reverend Greene turned the wagon down First Street toward the clinic. As they pulled to a stop, he set his hand on Jane's. "We're all praying for her."

"Thank you." Jane patted his hand, then reached over to clasp Reverend Lyons'. "Thank you both."

She climbed from the wagon and took the stairs to the balcony rather than heading through the clinic. Inside Willow's room she found Jesse reading to her. "Jesse."

"Hey, Ma." Jesse rushed over to give her a quick hug. "Pa's downstairs with Lee and Marjorie. I wanted to sit with Willow for a while, so Bonnie went downstairs. Can I stay at your place tonight?"

"You're always welcome. If your pa says yes, then I'm happy to have you." She kissed the top of his head. She moved to Willow's side to press a kiss to her forehead. "Hello, Willow."

The girl barely stirred. They had her propped into a nearly sitting position. Jane brushed some hair back from her forehead, concerned at the warmth she felt there. "How long ago did Bonnie leave, Jesse?"

"A few minutes ago. Said she'd be back with another treatment and some quinine." Jesse perched on the bed opposite Jane. "She gonna be alright, Ma?"

"I certainly hope so Jesse." Jane left the uneven perch she had on the edge of the bed to sit on the chair. "We're going to fight to make certain she does. We don't give up on family."

"Ma?"

"Yes?"

"What's gonna happen to Uncle Mike?"

"I don't know." Tears welled too fast for her to stop them. They flowed down her cheeks and blurred her vision. Arms wrapped around her, slender but strong. "Oh, Jesse. I don't know. I'm praying he recalls something, but if he doesn't I don't know what will happen."

"I'm sorry. I shouldn't have asked."

"You're allowed to ask. You didn't do anything wrong. I'm just quite emotional right now." She returned his strong hug, holding him close. "Just like with Willow, we're doing everything we can to save Uncle Mike. If anyone can save him, it's your uncle and your sister."

"Willow."

"What?" Jane blinked away tears to find Willow had her eyes opened. She took Willow's hand in her own. "Hey there. It's good to see you awake."

Willow offered a weak smile. "Jesse was…reading."

"He was." Jane smiled at her son. "Why don't you get back to it? I'll go get Charles to examine her since she's awake and get her that treatment Bonnie said she was getting."

"Sure thing!" Jesse raced back to grab his book and start reading again.

Jane stepped out of the room, but didn't make it two steps before she had to lean against the wall. She felt she couldn't breathe any easier than Willow as everything pilled on top of her. She released several long breaths to keep from falling into a fit of hysteria.

The last thing she needed was people fussing over her more than they already were. She needed to remain strong and pray that Willow would show even more signs of improvement. Though she'd had these two newest wards for only a year and a half, she cared for them as her own children. To lose any more children would be cruel.

For now she'd get Charles to reassure her this was a good sign. She needed more good news. Cole's lack of response over Willow's state of health had furthered her nerves too much. Not even Faith's wonderful news could push back the growing fear in Jane's gut.

First, Charles. Then she'd go meet the train. Maybe, just maybe, Cole would be on it.

If it were not for hope, the heart would break.
—Thomas Fuller

Jane climbed the steps to the depot. Tom stood beneath the sign for The Hangman's Inn so he could take care of their clients today. He nodded her way but blessedly said nothing. She'd come merely to watch and hope. Before she did so, she headed into the office. "Norman?"

"Nothing Janey. Same as every day." Norman leaned on the counter. His familiar lined features scowled. "Why ya still lookin'?"

"What?" The words blasted her melancholy to dust.

"Took longer than we all thought, sure. He finally done scared off after that stunt ya pulled."

"I—what stunt?"

"Hammy's been sayin' all over town you all but asked him to marry ya. Maybe that did it."

Jane stared at the man she'd considered friendly, and even more so Cole's friend. Words failed her, all responses disappeared. Thankfully, she didn't need to struggle to find them.

"Norman!" Kat emerged from the back room. Anger flooded her features until they were nearly red as her hair. "Don't you dare suggest such a thing. That's a horrible thing to say."

Jane stepped away from whatever Norman might reply to rush outside. On her way to the bench, Tom grabbed her hand. At his gentle squeeze, she turned to face him. "What?"

"You're troubled."

"This isn't news."

"More than you were when you got here a second ago. No telegram?"

"No. And…" She didn't want to say it aloud. It was bad enough Norman had. "I'll survive. I always do, even when perhaps I shouldn't."

"Jane."

"I haven't given up hope. I'm tired, worried, scared to death, and I ache with missing him. I still have hope. Right here." She set her hand on her stomach.

"Do you need Leanne tonight?"

"No. Jesse is staying the night. That'll be enough." She pulled away to take a seat on the bench. The train wasn't far off now. Cole would be on it this time. He had to be to stop all of this nonsense. That's all there was to it.

"Jane." Kat sank onto the bench beside her. "I'm so sorry."

"For what? He didn't say anything half the town isn't thinking."

"That isn't true."

"It is. I've got an ear for gossip even if I don't spread it. You think I haven't heard the whispers and seen the pitying looks?"

Kat's hand rested on Jane's. "Those that know you don't truly believe."

"Norman knows us." Jane squeezed her friends hand. "I'm afraid I had too much fun with our scandal before he had to leave, and that he's not returned as expected…"

"Jane."

"The talk is bound to happen."

"Well, it's awful."

"What is? That after four years of devotion people still suspect either of us would run away? I suppose it is. It's our own fault."

"Don't say that."

"It's nothing we don't encourage in what we thought was good fun. After all, no one truly knows what happens behind closed doors." Jane tried her best to put some conviction behind her words. Unfortunately, a numbness in her heart filtered into her inflection so clear she could hear it herself.

"I'm sorry anyway. Norman shouldn't have just blurted it out like that."

"At least he had the courage to say it. I doubt many others will do little more than whisper behind my back." The train whistle blasted close, weaving tension into Jane's limbs.

"Are we still on for Christmas day?"

"The Young's, the Turner's, the Jones', the Cooke's, Leanne, Patrick, and your family all gathered for an exorbitantly large supper at the Inn?"

"What about the Schaffer's?"

"They are still a maybe, but it's entirely possible. Lee hasn't decided if she wishes to make the trip into town or not, what with baby Marjorie. As for whether the feast itself is still happening, yes. My mother and Faith plan to be cooking. If rumor holds true, Cora is convinced she will be as well. I believe Lillian said she would be bringing gingerbread for the children.”

“Mother’s gingerbread is quite a treat.” Kat squeezed her hand gently. The train squealed to a stop at the platform.

Jane couldn’t seem to make herself take a breath. She half rose off the bench only to sink back down. Person after person filed out of the open doors, each heading this way and that. Some were familiar, many were strangers.

Across the platform, Nick greeted one of the strangers and led him away. One by one people filed from the train until it emptied completely. The platform drained of people slow and steady until only she sat there in silence with Kat still clutching her hand.

“Well.” A knot formed in her throat until no further words would come.

“Jane.”

“I’d best go.” Her nose burned with unshed tears. Tears she definitely didn’t want seen. She rose and straightened her cape. “I have much to do. The businesses won’t run themselves. Sally has another shooting lesson today. Thank you for waiting with me.”

“He’ll be back before you know it.”

“It’s too late for that.” Jane returned the hug as best she could. One foot in front of the other, she made her way off the platform. Norman’s words, ridiculous as she knew them to be, rang through her head. What was worse is she knew he wasn’t the only one saying such things.

The pitying glances over the past few weeks had been at first annoying, now almost intolerable. The situation with her brother, and now what was going on with Willow might be reason enough, she had no doubt they were saying what Norman had. The town did love a good rumor, after all. Cole leaving her had to be the juiciest bit they'd had in a while.

She slowed to a stop. Her mind raced against her wishes over every possibility there was. A storm that could cause damage to the lines so he'd not gotten one telegram. No, Norman would know about that. Plus, they'd sent letters as well. He could always send a letter if he couldn't send a telegram.

What could have tied him up so bad that he'd not reach out to her? Or at the very least to one of her brothers. If it was bad enough, she'd expect such a thing. If it was needed, they could spare one of her lawyer brothers if he needed one. Did he need one? With Christmas and the marshal's arrival so close, did she dare?

She should make the trip herself. Pack up the twins and take…who? Tom and Sally needed to remain to help however they could. Ada had to remain with the other children if Jane were to leave. Leanne would have to stay at her apartment for Alma. Kat couldn't go. Michael needed the Young's more than her paranoid idea to go after Cole did. Charles had a new baby and his clinic to worry about.

She could go by herself, of course. Pregnancy didn't negate her ability to travel, and she'd traveled by herself before. With Willow ill, she felt terrible leaving. She also felt horrible not knowing what was going on. She had to prove them all wrong. Cole wouldn't abandon her.

What was she thinking? She didn't need to prove a thing to anyone. Her heart knew, and that was enough.

No matter what she told herself a corner of her heart raced in panic. The portion of her mind that had learned to expect the worst raced over more possibilities. Had he been injured badly? Robbed? Or worse, killed?

The air thinned, her lungs tightened. Her vision tunneled until she couldn't see anything but the cobblestone at her feet. He wasn't dead. He couldn't be.

Jane! Cole's voice rang in her head, a yell in hopes of saving her. An echo of the past.

"*Jane*!" This time the scream came in Hammy's voice. "*Watch out.*"

She lifted her head and her vision tunneled on a set of flaring nostrils of a beast tearing down the road straight for her. The horse showed no signs of stopping and it was far too close. She spun at the same time the horse made to spin on the slick road.

The breath flew out of her lungs on impact. She flew she didn't know how far before hitting the pavement. Her mouth opened to fish for air, the wind had been knocked clean out of her. She gingerly tried to push herself to sit.

"Lady Jane." Hammy knelt beside her. "Lady Jane, are ya all right?"

Jane clasped his hand, trying to regain her bearing so she might answer. All that emerged was a groan as she dropped her head to the ground. Finally she managed a weak, "Ow."

The miniscule word hardly covered the aches and pains ratcheting through her body from the event, but it would do until she regained functionality of breath again.

"Jane, I'm so sorry." Matthew Coleman hovered over her. "I don't know what spooked Hunter like that. She's usually the calmest horse."

Her vision settled back into focus. A crowd now hovered over her. "Oh. Ow. Charles. Bonnie. I need…ow."

"Easy, Lady Jane. Doc's on his way with a littler." Hammy held her hand to his chest. "Leastwise that beast didn't trample ya. Just knocked ya couple feet."

"It felt more like ten feet." Every muscle and bone in her body screamed in protest of any movement. "Ow."

"I'm real sorry." Matthew held her other hand.

"It's not your fault. Horses spook." Jane groaned and tried to sit again.

"Jane. Charles brushed Matthew aside to bend over her. "What hurts?"

"Everything."

"The baby? Are you hurting there?" Charles brushed the hair back from her forehead.

"No. I don't think so." Another attempt at moving brought another groan. She didn't think she was seriously injured, but she'd be sore for days. "That was not fun."

Hammy chuckled. "You ain't hurt that bad, then."

"No more than my pride. Charles." She glanced at her brother. "We need to stop this happening so often. I really don't like you as my doctor."

"Hammy's right. You aren't hurt too bad. Let's get you on the litter." Charlie slid the litter up along her side. "And don't tell me you can walk. That blow dazed you pretty good. We're carrying and that's final. Cole isn't here to do it, we use the litter."

"Yes, sir." Jane knew better than to argue with his tone of voice. Besides, since every part of her ached right then she wasn't certain she could walk well enough.

The trip to the clinic was quick, if not smooth. Hammy insisted on carrying one end of the litter, which meant a fair amount of jostling. She didn't complain one second and thanked him profusely once she'd been deposited on the exam table.

Charlie moved and twisted her joints. "What happened?"

"I'm not certain. I was in a bit of a distraction. Mr. Hamm yelled at me to move, and there the beast was. I got bowled over by Mr. Colemans horse. I didn't have time to react and ow."

"Sorry." Despite his apology, he didn't cease the exam.

The door burst open. Tom, puffing and wide eyed, rushed to her side. "Lou. Hammy said you got knocked over by a horse?"

"It would seem so." She did her best not to wince too bad when Charlie got to her knee. "Oh, Charles. Stop."

Her skirts moved. Charles hummed. "Your knee is swollen. We'll wrap it and see how you do supporting your own weight."

"Jane, Jane, Jane. What am I to do with you?" Eunice walked into the room. She promptly kissed Jane on the forehead. "I fear I'm going to have to lock you away so you stop getting yourself hurt."

"That may be her safest option," Charles agreed.

"Would you all stop? This was a freak accident. My mind was elsewhere, and the horse spooked. I didn't see it coming until it was too late." She propped herself on her elbows. The action only made her body ache rather than scream in pain. "I'll be fine, right Charles?"

"I'd like to keep you here to observe, and of course have Bonnie check on the baby."

"That's completely impossible. My children, Charles." Jane accepted Tom's help to sit. "I will rest. Truly, I don't think my body will allow otherwise. I'll permit Bonnie to check on me as often as you feel necessary. More often because I'm panicked over it."

Charles eyed her quietly.

"I swear it." Those damn tears were too near the surface far too often for her liking. They spilled onto her cheeks, hot streaks slipped along her skin. "This baby is everything to me. Everything. I can't…I won't…I…Oh."

Eunice folded Jane into a tight hug, running her hand over her curls. Soft soothing sounds carried to her good ear. As Eunice's hold lighened, Jane could hear her fully. "My darling girl."

Charles squeezed Jane's ankle. He winked at her, a suspiciously wicked smirk in place. "Do you mean it, Ma?"

"Of course." Eunice cupped Jane's cheek. "I won't leave her side."

"What?" Jane sniffled against the tears that would not end. She studied each person in turn, trying to understand what had just happened. "What?"

"Ma is going to stay with you to help care for the children while you recover." Charlie's grin broadened. "Don't you worry. She'll love every minute."

"And your pa will help Tom with the casino. You won't have to worry about a thing but feeling better." Eunice patted her shoulder.

"But…what?"

"We'll take that as a yes." Tom chuckled boldly, not bothering to hide his amusement. "I say she should rest at least until Christmas, right Charles?"

"Oh, at the very least." Charlie's laughter joined Tom's.

"This is cruel and unusual punishment," Jane protested.

"Maybe, but what is it Cole always says?" Tom leaned on the table. "You have a habit of getting yourself near dead."

"But…"

"It's settled." Eunice clapped her hands together. "Thomas, help get your sister home. I'm going upstairs to check on Willow, then I need to make a stop by the mercantile to get something for a diversion to keep Jane busy. Until I get to the apartment have Sally keep her tied to a chair if need be."

"Yes ma'am." At Jane's next protest, Tom wagged his finger at her. "You don't ignore Ma's orders. Nobody ever wins if they try."

"But…"

Charlie's laughter boomed free. "This is going to be fun."

*Do not anticipate trouble,
or worry about what may never happen.
Keep in the sunlight.
−Benjamin Franklin*

Sally pinned her last unruly curl in place. Sometimes she missed the days she let it fly loose as a whore. It was at times less work, and at others more. Perhaps tomorrow she'd let half of it loose from her usual style. She gathered her reticule and headed down the steps, expecting Jane to be in full-on chaos already. After all, it was already nearly nine.

No sound greeted her on the way down. The living room sat strangely empty, a weird silence filling the apartment in place of the usual chatter. Seeing no sign of Mams, Sally wondered if she'd taken the children out to give Jane peace. She glanced toward Jane's bedroom. The door sat open, another rarity.

A glance inside revealed the cause of the oddness. Jane, still sound asleep at nearly nine in the morning. What was more, she was surrounded by children. Jesse sprawled on

Cole's side of the bed. The twins curled against Jane's right. Even Jaybird had joined the party to sleep across the foot of the bed.

Sally leaned on the doorframe, studying the scattering of bodies. Jane showed no sign of stirring. A purple bruise blossomed across her jaw. If that and the knee were the worst she got for what had happened the previous day, Sally was grateful.

Heavy footfalls hit the steps. Sally darted toward them to hush Tom. Eunice was behind the man and stilled at Sally's warning. Sally kept her voice low, "Ma's still sleeping, and she's got lots of company in that bed."

Tom moved near silent now to peek into the room. He nodded to his mother. "The kids."

"I've got her, and them. You two go on about your business." Eunice ushered them both out the door.

Sally stood rooted to the spot. Her eyes on the now closed door. "Is she gonna be alright, Tom?"

"She will be. Eventually. She's got to get her mind straight. Can't blame her, but she's worried about too many things."

"We all are."

"Ah yes, but her usual coping strategy is to turn to Cole. She's leaning on you kids for now." Tom led her toward the casino. "That's a good sign, believe it or not."

"She's going to be miserable trapped in the apartment with Mams guarding the fort."

"Ma can handle Jane. She won't let her be bored and will keep her as distracted as Jane lets her. Ma doesn't tolerate whiners."

"She'll never forgive you for helping trick her into that."

"You know, Sally. There's a lot your ma wouldn't forgive me for if she knew. I'm not worried about trapping her into staying put to heal. Good thing on our side this time is that baby. She'll do anything to protect the child that still lives and grows."

Sally paused midway through the casino to lean on the railing. The pit was empty this early in the day. "What are we doing about Pa?"

"I've got some inquiries out on someone becoming available to head to California and check on the situation. Jane'll be upset but I sent a letter yesterday telling Cole of the baby. If that doesn't get a response, I'll join her in worrying something's really wrong."

"What's he doing out there? You don't seem as concerned as Ma yet."

"Can't tell you that, but I can tell you it could be a big mess he has to clean up. The sort of thing he may be dealing with could distract a person and keep them busy." Tom's keen eye studied her. "I see your wheels turning. Let it go, Sally. That's for your pa to tell you when he's ready."

Sally held up her hands. "Fine. Fine. I'm just worried." She couldn't fault him for saying it, she'd said as much to Arthur not so long ago. Speaking of, Arthur himself headed their way. Sheriff Schaffer followed right behind him.

Arthur nodded to Tom, then smiled Sally's way. "Good morning."

"Morning. What brings you by so early? And how's Cora doing?" Sally was relieved that since his Ma's accident, and her punching him, they'd finally been able to sit down and talk. After the strain of his return, it felt like they'd come to a semblance of friendship again.

"Ma's doing great. She wants to get out of the clinic so she can shop for Christmas dinner. Keeps telling the doc that she's up and about and she needs to get back to it." Arthur leaned closer, a crooked grin forming. "I'm pretty sure they think she'll overdo it because she's Ma."

"Just like my ma." Sally grinned as David and Tom chuckled in agreement.

"Exactly. As to why I'm here, I'm taking Alma to the mercantile so she can shop before it gets busy. She said she wants to get presents for your ma and pa." Arthur touched her arm. "You're welcome to join if you want. She might like a girl's opinion on what to get your ma. I won't be no help. For that matter, you can help me get something for my ma."

Sally laughed at the helpless puppy look he tossed in for good measure. "You are hopeless. I might just join you despite the attempt at pity. I need to eat something first, though."

"Perfect. I was gonna let Alma eat first, too. We'll meet you in the restaurant."

"Thanks." Sally called out as he walked away, "Ma was asleep when I left. Don't ring the bell and knock quietly. Mams is in there."

"Got it." Arthur disappeared down the hall.

"David." Tom's greeting and tone were curt. Neither he, nor Ma, had fully forgiven David. At least now they were being civil. More so Ma than Tom. "What brings you by?"

"Lee and I were talking last night, and we thought maybe Jesse would like to stay here for the week until Christmas. What with Jay's sister in the clinic and…everything." David cleared his throat. The awkward silence lingered only a moment longer. "Jesse's worried about his ma, and Jay.

We're worried for Jane, too. I thought it would make her feel better to have Jesse stay over some extra nights."

Sally smiled brightly at the sheriff. She went so far as to half step in front of Tom when he grunted darkly, a threat he'd say something nasty. "That's so kind. She had all the kids camped on her bed with her last night. Although I don't think Jesse was much of a comfort the way he took over half the bed."

David chuckled. "He's ended up on the floor a few times. I might suggest to Jane she not let him do that again. He could make her injuries worse the way he tosses and turns."

"Probably." Sally cast a pointed look at Tom. "Isn't that nice, Tom?"

"Sure." Tome nodded to David. "Same as Sally told Arthur. If she's sleeping, let her. Don't think she's slept much these past couple of weeks."

David moved around them, then paused. "Have you two had any luck? God willing, I'd like to get him out of jail before Lewis arrives. Before Christmas if I can."

"We're following some leads." Tom was vague enough about it, which told Sally he didn't trust the man to follow those leads with them. "Don't worry. I'll let you know soon as we figure out who it was."

Soon as David made his way down the hall, she turned to Tom. "Should Molly and I get to the purpose of our visits immediately, then?"

"The sooner the better. At least you've already established a flirtation with both them boys." Tom leaned on the railing, surveying the empty casino. "Whoever was visiting Daisy would need a replacement. Our place is more likely than Leanne's, but I'll be up there the next couple of nights. Leanne hasn't had anyone new lately, or even anyone stepping up their visits, but I'd like to have a gander for a couple nights myself."

"I'll let Molly know. We'll go visiting Wil tonight, and Garit tomorrow night. Hang out for a while, make friendly-like. I'll make nice with more of the whores, too."

"Good girl." Tom cleared his throat as Arthur and Alma emerged from the back hall. "Shooting lessons at two today, after you and Alma have had lunch, then you're free."

"You know Ma will want to come to those lessons." Sally frowned. "Although all she does is make me look spectacularly awful."

"You're improving. You'll get there." Tom squeezed her shoulder. "Go with Arthur and Alma. I'll think about letting Jane come to keep practicing with her right hand as well."

"See you at two, then." Sally turned to follow Arthur and Alma toward the restaurant. In private meetings about the case, they'd decided to check out the brothels for anyone that might have ramped up their visits after Daisy's murder. Tom certainly could handle The Golden Touch himself, but it was easier for him to check on Leanne's place since they were involved. Molly or herself making regular visits to La Maison de Minuit would seem odd.

Seeing as she and Molly had been making regular visits to the saloon lately, they'd spend a little more time there. It wasn't a burden by any means. She found she had fun there when Molly or Patrick was with her, especially now that she wasn't a whore and could enjoy the atmosphere. Plus, it tended to make them all a bit randy and eager to return to bed. That was definitely always a fun end to the night.

Arthur tapped her hand. "Sally?"

"Hm?" It was then Sally realized she'd sat at the table with him and Alma. The waitress stood there awaiting her order. "Oh. Goodness. My mind was elsewhere. I didn't even realize I'd sat down yet."

"I could tell." Arthur laughed. "Do you want your usual?"

"Yes." Sally's stomach growled at the suggestion. "Extra bacon, please."

Arthur gave the waitress her order, then turned toward her. "What were you thinking about?"

Heat rose to her cheeks, sure she couldn't tell Arthur the naughty direction her thoughts had taken. Instead, she shrugged. "Nothing. Everything."

"Do you think you can join the conversation now?" Unlike a few weeks previous there was no nastiness in his tone. A light tremor of laughter lingered, though. "Or shall I focus all of my attention on Alma and pretend you haven't joined us?"

"No, you beast. I'm here now. Goodness." Sally joined his laughter. Even Alma smiled. Sally was relieved to see Alma smile even a little. Her moods had been driven more toward fits than calm the past couple of weeks. Sally leaned toward Arthur. "Thank you for helping with her so much. Ma told me what you did with her when she had problems."

"I'm happy to help. I like Alma. She's a friend. Just like you."

"And you are a wonderful friend to both of us. Isn't he, Alma?"

Alma nodded quietly. "Yes. A good friend."

Enjoy when you can,
and endure when you must.
-Johann Wolfgang von Goethe

Jane leaned against the cutter so she could keep weight on her good knee. Sally stood feet away with her weapon. Tom leaned on the cutter beside her. Though his gaze didn't flicker from Sally, he muttered under his breath. "Let her be. She has to learn."

"Then she needs a better teacher," Jane murmured.

"Keep that up and I won't give you a turn."

Jane stuck her tongue out at the back of his head.

"I saw that."

Sally took aim at the target and fired. The bullet hit way off the mark, but at least this time she'd managed to hit the target. Sally muttered her frustration as she lined up for another shot.

"Sally, breathe. You're holding your breath." Jane pushed off the cutter, but Tom pushed her back down. "It's ten feet. I can walk ten feet."

"Deal was you're only on your feet when you're shooting. You're supposed to rest that knee." Tom clapped her on the back. "I can handle teaching the girl to shoot."

"Clearly you can't or she'd be doing it by now." Jane folded her arms across her chest. The whole time he walked to Sally, she glared daggers at his back. The insolent man probably thought she should be grateful and fawning over the fact he'd let her emerge from the apartment at all. Or that he got her away from the knitting lessons that were going well, much to her chagrin.

He was wrong. She wasn't at all grateful. When he got back to her side, she ignored him to focus on Sally's next attempts. When some of them were even worse, she scowled at her brother. "Can I try now?"

"Fine. If your knee hurts, I don't want to hear it."

Jane used his path through the snow to get to Sally's side. The girl was reloading her weapon, cursing under her breath. Jane waited until she'd finished loading and lifted her head. Jane set her hands on her ward's shoulders. "First things first, you're too tense. You'll never hit any target that way."

"I just don't understand why this is so difficult. I mastered fighting well enough."

"Firing a weapon isn't fighting. It's something all together different. Also, it takes a lot of practice to get skills enough for a good aim. If it helps your frustration any, Cole can't fire my weapon to save his life. Always misses the target with it."

"Really?"

"Yes, really. Zeb tried to convince me to buy something else, like a Derringer. I wanted this one." She patted the Remington under her right arm. The one on her left for her right hand was a Colt 1849 Pocket. Smaller and easier for her less-dominant hand to handle. "For my right hand I've got something that suits my weaker side much better. You've seen I'm still not accurate with it."

"Do you think it's the gun?" Sally studied the weapon in her hand, a fine 1860 Army Colt that Thomas had given her to learn with.

"Not at all. Thomas has let me fire with that. It's lighter and less cumbersome than many." Jane turned Sally toward the target. "You need to remember to breathe. Before you fire, as well as after. Relax your shoulders and look down your sights."

Sally adjusted her stance, but her shoulder remained taut.

Jane leaned down to push Sally's leg. It shifted slightly forward. She set a hand on Sally's tense shoulder to push it down. "You know what's going to happen when you fire."

"Recoil."

"Don't brace for it, don't anticipate. Breathe. Line up your sight and pull the trigger on an exhale. Keep your eyes on your sights, don't try to see how you've done until after the full shot has been fired."

"But isn't it fired once it leaves the barrel?"

"No. The whole process is the firing of the shot. Now, keep that shoulder relaxed. Aim. Breathe."

Sally stilled as she leveled the weapon toward the target.

Jane took a few steps back. "Breathe. On the exhale."

After a few more exhales, Sally pulled the trigger. The gunfire cracked through the air, the target fluttered in the distance. Sally lowered her weapon, then gasped. "Ma!"

"I see." This time the bullet landed much closer to center, a couple inches to the right. "Well done. Keep trying. Remember what I told you."

Tom's brow furrowed on her return.

"No wonder Clara shot you people if that's how you teach someone to shoot. I swear." She leaned against the cutter again.

"I thought you didn't remember what you were taught."

"I don't. I just know what works for me."

"She can't always hold and breathe."

"No, but she can't learn to shoot fast if she can't shoot well. If you know how to shoot properly in controlled situations, the instinct comes when its needed."

"Even if you don't remember, apparently."

"True," Jane agreed. "I hardly had time to think when I shot that Indian that was about to shoot Cole. In fact, I passed out right after. It was instinct and protection. I had to have known how to shoot first to have managed it, though. Whether I remember or not, the knowledge is in this odd brain of mine."

"Brain's not the only thing odd."

"Runs in the family."

"There she is." He nudged her arm. "Keep that fire."

"Don't say things like that. It reminds me of him." Jane rubbed her hands together. "I'm attempting complete distraction. It isn't working well, but it's working."

"I suppose that's what counts."

"It was sweet of David to offer to let Jesse stay all week."

"He's your kid. He can stay however often he wants."

Jane didn't flinch at the venom in his tone. A bit of amusement flickered to live. "Still mad at him, then."

"You are too."

"I suppose I am. He's still a good man. He just had the unfortunate misstep of being a large idiot about this case and arrested the wrong man."

"We'll get the right one."

"I know you will. I worry for Michael, but I don't worry that you will succeed."

"Thanks for the vote of confidence."

"It's well earned. Outside of your misstep with Joe, you've proven rather capable. Sally has shown herself to be quite talented as well. I have no reason to doubt the pair of you will get the task done, even if you don't bother to fill me in on the details."

He snorted.

"I'm not Clara. I won't go blabbing your secrets and deceptions all over town."

"I know you're not."

Jane held her silence. Perhaps he'd just tell her it's none of her business. It wasn't. She wasn't the detective, but she also wasn't blind or obtuse. When not lost in her sorrows, she was also observant enough to know Tom and Sally were up to something along with Molly.

"No point in getting anyone's hopes up unnecessarily. There's no proof of anything yet. Only some suspicions we're chasing."

She straightened as Sally replaced the target. "I know your reasons for keeping things quiet. Blame my curiosity for wanting to know more. If you'll excuse me, it's my turn."

Jane popped the straps over her guns' handles a withdrew them as she limped toward the spot where she'd fire from. A few feet further back than where Sally had stood.

First she raised her left hand, aimed toward the target and breathed slow and deep.

In rapid succession, she cocked the hammer and shot six times at the target. Without taking any more time than it took to switch her stance, she did the same with her right. She settled the weapons back in their holsters and headed back to Tom's side without ever checking the target.

She didn't need to anyway, Sally race toward it as she walked back to the cutter.

Tom glanced at her holsters. "You're going to be spending some time cleaning and reloading tonight, and best hope we don't run into trouble on the way."

"Don't be dramatic. I've used my weapon more in the past two months than I have the entire time I've owned it. I don't often have the need. Besides, the cleaning and loading are soothing."

"I still say you'd do better to have a rear loader for one of them. In case you might need a quick reload in some fool situation you manage to get yourself into. Zeb has a nice Colt open top in the shop."

"What situation could I possibly get into that I would need more than twelve bullets?"

"Knowing you, could be anything."

"Ma!" Sally ran up with the target in hand. "How'd you do that?"

In the center of the target was a near perfect hole made by her first six bullets. About an inch around it in a perfect circle sat the next six shots. Tom snatched the paper from Sally to study it. He shoved the target at Jane. "Showoff."

"I told you I didn't need a rear-load." Jane handed the target back to Sally. "I wish I could tell you the secret.

Unfortunately, I long ago forgot it. Just keep practicing. You did much better today. Didn't she?"

Tom grumbled and stormed away with another target.

Jane grinned broadly at his retreating hunched, tense form. "He's so mad he's going to miss terribly. This ought to be rather fun."

"But he's always such a good shot."

"I have a feeling when he's trying to prove something, that won't be the case."

Sure enough, after he'd made his shots he didn't even go after the target. He came back to the cutter still stewing. "Let's get you back. You need to clean those guns."

"Sore loser." Jane settled into the cutter without argument. Once Tom got in the middle with Sally on his other side, Jane leaned closer. "That's what you get for tricking me into imprisonment."

"Wait. You could shoot that good with your right hand all along?"

"I could."

"Jezebel."

*Friendship makes prosperity more shining
and lessens adversity by dividing it
and sharing it.
–Cicero*

Jane set the teapots on the table as the first flakes began to fall outside. Only a few days left until Christmas, and the weather promised to be cold and snowy right up until the day. The Inn was down to a handful of guests, most of whom were in town to visit family. They expected another few guests before Christmas for the same reason.

The supply run that had arrived that week mostly consisted of one Christmas gift for each child in the settlement, even those not displaced by the tornado. They'd included food, but Jane had bumped her donation to make certain every child got a gift in honor of the holiday.

Colleen, Cora's assistant cook, walked over with a piping hot cobbler. She set it in the middle of the table. "There you go. It's my special recipe."

"Oh Colleen, it smells divine. Are you certain you won't join us today? There's a few hours before the supper rush. We'd be pleased for an extra place to set."

"Would that I could, but I gotta go see that Seth gets to work. Ma's going through one of her tryin' times and can't do it." Colleen's mother, Dee, had been ill for several years. Charlie had recently found a diagnose that matched her symptoms in a rare and newly recognized disease, multiple sclerosis.

"The poor dear. Tell Dee we're all praying for her. You let me know if she needs anything."

"I will. Thanks, Jane."

Jane grabbed plates after she left now that they had a cobbler to feast upon. It would be a special treat, seeing as they usually only had small treats.

"What is that deliciousness I smell?" Cora stepped into the kitchen. "Did Colleen make her cobbler?"

"Cora!" Jane rushed to wrap her friend in a hug. "Yes, Colleen made us cobbler. I asked her to say, but her ma is unwell again. I'm so glad Charles finally released you. You look well."

"I feel good. Charlie is convinced I'll feel different once I start actually working again. For the moment outside of some lingering aches, I really feel wonderful. I'm certain you can imagine."

"I certainly can." Jane had been shot twice in her life, and it was a fate she didn't care to suffer again.

"I had to swear I wouldn't do anything too strenuous, even with Christmas dinner."

"It's a good thing you have help to cook that enormous feast, then."

Cora glanced askance at Jane.

"Not me. Heavens, no." Jane laughed along with her. "I'm talking about Ma, Faith, and Lee."

"That is a blessing. Plenty of hands to cook the feast. Did you order the food?"

"Everything on your list. I even ordered extra of some of the common staples just in case." Jane took her usual seat. "Even Lillian is bringing something. Gingerbread."

"Delightful. One less dessert to be made here." Cora sighed her way into a seat.

Jane's response was waylaid by the appearance of Kat. She met her friend's eyes hopefully, but the subtle shake of Kat's head spurred a wave of grief through her so fast she forgot herself a moment. Thankfully Kat made her own enthusiastic greeting with Cora, which allowed Jane a minute to regain herself.

Rather than let them see how deep her upset, she went to grab forks and a large spoon for the cobbler. She exchanged pleasantries with the staff that remained to serve the handful of guests food and snacks. By the time she returned to the table, Lillian had joined the group. Jane also had better control over her emotions. She dispersed the forks among the plates before returning to her own seat.

Faith entered moments later, making greetings all around and setting a box in the middle of the table. "I didn't realize there'd be cobbler. Cora left behind some kitchen tools at the mercantile and I had a mind to make something. I brought a treat I used to make back home. Beignets."

Lillian opened the box to reveal puffed pillows of fried dough sprinkled liberally with sugar. "Oh my."

Jane eyed the pastry. Her stomach rumbled at the sight and smell of the delicious treats. "My goodness, I'm glad I can indulge in both, for I wouldn't know how to choose."

"Choose what?" Lee smiled warmly as she approached the table. "Hello, ladies. I'm so glad today is Reuben's day to manage the hotel. David took Marjorie since Tom's on duty. It's been far too long since I've been able to make tea."

"It certainly has been too long. Why is Reuben working today? I thought he usually took the weekend." Jane scooped a beignet onto her plate.

"With the arrival of our new assistant manager, Sean, we've adjusted our days. I asked for Thursdays off, and David has arranged his schedule so he has them off as well, this way I can come to tea more often." Lee settled into a seat. "Where are Leanne and your ma?"

"Leanne won't be able to make it today. She's been such a dear and helping me so much here. She had business to attend to at the brothel. My ma is off spoiling my children." Jane sipped her tea. "They're all over at the clinic with Willow playing games and eating sweets."

"A grandmother must spoil her grandchildren." Lillian scooped some cobbler onto her plate. "It can be no other way."

"A rule she lives by," Kat muttered drolly.

"Please, you spoil your children all on your own. You and Jane both do." Cora chuckled low. "Then again, they are some of the kindest children, so I doubt a soul would complain."

"As are your boys." Jane scooped some of the cobbler filling on top of her beignet and took a bite. She moaned in delight as the light pastry all but melted against her tongue. A burst of berry flavor from the pie added a note of tartness to the sweet. "Oh heavens. Dear me."

"What?" Kat's eyes widened. "Is something wrong?"

"No, not even a little bit. These two together. So good. I could eat myself into a stupor if left to my own devices."

Everyone laughed, but all did as Jane just had. Once their collective delight had calmed, Kat broke the delighted pleasure. "Has anyone seen Miss Bee? I went by to pick up the girls' Christmas dresses and the shop is closed."

"Closed?" Jane licked filling from her fingers without a care to decorum. "That's odd. She was filling an order for me as well. Of course, I didn't expect the measurements to be right, but I had hopes. Why would the shop be closed so close to Christmas?"

"That is strange. I hadn't any luck finding a replacement yet, so she'd have no reason to leave." Lillian frowned. "I doubt any of you would tell her we were seeking a more talented dressmaker, so she couldn't have heard out of turn."

"Certainly not," said Kat. "Not with orders still in line.

Jane absentmindedly dipped her beignet in the cobbler. "Did you hear anything when you knocked? See anything? Maybe she got hurt somehow? Perhaps tripped because she forgot her glasses again."

Lee covered a giggle with a cough. "That's terrible, Jane."

"Terrible, perhaps. Not out of the realm of possibility, though." Jane took another delicious bite.

"Perhaps we should send the deputy to check on her?" Faith sipped her tea. "To be for sure she isn't injured or ill and in need of a doc?"

"Excellent idea." Jane nodded to Faith. "I'll speak to Thomas when we're done here."

"Well, then." Lillian dabbed the corners of her mouth. "First order of business?"

"Roof damage," Jane suggested. "Between the tornado earlier this year, and the series of blizzards in the winter, there have been several businesses and homes that have had some major damage. Mr. Hamm has done his best to keep up, but it's mostly patch work."

"That is an excellent point. Even we have a leak at the depot. Hammy patched it after the tornado, but with the fluctuating temperatures and weight of the snow it's gone right through." Kat leaned forward. "I know plenty of businesses would be relieved for the assistance."

"Denizens of the settlement as well." Lillian jotted a note down in the notebook she'd set on the table. "How could we best be served to produce such a team? What tools would be best for expediency?"

The next hour passed in a whirl of discussion until every bit of cobbler and last crumb of beignet were long gone. Gossip and work passed between them until Jane felt quite tired from the hubbub. As the kitchen cleared of her friends, and only Kat remained, Jane allowed the grief to sink back in.

Kat walked with her back to her apartment. "Is there anything I can do?"

"No. You've done it. I'm afraid I simply must continue to wait and wait some more. I'll continue to pray with all I have that Tom is correct and he's likely fine." Jane led her friend inside the apartment. "How is Cindy doing?"

"She was very excited to spend Christmas with all of her favorite men. She's disappointed." Kat sighed heavily. "And she misses him. I didn't realize quite how much he'd become a part of her life the past few years until he was gone."

"I know the feeling."

"Are you truly all right?"

"No, but I am doing well enough to get by."

"Is that supposed to be enough?"

"It has to be."

The first duty of a man is the seeking after and investigation of truth.
—Cicero

The saloon burst at the seams with people. So much so that both Garit and Wil were working. Perhaps it was the approaching holiday or the chilly night that brought so many people. Sally wondered how it would look if there were cowboys in town as well.

The crowd had the possibility of being detrimental to their continuing investigation. Sally and Molly were there anyhow. In the end they knew even the smallest possibility of getting some clue would help.

Weeks of searching had left them with only a few names. They had managed to find Daisy's records, but she didn't use names. They'd matched about seventy-five percent of the names, and most of them had been cleared of any wrongdoing.

Sally spun her glass on the bar, her focus on the mirror behind the bar so she could watch the crowd without being obnoxious about it.

"Quite a crowd tonight." Molly didn't bother with the mirror. She spun on her stool and leaned her arms on the bar top. "Plenty of familiar faces, too."

"Many of these men are here every night. It's those playing with the talent we're worried about." Sally took a big sip of her whiskey. They wouldn't make progress sitting here. She set down her glass. "I'm going to make a circuit around the room."

"Me too. Meet you back here for another drink."

Sally hopped off her stool. Over the past week she and Molly had made nightly visits to the saloon. Sally had taken a page from her ma's book and interacted with all of the clientele. Jane had professed gratitude that Sally had taken on the overseeing of the business. Sally hadn't told her the real reason for her visits. The last thing she wanted to do was get her ma's hopes up until they had something solid to help Mike.

Saly wove through the tables much like her ma did when she visited the saloon. She spoke to everyone she came in contact with, waved over whores for men that needed some cheering, and took mental note of those doing well at the two poker tables to get them more alcohol.

Sally paused at a table near the windows. "Hammy, how are you doing tonight? Do you need another beer?"

Hammy's head wobbled on its way up to meet her gaze. A goofy grin plastered on his scruffy face. "Ah. Lady Jane. You're the best."

"Hammy." Sally didn't like the distinct slur to his words. The man slurred often, but this seemed like more. She perched on the seat beside him. When he reached toward her, she set her hand on his. "It's Sally. Not Jane."

"Janey, Janey. S-S-So sweet." He patted her hand. After a second he leaned toward her. His seat became precarious as he swayed again. "I'm givin' it all to ya."

"Hammy, it's Sally. How many drinks have you had?" Sally cupped his cheek, studying the glazed over eyes. "Hammy?"

After a few slow blinks, he seemed to come to himself. His eyes focused on her clearer than they had. "Sally."

"That's right, Hammy. Have you had too much beer tonight? You called me Jane."

"Mrs. Mitchell. Good. Kind."

"Hammy, I think you need to get yourself home and sleep off the beer." Sally helped him to his feet. When he stumbled after one step, she frowned. She glanced at a nearby table where several familiar faces sat. "Carl. Would you be so kind as to take Hammy home? I think he's had a bit too much beer tonight."

"Every night, ya mean." Carl rose to loop himself under Hammy's arm. "I got him, Sally. I'll make sure he gets tucked in for ya."

"Thank you, Carl. There's a free drink in it for your efforts."

"Much obliged." Carl helped Hammy to the door.

Sally felt drawn to follow. Her concern for Hammy overrode her need for further investigation at the moment. The men made stumbling progress down the steps. The last thing she wanted to do was give her ma another reason to worry, but she thought Jane would want to know. No, she'd tell Tom. He could check on the man to be sure he was alright before she worried her ma.

Once the pair turned the corner, she made her way back to the bar. Garit leaned on it across from her. "Sendin' away one of our best customers? Tryin' to hurt the business?"

"That would be true if Hammy ever paid for a beer. You're plenty safe."

"She's got a point." Wil's laughter rang through the saloon, boosting the mood. He clapped Garit on the shoulder. The two men got in a playful shoving match before settling again, full of laughter. The bump in business had done wonders for both of their moods. Wil mumbled something in German before moving back down the bar.

In a sharp, yet somehow playful tone, Garit called after him in the same language. He narrowed his eyes when he caught Sally staring. "What?"

"Nothing. Nothing at all. You're in a good mood tonight is all."

"I'm allowed."

"For sure. It's so rare, though. Wil, sure, he's a laugh on a regular basis. You've been nothing more than rude and insolent since I first stepped in here."

He leaned close until they were nose to nose. "You ain't seen rude, lady."

"Of course not." She didn't balk one bit at his threatening stance. She waited patiently for him to back up. It wasn't long before he settled back on his side of the bar in a more casual lean. Sally knew a play when she saw one. Wil and Garit both had one. She couldn't figure out what on earth it could be yet. Instinct told her both Tom and her ma knew.

"Sally." Molly plopped into the seat beside her. Before saying whatever she'd come to say, she turned her brightest smile on Garit. "Guten abend, mein Herr."

"Du sprichst Deutsch?"

"I do speak German. Quite well, actually." Molly batted her eyelashes. "I'm a surprising woman. Didn't you know?"

"Ja." Garit nodded. He glanced at Sally, then back to Molly. "There's a lot of that around these parts."

Molly turned to Sally when he walked away to fill an order. "As I was saying. Do you know who the dandy is with Rose?"

Rather than directly seek out and study the man Molly meant, Sally allowed her gaze to sweep the room. She only allowed a few moments extra hesitation at the man Molly pointed out.

Sitting near the steps in the back a familiar man sat in well kept clothes, not too fancy, but not usual clothing for most of the men that frequented the brothel. Men like him usually went to the casino. He had a good grip on the whore in his lap. Though Rose smiled, her shoulders were tense, her fingers gripped on the arm of the chair. She wasn't happy to see her visitor.

"Reuben Miller. He's one of the managers at the Sage Brush."

"You know, I came in here on the regular before you started joining me. I don't recall seeing him before this past week that we've been in here daily. I mean, not ever. Not in town, not in the mercantile, not anywhere."

"He bach's on a small claim south of here. I hardly ever see him in town either. He doesn't attend our church, I believe he went to Glorious Valley with Eckles. I think he perhaps goes to the mercantile once a month, otherwise I know little about him."

"He's a weaselly sort."

"That's what ma says. Rose seems to think so, too."

Molly hummed, tossing back her whiskey. She slapped the bar for another.

Sally gestured to Peony as she made her way through the crowd toward a sure-fire no. Peony pouted, but moved to Sally's side. "Yeah?"

"Don't bother. You approach Leon, he'll remember he's got a wife with a rolling pin and bolt out of here without paying for his tab, much less a whore." Sally tugged Peony closer. Several gazes had turned their way at the motion, most leering. A good distraction. She could ask questions in safety. She fiddled with the girls hair to fix a ribbon that sat askew.

"Ah. Too bad."

"Tell me about Reuben."

Peony had the decency to not blatantly stare at the gentleman in question. As Sally adjusted the ribbon at her throat, she arched her back for better access. "What do ya wanna know? I don't know much."

"Has he been coming around long?"

"A couple months, maybe. Real quiet type unless you're what he wants."

Sally pondered for a moment. She fiddled with the girl's skirts to tug up her stockings, revealing the skin of her thighs in the process. The men at a nearby table stared blatantly now, practically salivating. "Is he rough?"

"Nah."

"No, I don't mean that rough. Not so violent these two would kick him out, but enough to get in some pain?"

Peony frowned, adjusting her corset back and forth. "Maybe."

"Here." Sally gave the corset a sharp tug down, then another up. Peony's bosoms bulged at her efforts. With a tug and twist of the corset strings, the plump reward for the small effort remained. "Now, here's another tip. I know I busted Zeb's nose, but he's a good one."

"Zeb?" Peony gave her an incredulous look. "No."

"He likes a good mouth job before he goes for the goods. Makes it take less time for a decent payback on the monetary side." Sally winked. "Next time I'll give you the best tip for your pleasure over money."

"I'll keep that in mind."

Molly nursed her drink, her focus on the girl as she sidled off toward Zeb. "Turning over your tips of the trade?"

"For this town, anyway. I have no intention to ever whore here again." Sally stood again. "Garit, would you please load up three beers, five whiskeys, and a gin?"

"Since you asked nice." Garit flopped a tray on the counter before he moved to fill the request.

Molly eyed the tray. "What are you doing?"

"I'm tending to customers, of course." Sally took the tray soon as it was full. She wove among the tables again, exchanging alcohol for money. At the table with Reuben, Sally set the gin down in front of him. "Three bits, Mr. Miller."

Reuben tossed the money on the table. "Thanks."

"Did you want a room? I can recommend bed three for five dollars more." Sally studied Rose, who turned her wide-eyed gaze on her. For the first time she realized the dark hair falling in waves down the girls back was stunningly similar in color to Daisy's.

"Perhaps I will. What do you say, Rose?" Reuben stood with his arms still tight around the girl. Her toes had barely brushed the floor when he threw the money on the table. He tossed back his drink and led the whore to the stairs.

Sally waited until they were almost up the stairs before she carried the tray back to the bar. She sidled up to Wil. One finger hooked into his trousers, she dragged him away from the bar to the storeroom. All for the sake of those goggling, she pressed against him before she shut the door with a solid slam.

Instantly she backed off the man to lean against the shelves across from him. "Do me a favor, would you?"

"Seems like I already am, seeing how you dragged me in here."

"I know you're good to keep a secret. Busy though it might be out there, if anyone hears me asking questions…"

"You asked Peony plenty of questions."

"Nobody cares what whores say to each other, especially when they're touching each other."

"Fair enough point."

"When Rose is done, I want her taken out of circulation for the night."

Wil frowned. He crossed his arms, leg lifted to rest on a shelf. "No."

"I worded it wrong. It's not a favor, it's an order."

"You don't got that kind of power."

"I do if Ma says I do, and this is important. No one else is to touch her until I talk to her tomorrow. I have some questions for her."

His brow rose. "If I must."

"You must. It's important or I'd never ask."

"Will do."

"Good. One more favor."

"You're pushing it."

"We've been in here several minutes. Proper dishevelment and behavior upon departing will be required."

He chuckled low. "You're good at the game."

"An expert, you might say."

"Then let's give them a show."

Some rise by sin, and some by virtue fall.
-William Shakespeare

A brisk three raps on the door startled Sally out of a dead sleep. She pushed onto her elbow and brushed some unruly curls out of her face.

The presence of a warm body behind her stirred the last bit of sleep from her brain. She spun quick, nudging the woman beside her. "Molly. You fell asleep."

"Hm?" Molly stretched luxuriously. Another knock on the door got her attention enough for her to look around the room. "Oh. Oops."

"Oops? What if Ma had caught you."

"Who cares? I was comfy."

Sally pushed her from the bed. Molly landed with an oomph. On her rump in an undignified position, she narrowed her eyes at Sally. "Rude."

A third knock was accompanied by Tommy's sharp voice. "Sally. Wake up. We gotta get to the mines."

"What?" Sally flew to her feet. She threw on her robe as she rushed to the door. "Tommy? What's going on?"

Tommy stood, fully dressed, a hand on his holster. His brow furrowed in a grim expression. When he glanced behind her, there was a flicker of surprise. "Oh, Molly."

Heat rushed to Sally's cheeks at being caught. She straightened against the embarrassment. "What is this about the mines?"

He nodded to Sally. "Get dressed quickly. Molly, you might as well too. We need to get there before the men go tramping through."

"Tramping through—never mind, I'll get answers later. Getting dressed." Sally closed the door on him. She rushed into clothes quick as possible.

Molly did the same, whipping her hair into a knot faster than Sally had a dream of with her curls.

Instead, she tied back the top half of her hair to keep it out of her face, leaving the rest loose. She pinned a hat in place and grabbed her notebook. Neither of them said a word in their rush to get dressed and outside. By the time they'd reached the front porch, Tom had horses ready for all three of them. He hopped on Brag, offering Bluff to Molly.

Sally swung into Agatha's saddle and followed Tom as he rushed through town toward the mines. Though she'd gone to the hill north of town, Sally had never been to the mines herself. From the hill and parts of town you could see the mines working tirelessly to reap gold and silver from the rock.

The horses slowed on the curving, rocky path up into the hills. A crowd gathered near one mine entrance. David and one of his deputies, Simon, stood sentinel. David frowned when Tom dismounted. "They can't go in there. It's too dangerous."

"Oh, really?" Sally straightened, indignant at the suggestion she couldn't handle a mine.

"You shouldn't, your ma would kill me."

"But I suppose it's fine for Tommy or any other man?" Sally brushed right past him to grab a lamp. She'd made it several feet inside before she heard footsteps behind her. Tom drew close, a bright grin on his face. "What?"

"Not a damn thing. Proud of you is all." Tom waited for Molly to catch up with her own lamp. He held his aloft to point down the shaft. "Kevin Doyle discovered her this morning. Charlie's probably in there with Andrew by now."

"Discovered...her?" Sally stepped deeper into the cold, dark tunnel. Her dress would be a mess. She should have thought to grab an old chore dress. "What female would be in a mine?"

"You're in here."

Sally paused long enough to glare at him.

"There's been a few female workers in the mines, in fact there's still at least one. Hard to tell seeing as she wears trousers and keeps her hair short." Tommy ducked as the tunnel narrowed. "This isn't a miner, though. Not by a long shot."

"Then who?" Molly kept pace with them easily. Being the shortest of the group, she had no need to duck under the low ceilings.

"Miss Bee."

"The dressmaker?" Sally almost stopped in her surprise. Curiosity proved a fiercer power that drove her ever forward. "Ma said she hadn't been open so they could get the Christmas dresses for the younger children."

"I went by the shop yesterday to see if anything was out of sorts, but it was clean as a whistle. I would have said she stepped out for a minute and forgot to come back. Apparently when Doyle reported for work, he was first in the tunnel. Found the body and hightailed it to the Sheriff'." Tommy lifted his lamp. "I see them."

Sally moved forward quicker now that she could see the lamp in the distance. Sure enough, Charlie and Andrew were both bent over the body. The dressmaker lay sprawled across the stone floor of the tunnel in a puddle of her own sick. A strong, acrid smell hit Sally's nose. "Oh. How much did she drink?"

"Enough to kill her, I believe." Charlie clicked his bag shut. "Or it would have if the elements hadn't gotten to her first. It was bitterly cold last night."

Tommy circled the body to the other side. His lantern swept across the tunnel floor. "Not a sign of liquor in here. What would bring her into a mine shaft? In the middle of the night, no less."

"Where's she been for the past four days?" Sally added to his questions with her own. "And since when did Miss Bee drink? The woman tutted at Ma every time she spoke of alcohol. Miss Lil said she was part of the Temperance League in Denver and had designs on starting one here."

"Those that protest the most often have the biggest problems." Andrew rose. He hit his head on the low ceiling, grunting and glaring at the rock. "Perhaps she'd been hiding it from everyone. I've seen it happen in the finest families as much as the poorest."

Sally opened her mouth to breathe through it so the smell wasn't as bad. She knelt next to the body. "Is that bruising around her mouth? Or is from the cold? Or perhaps lack of oxygen?"

Charlie lifted his gaze to her. His brows rose. "It could be any of those things. I'm impressed."

Sally smiled her appreciation at the compliment. "Tommy, I'd like to go with Andrew for the autopsy. You and Molly can see if there are any clues to follow in here."

"Good idea." Tommy nodded. "You good with that, Molly?"

"I don't mind getting my hands dirty." Molly winked at Sally, a wicked grin twisting her dainty lips. "Let the princess go do science."

"Princess, am I?" Sally chuckled low, then bounced to her feet. By the grace of a last second thought she managed to duck her head before she smacked it as Andrew had. "You behave. Uncle Charlie, should I send someone in to help move her?"

"If the brute helps us load her onto the litter, we can get her out together. If you'll carry the bags." Charlie dusted some grit from his pants. "Would you?"

"Of course." Sally scooped up her lamp and the bags. "What do I tell David, Tommy?"

"Give us an hour. The men will have a late start today." Tommy leaned down to help get the body on the littler. "With two of us, it shouldn't take more than that. Maybe see if Simon can bring us down a few more lamps."

"You got it." Sally moved back up the mine shaft to the entrance. The sunlight momentarily blinded her after the darkness of the shaft. She blinked away the spots to find a restless crowd muttering some feet away. David and Simon had been joined by none other than Henry Daugherty. "Mr. Daugherty."

"Miss Sally. Is what David is telling me true?" Concern lined the town founder's features. He glanced toward the shaft. "There was a woman found dead in my mine?"

"I'm afraid so. It was Miss Bee, who's been missing for a couple of days." Sally noticed Rusty Piper hovering nearby, pencil scribbling away. The crowd lingered, all staring at the mine where Miss Bee's body would soon show up. "Oh dear. We need something to cover her. The whole crowd doesn't need to see her like that."

Simon moved quickly to grab a tarp from some nearby scaffolding. "This should do."

"Well enough, I suppose. Could you take some more lamps down for Tommy and Molly as well? The more light they have, the better." At his nod, she smiled. "Thank you, Simon. David, they said they'd need around an hour. I'm going with the doctors for the autopsy."

David turned to Henry. "Mr. Daugherty?"

"They can have all the time they need. I'll send the men home with pay today. They can return after Christmas." Henry turned to the crowd of miners to make his announcement.

David drew Sally closer to the mine entrance away from the gratitude of the crowd after Henry's pronouncement. His voice lowered after a glance toward Rusty. "What's the word on what happened?"

"Honestly?"

"Please."

"We have more questions than answers right now. She definitely had a lot of alcohol in her, but like Tully, all accounts say she didn't drink."

David's brow furrowed. "You think the person that did that to Tully did this to her?"

"We don't know yet if it was done *to* her." Sally shifted when the doctors emerged with the body. "Even if she did that to herself, how did she end up in a mine shaft? More so in the middle of the night? The docs think the cold might have killed her, but they won't know until Andrew finishes his autopsy."

David watched the doctors push the litter into the wagon bed and closed the tail. "I tend to agree with the questions you've set and I have a few of my own. This is all very strange."

"Welcome to the party." Sally couldn't keep the sarcasm from her tone. At David's sharp look, familiar prickles of embarrassment flared across her chest. Not to be intimidated any longer, she lifted her chin in defiance of his look, and her own embarrassment. "Everything has been odd. It's about time you caught on."

"Sally."

"I'm going to the autopsy. Whatever you ask Tommy will be passed on to me, I'm sure. Excuse me." Sally darted to her horse and leaped into the saddle. She spurred on Agatha until she'd passed Andrew and Charlie in their wagon.

Once in town, she swung around the long way so she might pass the dressmakers shop. Though she didn't try to go in yet, she pondered going in later. Perhaps she'd take ma along. With her exacting memory, ma would know if anything was out of place.

Sally moved on to the clinic, but was still there near five minutes before the doctors. When they arrived, she pushed open the door for them, carrying their bags in behind them.

By the time the men had Bee on a table, Sally had grabbed one of Daisy's old large aprons and tied it around herself. "Tell me how to help."

Charlie stepped aside to give her room. "I'll leave the two of you to it."

Andrew nodded to Charlie. "I'll have Sally keep you posted as to where I am and when I'm done. At the very least the cold preserved the body for us."

"Not certain I'd call that a blessing," Charlie muttered on his way out.

Sally rubbed her hands together. "What first?"

"We set up the instruments, and then we begin with observation."

"Observation I can do."

"We'll see."

If you would be a real seeker after truth,
it is necessary that at least once in your life
you doubt, as far as possible, all things.
–Rene Descartes

Since Henry had given them free rein over the mine shaft, Tom and Molly had spent several hours combing the entire length of the site of Bee's death. Most of what they'd found could be attributed to miners going in and out on a regular basis. He'd hoped for more.

In front of the mercantile David and Simon broke off from their group to head to the jail. When they were out of hearing range, Molly spoke beside him. "All right, out with it."

"I wasn't going to say a word." It was only part lie. He'd wanted to say something since that morning, but he'd debated on whether it was his place. Sally was her own person now.

"Liar. You're protective of her, much as a pa would be."

"She has a pa."

"She only started calling him Pa a few months ago. You've been her mentor."

He grunted his disagreement. This argument was one he wouldn't have. "Fine. She's not a toy."

"I never claimed she was." Molly turned in her saddle to face him. After several hours in the mines she was downright filthy. Her eyes shone through the muck. "We're having fun. Both of us. That's all."

"Sally doesn't have the years we do to figure that out."

"She spent near two years as a whore at the tender age of thirteen. She's no fool. What she has been up until recently is repressed. Afraid to do anything wrong because she didn't want to lose the good thing she'd stumbled on.

"That I knew." He'd seen it, too. So had Jane. They would've had to have been blind not to. All Sally wanted to do since being taken out of the whore life was please Jane as if she were her real ma.

"Once she figured out how to relax and let herself be whatever she wants, she's been learning like never before. The girl has a good memory, and skills to boot. She may have had them before, but in the past few weeks she's excelled beyond even your expectations."

"She's still young."

"Are you saying I'm old?"

"You're not young, haven't ever been."

"I was before."

"Days you like to forget existed. Do you even remember your real name?"

Molly's sharp eyes darkened. She changed the subject right back to Sally. "I'm much closer to her tender age of what we assume is eighteen than you are. I got fed into this life early instead of whoring like her."

"She's one of ours. I won't have her hurt."

"She won't be. Don't you worry." She urged her horse closer. "It's good you're so protective of her."

"She saved my life."

"That all?" Her brows rose until the whites of her eyes shone out of her dirty features. "You've never dug deeper than that after she saved your life, did you?"

"Why would I?" He didn't know why he felt offended by the insinuation, but his defensive hackles rose. He thought about moving on so he didn't have to hear where she was going with this.

"Because you do it to everybody. You can't help yourself, never could. This one you treat like family and yet you've never looked. Never dug deep into who she was and where she came from."

He urged Brag forward a few steps, done with the conversation he'd lost control of.

Molly followed him step for step. "She even looks like family."

Tom couldn't deny that. No one could deny the striking similarity between Jane and Sally. Even Cole had commented on it. He'd noticed it, too. After Sally had lost the face of a whore and stepped into her role as Jane's ward, the similarity had grown into an uncanny likeness. He shook his head. "It's not like it's possible for Clara to have been her ma. She would have been a child herself."

"Fifteen, right?"

"Yeah. She didn't leave for Utah until she was nearly sixteen. And it isn't possible."

"Your family is so large, though. Your ma has what, nine brothers and sisters? Five sets of twins all with the possibility of making babies themselves."

Tom couldn't argue that point. It was a possibility he'd rather think about than the other. "At least three ma hasn't talked to in years."

Could Sally be blood after all? It seemed infinitely impossible that odds would bring the girl right to Jane's doorstep. Then again, what odds would have her near death stumble into the town her ex-husband had called home all those years ago?

"There's the look." Molly 's lips formed a crooked smirk. Damn woman thought she'd gotten him good and distracted.

"There's no look. You're trying to make trouble so that I'll forget you've been playing with her. It won't work."

"Sure, sure. That's what I'm doing. You're a damn Pinkerton, Tom, and you never once bothered to look deeper."

"Saw no need."

"Not even to look for Sally's actual ma?"

"No. I promised I wouldn't, based on what little she's said her and her ma didn't get along at all. Jane made her send a letter to her some years back. Jane sent it to Patrick, who mailed it from St. Louis. I didn't nose on it."

"So strange for you."

"Knock it off."

"Fine, fine. I'll leave it alone. Let's go check on your special protégé and see what she's discovered during the autopsy. Shall we?"

Tom waved her ahead of him. He followed behind in silence. With what they were currently dealing with, he didn't need Molly of all people pointing out he might have missed something. He hated missing something big as this would be. It meant there were other things he could have missed. Things vital to those he cared about.

Jane's turmoil nagged him, exacerbated by this new unease. Cole's continued silence became more suspicious with every passing day. He'd heard the mutterings and gossip around town that Cole had run fast and far when the suggestion of marriage came along. Tom knew different. Jane knew different, but that didn't mean Jane was immune to the mutterings. She put on a good face in public, but she'd expressed her concern to him and Nick on a few occasions.

After he got cleaned up from the mines he'd send out a few more telegrams. There had to be someone available to head to, or already in, California. That matter was far more pressing than Molly's preposterous musings. He didn't need Jane getting so distraught that she could lose the child she carried. He didn't want to lose his sister again, and that may well do it.

At the clinic, he dismounted in full distraction. His attention was drawn by Molly's throaty chuckle. "What is it now?"

"I got your wheels spinning. That's so fun."

"No you didn't. I'm thinking about Cole's absence. You don't know anyone out in California that could head into Hell, do you?"

"Not at the moment. Most of my contacts are out east, and a few in the south. You'll have better luck after the new year. I know C.B. and F.P. are both wrapping up jobs around then. Have you reached out to Russ and—oh, I don't know— offered to *pay* for some help?"

"I have too many favors at hand to call in to bother paying. Unfortunately, everyone is tied up right now. It's a busy year, apparently."

"You're just lucky I'm having fun training Sally. I've gotten five offers this month alone. Only took the shortest two." Molly pushed open the door to the clinic. Bright laughter rang through the clinic to meet them.

Tom followed the laughter back to the kitchen. There he found Sally and Andrew in near-tears with laughter. Sally smacked the table, holding onto her waist with her other arm. Though she spotted them, she couldn't seem to get a hold of her laughter.

A glance toward Molly gave him a glimpse of a stricken look. She caught him staring and schooled it back into her practiced smile.

Tom leaned closer. Under the continuing laughter of the other two, he spoke quiet. "So there's no feelings? None at all?"

"Shut it," Molly muttered. Her cheeks darkened under his continual look. Felt a little good to turn the tables after she'd blindsided him on their way here.

"Oh. Oh. Oh." Sally worked herself toward stillness, but clearly still couldn't speak. Chuckles shivered through her every time she opened her mouth. She wiped at tears that had sprang free in her ceaseless mirth. "Hi."

"Hello to you, too." Tom nodded to the still laughing doctor. "Andrew."

Andrew waved. He made some semblance of trying to collect himself. A few *ha*'s emerged on his way to speech.

"So sorry. Sally has been sharing stories. I have to say they're as amusing as her ma's."

"Where do you think she gets them from?" Tom winked at Sally. "If you're ready, I'd like to know what the word is on Bee."

"Right." Sally cleared her throat. With the ring finger of each hand she dabbed along her eye's water line to dab away any remaining tears. "Uncle Charlie was right. Alcohol and exposure did her in. How she got into the mine shaft we don't know, but there was something interesting."

"Her front teeth were broken," Andrew chimed in. "And there was some bruising at the back of her throat."

"It looks like she didn't drink all of that alcohol willingly, much like Tully." Sally brushed at a stray curl. "If any of it was, that is. We can't know for sure, of course."

"Not until we find out who did it," Molly finally entered the conversation. "Tom and I found little that couldn't be attributed to the miners. Except for one thing."

Tommy pulled a handkerchief from his pocket. "It's nowhere near dry so we can't yet tell what it is, but there was some paper in the sick she left on the floor. From what I can see it looks like part of a book page. If the acid didn't eat away all of the ink, we should be able to figure out what it's from."

"If it's anything Ma read, it'll be no problem."

"That's what I'm hoping."

Everything that deceives
may be said to encant.
–Plato

Sally took the time to clean herself up from the mines and autopsy and get changed before she made her way to the brothel. They'd gotten up so early to head to the mines it was still only nearly ten in the morning.

Such an hour would be early for the whores to be up and about, but she would take her chance to catch Rose. She'd invited Tom to join her, but she wasn't sure if he would. He'd seemed awful distracted on their way back to the Inn. She wondered if he was upset about the state he'd found her in with Molly that morning.

If that were the case she hoped he'd just out with it. She had learned to not be embarrassed, especially around those close to her. Then again, Tom had always been protective of her. She thought about all the time he'd had around Molly. Had he said something to her?

"Good morning, Sally." Ada sat on the floor with the twins, or at least Colton. He worked intently on the slate before him. Clara danced around on her tiptoes even though there was no music to be had that morning.

"Good morning, Ada. Looks like you have a handful." Sally tried to cover her smile by putting on her cape.

"Every morning with this one. I think she's excited. Jane suggested they might go on a r-i-d-e in the c-u-t-t-e-r."

"Ride," Colton said suddenly.

Ada's eyes widened and she turned toward the boy. "What?"

"Ride." He didn't look up from his task, even as Clara squealed in response to the repeated word.

Sally stood frozen, cape still half on. "Did he just say what you spelled? Could Pa have been right? He can read?"

"He's not yet three," Ada protested. "It would seem he knew that word, though."

"We're going to have to watch what we say, and spell, I guess." Sally chuckled. "Ma will be happy, at least. She might have someone to compete with her in the memory area."

"I think she has enough of that with all of her brothers." Ada tried to contain Clara's enthusiasm. The young girl twirled right away from her. "Oh, bother."

Sally ducked toward the door. "I'll leave you to it."

"Thanks," Ada muttered drolly.

Sally closed the door as Ada went for Clara, who squealed and climbed right over the back of the sofa. Still laughing, Sally headed for the brothel.

The doors were still locked, which was not surprising at this time of day. She pulled her keys from her reticule to let herself in.

When she shut the doors, a loud click met her ears. Wil called out, "Who's there?"

"It's me." Sally stepped further inside. Wil stood at the top of the steps with his weapon trained right on her. "Good to know you're on alert to the slightest sound."

Wil lowered the weapon to his side. He rubbed a hand over his face. "What the hell do ya want? It's damn early for visiting."

"I'm not visiting you."

"It's early for the girls, too." He walked down the steps, gun still in hand. A huge yawn split his face. "What's the deal with pulling Rose off the floor? I had a couple asking for her. Could've made your ma and pa some more money."

"I had my reasons." Sally poured him a whiskey. "Here, drink. Won't wake you up but it might make you less grumpy."

"Insolent women in my saloon at indecent hours makes me grumpy."

"It's ten in the morning. That's not indecent."

"It is to me." He tossed back the whiskey. "You oughta remember."

"I was always an early riser." Sally poured herself a whiskey before refilling his cup. "Up at eight no matter what. Some nights I got maybe two hours sleep."

"Still managed to be the prettiest flower in the field, I bet."

"Not with all that makeup on. Besides, it was Primmy who was prettiest. She's quite a beauty. You might know her. She works as a waitress over at the restaurant. Goes by Bella now."

"She was a whore, too?"

"There's a few of us Ma and Pa sent into the world. The rest kept whoring elsewhere, except Bluebell. She went to work for Leanne." Sally leaned on the counter. "Based on what happens when I talk to Rose, there may be another customer to keep an eye on. Probably not kick out quite yet, because I want to keep an eye on him."

"Am I going to know why?"

"Eventually."

"That's good and vague."

"I imagine if my gut proves true, everyone will know soon enough."

"I'm intrigued."

"Good. Ma always did say to leave them wanting more."

He snorted, tossing back his fresh pour of whiskey. "I'm gonna get cleaned up."

"Please do." Sally paused at the door lock rattling. The door creaked open a moment later. "There you are, Tommy."

"I went to see Hammy like you asked. Oh, morning Wil."

Wil nodded to him. "Morning. If you'll excuse me, I'm gonna go wash last night off me."

Tommy tipped his head in return before he moved behind the bar with Sally. "Hammy looks fine. He has a headache is all. Said he drank too much, hardly remembers last night. Otherwise, he seemed like the Hammy we know and love. I suggested he go to the clinic to get something for the headache, but he said he's got work to do."

"At least he's all right. He had me worried last night. I didn't want to worry Ma about it if I didn't have to, she's got enough worrying to be getting on with." Sally leaned on the bar. "We'll probably have to wake Rose if we want to talk to her without any nosey Nellie's."

"I'll leave that to you. I'm going to grab a beer."

"Yes, sir." She circled the bar. "I'm expecting Andrew to arrive soon to give her a quick exam as well. In case anyone knocks, it's probably him."

"Got it."

Sally headed for the back rooms. On the left stood a room that hadn't been there in the old saloon. Pa had added a third room for the whores to give them more space. Inside she found several of the younger whores in various stages of sleep. To her relief, Rose was already awake.

Rather than disturb the others, she waved for Rose to follow her. As Rose made her way out, she whispered. "Why'd you put me out last night?"

"Come with me and we'll talk about your last trick." Sally led her onto the main floor. Tommy sat on a stool nursing his beer. "Rose, you know Tommy, right?"

"Sure thing. He's Jane's brother." Rose smiled at him. "Too bad he prefers the fancy place."

Sally chuckled when Tommy slurped his beer rather than reply. "What can you tell me about your last trick last night? Reuben."

"Pays good. Sloppy. Can't do the deed half the time, makes me diddle myself instead." Rose flopped into a chair. "Gets upset when he can't. That's when he gets rougher. So, it happens more often than not."

"How bad does he hurt you?"

"Not bad. A few bruises, but not enough I'm gonna go whinin' or nothing." Rose flipped up the dress strap that flopped down. A tick that Daisy herself had often had, even after she left whoring. In the light of day the similarities weren't as obvious as they had been at night, but they were still there. "We didn't used to see him much when we first opened. Maybe once a fortnight."

"Has he been around more lately?"

"Yeah. Now he's always askin' for me. It's gets tedious, that's why I got mad when ya urged me to take him up last night. Sorry. Is that why I'm in trouble?"

"You're not in trouble," Sally reassured her. A knock on the door pulled her attention away from the whore. "That'll be Andrew."

"I'll get him." Tom let the young doctor in. "Andrew."

"Mr. Young." Andrew stepped inside and removed his hat. He grinned when he noticed the women. "Sally, always good to see you. Hello, Rose."

Rose nodded to him. The presence of a young man had her arching her back and leaning forward. "Mornin' to you, doc. It ain't your usual day."

"No, it isn't. Miss Sally asked me to stop by in case you needed any assistance." Andrew set down his medical bag on the table. "Is there something ailing you?"

"I'm fine," Molly stated. She smiled. "You can check me over if you like, though."

"I actually wanted you to check her for bruises from a trick last night." Sally pretended not to notice the flush blooming on her friend's cheeks. She gestured to the rooms across from the bar. "If you'd prefer, you can use a room."

"That's up to Rose." Andrew's tone maintained its professionalism. The blush faded nearly as quick as it had risen.

"Nah. It's fine. Don't gotta look at my privates. He didn't go near that."

Sally stepped away to where Tom sat at the bar. "Am I crazy?"

"If you were, I wouldn't stopped you long ago. He sounds like a good possibility." Tom pushed aside his beer. "The problem is getting proof, and a confession if it's him."

"He started coming around more often after Daisy was murdered. He favors a whore with a similar look to Daisy." Sally pondered the situation for a moment. The man was looking for a ghost with another human. What if they gave him what he was looking for?

"What are you thinking?"

"I'm thinking we take our lead from Dickens."

"Come again?"

"A visit from the ghost of whores past." Sally kept her voice low, and her gaze lowered. Maybe Tom would think her crazy. "We should use Molly. I bet we could doll her up just right to have an air like Daisy. Her hair color's a little dark, but it may work."

Tom didn't protest or dissuade the notion. "She may have a wig that's closer to the right color."

"She might."

He nudged her arm. When she looked up, he wore a grin. "You're doing really well."

"Thanks."

"Now." He jerked his thumb over his shoulder toward Andrew. "What're you doing with that one?"

"What do you mean?" She furrowed her brow. When his meaning sank in, she scoffed. "Oh. He's a friend is all. He's completely sweet on Bonnie. It's kind of adorable how smitten he is."

"Wanted to make sure you knew that and weren't getting moony."

"I'm moony over no one, rest assured." Sally patted his arm. It was sweet he was worried for her and her heart. "Thank you for worrying over me. I'm really fine."

"Good."

"All done," declared Andrew.

Rose was already on her feet. "Are ya done with me?"

"We are. Thank you, Rose. I'll be by later tonight again. If I have any further questions, do you mind if I ask them?"

"Nah. What about Reuben? If he comes back."

"Take yourself out of circulation. Say ma had to adjust your monthly schedule. It happens the longer you work with other women." Sally ignored Tom's grunt of surprise.

Andrew moved behind the bar to wash his hands in the tub. "She has some bruising on her ribs, nothing so severe I'm worried. It was hard to see because she covered it with powders, but she has some light bruising on her neck as well."

Sally frowned. "I'm definitely going to have more questions for her tonight."

"Did you need anything else?" Andrew dried his hands. "I've got an appointment at the clinic soon."

"No, that's it. Are we still on for lunch?"

"Of course. I told Bonnie."

"Good." Sally led him to the door, closing it behind him. She turned back to Tommy. "How do we go about doing this now?"

"Priority is getting Daisy's case solved so we can get Mike out of jail. I'll talk to Molly about getting herself to look and act more like Daisy. I knew her better than you did."

"Good. Then we can—"

A sharp whistle cut through town loud and clear. So loud they had no trouble hearing it even with the doors closed. The Young emergency whistle if she'd ever heard it. Sally met Tom's eyes, then rushed from the saloon to the porch.

The whistle repeated from their left. Jane stood on the porch of the jail waving frantically.

"Damn it, Mike." Tom took off like a shot.

Sally followed right behind. "What could it be?"

"No idea."

Have patience awhile;
slanders are not long-lived.
Truth is the child of time;
erelong she shall appear to vindicate thee.
–Immanuel Kant

Jane rushed back into the jail. Michael stood right where she'd left him. His face pressed to the bars; hands wrapped tight around them.

She set her hands on his, inhaling against the hope that had flared. "I can't believe it. Do you really mean it?"

"I do." Mike actually smiled for the first time in weeks. The hope she was trying to push down in fear it wouldn't be true shone across his face. "I feared the worst reasons for why it wasn't happening until now."

"What is it?" Tom burst into the jail so fast he almost smashed right into the bars. He stopped short, hands braced against them. "What's happened? What's wrong?"

"Nothing's wrong." A squeak of excitement escaped through her voice. Jane found herself laughing. "Michael is remembering!"

"He's what?" Sally came to a stop beside Jane. "Everything?"

"Bits and pieces mostly. Especially what happened after that second bottle of whiskey." Mike grimaced. "I remember why I started drinking again after Jane knocked some sense into me, though. It's a start, a damn good one."

A few seconds later, Nick burst in. "Sorry for the delay, I was in an appointment. What's going on? What's the problem?"

"I'm remembering," Mike said to Nick. For the first time since he'd been put in jail his voice wasn't deadened by lack of hope. Life shone through the gruff notes still carried by the lack of regular use of his voice. "It started last night when playing checkers with Jesse."

"David Jesse Schaffer." Jane turned on her ex-husband. She did her best to maintain a glare when he grinned at her. "What on earth was Jesse doing in the jail?"

"Don't give me that tone. Jesse is in here all the time, at least he was before Mike was arrested, I've kept him out much as I could since. He wanted to visit his uncle." David didn't have the decency to look properly reticent for his actions. Maybe he knew she wasn't truly mad at him. "If it helped Mike, why are you complaining?"

"Oh, hush. You terrible man." Jane turned back to Mike. "Tell us."

"Wait." Nick held up his hands. "David. As his attorney—"

"Say no more. I was wondering when Jane was going to demand. Surprised she didn't before she even called you lot." David pushed through them to unlock the cage. "You can all join him, but he can't come out yet. We still don't know who did it, or if the memory is relevant. Especially seeing as he's still having trouble after the second bottle of whiskey."

Jane didn't wait to be told twice. She bullied her way past both her brothers to wrap Michael in the tightest hug she could manage. He hugged her back, body shaking with a brief spat of tears. "I needed good news. This is wonderful."

"It's not freedom," Mike said in an undertone. "You heard him."

"But it's a step. Maybe it's something Sally and Tom can run with." She rubbed his back until his shaking stopped. They parted and sat beside each other on the cot. She took his hand in hers to keep a supportive hold on some part of him. Nick and Tom had brought a couple of chairs in the cell during their hug.

Sally rushed over to hug Mike as well. "Things are looking up. Ma's right." She retreated back out of the crowded cell to linger in the doorway.

Nick pulled some papers from his attaché. "Tell us what you've remembered."

"Jane had just given me the what-for at the saloon."

"A well earned one," she said quietly.

"And how," he agreed. "I admit, I still wasn't happy. Her words had the impact they were supposed to, though. Cut through my circling thoughts. I was going to go home to dunk my head in a bucket of cold water."

Nick scribbled quickly across his paper. "So you left the saloon to ride home."

"I couldn't remember what I'd done with my horse." Mike grimaced the admission. He pulled his hands free to rub along his thighs as though they were cold "She might have cut through the nonsense but I still had a head full of liquor. I decided to walk."

Tom leaned back in his chair. "On a path that took you right past Daisy's, I'm guessing."

"It's the quickest way home, and I already said I wasn't thinking clear." Mike's hands shook their way to his head. He ran his fingers through the tangled locks. "I didn't go to her place, I know I didn't. I swear it."

"You don't have to defend yourself to us. We know you didn't do this." Jane clasped his hand in hers again. "Just tell us what happened."

"I saw her letting someone in." Mike flinched, pinching the bridge of his nose. Jane hadn't missed the tears that had made an appearance right before. "A man."

Both Tom and Sally leaned forward at this news. Tom broke the silence. "Did you know who it was?"

"Of course I did. I couldn't believe it." Mike's hand slapped to his knee. "I'd worked with him for two years."

Jane didn't miss the significant look that passed between Sally and Tom. They knew something, that much was clear. She turned her attention back to Mike. "Who?"

"Reuben." Mike shook his head, clearing his throat. "He knew how I felt about her. It didn't matter. He still went to her to use her services. I didn't dare go near the place because I was so mad once again. Instead, I went home and dragged out all the whiskey. I drank until I don't know how long, but I was home doing it."

Sally spoke quietly, "Your assistant manager, Rueben Miller. You're sure it was him?"

"Yeah. I think I'd know who it was. I've been working with him for two years now." Mike lifted his gaze toward Sally. "They seemed familiar enough, seeing as she welcomed him in."

Sally glanced to Tom, her brow raised in a silent question. At his nod, she stepped back in to kiss Mike on the cheek. "We're gonna fix this, Uncle Mike. Just you wait and see."

Jane turned to Tom when Sally darted from the jail quicker than a jackrabbit. He gave her only a short shake of his head. She'd press the matter later, now wasn't the time. She rested her head against Mike's shoulder. "It's something. It's much more than you had. Wait, sorry. I know that's no less frustrating. I about took Cole's head off for saying that to me once."

The instant she said Cole's name, the joy she'd been basking in took a brutal hit. She kept leaning against Mike so he wouldn't see if she hadn't managed to keep her expression schooled. Unfortunately, Tom could still see her. His razor-sharp focus stayed on her while Nick began a series of questions.

By the time Nick finished a steady stream of inquiry and began to write, Jane though she had much better control of the stray panic, or grief. She lifted to her head to smile at Mike. "This is good. Very good. Believe it."

"You may have to keep believing for me." Mike folded her into another tight hug. "Do you think you can do that for me?"

"I can. Forever if necessary." She held on as long as he needed her to. When his hold loosened she rose. "I'll let Nicholas finish with you. I'm going to go tell Kat and Cora. They've both been so worried about you."

"I know. Cora's stopped by to see me a few times." Mike squeezed her hand. "Come back soon. I'm going to need reminders."

"You can't stop me." She kissed her cheek.

Tom leaned in for a quiet word with Nick. Before she'd made it to the door he'd followed, but stopped for another word with David. She paused at the railing outside, certain her crafty brother was following her to check on her.

She wasn't wrong. He leaned on the railing beside her. "In a couple of weeks I'll have a body to head out there. He's on a case, but it's almost over. He's he best."

"You said that about Joe." Try as she might, she'd been unable to keep the bitterness from her tone. She was both furious at, and worried about, Cole.

"That's not fair." In a rarity, Tom actually sounded wounded by the attack.

"Sorry. I'm worried sick."

"I'm getting there, too. I wasn't before, not as much as you." His fingers ran along his short beard before his hands clasped together. Eyes narrowed as though the main thoroughfare was full of suspicious sorts. "I thought maybe his pa had left a mess of families behind and he was busy dealing with that. It's been too long now, though."

"It was too long from three days after he left Fresno. That's the last time I heard from him." She ran a hand along her stomach.

"He's not much of a writer."

"No, but he promised. Plus, he was so worried about me disappearing because of the miscarriage. I struggled so much after it. He was so worried about me. It was his biggest argument for not leaving at all."

"I'll try to get my friend to hurry on his case so he can get out there sooner."

"I should go." Jane turned toward the western mountains. "I need to."

"How do you think you're going to manage that?"

"I haven't figured it out yet, but if I don't hear something soon, it's happening."

He set a firm hand on her shoulder. "I'll go with you."

"You can't. You have to help—"

"Sally's all but handling it on her own. That girl's got a head on her for this detective work. Stepping right into her own now that she isn't so scared. She even dressed down David this morning and everything."

She turned from the mountains to face him. He wore a crooked grin, his chest puffed in pride. "I'm sorry. She did what?"

"He tried to tell her it wasn't safe for her to go in the mines."

"He did, Charles did."

"I know. Your girl pushed right past him pointing out that he wasn't about to keep me out."

"Good for her." Jane couldn't be more relieved for the boost in confidence Sally had seen these past weeks. "I worried. She's been so focused on being good and following rules I think she lost herself in there. It's funny."

"What is?"

"If Superintendent Paxil hadn't been such an ass, none of this might have happened. I wanted to kill the man back then. Now I'd like to shake his hand."

"It would've happened in its time." He tugged her into a one-armed hug. "You raised her good these past couple of years. It might have taken her longer, but she would have come into her own."

"How many would she have hurt in the process? She might have married Arthur, and that would have been a mess when she realized it wasn't what she wanted."

"If we lived in 'might haves' we'd be a sorry sort. What with all that might have happened if Clara had never run the first time. Or if I might have convince her to come with me one of those times I found her."

She shuddered at the idea. "You're right. I should just be happy things are the way they are. Well, except for my missing man."

"Except for at."

"Christmas is in a few days. I'll remain for that, and a few days after to ensure all of my affairs are taken care of. Then I'm going."

"I'll come with."

She clutched his hands tight in gratitude. A protest lingered. "You don't have to."

"Don't care. I'm going."

"If you must."

*Hope in reality is the worst of all evils,
because it prolongs the torments of man.
—Friedrich Nietszche*

Jane leafed through the pile of books on the desk. One by one she organized them into stacks of where they'd go in the library. Her mother had agreed to let her come to the library unaccompanied because she'd improved so much by resting during the week.

Besides, the next two days the library would be closed for Christmas Eve, which was also a Sunday, and Christmas day. Her hope was to get the placed cleaned to her satisfaction before that. The last thing she needed was to return to a chaotic library on Tuesday. Or maybe she did need it. Having a chaotic library would keep her mind and body busy.

The absolute stillness in the building both soothed and riled her discontent. After a week stuck in her apartment well overfull of people, it was nice to have calm and peace for a few hours. Unfortunately, that same quiet allowed her mind to wander.

Worse, it allowed the worry back in.

She'd already told Eunice of her plans to leave if she heard nothing from Cole in the next few days. Her ma had surprisingly encouraged the notion. She'd been all to happy to point out she'd be there to help care for the children.

The increase in hope over Michael's fate helped, too.

Her biggest guilt lay in leaving Mike before they knew for sure what would happen. Jane prayed that Tom and Sally would find a resolution to the matter sooner rather than later. Either way, she trusted them to see he didn't pay for a crime he didn't commit.

She set the last book in place. The shelves on the upper floor all stood neat and tidy. There were still large gaps in many shelves. Gaps she hoped to fill over time. A well-stocked library seemed one of the best gifts she could leave the town when it came her time.

Back at her desk, she sat with a heavy sigh. For some reason she found herself drawn to the drawer at her side. Withdrawing a Poe book, she dusted off the cover. Almost casually she flipped through to a poem she knew all too well. One that Cole had learned once upon a time. She wondered if he remembered now that it was no longer necessary to dig into Clara's past.

She traced her fingers along the words with a gentle touch. *And neither the angels in Heaven above nor the demons down under the sea can ever dissever my soul from the soul of the beautiful Annabel Lee.*

Clear as any memory surfaced the first time she'd told Cole of the poem. How it was everywhere in Clara's things. He'd tugged her toward him. *Come here, Annabel.*

"Neither the angels nor the demons can dissever our souls." She slammed the book closed. The sharp snap echoed through the empty library. "Clara thought that, too. Yet her and David were ripped apart."

She almost threw the book back into the drawer, but her affection for all books, even the ones that upset her, kept her from the violence. Instead she slid the book back into place, then slammed the drawer itself. The quiet was definitely worse for her disposition. Perhaps she could close early and return home. After all, who truly needed the library on the eve of Christmas Eve.

The door slammed open, startling her from her musings. Kat stood there smiling so bright, Jane wondered how she didn't tear at the seams. "Jane!"

"Goodness, Katherine. That was quite the entrance. Dare I ask the reason?"

"We just got word. Good word." Kat's smile didn't break. "There was a storm in the mountains near Fresno. Several towns lost their telegraphs for at least a week. Including Holle Creek."

"What?" Jane flew to her feet. So deep was her relief she crushed Kat into a hug before she had confirmation. "Please tell me you aren't kidding. Tell me I heard you correct. Cole hasn't received a telegram since—"

"At least a week." Kat held Jane's hands tight in her own. "It'll still be a few days before they get all the towns connected, but a day or two after Christmas we should be able to get through again."

"Thank heavens." Jane sank into a chair. Relief stole every bit of strength from her legs. She felt as though she'd run the length of the valley as the panic eased out, leaving her weak. "Oh my. What a relief that is. Unless…"

"Stop that right now. He's fine, I'm certain of it. We'll hear from him in no time." Kat knelt in front of her. "You now need to relax. Enjoy your Christmas."

"Pray that he's on today's train?"

"You can do that, too. If the storm was like they said, he's likely still trapped in Holle Creek, though."

"A storm. It makes perfect sense."

"Precisely."

"Oh goodness." Jane clutched her heart a moment as it raced back into life. Into hope. "Oh, I was going to close up early anyway. Let's go celebrate. Cocoa at Cora's."

Kat laughed. "Cocoa? Not tea?"

"No. Not tea. I want a real sinful treat since my sinful dessert is so far away."

"Jane." Kat chuckled over her admonishment. "I'm glad you're feeling better."

"Much. I didn't realize how worried I'd been until the worry was relieved." Jane threw on her cape and grabbed her muff. "Tell me you'll join me. We'll try to snag someone else for fun if we can."

"Sounds like a good idea. I wonder if we can figure out a way to get Leanne down the hill. You're in such a good mood, she'll have quite a bit of fun with that."

"Excellent idea. How best to get a message to her?" Jane locked the door. When she turned, she froze. Walking down the street alongside Sally was a ghost. The keys clattered to the porch. A strangled gasp was all she could manage as she pointed toward them.

Kat half-shrieked. The noise was enough to make both young women turn.

Jane's heart slowed from its rapid pace when the woman's face came into view. "My God. I thought that was Daisy."

"Me too." Kat gripped the railing, breathing hard.

"Sally Ann," Jane called.

Sally approached with who Jane now knew to be Molly at her side. "Ma?"

"What in heavens are you doing? Are you trying to scare us to death? We though that was Daisy with you."

Sally's brows turned down. "I'm sorry, Ma. We were testing something."

"You meant to look like Daisy, then?" Jane cast a sharp look at Molly. "That's simply cruel."

"Ma, it wasn't meant to be." Sally moved closer. "There's a reason. A good one. I promise. You gotta trust me."

"It's just a wig, and a dress. The cape as well." Molly lifted the hood of her cape to cover her hair. "We have our reasons, Jane. Tom knows about it and everything."

"Sorry." Sally glanced between Kat and Jane. "I didn't expect you to see her. We were heading out for—"

"A walk," Molly interrupted. "We probably won't be back until late."

Jane scooped her keys from the porch. "Don't you dare go anywhere near the jail, do you understand me?"

"I promise." Sally grimaced slightly. "I'd never do that to Uncle Mike."

"See that you don't."

"We'll keep her hood up, too."

"Please see that you do." Jane exhaled a breath in hopes it would calm her further. "By the way, Sally. Katherine just brought me some good news, of a sort. There was a storm out where Cole is, and it knocked out the telegraph wires. They've been down a week."

"Really?" Sally brightened. "That's great news. Think he's on his way back, then?"

"I'm hoping. If nothing else, perhaps we'll finally hear from him in a couple of days."

Sally hugged her tight. "That's wonderful. If you'll excuse us."

"Of course. Go do what you need to do, but please be aware of others." Jane nodded to them both. She waited until they walked away to turn to Kat. Kat still stared at them wide-eyed. Jane shook her head. "I don't know, but I imagine it has something to do with Daisy's murder so I won't push."

"That was surreal."

"You're telling me." Jane laced her arm through Kat's. "Now, how do we get Leanne down the hill?"

"I could send a telegram to Mother and see if she can send someone over to let Leanne know we're looking for her."

"As long as you're doing that, ask your mother to join us. Lillian would be find company."

"Perhaps they could swing by and grab Faith on their way in."

"That might be difficult. There may be a crowd in the store buying presents." Jane was pleased that already people had begun to come around to using the mercantile. There were still a number of hold-outs, but with Lillian and Graham using the store, more people were going.

"Fair point, but we can try." Kat stopped short. "Is that— *fire*!"

Jane lifted her head at Kat's shriek. Her jaw dropped as she spotted the fire in the distance. Realization dawned on her as the only building it could be. "Heavens. It's the church!"

As Kat screamed *fire* again, Jane ran toward the bell. She gave a good tug on it. Within moments strong hands replaced hers, pulling the cord with greater ease than she had. She nodded to Wil, thanking him for taking over as people streamed into the streets, then rushed toward the meadow.

"I hope the Reverend's weren't in there preparing for service." Jane rushed to follow the crowd toward the building inferno. Fortunately Eli and Mark had found a small home in town that had been gifted to them anonymously so no one was living in the church. However with Christmas Eve the next day, they might have been at the church to prepare.

"No, there they are." Kat dragged Jane toward the two men who stood some distance from the burning church. Kat touched Eli's elbow. "Reverend Lyons, Greene. Thank heavens you're alright."

"We were planning on going in to finish setting up for Christmas Eve service at two." Reverend Lyons took her hand. "All of the Christmas gifts were in there to be put on the tree."

"Forget the gifts." Jane moved to Reverend Greene's side. "You are both safe, and that's what's important."

"Our church." Reverend Greene couldn't seem to tear his eyes from the blaze.

"Mark," Jane soothed. "Remember what it says in Matthew eighteen, verse twenty. 'For where two or three are gathered in my name, there I am in the midst of them'. The church is a building. Your congregation is still here, and we are with you."

"Thank you, Jane." Reverend Greene, patted her hand. "We will have to figure out what to do for Christmas Eve."

"And we will. We were just about to gather our friends for cocoa and conversation. There is no better group of people to figure out a problem, if I do say so myself." Jane turned back to the church. Already the flames had receded as men and women all worked at putting out the flames with snow and water gathered in town. "Once Christmas is over, we will get a new church built. We were outgrowing this one anyhow."

"Until then, we will give sermons on the porch of, or the stage within, the Inn if we must." Reverend Lyons said brightly. "Jane is right. As long as we have people gathered in His name, we will still have church."

"Well said, Eli." Kat grinned over at Jane. "I believe I'll go send that telegram. If Mother isn't already on her way down to see what's happened, that is."

"You send the telegram. I'll see to getting these fine gentlemen over to the Inn. It will be some time before the fire is out, I know from experience."

"I just don't know how this could have happened." Reverend Greene turned with her. He waited for Jane to take Eli's elbow to guide him.

"I don't know either, but we will take care of it."

Nothing is easier than self-deceit.
For what each man wishes,
that he also believes true.
—Demosthenes

Sally slowed Agatha at the edge of town to glance back toward the smoke billowing in the air. They'd heard the emergency bell clang before they'd ever left the barn. Molly had somehow convinced her to continue on their task. She knew what they were doing was important, but she worried if anyone was injured or needed help. "We should go back and help."

"Help do what?" Molly didn't turn back. She did slow Brag beside Sally. "You know with that bell clanging everyone and their brother is running to help. This actually works to advantage. They'll never hear that cacophony out at the hotel."

"True."

"And this means just about everyone here in town is distracted by what's going on that way. They'll never notice us or where we're heading."

"They can notice me. It's you we'd prefer they paid no attention to."

"Precisely."

The logic of it was clear and simple, but Sally worried for whatever had happened. What building was on fire now? Would they be able to put it out as quick as they had the livery? She took small comfort in knowing it wasn't the Inn, they would have seen it when they left the barn.

Sally finally turned away from the chaos to spur Agatha on in a good clip right out of town. She eyed Daisy's old house as they passed. The small homestead had been left to Cole in Daisy's will. Everything had been left to Cole, actually. What little resources she'd possessed had all been left to Cole. Nick had taken it upon himself to change all the locks and present Cole with the new keys before he'd left.

The very key she'd snuck out of the desk drawer the night before to give to Tommy in fact. Her mentor had also managed to get Mike's keys to the hotels. They'd spent half the night getting things set for their plan today.

A simple set of tricks set to haunt the man they suspected had killed Daisy. Illusions such as Molly had proved rather adept at planning and performing.

If all went well, they'd have either a confession, or one scared man running for his life.

Or both.

They made good time out past Daisy's house to the Sage Brush. The horses were pushed at a good clip so they crossed the miles in minutes. When they got some fifty yards away in the cover of trees, they slowed to a stop. Molly swung out of her saddle to tie Brag to a tree.

"I'll wait here." Sally clung to the edge of the woods. It wasn't quite dark enough for them to be well hidden by darkness. Luckily the time of year and pitch of the mountains meant they'd get dusk within the hour, and complete darkness soon after. All before five o'clock.

"Give me twenty minutes."

"Thirty, more like. Please be careful. It will be slick around the waterfall."

"Thirty then, but don't be too generous. Don't forget you need to stall him after to give me time to get back."

That was the tricky part. If he was scared enough, would she be able to stall him long enough to give Molly a chance to enact the next part of their plan? "I'll use my best diversions."

"Good. Don't you worry about me. You haven't seen me in action."

"I've seen you in plenty of action. I'll still worry." Sally matched Molly's wave, if not her smile. As the woman disappeared into the woods, Sally pulled the pocket watch from her bodice to note the time. Within the twenty minutes the device would be utterly useless in the dark. She had matches to check the time after, but it wouldn't be necessary. She'd leave in ten and take a slow approach until Molly gave her signal.

Sally kept an eye on the sun setting over the mountains. Her ears strained for the sound of anyone passing by. No one came, not that she was surprised by this. This close to Christmas the clientele at the Sage Brush was low. Plus with it being winter the waterfall was little more than a visual treat. There'd be no swimming. Add to that the fact there was no longer a doctor on staff with Daisy gone, the draw had lessened.

She hoped once his name was cleared Michael would be able to resolve all the difficulties with the hotel and get it back to running as well as it had in recent years.

Sally urged Agatha forward in an easy walk. When the hotel came into clear view, a spark of light from a match lit near the very edge of the wrapped porch. Molly was in place already.

With that knowledge, Sally urged Agatha into a more rapid, normal pace to the hotel. She drew to a stop at the hitching post as Molly stood. The woman no longer had a cape on, only Daisy's typical dress. Her wig was styled much in the way Daisy always had. The well-lit porch illuminated her in an eerie light that helped their efforts.

Molly walked close to the office window. She dragged her fingers along the panes to emit a squeaking cry Sally could hear from where she sat. In a few short seconds, Molly burst into a run to tear around the corner of the porch. Much like Tom, she managed to move almost silent.

Sally alit from her saddle and tossed the reins over the hitching post. Halfway up the steps, the front door burst open. She allowed a gasp of surprise. "Reuben?"

Wide-eyed, Reubens gaze swept back and forth along the porch. He completely ignored Sally. He raced to the end of the building, staring around the corner.

Sally finished climbing the steps. Casually she approached the man, in no rush. The longer he took to come to his senses, the longer Molly had to get into position for the next part of the plan. She peeked around the corner beside Reuben. "Are you looking for something?"

"Did you see anyone out here?" A note of panic in his tone proved they'd spooked him already, and they'd just gotten started. He spun to face her. "I thought I saw…"

"I didn't see anyone as I rode up, and then you came out." Sally furrowed her brow, doing her best to project concern in her tone as well. "Is something wrong?"

"No. No." Reuben shook his head. He turned to look down the porch again. Only squares of light from the window remained to be seen. "What are you doing here, Sally?"

"I came to see Lee. I wanted to talk about Ma's present."

"Lee no longer works on Saturdays. It was part of our agreement with this new manager Nick hired." Reuben adjusted his jacket, straightened his tie. He was getting himself collected again. Likely dismissed the event as imagination.

"Oh, that's right." Sally groaned. "I'd totally forgotten. I had hoped to find out if she'd had time to finish. She's been so busy of late."

Reuben strode back into the hotel. "You'll probably find her at home with her family."

Sally didn't miss his sneer at the word 'family', but chose to ignore it. She leaned on the reception desk he moved behind. "You're probably right."

"Well, then. If that's all you needed." He closed the counter with a snap of finality. She didn't mind. Behind the reception desk with it closed was right where they wanted him. "Was there something else I could help you with?"

"I suppose not." Sally stood, but then stopped as she took in the lobby. The entire area had been decorated the day before for Christmas. Lee had bedecked the entire area with aplomb, and the help of several friends. "Why aren't the

Christmas decorations up? Uncle Mike and Lee would definitely want them up."

"I took them down. We don't have enough guests to appreciate them."

"Even a few guests would appreciate them." Sally tried to control her temper over all the work Lee had put in destroyed in a day by the man. She released a controlled breath to regain her cool logic. "As would the staff. Those that have to work on the holiday always appreciate allowing a Christmas feel. They can celebrate together in their off time and with their families once they are able to return home."

A tinkling of glass interrupted whatever reply he might have made. His attention flickered behind her. A frown creased his features. "Did you open that door?"

"What door? And how could I have opened a door? I've been standing right here in front of you the whole time." She turned to face the door behind her. The doctor's office door sat half open. A wall of shelves full of bottles twinkled in the lamplight from the hall. She, of course, knew the entire layout of the office really well. The night before she'd helped set everything up for the next show.

Another tinkling of glass sounded from the room. The flash of a skirt flickered past the door opening. Even with the room dark, the hall lamps and the bright ribbons on the skirt had made it visible. Sally pretended to notice nothing.

"Did you see that?" Reuben seemed frozen solid in place.

"See what?" Sally circled around to where the counter opened as though looking for a better view. "I see a dark room, some bottles."

A few moments later she appeared, putting a bottle on the shelf. Long auburn hair brushed along bare arms. Delicate fingers pushed the bottle in place.

A weird, choking cry came from the man beside her. "Get—get out."

"What did I do?" Sally tried to appear offended.

"Not you. *Her*." Reuben moved toward the exit.

Sally leaned on the counter right where he'd have to lift it. "Who are you talking about?"

The woman inside half-turned toward the door. Right as her face would have come into clear view, the door slammed shut. A lock clicked.

Reuben fought with the counter. "*Move*."

"Reuben, what—" Sally yelped when he shoved her off the counter hard enough she lost her balance. She hit the floor with a thump as the countertop banged open.

Reuben charged the door, banging hard on it.

Sally mentally counted the seconds it would take for Molly to remove the strings and slide from the room via the window. Not to mention the likely fifteen, maybe twenty minutes it would take to get to her horse in the dark. Before she'd come close to how long Molly needed to escape the room without being seen, Sally knew they had plenty of time.

Rather than getting his keys, Reuben banged on the door. He hollered to be let in, and even kicked the footplate several times. He pushed and pulled in a panic she had no intention of cooling quite yet.

It took him nearly five minutes to get his head enough to remember he had keys. If he bothered to pay her any mind she fully intended to seem puzzled, perhaps concerned for his well-being. He seemed to have forgotten she was even there just yet. She also didn't want to interrupt the tirade. The whole plan was for him to fall apart anyhow.

When he flung open the door, she trailed behind him into the office. She glanced around the room quietly while he searched high and low. In his distraction he easily missed her checking above the door to see if the hook was gone. It was, thankfully. That was going to be the hardest part. None of them figured that she'd have to manage to pull all evidence from the back of the door. Even if he looked behind it, he'd be looking low for a person. The strings and hook above the door were most likely to be seen, and all evidence appeared to be gone.

Cold blasted into the room when he flung open the window. He half-hung out the window looking up and down the porch. "Where did she go?"

"Where did who go, Reuben?" Sally moved deeper into the room. "I don't see anyone in here. Not that that's surprising. Dr.'s Young and Cross only fill in a couple days a week, and certainly not this weekend."

"You didn't see her close the door?"

"Who?"

"You didn't see…" He pulled a kerchief from his pocket and dabbed the moisture from his forehead. "You had to have seen."

"What are you talking about? The door was never open." She leaned against the chair Daisy had used for the facsimile of an exam she'd done for the wealthy clientele looking for quick fixes and snake oil. "Are you well?"

"It was open." He shoved his head back out the window. "I saw her."

"Reuben." Sally pulled him from the window and shut it against the cold. "You don't look well. Come, let's get you a drink and calm your nerves."

He didn't fight her lead all the way back to his office. When she pushed him into the chair, he stared out the window.

She poured him a scotch, Daisy's preferred drink, and set it before him. "Drink, Reuben. You look a fright."

He took the glass and slurped it down. "You didn't see anything?"

"I'm afraid not." Sally perched on the edge of the desk. The man had panicked so long that with time for saddling his horse, she felt safe to end the distractions and see him on his way. "You don't look well. Why don't you head home? I'll stay here until the night manager arrives."

"I can't. You're not allowed."

She lifted her chin, ready to lay into him for his insolence, but schooled her thoughts quickly. It wouldn't do to get into an argument right then. "Mike is my uncle, as is Nick. I'm allowed. I'll make sure they understand. Go home, get some rest."

Reuben's gaze lifted toward the now-closed clinic door.

"Come now." She urged him to his feet. Gently she pulled him from the office. "Larry will be here in a couple of hours. I don't mind staying."

"I think I might." Reuben rubbed his hands over his face. "I think I might."

Sally guided him toward the back where he could exit by the stables and gather his horse. The man made slow progress, but the moment he disappeared into the barn she raced through the hotel and out of the front. She'd had a suspicion he'd go toward Daisy's instead of his own place.

She pulled back into the shadows to witness the departure.

Five minutes later the horse came around the hotel slow and steady. Reuben had a lamp with him. He glanced around when he passed the porch. Sally clung tighter to the shadows, glad her cape's hood covered her light hair.

The lamp bobbed and swayed as Reuben moved down the lane. He still didn't rush. Perhaps the man was still in shock.

At the end of the lane the lamps movement paused. Sally could imagine the man looking back and forth toward home and town. The lamp turned left to head north toward town, rather than south toward where Reuben's homestead was.

That meant he'd meet another surprise from Daisy at her small homestead. Another few moments of haunting for him. A haunting to rival Ebenezer Scrooge's. Sally only hoped Molly had had enough time to get set in her next track before the man arrived.

She wished she could witness the event, but she did have to wait until the next manager arrived. Hopefully Tom had shown up to help Molly instead of being distracted by whatever had happened in town.

Tomorrow she'd learn the end results. For the moment, she closed the door to the hotel behind her and settled into the office chair. She hoped against hope it would all work.

For there'd be no better gift for her ma than to have Uncle Mike free.

Well, except to have Cole return home.

Peace visits not the guilty mind.
—Juvenal

Sally yawned her way down the steps. The sounds of screaming laughter and playing from the children reached her before she hit the bottom. Warm hands cupped her cheeks before she'd opened her eyes at the end of the yawn.

"Good morning, dearest." Eunice kissed her cheek. "Your ma is out getting the casino set for a proper Christmas Eve service. I'm minding the children. Do what you need."

"Thanks, Mams. What about Alma? All this joy might send her into a fit."

"Your ma has already seen to her care. She is in the family box watching the activity with one of her favorite books. Seeing how raw her nerves were, Jane wanted to keep her in sight. Said she'd take her to see Willow after a spell."

"I guess everything is covered." Sally wondered at how ma had adapted to her regular absences of late. Then again, she had the extra hands of her parents and James to help out where Sally's presence was lacking.

"There are always things to be done. Don't you worry. If you haven't plans of your own, I don't doubt Jane will set you to a task." Eunice chuckled low. "Go on, enjoy your day. I'm going to enjoy the rest of my grandchildren. I hope you'll be with us for the Christmas Eve service and after, though. I haven't had enough time with you."

"I will be. I only have a few things to get done today." Sally kissed Eunice on the cheek before she left the apartment. Inside the casino Jane directed the placement of a modest tree on the stage from her seat in the audience. At least she was still resting as directed. A pile of plainly wrapped gifts lay to Jane's right. "Ma?"

"Good morning, Sally." Jane kept her attention on the stage. "A little more to the left, Edgar. That's it, perfect. Thank you. Would you go to the mercantile and see if Faith and Abe have finished gathering the gifts for the tree? I only have half of them here."

"Will do, Janey." Edgar hopped from the stage.

Sally descended into the pit. She circled the stack of gifts. They were all small, plainly wrapped, but there were dozens upon dozens. "You said last night that everything burned with the church."

"The ladies got together yesterday, Sally. Where do you think these came from? Lillian, Katherine, Leanne, Faith, Lee, and myself put together the bulk of it. Our mayor helped take up a collection to see to it that everyone in town that attends service has a gift on the tree. They're mostly small trinkets, candy for the children and such, but everyone should have something."

"Ma. This is so much. Are you sure you got everyone?"

Jane cast her an offended look. "You're asking me?"

"Right. Silly question." Sally felt heat rise to her cheeks. Of course. If anyone could ensure everyone was cared for it would be Ma with her exacting memory. "I keep forgetting your memory is far better than mine is."

"I wouldn't say far better. Yours is good enough in the things that are important to you. Plus, you weren't raised from birth to memorize lines." Jane sorted through the gifts. "What are you up to today?"

"I have a few errands to run." Sally kept her answer intentionally vague. She and Tommy had agreed not to get any of the Young's hopes up unnecessarily. Though by all reports from Molly and Tom, the final stage of Reuben's haunting had left him running quick as a jack rabbit back to his own place. Far as she knew, he hadn't made a move to confess to anything so far. "I should be back in time for supper and service. If that's all right, of course. Did you need my help with anything?"

"Not with anything other than what you're doing." Jane's gaze fell on her. A sharp understanding in her eyes. Perhaps she had an inkling of what was going on after all. Or perhaps she just hoped as much. "Your grandmother has things handled with the children, and I have things handled here. I heard word Wil is opening the saloon early for the holiday for some reason. I'm not one to ask questions."

"Yes you are." Sally matched Jane's teasing tone easily. In truth, they'd asked Wil to open early in hopes Reuben would show up so they could keep an eye on him. Also for one more possible visit from his ghost. "I'll swing by the brothel on my way. I'll see you at supper."

"See you then." Jane wove through the seats toward the bar.

Sally took her cue and high-tailed it out of the Inn. On her way past the saloon, she spotted Wil on the porch smoking a cigar. "Morning."

"Morning." He dipped his head in greeting. Several whores lounged near him to advertise the saloons early opening. "Slow start."

"This early in the day I'm not surprised. I'll stop by after a bit for a drink."

"Look forward to it."

Sally continued her stroll down the street at an easy pace. The handful of folks she passed each got a nod and a greeting. In the distance, Tom lounged on the jail's porch, feet on the railing. Noting his stance, Sally didn't rush toward him. Clearly nothing had happened yet, so she kept her easy pace. She took the seat beside him. "Good morning."

"Good morning." He sipped from his canteen, gaze wandering the street endlessly. The man was always at attention, watching for danger. A skill Sally still had to learn. "Sleep well?"

"As well as can be expected with Uncle Mike still inside." She glanced toward the open door. Despite the cold, it sat propped open. She could see Mike lying on his cot, arm draped over his eyes. "How is he doing?"

"As to be expected. I'm afraid Jane's prediction that he'll never be the same will prove true." A tightness took over his tone. His eyes crinkled as though staring at a blazing sun. "Not so much the time spent in there, though that's bad enough. His own doubt over his innocence. It's something that changes a person."

"Ma said as much." Sally shivered from something other than the cold. She cleared her throat. "Ma and the ladies bought gifts for everyone to place on the tree."

"I knew those ladies were up to something. Soon as I saw them gathering after the church caught fire."

"That is the strangest thing, the church catching fire."

"In a virtual sea of strange things of late."

"You're telling me."

"That's something hard to figure, though. By the time it was put out there was probably no footprints to be found. They'd have been melted or trampled. No one saw anything, but by the time Kat saw the fire, it was well caught on. Could have been burning a while."

Sally pondered the puzzle. "Stove, maybe?"

"Cold as ice. Isaac was supposed to light it for the Reverends earlier in the day, but he was running late on his chores and hadn't made it yet." Tom tilted his head to the side. "Show time."

She made sure to school her reaction. When she turned toward the street, she made it slow and casual so no attention was drawn to their conversation. Sure enough, Reuben rode up to the saloon. He'd get a nasty surprise when he arrived. Molly was in place, ready to walk away from the entrance when he got in sight.

With help from the whores inside to hide her escape, she'd slip into the secret room built for the vault. The door wasn't visible to anyone that didn't know it was there.

Will would set her free soon as Reuben took his leave, which would hopefully be right to where she and Tom were sitting.

She took the canteen from Tom, drawing a sip of water while the man climbed the stairs. At the top he paused, then backed down two steps. Then two more. Once again Reuben was giving Molly plenty of time to cover her tracks.

He seemed to get a grip and climbed the stairs again, entering the saloon. Sally sighed as he disappeared from sight. "Once again I'll miss the show."

"You could have waited in the saloon. It's not like you're a stranger there."

"I know, but I was there last night at the hotel. I'd hate to push the luck of coincidence cluing him into anything. I'm far more appropriate here visiting my dear uncles on Christmas Eve."

"Dear might be a stretch."

"Fair enough point." She pushed herself to stand. "I'll head inside and visit with uncle Mike. Will you give a heads up when he heads this way?"

"When? Good optimism. We can't know that he will."

"I'm feeling hopeful."

"Then I'll let you know."

Sally stepped inside. David sat at the desk reading quietly. Occasionally he cast a worried glance Mike's away. At Sally's entrance, he stood. "Sally. It's good to see you."

"And you as well. Will you be at services tonight?" It didn't escape her notice that Mike didn't even raise his head at her entrance. The hope he'd had so recently over his recovered memory seemed to have faded.

"We plan to be. Simon will be guarding tonight unless something comes up that I need to be here. Lee, Marjorie, and Jesse will be there without a doubt."

"Ma will be pleased."

"For them, maybe not so much for me."

She smiled warmly. "She's softened toward you of late."

"A little. Not enough."

"She will. Soon. I hope you don't mind me visiting Uncle Mike."

"Of course not. Let me open the cell for you." David drew beside her, speaking low. "Having the door open seems to help his disposition."

"Holy shit," cried Tom.

"Hold that thought." She set a hand on David's arm to stop him from opening Mike's cell. Through the window she could see Reuben walking toward the jail. That's what had riled Tom for sure. "I think you're about to have company. I'll sit right here."

"Are you sure?" David's confusion creased his features.

"Yes. Go on." Sally took a seat next to Mike's cell. Another chair sat on the opposite side of the bars. "Uncle Mike."

David turned when Tom's bulk shadowed the doorway. "Tom? What's going on?"

"You're about to find out." Tom took a seat on the Sheriff's side of the desk, leaving David's chair empty for him.

Mike finally lifted his head from the pillow. When Reuben entered, he sat straight up. He blinked a few times, then turned his gaze on Sally.

She nodded subtley, then patted the seat beside her.

"Sheriff." Reuben's voice scratched along the word like sandpaper on metal.

"Mr. Miller." David stood behind the desk rather than take his seat. "What can we help you with today?"

"I—I—I did it."

"Did what, exactly?"

"Killed her. Daisy."

The excellence of a gift lies in its appropriateness rather than its value.
-Charles Dudley Warner

Jane awoke with a start to utter silence. As it had every morning since Cole had left, her heart stretched out its aching loss for the warmth that didn't encompass her. She rolled to her left where he always laid. The empty space drew her to run her hand along it.

The night before she'd pulled every Christmas present out of its hiding place, save for those she'd gotten for Cole.

"Merry Christmas," she whispered to the emptiness beside her. "Wherever you are."

Every morning for the past week she'd woken surrounded by children. Not once had any of them, nor anyone else, allowed her time to malinger. This calm moment was both a blessing and a curse. She appreciated the moment to think of him, long for him, and also hated the silence. At the same time she wished those wishing to comfort her had allowed her these moments of longing.

While the quiet lingered, she closed her eyes. An image of Cole's ice blue eyes sparkling with laughter rose in her memory. A wicked smirk, a teasing touch across her hips. The husky whisper of *come here*. The way they'd spend their first few minutes of each and every day wrapped in each other in the quiet of their room.

She could imagine the way his hand would dawdle over the swell of her stomach awaiting a sign of life from the child within. As if it were happening right then, Jane set her own hand on her stomach. She opened her eyes to the empty pillow beside her. "We're here. Waiting for you. You have to know that. Feel it. Wherever you are."

Movement within bumped against her hand. "Come back to us."

One swift, sharp jangle from the bell to the living room interrupted the quiet spell. She'd hoped for more time before the chaos of her apartment and family, followed by the even greater chaos of the massive dinner with staff, friends, and family gathered in the restaurant. Once she added in visits to the clinic to see Willow, and to the jail to see Michael, she wouldn't have another moment to breathe the whole day.

She exhaled the rising tension at the thought of her busy day. With a deep inhale she tried to gather the strength for another day. The knowledge that she'd be able to send another telegram to Cole the next day helped her mood some. The thought that maybe she'd even get one helped her rise to face the day. She threw on her robe on the way the door.

The familiar and heart-warming chaos of the children greeted her upon her exit. At her arrival the younger children raced toward the stockings, except for Jay who still wasn't used to the tradition. The previous year he and Willow had avoided most Christmas activities. Jesse dragged Jay to the stockings and soon they were all tearing in.

Eunice handed Jane a mug of tea. "Merry Christmas."

"Merry Christmas." Jane kissed her cheek, then went along to do the same with her pa, Tom, Sally, Nick, and Alma. By the time she managed to sit there was a knock on the door.

"I've got it." Sally leapt from the sofa to open the door. She exclaimed. "Uncle Charlie! What's this?"

Jane moved to stand again, seeing her brother and Millie both enter. Millie held George, but not for long as the second she'd seen him Eunice took the child from her arms. Jane nodded to Charlie. "Charles. I wasn't expecting you until supper."

"I wanted to deliver a surprise gift." Charlie winked a second before he stepped aside to reveal Willow standing behind him.

"Willow!" Jane rushed forward to sweep the child into a hug. She was quickly pushed aside by Jay who dragged his sister into the merriment. Jane clasped Charlie's hand. "She's truly free to come home? I thought you said it would be another few days at least."

"I wanted to surprise you." Charlie hugged her tight. "She'll need to continue treatments at home, but I know you, Ma, and Ada can manage."

"This is about the best present I could have gotten." Jane turned to watch the children playing with the small trinkets and treats she'd put in their stockings. Willow was already ensconced with the rest of the children, chatting as eagerly as the rest. For a moment they seemed a complete family. Only missing a few pieces. Her heart twisted again. "Just about the best."

Charlie pulled her into another hug. Thankfully he offered no words of comfort that were likely to set her crying. He released her quick enough to avoid such a fate as well. Instead, he waded through the children toward the stack of presents under the window.

Jane sat on the edge of the settee and presents were handed around. While presents were exchanged, opened, and exclaimed over, she sipped her tea. For every gift handed her way, she made her own exclamations of delight and thanked them all.

When the last present had been unwrapped, the children got lost in play. Sally and Alma both read one of their new books. The men headed outside to tend to the animals. Seeing her chance, Jane rose to get herself dressed and enjoy a few more moments of peace.

Though the spell of her morning had been wiped away, perhaps she could find another moment for such thoughts. She didn't realize Eunice had followed her into the room until the door closed not by her doing. A small cry of surprise startled free. "Goodness. I didn't know you were following me."

"I merely wanted to check on you. You don't look well. Tired."

"I am tired, but no more than is to be expected." At her mother's look, she couldn't help but admit, "Fine. Perhaps a little more tired than usual. I don't sleep well when Cole isn't here. The children try, but it's not the same. I think lack of sleep is causing these headaches."

"I know how difficult it can be." Eunice smiled sadly. "Add in all your other worries. Willow, Michael. I myself haven't slept well since he was put in jail."

Jane perched on the bed beside her mother. "I feel terrible worrying so much over Cole. He's a grown man and is capable of taking care of himself. The news of the storm relieved me for a time. It's just—I know what he's going out there to face. I have no reason to worry that he'd…"

Eunice set her hand on Jane's. "We always worry. Just as we had no reason to doubt Mike's innocence, we still worried that the rest of the world wouldn't see it the same. It's perfectly natural to worry."

"It seems so silly when there are so many greater things people are dealing with. I mean, your son is in jail for a murder he didn't commit."

"Greater troubles elsewhere don't impact the troubles you're dealing with." Eunice pulled Jane close until her head rested on her mother's shoulder. "Plus, there's something else. Something so simple, yet so deep that it affects everything."

"What's that?"

"You miss him."

"I do. So much." Tears burned at the back of her eyes until they slipped free. "If I'd heard anything I imagine it would be lessened."

"Most likely it wouldn't. Missing those you love doesn't lessen with correspondence. Believe me." Eunice sighed. "When your pa would need to travel for even a few days my moods were affected. Being so far from most of my children affects me as well."

"I'm sorry they all came here."

"My worry is eased knowing my precocious child drawn to trouble is being watched over by so many of her brothers."

Jane laughed weakly, too amused to be annoyed by the statement. "I suppose there is that."

"It's a blessing and a curse."

"I should let you go. There is much cooking to be done." Jane blew out a long breath. "I'll be all right. Once I gather myself together, it will be as if I weren't this ridiculously despondent."

"As will I." Eunice sighed alongside her. "We can sit here a few more minutes."

"If we must." Jane smiled when her mother chuckled. After all, neither of them made one motion toward departing their embrace. "Can I tell you something?"

"Of course."

"Cole and I are married."

"I suspected as much." Eunice patted her hand. "Even if you weren't, you were."

"That makes no sense."

"I disagree. It makes perfect sense. Anyone with eyes can see how much you two love each other. Even if you try to brew up scandal at every turn you have been rather devoted from early on if your brothers are to be believed. Although sometimes they like a good tale to spin."

"They weren't spinning too much. We have been, even when we didn't want to be."

"When did you marry in the legal sense?"

"Three years ago, right after I became partner in the Inn."

"I see." Eunice squeezed her hand. "Why haven't you told anyone?"

"At first it was because we didn't do it for anyone else, and it was a little game. Then it became habit. Right before

Cole left we decided to reveal the truth on his return." Jane straightened, determined to get herself together before facing the rest of their gathering. "I wish we had. I'm tired of the whispers over his departure. They work on my nerves."

"As they should. Although even if you had, they'd still gossip."

"Quite true." Tension remained woven through her muscles, but Jane rose from the comfort of her mother. "We shouldn't dawdle longer."

"There is much to be done." Eunice brushed a lock of curls behind Jane's ear. "You can always talk to me, my darling girl. I know sometimes you don't feel like my daughter, but I am always a safe space."

"I know. Thank you."

*The spirit in which a thing is given determines
that in which the debt is acknowledged;
it's the intention, not the face-value
of the gift, that's weighed.*
—Seneca

Jane wove through the tables setting silverware down at each place. A low hum of cheerful activity reached through every part of the restaurant and into the casino where the children played. In the kitchen Patrick chatted cheerfully with the working women, his foot absently rocking the bassinet that held George and Marjorie.

Staff, guests, friends, and family alike gathered in pockets of discussion. Jane tried to convince herself of paranoia. It only *seemed* like several of the groups would glance her way every few minutes. Her hearing being what it was, with her right ear near deaf from scarlet fever a few years back, she wasn't able to easily eavesdrop to reassure herself over such a silly thought.

Christmas day wasn't the day for such suspicion and worry. She tried to shake off the thoughts to return to her task. Once the tables were set she moved to where Tommy stood. "Think they'll allow me in the kitchen?"

"Not on your life. We all want good food today." Tommy clapped her on the back.

"Rudeness." Jane smacked his belly. "You'd best be careful. I'll make a special trip simply to fuss with your plate if you keep it up."

"I'll shackle you to the desk before I let you fiddle with my plate." He leaned on the registration desk. At first his voice was too quiet to hear clearly, even deep as it was, from her right side. Then he turned to level his gaze on her. "I said, why do you look so morose?"

"I don't look morose."

"Not all the time, true. I've noticed your consternation while you've walked around setting the tables."

"It isn't consternation. More paranoia."

"It's not paranoia if it's true." Tommy nodded toward some friends and staff gathered near the stairs. "They're curious. Some a little suspicious. It seems over three years of devotion didn't stop them from wondering when he'd turn tail."

"Norman asked me flat out last week. It hasn't helped my nerves."

"He spent the better part of fifteen years the consummate rake, don't forget. That's all any of them bothered to know before you came along. Plus, they don't know about…" His gaze flicked briefly on the ring she wore. She didn't wear it in the traditional location, and it had been her grandmother's so they could pass it off as an heirloom, not a wedding ring.

"And they love to gossip." She turned away from the scene to glance in the kitchen again. With her left ear on him now, she leaned against the counter. "Please tell me that isn't all they're discussing. It has to be boring to be so set on one subject."

"Nah. There's plenty to gossip about."

"I suppose that's true."

"There's Mike, Cora's shooting, the church fire, all sorts of gossip to fill their coffers." He squeezed her arm. "I merely wanted to reassure you that your paranoia isn't unfounded."

"Is that supposed to help or hinder me?"

"I hadn't figured that out."

"Maybe you should have." She elbowed his side, chuckling with him. "Because it might be making me feel rather worse."

"I'm not too concerned."

"Oh?" She turned to study him more intently. Something was up. His stubbornly dark and angry features of late were far lighter. A spark lit in his eyes she hadn't seen in quite some time. "What has you in a mood?"

"No mood."

"Liar."

"It's Christmas. I've got my woman in the next room. I've also got my overly annoying sister pestering me."

"Speaking of—where is Nicholas? More so, where's David? I thought Simon and Bruce were covering duties seeing as they're bachelors. For that matter, Bruce should be here for first dibs, with Simon coming after."

"How on earth am I supposed to know what David is up to, woman? Why are you so damned nosey today?"

"Oooh, you're defensive. What's going on?"

"Nothing." Despite his words, he wore a wicked sort of grin. "Go enjoy your day. Make sure your children aren't tearing apart the casino. I'm sure David will be along soon enough. His wife and children are here, after all."

"No, no." Jane held her finger in front of his face to stop him moving. She'd seen the look he bore before. "No, sorry. You've got that same look about you."

"There's no look."

"There is, and you are wearing it. It's the same look you had when you helped Cole arrange to have every boy in town bring me a fresh caught fish from the creek."

Tommy laughed outright. "That was hilarious. The look on your face. It took you weeks to get the smell out of the library."

"It was not funny. I've moved libraries and the odor still lingers in some of the books."

His loud guffaw startled silence out of every conversation for a moment before the hum resumed. "I'm surprised you didn't simply replace them."

"I'm not going to throw away a perfectly good book. I air them out every chance I get." A small kick to her belly drew her hand to the spot it had landed.

Tommy's gaze drifted to her hand.

Before she could say anything, Nick and David entered the Inn together. They paused in the doorway, both grinning broad as anything. Nick opened his mouth first, but he only shouted, "Ma!"

Jane left Tom to approach the pair of men. "What are you two doing? You're late."

"We are," Nick agreed. Already his grin had been replaced with his usual stoic expression. She couldn't deny the light of laughter dancing in his deep blue eyes.

"But with good reason." David squeezed her arm in reassurance.

"What reason?"

Eunice emerged from the kitchen, wiping her hands on a towel. "What is all the shouting about, Nick? We're very busy, you know."

"Believe me, you won't mind." Nick didn't allow time for further protest. He moved aside, and David followed suit.

Climbing the steps toward him, his head down, came Michael. He lifted his head at Eunice's scream. A smile barely managed to form before his mother crushed him into a hug.

Jane clutched David's arm tight, unable to find words. It seemed incredible he was standing there being brutally hugged by their parents. Hope flared against the doom that had been pushing her down for days. She turned to David. "What's this?"

"He's free. There's been a confession." David wrapped an arm around her shoulders. "I'm sorry it took so long, and I arrested him so quick. It's your kin you need to thank for this, though. I don't know what they did, but Reuben was scared silly."

Jane looked back to Tommy, who had been joined by Sally. The pair watched Eunice and John gushing over their son. Each of them wore a huge, bright smile. Though Jane wanted to see her brother, she figured Eunice would take some time. Instead, she crossed to Tommy and Sally. "You two did this?"

"With Molly's help, and a little inspiration from Ebenezer Scrooge." Sally's grin grew more when Jane clasped her hands. "I'm only sorry we scared you first."

"I don't even care. Thank you." Jane hugged her tight, then moved on to Tommy. "You have both made Ma's Christmas. Mine, too."

Tommy offered a gruff grumble to her brutal hug. When Mike approached, Jane stepped aside so he could thank his brother and niece. Jane remained silent during the exchanges, studying her brother's features intently.

He smiled and expressed gratitude, everything he should be. A tightness lingered in his shoulders, and his eyes were tired. He was pale, no flush of life and color. The man was exhausted and overwhelmed already. He'd been alone, despite their frequent visits, for too long. When he finally turned her way, she held out her hands.

He ignored them to pull her into a crushing hug. Without argument, she returned it in kind. They both held on for a long time before Mike finally spoke. "Thank you."

"Me? What did I do?"

"You always believed. You got angry for me when I couldn't. You let me feel whatever I was feeling without judgment."

"I've been there, remember? Maybe not as long as you were, but I was there too." She released her tight hold so she could meet his gaze. His smile didn't reach his eyes. Pain lingered there instead. "Keep your coat on."

"What? Why?"

"Meet me by the door in a few minutes. Go on." Jane dashed back to the apartment to get her thick wool coat. By the time she returned, Mike stood talking to Cora and Leanne near the door as she'd asked. "Cora, if you don't mind, I'm going to steal my brother. We'll be back soon. How long until supper?"

"No worries. We'll all have plenty of time to chat now. And we have about another hour until supper is ready." Cora gave Mike's hands another squeeze before she and Leanne returned to the kitchen.

Jane laced her arm through Michael's and steered him out of the Inn. They walked through the quiet streets in total silence. Mike didn't even ask where they were going. She wondered at his lack of curiosity. "You're not going to ask?"

"No. I think I know."

That explained it. Then again, the direction they walked led to only a few places. "All right, then. How are you really doing?"

"I don't even know." Mike sighed deeply. "Reuben came to the jail yesterday and admitted everything. I sat right there as he confessed."

"Wait. Yesterday?"

"Yes. I think they wanted to surprise everyone on Christmas and took their time releasing me. I mean, my cell door stood open and I was able to walk about freely. David offered to let me sleep at their place last night. I almost took him up on it. Part of me wanted to kill Reuben myself, the rest of me was just…"

"So very tired."

"Yes."

"You've been fighting everything for weeks. Christmas was a terrible day to release you. I mean, it's lovely for all of us, but far too much for you to bear. So many people gushing."

"So very many."

"Here we are." Jane pushed open the gate to the cemetery, leading him through the crosses to the one they'd come for. "Would you like privacy?"

"No. Yes. I…"

"I won't be far." Jane kissed him on the cheek, then looked down at Daisy's cross. "She knows the truth. Remember that."

"Thank you."

Doubt is not a pleasant condition,
but certainty is absurd.
–Voltaire

Jane kept Mike at her side as much as possible so he wouldn't get overwhelmed by all of the joyful glee over his release. When it came time for supper she dropped him in place at the table, assuring him she would be gone only a few minutes. She then headed toward the office for the special bottles of mead she'd ordered.

General chaos still ruled the restaurant as food was carried out to the large table they'd set up as a buffet for easier dining. It would take far less time for everyone to get their own food at one place than to hand around endless platters.

The children hovered near the dessert table. Clara tried to grab nearly every dessert in her tiny reach, with Jesse keeping her hands off the food. Sally held Colton, pointing out the various treats. The young woman snuck both of the youngest children one of Lillian's gingerbreads. She flushed when she caught Jane watching, but grinned and shrugged. She mouthed *It's Christmas.*

Jane shook her head, slipping into the office to grab the mead. While gathering it, a conversation that had to have been quite close by reached her.

"Wondered why he didn't skip out sooner. All them kids they got? Musta been driving him crazy." Edgar, of all people, spoke in a low, deep tone that carried under the reigning din.

Phyllis' voice wasn't as deep, and Jane had to strain to hear it. "Thought he was happy, though…well, then the brothel came along."

"I knew it then," agreed Edgar.

Jane intentionally rattled the case of bottles as she left the office. Mike offered a protest to her lifting and came to free her of the burden. Jane thanked him, her gaze fixed on the small group of staff near the reception desk.

They all quickly looked anywhere but her, exclaiming over the table brimming with food. The near constant headache she had any longer pressed behind her eyes until her vision blurred a moment.

She shouldn't be mad at them. This was all her doing. All her own fault, really.

In recent months they'd truly been playing the game of scandal without shame. It had all been such a laugh, but it didn't feel that way any longer. And Edgar? He'd been employed at the saloon before it became a hotel. He'd seen so much of her and Cole's relationship as it had grown. He, at least, had the decency to look abashed at being caught.

Millions of words bubbled in her head, but she burst each one with her own anger and instead went to her seat silent as a church mouse. Slowly everyone came to sit at the table. Little by little the bustle settled into quiet murmurs.

Whispers of conversation reached her good ear as the final trays made their way to the buffet.

Flickers of Cora, and Mike, the brothel, Cole, murder, fire, and back to Cole. She closed her eyes and wished for the briefest moment to be deaf as Lizzie. Now that she paid attention, she could hear it all, and she'd rather she couldn't. There was enough to worry about.

Yet, how dare they?

Reverend Lyons cleared his throat as he rose to his feet. Jane tried to release the tension of anger, knowing it could only help her pounding head. She feared it instead erupted into the grip she had on her brother's hand while Eli offered his blessing over the meal. While everyone moved to get food from the table, Jane sat quiet to wait her turn.

In truth, her appetite had fled. Her anger hadn't only made her headache increase, but flared the uncomfortable indigestion she'd been suffering as well. She didn't miss the fact that both Mike and Tom cast worried looks her way. It would do to have them fuss over her.

To appease them, she rose with her plate to get some food she didn't much feel like eating. Children bustled around her and darted back to the table. Several people still had to get food and moved toward the buffet as well.

When Mike joined her with his own plate, she released a shaky breath.

"At least in jail I didn't have to hear them discussing me and my troubles right behind my back," he muttered.

"I'd say you get used to it, but when it's painful it's harder to get used to."

"Anyone that says he'd leave you is a fool." Mike's brief comfort helped, only to be interrupted by another.

"But then why ain't he back?" Norman reached over to grab some more potatoes for his plate.

"*Stop it*!" Jane didn't realize she was going to shriek until the high tone erupted from her lips. The plate she held dropped from her shaking hands to clatter to the table. She spun on the gaping crowd. "He's your damn friend. Has been for years. You should know him by now. He's not gone. He wouldn't leave me. Leave us, damn it. We're married!"

Pure, undiluted silence fell over the room like a blanket of thick snow.

Jane's racing heart settled into embarrassed calm at the tableau before her. Nobody moved a muscle except her mother, Thomas, and Leanne. The three of them had known. Even Kat was still, but humor danced across her features.

A hand touched her arm gently. Mike spoke into the silence in a gentle tone. "You're what?"

"Married. For three years now. He loves me and he didn't turn tail. He wouldn't. We agreed to this child together, it wasn't…it isn't…oh."

Tears burst from their confines. Jane tore through the room at their first appearance. What an outburst. Why couldn't she have held it in for a little longer? Mike had far more right to anger than she did.

She slammed her bedroom door, locking it tight behind her. The silence in the room mocked her. Why she'd come here, she didn't know. He wasn't there, hadn't been for weeks.

All of the wonderful surprises she'd received for Christmas. Willow's return. Mike's release. She should be eternally grateful, and the gratitude was there. Yet she still looked for one more miracle. One she had convinced herself wasn't coming when he hadn't arrived on yesterdays train. Or she thought she had.

A key turned in the lock. Jane spun in surprise. Before the door opened a renewed flame of hope that Cole had returned rose unbidden. The appearance of Tom instead doused that flame harshly. She sobbed, flinging herself onto the bed.

The door lock clicked again and the bed shifted as Tom sat beside her. He said nothing at all while she cried. Only form of comfort he offered was to rub her back. He held his silence until she began to gather herself together. "That was quite the show, Lou. They'll be talking about it until the sweetheart dance. Maybe even beyond."

"Not helping," she mumbled into the bed.

"If you were looking to end the gossip, I gotta say that was the wrong way."

"Still not helping."

"I told him."

That gave her pause. She sniffed back further tears. His words could be interpreted in so many different ways. She pushed off the bed to sit. "Elaborate."

"I told Cole about the baby. In my last letter and telegram both. Sent them about four days ago. I figure if we don't hear anything by the time the telegraph is fixed, there's a real problem."

"I can't be mad about it." She offered a weak smile when he looked at her askance. "Maybe I should be, but I only want a word, just one. Knowing about the storm helped for a bit, but now I worry that something happened during the storm. What if he's injured? I doubt there's a doctor in that town. What if..."

"We aren't going to even think it." Tom wrapped an arm around her shoulders. "So don't you dare even say it. He's fine. Idiot probably didn't think to head down the mountain to ease your mind. He's not really quick up there, you know. Years around you and he still isn't quick."

"Stop it." Despite her attempt to scold, she laughed. For the brief moment it lasted, the cheer felt good. When Tom really worried, she knew she should be panicked. If he wasn't there yet, she could maintain a semblance of hope. "Even you've been impressed by him a few times."

"I guess so. The case for the casino impressed a lot of people. I'm pretty sure they all think you wrote it."

"They're wrong. That was all Cole." Jane rested her head on his shoulder. "Well, I've gone and made a scene. Now I look a fright."

"You really do."

"You're a jerk."

"I am. You'll get no argument here. This jerk is going with you to California if there's still no word in the next few days. Before the new year arrives we'll be on a train."

"Thank you. I shouldn't think the worst, I know it."

"Your lifetime of experience leads you down dark holes. I understand that."

"I know you do, and I appreciate it." She pushed to her feet. It would be best to get cleaned up. She crossed to the basin to cool the heat of tears that lingered on her cheeks. A glance in the mirror showed the blotchy evidence of her breakdown. "What a mess. I hope I didn't upset Alma with my little display."

"Alma is fine. She was in the casino with Arthur, Shelly, and Cord. Arthur got her food for her so she wouldn't have to face all the jubilation, especially with Mike's return."

"Arthur I understand. Shelly and Cord?"

"They're friends of Arthur's. Their parents work here, you know. He has to go back to Denver soon. I think he wanted to make sure she had someone other than you, Sally, and Leanne to help."

"Cora raised a fine young man. I do hope he finds someone that wants the same life he does." Satisfied with her appearance, she turned back to her brother. "Shall we? I might as well face what chaos my pronouncement has wrought."

He offered his arm. "Let's go enjoy the chaos."

"Sounds like—Sally."

Soon as the door had opened, they found Sally at the apartment door. "I came to check on you, Ma."

"I'm better now, thanks to this brute."

"You and Pa are really married?"

"Yes. We really are." Jane grunted at the impact of the hug she got from Sally. "Goodness."

"That's so wonderful." Sally straightened as though she hadn't nearly squeezed the life out of Jane with her hug. "I'm going to warn you now, Jesse is beside himself out there. Upset he didn't know, but so very excited. Of course, hardly anyone knew."

"This is true. For a long time the only souls that knew were Tom, Nick and Leanne. You know what, I have a feeling this explanation is going to bear repeating often. Let's go to the feast so the story might be shared far fewer times."

"I just wish Pa was here to tell the story with you."

"He was supposed to be. We'd both agreed it was time to share it, and planned to upon his return. I simply couldn't stand the rumors and muttering any longer and lost control." Jane kept her arm laced with Tom's as Sally closed the door. "Tom and I are going to go after him if he doesn't send us any word in the next few days."

"I can go. Tom should stay." Sally cast a nervous glance at her uncle. "You've got—"

"You have things handled on the detective work. You've also proven capable of handling the library, brothel, and casino these past weeks." Tom brushed off Sally's protest. "Plus, you'll have Ma and Pa to help, as well as James. They won't be leaving for a few more weeks."

"I—you want me to handle the investigation myself?" Sally flushed. Her fingers danced nervously over her reticule.

"You've got Molly to help."

Jane squeezed Sally's hand. "You can handle things. We've seen how capable you are. Don't worry so much."

"I didn't think I was ready. There's still so much to learn."

"Nothing says you can't learn while you work. Most people learn that way."

As a cure for worrying,
work is better than whiskey.
—Thomas A. Edison

Jane wiped down the bar around the glass of beer she'd set there. Hammy was several minutes late, which was unusual for him. She imagined the discussion around the new church was running late. Right as she was about to take the beer back, she spotted him entering the casino.

She smiled at his approach. "Mr. Hamm. You're running a few minutes late today."

"Sure am, Mrs. Mitchell." He wasted no time using her revelation from Christmas Day to his advantage. "I want to do the church like the Reverends want. The council sees it different. 'Cept for Kat, she was on my side."

"As all of them should be. We've no need for something obscene. A church isn't about the building, it's about the congregation. We proved that with our Christmas Eve service right here in the casino, where services will continue to be held until they're able to find something else."

"Really? You're gonna have church here?"

"We are. I spoke to Reverend Greene about it after the Christmas Eve service. There's enough space, and we don't offer gambling on Sundays."

"That's right good of ya."

She squeezed his hand. "You stick to your guns on the new church. Kat and I will have a chat with Lillian and see if we can't get more minds on our side."

"Much obliged." He slurped his beer. "Ya really been married so long?"

"I really have. Granted, you started calling me Mrs. Mitchell before it happened, but I never minded." She kissed his cheek when she saw Mike enter. "Finish your beer, I'll be right back."

Mike hugged her the moment she got in range. "Hey."

"Have you slept at all?"

"Too much. I've been asleep since I left here. A whole day and a half. In the hotel."

"The hotel?" Jane led him to a chair and took the one beside him. "Why the hotel?"

"I think I'm going to sell the homestead. Maybe I'll build one closer to the hotel." He rubbed his hand over his face, which erased some of the sleepiness that lingered there. "Either way, since we don't have a lot of guests right now, I'll be staying in the hotel."

She understood. The homestead likely reminded him too much of Daisy and life before jail. She never went back to her homestead after she'd survived her hanging, insisting David keep it for him and Jesse. He still lived there with Lee. "That sounds like a good idea. Will you be hiring someone else to help?"

"I asked Nick to find someone. I'm not trusting myself too much right now."

Jane set her hand on his. The last thing she'd do was chastise him for such a thought. She'd had them herself when she and Cole had been betrayed by a member of their staff. "It's difficult when people we trusted betray us."

"Are you talking about Reuben? Or Daisy?"

"Yes."

"I sure can pick them."

"You can. Daisy was different, wounded. You would have found resolution if she hadn't been killed. Reuben is the anomaly, and he's one man. Outside of him, you've already surrounded yourself with good people." She lifted a brow when he turned a glare on her. "Don't give me that look. I know all too well at you're feeling. Well, maybe the exact same thing didn't happen, but we were betrayed, too. By people we trusted. It's even happened to Thomas."

"It stings like mad."

"It really and truly does."

"What does?" Tom flopped into the chair across from Jane. "Brothel's good. Wil and Garit thanked us again for Christmas dinner."

"I'm glad they decided to make it over." Jane kept her hand on Michael's. "As to what stings, we were talking about betrayal by people we trust."

Tom's gaze flickered across the room before it returned to her. "That so?"

"What with what happened with Iris a few years back, and with what Michael's going through now. Why? Do you have something else to tell me?" Not for the first time Jane saw the flicker of guilt that crossed his features. Much as it had in the moments before he'd revealed he'd found Clara three times when she'd been hiding from her old life.

"Nah. I already told you, remember?" He turned to Mike. "We're resilient folk. With time it'll pass. Always does."

"It won't if Ma keeps doting. I'm glad she's here, but it's a lot." Mike scratched the back of his neck. "I'm relieved she's distracted by Jane's horde of wildebeests for most of the day."

"My children are not a horde."

"I beg to differ." Mike laughed softly, a wonderful sound that she couldn't deny for her own annoyance. He squeezed her hand. "I think Tommy can agree. When they set on attacking, it's a horde without a doubt."

"He's got a point." Tom chuckled. "I have to say I'm glad you decided to have all of these children. I never wanted any myself. You having so many means we aren't being berated by Ma to have them."

"Just for that, I'm going to tell her to hassle you to death about children."

"Devil woman."

Jane laughed heartily for what seemed the first time in ages. Hope didn't seem so out of reach with her brother out of jail and Willow out of immediate danger. All that remained was for a telegram to arrive and she'd be able to breathe again for real.

Tom kicked her shin. "You listening?"

"What? Oh. No. Sorry."

"I was just at the depot. Norman said he hasn't heard that the lines are fixed yet. He's hoping to hear something by the end of the day. Then you gotta give it time, there's a backlog."

"Patience may be a virtue, but it isn't one of mine." Jane's shoulders slumped. She knew he was right, of course, but she couldn't help hoping. "I'll do my best."

"I still can't believe you kept your marriage hidden for three whole years." Mike shook his head, leaning back in his seat. "You got married and didn't tell me. I thought you couldn't keep a secret from me."

"Our marriage had nothing to do with you. The only reason this idiot knew was because Cole needed his help in asking me. They both did horrible with it, but that's another story."

"One I'd really like to hear."

Jane leaned forward, eager to share the more detailed story with her brother now that all was out in the open. "Do you remember the fight Cole got in with Al?"

A crash behind her startled Jane to his feet. Hammy and Olive lay in a tangled pile on the floor along with the tray of drinks that had made the crash. Glass sparkled on the carpet and Hammy struggled to get to his feet all while apologizing profusely.

"Gilbert." Jane rushed to his side. "Please be careful. You'll cut yourself."

"S-s-sorry." Hammy stumbled a bit when Tom hauled him to his feet quite fast. "I didn't see ya."

"No harm, Hammy. Right, Olive?" Tom brushed sparkles of glass from Hammy's coat.

"Just stunned is all." Olive got to her feet on her own, brushing her own skirt. "He musta moved same time as I backed away from the table there. We collided. You all right, Hammy?"

"So sorry," Hammy mumbled. His hands brushed over his head several times. "Head. Hat."

"Right here." Mike scooped the hat from the ground and dropped it on Hammy's head. He urged Hammy away from the glass he was still walking over. "You've got a few cuts from the glass there, Hammy. Why don't I run you by the clinic on my way out? I'm heading that way."

"Nah." Hammy's hands shook as he rubbed them along his coat. "I'm always cut up anyhow. No harm done."

"Hammy, please. For me." Jane clasped his hands in hers despite the blood and possible glass still covering them. "Let Charles give you the once over and I won't say another word about it."

"Aw, Lady Jane. All right, I guess. If ya insist." Hammy's cheeks darkened. "For you I'll do it, Mrs. Mitchell."

"Thank you." Jane kissed him on the cheek. She leaned close to Mike before he moved to follow Hammy. "Have Charles check him. He stumbled at supper yesterday, too."

"Will do." Mike kissed her on the cheek, then led Hammy from the casino.

Tom turned his attention to Olive. "What about you? Any bumps we need Charlie to check on for you? The pair of you took quite a tumble."

"Yes, you did. Did you get cut at all, Olive?" Jane moved forward to her waitress.

"Nothing hurt worse than my pride." Olive gestured to the floor. "Never dropped a drink once. Now look at this. What a mess."

"Accidents happen. Don't you worry about it. We'll clean it up." Jane picked the tray up off the floor. "If you're certain you're fine, go ahead and keep on with what you were doing. Tom and I have this handled."

Jane stared at the mess of glass and soaked carpet. "I'll grab the broom. Will you get the towels for me?"

"On it."

Together they set about cleaning the mess. It took almost a full hour before the glass was cleaned away to Jane's satisfaction. When she grunted her way to her feet, John emerged from the back. A crooked grin creased her pa's features. "Having trouble getting to your feet?"

"Let me attach a child to your belly and we'll see how well you move, Pa." Jane laughed despite her complaint. "What are my children up to?"

"Alma and Sally went to the library. Sally's friend joined them."

"Molly?"

"Yes, Molly." John led her to the bar and sat her on a stool. He circled around behind. "I came out here to get you to rest a while. Your ma said you haven't been feeling well and should be taking it easy."

"I don't know the meaning of those words."

"You know the meaning of all the words." John chuckled as he poured them both coffee. "I have found in many years of marriage that when Eunice says so, you do it. Almost every single time she's right."

"Maybe you should talk to Cole."

"I think Cole knows my secret already." He sipped his coffee, scanning the room. "Business is good for this early in the day."

"Most folks are still off due to the holiday. I think most of this week will be good business."

"Good news."

"Always." Jane sipped her coffee, studying the half-crowded floor in interest. "You know, I think I'll send out word that there will be an extra night in the Gold and Silver rooms this week. Should liven the place up even more. The Burlesque is scheduled for Friday and Saturday both, so we'll throw in some gambling for the high rollers."

"Even better." John poured another mug of coffee. He slid to Tom when he walked behind the bar. "Son."

"Pa." Tom sipped his coffee. "We've got things handled here, Jane. Why don't you go relax?"

"Why does everyone keep telling me to relax?" Jane polished off her coffee. "Telling me to relax has the exact opposite effect. You are aware of this."

"I'm just trying to help." Tom held his hands aloft. "If you'd rather sit and stress, that's on you. Maybe you can knit and stress since you've taken a liking to it."

Jane narrowed her eyes for his jab at the new hobby her mother had foisted on her that she was loathed to admit she enjoyed. It did help her sit still while still feeling busy because her hands were working. "What I would rather do is continue to sit and enjoy my business. Sally has the library handled and you already told me there was no word at the depot, so what else am I going to do?"

"Sorry, sorry."

Jane hopped off the stool. "Then again, something smells really good. I'm going to go peek in the kitchen and see what Cora's up to."

"Leave some for the rest of us."

"Hush."

*Blessed is he who expects nothing,
for he shall never be disappointed.
-Alexander Pope*

Jane ran the final calculations in the ledger and was pleased with what she saw. Despite the low clientele in the Inn at the moment, they were still doing well. The brothel and the gambling rooms both had much to do with the matter. She was relieved they had them.

A tug on her sleeve brought her attention away from the numbers. Willow stood beside her, hands behind her back. "I have something for you."

"You do?" Jane shut the ledger in the desk and locked it in place. She shifted so she could face Willow directly. "Whatever for?"

"Christmas."

"That's very kind. I wasn't expecting anything at all. Somehow all of you children have surprised me anyhow."

Withdrew her hand from behind her back. She held out a reticule to Jane. The entire thing had been beaded intricately with flowers and vines. A hummingbird hovered over one of the flowers.

"Oh. My goodness." Jane drew the purse closer. She ran her fingers over the intricate beadwork covering the front of it. "This is beautiful, Willow. You did this for me?"

Willow nodded quietly. "I sold some to Mrs. Kilmurry for the purse. She…she said you liked to wear these."

"I very much do. I always wear a reticule on me. This is absolutely stunning. I'll wear it proudly. Thank you." Jane pulled her into a warm hug. The girl responded with one of her own. Jane sighed happily in relief. She knew there was still a ways to go, but she finally felt like they were making progress.

When the hug finished, Jane rose to immediately replace the purse she'd been wearing with the new once. Once all of her supplies were moved, she turned this way and that to show it to Willow. "What do you think?"

Willow smiled shyly. "It matches."

"Would you look at that? It does match my dress today. Good thing, too. I have errands to run. I'll wear my cape so everyone can see it." Jane cupped Willow's cheek. "Thank you very much. It's a beautiful present."

Willow hugged her again, then rushed off to join her brother at the checkerboard. Jesse had gone home to stay with his pa again the day before, and Jay seemed lonelier for it. Soon as they began playing, Jane nodded to Ada. "I'll return in a couple of hours."

Ada paused the story she'd been reading to the twins to acknowledge Jane. "We'll be here. Willow and Jay finished their lessons early with you here this morning. I'm allowing them play for the afternoon."

"They're welcome to it. Willow isn't due for another treatment until bed, so everything should be done for the day. Except those darn hounds."

"I do the dogs," Jay said even as he focused on the board.

"Then that's settled as well. Thank you, Jay." Jane leaned down to kiss each twin on the cheek before heading to the door. She swung her cape on and stepped into the brisk day. Thankfully it wasn't brutally cold seeing as she wanted to wear her cape.

Her ultimate destination was the mercantile to order supplies to the Inn, but first she wanted to get to the depot in hopes there would be something there for her. Anything, really. Even the shortest of notes saying he was fine would be enough.

Garit nodded from the porch of the saloon, a gesture she returned out of habit more than intent. She paused in front of the dress shop, turning to face it. Though Sally had asked Jane to go in once to see if anything was out of place, that was the last she'd heard of it.

Sally hadn't mentioned anything about Miss Bee's death in some time. Neither had Tom. For that matter, she never heard them speak of the odd deaths and events that had plagued the town over the past six months or so. She didn't doubt they were doing whatever they needed to do.

Was she egotistical for not thinking further on them recently? Had she become so wrapped in her own distraction and worry that she simply ignored the chaos around her unless it involved her directly? Certainly she'd been wrapped in Daisy's murder, but more so what it had done to Mike.

She shook off such thoughts. It wasn't as if she herself was a detective or had any aspirations of such things. Even if her curiosity could rarely be sated, such a thing was not her lot in life. She'd leave it to Sally. Still, she'd make certain to ask the girl later if she'd made any headway.

Now distracted with the wonder of when they'd get a new dressmaker, Jane made her way to the depot. She'd barely made it inside before Norman barked, "There ain't nothing."

Kat turned from her seat at the telegraph. Her brows turned down. "I'm sorry, Jane. We haven't heard anything from Holle Creek except their general broadcast that the lines were back open yesterday."

The familiar nagging worry clenched tighter in her gut. Three days since Christmas. A full twenty-four hours after the telegraph lines had reopened. Still nothing. By then he should have received Tom's letter telling Cole she remained pregnant. For that matter, he should have received the backlog of telegrams from her, as well as her own letters sent over the course of the past month. Yet, there was nothing?

She couldn't keep standing there like a pitiful creature. Her mind raced for something to say.

"Perhaps he's still planning to surprise me by arriving on a train." Her own voice sounded foreign to her ears. Hollow, emotionless. The bitter twist of disappointments knife into her hope left her raw.

"Of course." Kat circled the desk to her side. "That's likely all it is. He's going to show up and be completely taken aback at how much we're ready to knock him down for his lack of communication. He simply figures you don't need daily updates. You'll see. He'll be on tomorrow's train for certain."

"For certain," Jane repeated though she didn't believe it. "I really must get to the mercantile. I have an order to place. Excuse me."

Kat pulled her into a warm hug. "We'll be keeping an eye out for any word. I'll get it to you the second it arrives. I promise."

"I know you will." Jane squeezed Kat's hand before departing the depot. Halfway down the street she realized she hadn't even shown Kat the lovely purse from Willow.

This distraction would do her no good. The disappointment couldn't be bothered to move out of her way, though. She made it to the mercantile without truly seeing where she was going or what she was doing. It wasn't until Faith's greeting reached her that she realized she'd walked the full distance to the store.

Jane placed her order, exchanged pleasantries, and got on her way as quick as she could. Making up her mind to submit to distraction, she headed straight to the library where Sally was. Inside she found both Sally and Alma in the tea area reading books intently. "Sally."

"Hey Ma." Sally marked her page and closed her book. "What are you doing here? I thought I was covering the library this week."

"I wanted to visit with you. I need some distraction."

"You do? Oh." Sally's smile fell. "Still nothing, then."

Jane glanced toward Alma, who despite being nose-deep in a book had her eyes on Jane. Somehow Jane knew that even if she couldn't express it, the young woman understood. "I'm afraid not."

Alma's fingers tapped on the book, and she rocked back and forth. No sound emitted, which meant her nerves were under control for the moment.

"What sort of distraction are you after? We do have a library full."

"Actually." Jane sat across from her. "I want to hear about your investigation. The whole thing. Everything you're doing, what you think. I know it didn't stop with Michael, and I know it started before."

"Are you sure?" Sally cast a wary gaze on Alma. "Now?"

Alma's presence was a problem, especially if the girl understood as much as Jane suspected she did. Jane thought a moment, then turned back to Sally. "You and Molly talk about it when you're here with Alma, so Alma has heard it before."

"True enough." Sally rose. "I'll make some tea, and we'll get started then. I could probably use a fresh pair of eyes on the whole thing anyway. I feel like I'm going in circles."

"Wonderful. I'm happy to be a new pair of eyes. I had a lot of help, but I did solve the mystery of my past."

"If only this were as clear cut as a mad man that could change his face."

"There's always a mad man, or woman."

"That's what the books say, anyhow."

The ideal man bears the accidents of life
with dignity and grace,
making the best of circumstances.
-Aristotle

Sally wandered through the shelves, placing books back in their places. For the moment she was alone in the library. Jane had taken Alma with her for the day. Ada had the youngers, and Mams and Pops were watching the hotel, while Tom watched the brothel. Molly had also decided to hang out at the brothel.

Sally didn't mind the quiet. With two more books she'd have finished her cleaning and could get back to her project. Jane and Tom had both reminded her that constant focus on the mystery could make the answers less clear rather than more, but she couldn't stop.

Soon as the last book slid into place, she rushed down the stairs into the siting area. Laid out across the entire table sat a wide stretch of paper Jane had got her from the butchers, along with several pencils. Sally procured her notebook from her reticule and flipped through the pages.

"I've thought this over and over, rearranged the pages several times," she muttered to herself. Flipping through the pages, she only half paid attention to the notes. "What if I thought about it in reverse for a change?"

She grabbed a pencil to draw a long line down the center of the paper. Toward the right side she made a mark with the date December 24, 1876. Above the date she wrote *Church fire*.

There was hardly a soul that thought the fire had been an accident. After all the stove had been cold, and it was the dead of winter with no sign of lightning in the area. Unfortunately, due to the heat of the fire melting the snow and the hundreds of feet stomping over the area to put out the fire, they had no hope of finding any clues in any proximity to the church.

Thus, alongside the words she scribbled, *Suspicious. No clues*.

One by one she went through all of the odd events and deaths over the previous six months. Cora's shooting, the shadow she'd seen the same night, Miss Bee's strange death, as well as Opal's. Then Chauncey's clear poisoning, and Ellis' less clear accident. She didn't hesitate to include Daisy, even if her murder had been solved. Her own attack, Ma's, Emily's, as well as Keller, Keenan and McKerney. Tully and Lucy were added as well. The whole timeline seemed both completely unrelated, yet also related.

Instinct spurred her on. She went further back than Keller's death to mark more significant events in the town. All events considered 'normal' and unrelated went under the line, while the oddities lingered above it. She included everything from the Centennial celebration, and the statehood, the brothel opening, the library opening, the tornado, and even Reverend Lyon's arrival in May.

By the time she was done the paper was covered in her notes. A foot lingered on either side of the beginning and ending events to add more as she thought of it. She pulled a chair out from the table and climbed up so she could look down at the timeline from a different perspective.

"Everything follows a course, but this one seems so uneven. Each attack that's similar is also different." Once again she pondered the idea of multiple attackers. "But how?"

Her turning thoughts froze when she heard a odd noise. She thought it was perhaps a scream or a yell. She climbed down from the chair and rushed to open the door. The winter breeze stirred along her skirts, but relative quiet met her otherwise. Only a few people wandered this street unlike the main thoroughfares.

"Help," came a muffled yell. "Someone. Please."

Sally darted from the library in search of the source. Despite the few souls wandering further down the street, she yelled into the emptiness. "Hello? Who's calling?"

"Help!" This time she could tell it came from the livery across the street.

She didn't hesitate a second, tearing in the building. A wagon sat askance in the center of the large stable, several more in a row behind it. The horses lining the right side of the barn snorted and stomped. They nickered, bobbing their heads in some upset. "Archie?"

"Help." It was weaker than the yell she'd heard from outside. "I'm…here…"

She found him under the wagon, one arm and his legs trapped by the wagon bed. His head had barely been missed by the wood box. "Dear God, Archie! What happened?"

"Someone…knocked…my supports. Help."

"I'll get help. I'll be right back." She didn't move when he clutched her hand tight. "I promise, Archie. I'll go scream real good and come right back. I won't leave you alone for more than a second or two."

"Hurry."

"I promise." She tore toward the doors and flung them wide open. Tom had tried to teach her the emergency whistle the Young's used, but she hadn't yet mastered it. Instead, she placed her hands around her mouth to scream. *"Help! Help! Tom! Hurry! It's Archie! Anyone, help!"*

Without waiting to see who responded, she ran right back to Archie's side. Less than a minute later she heard the brutal whistle of a Young. She clutched Archie's hand. "They're coming. That was Tommy, or maybe Nick. Either way, they'll be right here to get this thing off of you."

Archie nodded weakly.

"Archie?"

He grunted, his eyes opening again. "Sally."

"That's right. Stay with me, Archie."

"Sally," Tommy called into the livery.

"Under the wagon. It's Archie. The wagon has him pinned." Sally clung to Archie's hand, smiling at him as long as he kept his eyes open.

"Get out from there. You could be hurt." Tom grabbed her shoulder.

She shrugged him off. "I'm not leaving Archie. You guys need to get this off of him. Fast. He's losing consciousness again."

"She's not wrong." This from Charlie. "We need to move fast. Arthur, go get some more men. We have to lift this off of him immediately. I don't want to have to cut off any limbs today."

"Shhh." Sally soothed Archie at Charlie's words. "If anyone can save your limbs, it's Charlie. You're going to be fine. Hurting something fierce, but fine. You got that, Archie?"

He nodded again. Another low grunt emerged.

"Good man." She turned back to find Tom watching her. "He said someone knocked out his supports. This was no accident."

"Not really worried about that right now. The remaining supports can't hold this weight, Sally." Tommy frowned at her. "You need to get out of there."

"I told you. I'm not leaving him."

"He's unconscious."

"I don't care. I promised."

"Stubborn. Just like your ma. Fine. If I tell you to move, you do it. Understood?"

"I understand." Sally kept her hand tight in Archie's despite the fact his grip had weakened. Like Tommy said, he'd gone unconscious. "Please hurry. Please."

"We're working on it. This isn't like lifting a crate of your ma's books." Tommy shuffled about. "More like lifting the entire library's worth."

"Sally?" Arthur's face appeared near Tommy's legs. "You all right?"

"I'm fine. You guys worry about lifting this thing." Sally smiled at his nod, then turned back to Archie.

"Sally?" Charlie's voice reached her from somewhere amidst the mass of shuffling and muttered instructions. "I hate to ask, but do you think you can pull Archie free once we lift?"

"Yes." Sally didn't hesitate to answer. Sure, Archie was a decent sized man, but she'd once dragged Tommy out of a fire and he was bigger. "If I can move Tommy, I can handle Archie."

A chuckle went around the wagon from dozens of mouths. Graham's chortle sounded above the rest. "She's got a damn good point."

"All right. We're going to try on three. Sally, don't move him until we're sure he's free," Tom called from nearby. "Cuddy, watch that support. It's ready to go. It won't be there to help the second the weight shifts."

"Got it," Cuddy acknowledged.

Sally shifted as the count started, moving to grab Archie's shoulders. After three came a great deal of grunting and hollering around her. Someone called, "Sally, go."

Without hesitation she hauled the man back out of the gap between two men where her feet had been. There were plenty of hollers of complaint and strain, but she didn't stop for anything. Dragging him six inches at a time, she finally got him all the way out. "I'm clear."

There was more discussion in strained voices before a loud crash echoed through the building. Horses screamed and stomped at the chaos. Sally lingered near Archie's head. "Archie?"

"I've got him, Sally. We need to get him to the clinic immediately. Andrew, the skid." Charlie brushed her aside so he could examine his patient.

Tom hauled her to her feet, then off to the side to give her the once over. "You're learned too much from your ma. How to scare the pants off your family, first and foremost."

"I really need to learn that whistle." Sally stared at the wagon where it had fallen. Now flat on the floor of the livery. "Who's going to take care of this place for him? We don't know how long he'll be in the clinic."

"Or if he'll even be able to work after." Tom lifted his hat to scratch his head. "No hope of much in clues unless there's something else in the building. Too many hands around the wagon to get it off of him."

"We'll lock it up for now and come back. I want to show you what I've been working on." Sally sighed. "Especially now that I have to add to it."

Tom and Sally both thanked every man that had come to help, then closed and locked the livery. "I'll send Jim over to take care of the horses when he's done in our stables. At least the horses will be cared for. We'll find someone to help take care of the business while he's laid up."

She led him back to the library. The door still hung wide open as she'd left in such a rush. Inside, she moved to add coal to the stove, but something caught her eye. Or rather, a lack of something. She let out a squeak. "Oh no. It's gone!"

"What is?" Tom walked up behind her, scanning the sitting area.

"Everything." Sally ran her hand along the table where her timeline had just sat, as well as her notebook. "My notebook. The timeline. All of it. I left it right here!"

"What?" Tom's expression darkened. "You went and lost your notebook?"

"I…" Sally spun, staring at the stove where the fire burned much too happily for simple coal. The grate sat wide-open, and she knew she'd closed it. She knelt down to look inside. The remains of her notebook flickered in flame. The leather binding hadn't gone, smoldering and smoking. "At least it wasn't stolen, I guess. Oh."

Tom sighed when she sank to the floor. "You'll have to work on your memory, then. Write down every detail you recall in a new notebook. Once you've done that, I'll let you take a look at my notes."

"I don't have Ma's memory." She was fully aware she was whining, but didn't care right then. All that work gone up in smoke. "I can't."

"Then I guess you aren't the detective I thought you were."

"Maybe I'm not."

"Bull."

The secret of a good memory is attention, and attention to a subject depends on our interest in it. We rarely forget that which has made a deep impression on our minds.
—Tyron Edwards

Jane wiped the counter, trying to ignore the frustrated groans coming from the end of the bar. Sally had been sitting there with two notebooks open before her for nearly two hours. Every time she set her pencil to one, she let out another groan and slammed it back on the bar.

Tom had filled Jane in on the disappearance of the notebook that had occurred the day before at the same time as the incident with Archie. While Tom investigated that matter, Sally had been left to reconstruct her notebook. From what Jane could tell, Sally was failing miserably.

Jane made her way down the bar to her ward. "Sally."

"Ma." The miserable droop of Sally's shoulders carried into her morose tone. "I can't do it."

"You can, I have no doubt of that. You're trying too hard to make it perfect, to make it exactly identical to the old one. You can't do that, it won't work for you."

Sally's head flew up, her eyes wide. "Ma!"

"Yes?"

"You saw the notebook. You could recreate it."

"I cannot."

"Yes, you can. You rewrote every single journal after the fire. You can remember every detail, always could. You could recreate this."

"Allow me to be more precise, then. I won't. To do so would defeat the purpose of you doing it yourself." Jane leaned on the bar. "This is about your memory, not mine."

"But my memory isn't like yours."

"I believe we long ago established there aren't many memories quite like mine." Jane set her hand on the open notebook. "Take it one thing at a time. Don't try to remember in sequence or what was on every page. This doesn't have to be chronological. As you remember something, write it down. Then you move onto the next thing. You can rearrange everything once you have everything written down."

"But dates."

"Worry about dates later. If you can't remember what day it happened, write down what you do remember. When you've reconstructed all you can remember, or I suspect in some cases more than you had down, Tom and I can help with dates."

Sally tapped her pencil on the page in front of her. Then her whole body shifted. Excitement straightened her spine and raised her brows. "Oh, oh!"

"What?"

"I gotta go to the butchers. Excuse me, Ma."

Jane chuckled as she tore from the casino. She had no idea what Sally was talking about, but she didn't care so long as the young woman was excited again. Jane turned her attention back to the clock. Five minutes until one. If he was coming to the casino today, Hammy would arrive at any minute.

"What was that all about?" Tom plucked a bottle from the shelf to pour a drink.

"What was what all about?"

"Sally."

"Oh, I was encouraging her to stop trying to remember every precise detail from her notebook and to begin with one thing she remembered. I suggested she forget about chronological perfection and to work on one thing she remembers and keep goin"

"Good idea. That girl was tied up in knots."

"Thank you. It seemed to work, although why she'd run off to the butchers, I'm not certain. I gave her a length of paper from there the other day." Jane poured a beer in preparation of Hammy's arrival. "Are we set for Friday?"

"We are. Tickets are purchased. Are you packed?"

"I've been packed for two weeks." She set the beer on the counter. After a glance toward where Sally had disappeared, she turned her attention to her brother. "Are you certain you can leave Sally behind with only Molly now that her notes have been lost?"

"She's going to have to learn from her own mistakes. I've got plenty of faith in her." He lined up the drinks he'd just poured on a tray. "Do you?"

"Of course."

"Jane!" Kat waved from the top of the steps, a bright grin on her features. She raced across the pit to the bar. "This just arrived for you."

Jane took the thick envelope in surprise. There was no return address, but the handwriting was Cole's. It was so thick, she imagined there were letters for them all. Perhaps a backlog of what he couldn't send due to the storm. Relief made her nearly collapse on the spot. "Oh. Oh! Tom, look. It's from Cole."

Tom frowned at the envelope. Instead of happiness, he appeared cautious. "Odd."

"What? I bet it's all he couldn't send due to the storms." She tore into the envelope, unfolding the thick letter only to see the words *Decree of Divorce* at the top. She dropped the letter as though burned. "What the devil?"

Her heart stopped beating when Tom snagged the papers. She shook her head, buzzing filled her ears to block whatever Tom and Kat were saying. It couldn't be. There was no way in hell. No possible way. What was Cole playing at?

She ripped the papers from her brother's hands to scan the pages herself. Fast as she could, she read. By the decree he expected her to sell all of their holdings and secure the funds in an account in California. *All* of the funds. The children weren't even mentioned. "No."

A hard shake to her shoulder brought her attention to Tom. His brows furrowed into a fierce glare. "This has to be fake. I'll take it to Nick immediately."

Jane blinked rapidly against tears she knew she shouldn't shed. Tom was right, it had to be fake. There couldn't be any way Cole would divorce her without so much as a word. It couldn't possibly be.

"Lady Jane. What's wrong?" Hammy sat on his stool, his grin fading as he looked between the three of them. "Is it Archie? Did we lose him, too?"

"No," Kat answered in the lingering silence. "We still don't know if he'll keep his leg, but he's holding on."

"Y'all right, Janey?" Hammy set his hand on hers, the calloused warmth showing how cold her fingers had become. "You look like ya seen a ghost."

"I'm…" Jane shook her head, unable to form words. Her head spun with questions that had no answers, not until she saw Cole face to face. She had no idea how she was. Dumbfounded was perhaps the best word for it. "I…"

"Jane." Tom tucked the papers into his vest. "I've got this. Friday we leave."

"Friday." Jane took a bracing breath. On Friday they would go find him and demand answers for this mess. She gave Tom a nod. "Of course."

"Where you go-o-o-oh…" Hammy's voice trailed off in a garbled slur.

"Mr. Hamm?" Jane turned to face him to find a frightening sight. The entire right side of his face drooped. The beer he had crashed to the floor. "Oh my God, Gilbert!"

Jane tore around the bar to where Kat was already helping to hold the man up. Tommy disappeared, calling out he'd get help.

"Mr. Hamm." Jane helped Kat get him to the floor. She took Hammy's hand in hers, holding on for dear life. The man continued to try to speak, but she couldn't understand a word of it. "It's going to be fine. Charles will be here in a minute. He'll help you, Gilbert. Try to relax."

Janeb rushed his thinning hair from his forehead. She tried to soothe him as best she could while she waited for help. "My dear sweet man. I've got you. I'm not going anywhere. Just keep holding my hand."

"Jane." Charlie dropped to the floor beside Kat. The litter clattered to the floor behind him. "Gilbert, can you look at me?"

"Hammy kept his eye on Jane, continuing to babble incoherent words at her.

"Mr. Hamm, please look at Charles. Don't you worry about me, I'm not moving." Jane wiped her tears when he finally turned his attention to Charlie. She kept his hand clutched tight to her chest. Without a doubt she knew what had happened, and it wasn't the first time. Cole had told her about the first time Hammy had suffered a stroke. Daisy had saved him then. Charlie's grim face made her worry he wouldn't be saved again.

"He's not been well for weeks," Jane whispered. When Hammy turned his head to look at her, she smiled softly at him. "Have you? You've had some confusion, incoordination, and headaches. Everyone passed it off as his drinking. You've actually been ill for weeks, you poor man."

"Let's get him to the clinic. Jane, you can come, but I need to try to—"

"Do whatever you need to, Charles. I won't get in your way, I simply want to see him as soon as is possible." Jane kissed the back of Hammy's hand. "I'll see you soon. Don't you leave me yet, Mr. Hamm. I told you, I can't imagine a day you aren't there."

Jane released his hand to move out of the way to give them room to lift him onto the litter. It wasn't until he'd been carried up the stairs that she released the sob that had lodged herself at her diaphragm. A kinder man there never was, he didn't deserve this. It would kill Cole to hear what had happened. He'd always had a soft spot for Hammy. The thought of Cole hardened her against her sobs. He wasn't here, and he wanted to divorce her without a bye or leave?

Tom helped her to her feet. "Easy there, Lou."

Her tears had dried, a cold fury in her belly. "Send a telegram."

"What? Jane. After what Cole—"

"Cole will want to know this." She swiped the lingering tears from her cheeks. Fists clenched at her sides, she stared where Hammy had been carried from the room. "He may not care about me or the children any longer, but he cares about that man."

"Jane. You know this paperwork can't be real."

"Send the damn telegram. I'm going to the clinic."

The best portion of a good man's life, his little, nameless, unremembered acts of kindness and love.
—William Wordsworth

Jane sat perfectly still perched on a chair in the waiting room. Several townspeople filtered in as word of Hammy's situation made its way through the streets. Jane ignored their conversations, unable to block the turmoil in her own mind and heart.

Rather than deal with the heartache and doubt of the letter she'd received, she chose to focus on the matter at hand. She had to push down the violent emotions the divorce papers had left her with. The baby didn't need that stress on top of her worry and fear over Hammy.

Unlike every other incident in the town during the past six months, this one held no suspicions, no unusual circumstances. It was merely a tragedy. Pure, unbridled tragedy.

She'd meant what she'd said to the kind old man. She couldn't begin to imagine a day when he wasn't around. For years now that dear, sweet, gentle man had been a bright spot in some terrible days, and a downright happy note on good days.

It ripped her in two to witness it all crumbling before her.

She rubbed her hand over her heart at the deep ache running through it. An ache she could no longer be certain would completely disappear ever again. Life would be irrevocably changed.

Tom crouched in front of her. She didn't care what he had to say, she only needed the door she stared at to open. For Charles to emerge with a smile instead of anything else. A tap to her knee brought her gaze to Tom. "I sent the telegram."

"Thank you." She returned to staring at the closed door. "Don't say it. I can't hear it right now. Mr. Hamm is my concern right now. Not…not that."

"If that's what you want."

"It is." She folded her handkerchief between her hands. The tension and pull forced feeling through her chilled appendages. "Move our tickets, please."

"Already did, to next week."

"Thank you."

"I dropped off the papers to Nick and James."

"At the moment, I really don't care. Go see to the casino, please." Jane rose when Charlie stepped out of the exam room. A hush fell over the waiting room. Charles didn't appear relieved, but grim. Jane approached him. "Charles. Please tell me he isn't d—…"

"He's alive." Charlie set his hands on her arms. He held her gaze evenly, the grim expression not softening. "It was a severe stroke. Much worse than the one Daisy described in her notes. Even if he makes it through the next few days, he won't be the same."

"Do whatever it takes, Charles. Spare no expense."

"Jane. It isn't that simple." He couldn't be saying there was nothing they could do. There had to be something.

"Call in an expert, then. Make it simple."

Charlie pulled her to seat. "The damage he's suffered is traumatic. If what you told me about him being ill for weeks is true, then I suspect he's been having a series of strokes. Which means he is likely to have another."

The reality sank into the pit of her stomach. Her nose clogged with unshed tears. She closed her eyes against the earnest worry in his. "How long?"

"Days. Maybe weeks."

"You think days."

"Yes." His hand smoothed over her hair before he pulled her against him.

She collapsed into his comforting embrace while she digested what he'd told her. Charlie expected Hammy to die, and soon. The ache in her heart threatened to rip it right open, but she only allowed a few tears to slip free. For the time being she could remain strong. She had to, for Hammy. "I would like to see him."

"We're moving him to a room. I'll let you know when he's ready for visitors." Charlie glanced around the crowded waiting room. "He'll have no shortage of folks wanting to sit with him."

"I know. He's greatly loved." Jane swiped at the tears that now fell freely because she'd foolishly allowed a few to run free. "Please let me know when he's ready."

"Of course." Charlie kissed her forehead before returning to the room with Hammy inside.

Kat rushed into the clinic, right to Jane's side. "I wanted to send mother a telegram so she'd know what happened. What do the doctors say?"

"He's still alive, but Charles can't be certain for how long. He said the stroke was traumatic." Jane clutched Kat's hands. "He suspects it's been happening for a while seeing as Mr. Hamm hasn't been feeling well for some weeks now."

"Oh, that dear sweet man." Tears trickled down her friend's cheeks. "Where is he?"

"They're moving him to a room."

Tom cleared his throat as he rose from a chair across from them. "Jane."

Jane lifted her gaze to meet her brothers. She didn't have to ask what he wanted, she knew what they'd been talking about before Charles had come out. Even she was surprised by the venom that carried in her tone, "Tell James and Nicholas—tell them to make him bleed."

"Right." Tom slipped from the clinic with little more than a nod.

Kat released a shaky breath. "Even before the stroke he was so good and kind. He helped me when I wanted to leave Dominion Falls, when Mother was trying to marry me off. He worried about me, but he helped anyway."

"He stood up to Guy for me."

"Hammy?"

"Yes." A laugh burst free as Jane remembered the day she'd met Hammy. "Guy was forcing me to walk alongside him to gain an audience over some fool notion. He would not release my hand no matter that I'd asked him three times. Mr.

Hamm spoke up behind us and told Guy I'd said to let me go. He said it wasn't right to hold a lady."

"Sounds like Hammy." Kat sighed, her gaze wandering over the murmuring crowd still waiting, though they'd learned the man's fate. "Didn't he see to your care after you were shot, too?"

"You mean he set Lizzie and her mother to my care and reported back to Cole." The mention of her husband tugged away the happy memory. Her smile sank into a frown. Fortunately right then Charles appeared to let them know Hammy was settled into his room.

Jane and Kat followed him up the stairs to a room where a bed had been pushed right against a window with a view of the street. The view didn't matter at the moment as Hammy appeared to be asleep. Even in repose, the right side of his face drooped.

Jane sank into the chair near his shoulder, Kat right beside her. Her hand shook as she reached out to set it on Hammy's shoulder. "I'm so sorry, Mr. Hamm. You never deserved such a fate. I wish I had the power to make it all better for you."

"We all do." Kat clasped the sleeping man's hand in hers. "You've done so much for this town. I know every soul out there wishes we could do something for you."

Not certain she could form any further words without crying, Jane simply brushed her fingers along his cheek. Waiting hopelessly for him to wake, to speak. Somehow she thought it was less likely than Cole returning on the next train telling her this was all some horrible nightmare and to wake up.

It was a nightmare, but it wasn't likely she'd stir to consciousness from it.

Sorrow is the mere rust of the soul.
Activity will cleanse and brighten it.
–Samuel Johnson

Sally sighed in happy satisfaction. The butcher paper she'd spread across the table sat nearly full of notes. In no time she'd be able to transfer all of the details into her notebook. Recreating the timeline she'd made in the library had proven far more successful than simply trying to rewrite every word in her books.

The door opened and closed. Several minutes later a rustle of skirts entered the room. Sally only glanced quickly toward the figure to ensure it was Jane and not Ada or Mams. "Ma. Come, look at this. You were right. I was trying to remember it all the wrong way."

"That-that's good, Sally." Jane's voice cracked, and came out in little more than a whisper. Sally had expected a bit of excitement. When Sally lifted her head to take a better look, she noticed the pale, tear streaked lines of Jane's features.

Sally abandoned her task to rush to Jane. "Ma? What is it? What's happened?"

"Mr. Hamm. He, um…"

Shock and fear struck deep in Sally's heart until she could hardly gasp. "No."

"He had a stroke." Jane sniffed and shook her head. She pried her fingers free of Sally's grasp. They fluttered along her bodice. Jane turned this way and that a moment as if lost. "I, um…I need to lie down. Excuse me."

"Ma," Sally barely managed to call before the bedroom door slammed. Jane had already been so upset about Cole, this would be so difficult for her. She shouldn't go through it alone, locked in a room. Sally rushed to the door, knocking hard as she could. "Ma, please."

"Sally." Tom's entrance had been completely silent. He shook his head, his features stern as she'd ever seen them. "Not now. Your ma—it hasn't been an easy day for her. She needs some time right now."

"She said Hammy had a stroke?"

"He did. Right in front of your ma, too."

"Oh." Sally's stomach churned, and she set her hand over it. "How awful for her."

"Charlie doesn't expect him to recover." Tom cleared his throat. None of his usual humor filtered in his tone, it was flat as anything. His hat remained pulled low down over his eyes when he usually removed it when he entered the apartment.

Something was up. Something more than Hammy. "Is there more?"

"Nothing more you need to worry about right now."

"Then there is."

"I said it isn't your concern." He adjusted his vest, his gaze cast about the room. It came to rest on the table with her papers. "What's that?"

"Oh. I…" She cast one more long look at Jane's door.

"Leave her be."

Sally's shoulders sagged at the order. She crossed to the paper spread across the table. "This is what I wanted to show you yesterday. I suspect the original got burned along with my notebook."

"Show me now."

She hesitated, another glance at Jane's door.

"I'm going to give your ma some time before I go check on her."

"If you're sure."

Tom took a seat on the sofa. Hands clasped in front of him, he nodded. "I'm sure. Now show me what you did."

Sally perched beside him, staring at the timeline. The excitement and joy of mere minutes before eluded her. Rather than speak, she stared at the lines and notes running across the page along the center line. "Hammy?"

"Yeah."

"He used to pay for time with us, but then would just sit and chat."

"Still did at the new place, far as what Wil and Garit say."

"If we were having a bad night, he always seemed to know. He'd pay Cole for an hour. Then he'd buy us a drink and tell us jokes and stories."

"He's one of the good ones." Tom's voice was gruff. He adjusted his hat lower over his eyes. Though they carried on a conversation, his attention didn't waver from her sheet of paper. "Doubt there's a person in camp that would say a cross word about him. He liked to be happy."

"He likes for everyone to be happy."

"That he does." Tom sighed. "Cole once told your ma that Hammy had loaned him the money to buy the original saloon. Let him pay back without interest. Cole had a real soft spot for him."

"So did Ma."

"Jane loved him like family. Treated him as such."

"This has to be breaking her heart." Sally's voice cracked with tears.

"Among other things," Tom mumbled under his breath. His gaze fell on Jane's door. At this angle she could see his face lined with worry.

She wanted to ask what he meant, but knew she'd get shut down again.

He sniffed, extracting a handkerchief from his pocket.

"A stroke," she spoke quiet now.

"They're thinking it's been happening for a while. We just thought he was drunk."

"He called me Jane," Sally recalled. She lifted her gaze to the window. Her vision was too blurred with tears to see the paper clearly anyhow.

"I remember. I checked on him the next day."

"He couldn't hardly walk straight. I was worried, but didn't want to panic ma."

"She already was, I think."

She shook her head. "What if I'd sent him to the clinic instead of home?"

"We can't know it would have helped. He's had some troubles of late. Jane was good and worried about him, but she thought he was working too much. She tried to get him checked by Charlie several times. Maybe we could've stopped it, but I'm not the doctor so I don't know. Either way, it's happened, and it's bad. He can't really talk, and Charlie doesn't think he can swallow to keep sustenance."

Sally released a breath she hadn't realized she was holding. It expelled in a shaky tremor. "Is Ma going to be okay?"

"Eventually." Tom cleared his throat again. He swiped his nose one more with the handkerchief before he scooted closer to the paper. "Now tell me what you did here."

She blinked at her continuing tears when he tugged the paper closer. "I, um, right."

"Nothing we can do right now. We've got to keep pushing forward. Tell me what this is."

"I made a timeline of everything that happened. In my notebook I had to keep flipping pages. It had more details, but I wanted to look at everything whether it seemed related or not."

"Good thinking." His voice remained gruff, but otherwise seemed calm. He moved the paper around to look at everything she'd written. "What's this on the bottom?"

"Big events in the town. Some small events. Anything that stuck out, really. The tornado, the celebrations for the Centennial and statehood, Reverend Lyons' arrival, Bonnies, the opening of the saloon. Things like that."

"Tell me why you included them."

"I'm not entirely sure," she admitted honestly. "I wanted to see everything laid out together. All the things that have happened over the past year. I don't necessarily thing they're tied together, but I was looking for any sort of pattern."

"Did you find one?"

"Not really." She leaned forward to point out Keller's death and the Centennial celebration. "A few of the incidents, like Keller, happened right before something else, but it doesn't seem particularly tied in."

He pointed to the left of the timeline. "Why'd you start with Eli's arrival?"

"That's just what struck me as a significant event this year. Reverend Lyons was the first thing this year of major import. Before that, things were mostly status quo."

"Looks good for a start. It's lacking in details, though."

"I'll add those in when I put things in my notebook. This just gives me a rough sketch." A loud thump came from the bedroom. Sally glanced toward Jane's door again, wondering at would could have made so much noise they heard it out in the apartment. "Tommy?"

Tommy acted as though he hadn't heard a thing. He nudged her attention back to the sheet. "What are these?"

"I—what?"

"Up here at the top."

"What about Ma?"

"I'll check on her in a few minutes."

"But…"

"Sally." Tom's voice harshened. "I said I'll check on her. Tell me what you've written here."

She knew he was good as his word, but an unsettled feeling kept her stomach twisting. Rather than argue, she directed her attention back to the paper. Across the top of the paper she'd written several words or phrases that could seem random. Words like *whore, everyone loved him, succubus,* and *man of God.* "I jotted down some themes I found among many of the victims. Odd man out is Mac, of course. Nobody liked him, and he certainly wasn't a man of God."

"No. He wasn't. Was he?"

"And Miss Bee. Far as I could tell, she was never a whore. I sent a telegram to Seth myself to check and he found she'd been a spinster her whole life."

Tom nodded quietly. "This looks good, Sally. See about getting everything transferred. We'll check your dates later."

The back door opened. James stepped into the apartment with nary a greeting. He studied the pair on the couch before nodding to Tommy.

"I'm going to check on Janey." Tom crossed to his brother. They conversed in low tones so Sally couldn't quite catch what was being said. Before James left, he slipped Thomas some papers. With a fingertip to his hat in acknowledgment of Sally, he slipped from the apartment as quick as he'd arrived.

"What's going on?"

"What else around your ma? Everything. Keep working. I'll be out in a while."

Sally frowned as the man unlocked the door and slipped into the bedroom. The lock clicked behind him. "What the hell happened today?"

I have lost confidence in myself,
I have the world against me.
-Ralph Waldo Emerson

Tom closed the bedroom door behind him, locking it for good measure. He felt a little guilty for not going into it with Sally, but she would learn in time. Jane was still figuring everything out. Hell, so was he. He was too worried about Jane to go into how Sally or anyone else would react.

Of course, he was also worried about what would come out when Hammy died. His secret would be laid bare. Good intentions or not, he didn't think Jane would forgive him quickly. Not with everything else going on.

The room was dim. Jane had drawn the curtains shut. His first step crunched against the floor. A glance down showed him a broken picture frame. Glass shimmered on the carpet, but it seemed the photograph was still intact.

He bent down to grab the picture and dusted the glass off the photo's surface. The picture was from the opening of the new Hangman's Inn. Jane and Cole smiled brightly out of the picture, their beautiful new hotel behind them. Blurs of children tore across the porch behind them.

He remembered the day, perhaps not as clearly as Jane, but clear enough. He could even identify the blurred children as Isaac and Jesse, who'd made quite a game of playing along the wrapped porch. Other staff stood behind Jane and Cole. Cora, Chauncey, Edgar, and himself among them. Right near Jane stood Hammy, his hat gripped in his hand, an embarrassed grin on his face for being included in the picture.

He set the picture on the dresser for safety before moving toward the side of the bed where Jane lay. The mess she'd made of the room was impressive. His sister Clara had been extremely messy in her youth, and even some when she got her own place. Though public areas were always neat for company, her room had been tossed over with clothes and shoes. One thing Jane and Clara had in common was their love of clothes.

Jane and Cole's room in the saloon had always been a bit cluttered, but that was due to size. Jane had hardly room for her things along with Cole's. There'd been no real closet, and so she'd been forced to make do with what they'd had. Once they'd built the apartment and moved in, the room had been spotless.

This mess, though. It wasn't clothes tossed about carelessly. It was destruction. Broken shelves and picture frames, along with a wood mustang he recognized as Cole's littered the floor. He figured the large thump he'd heard with Sally was the shelf that had been torn from the wall and broken.

Jane curled on her side, staring at the closed window. Her hands ran aimlessly over the swell where the baby lay.

Another picture lay smashed on the floor beside her. This one a tintype that lay face down.

He picked this one up as well, recognizing their wedding picture. Neither of them faced the camera for this one. Cole and Jane stared into each other's eyes, bright smiles on their faces. With even greater care, he set this picture on the shelf above the bed. Out of respect to her temper, he turned it toward the wall.

Jane remained silent through all of his actions. Her gaze remained fixed on the stripe of sunlight escaping a small crack in the curtains. He perched on the bed beside her. It would do no good to interrupt her choice of silence, so he held his tongue.

After what felt like ages, but was likely mere minutes, she set her hand on his. He broached no argument as she pulled it against her stomach and held it in place. Two swift thumps hit his palm, followed by a long push before it disappeared.

A swoop of motion crossed again, and another bump before it settled.

"Baby's active," he said in an undertone.

"I'm fine. He's fine. Leave me alone."

"Not a chance."

"Go away, Thomas." There wasn't a lick of anger in her tone. No command. Her voice was monotone, deadened.

"Hammy lived his life with one goal—to be happy. He wouldn't want this for you."

She rolled to her back, staring at the ceiling. The silence lingered. He wasn't about to break it, she had to. Finally, she sighed. "I'm not Gilbert Hamm. I am me."

"And that old coot adores you."

"Someone should, I suppose. It's clearly not my husband."

Tom glanced toward the tintype he'd set on the shelf. Poised to argue. "I've seen different."

"I thought I had, too. It appears we were wrong. The infallible Thomas Young got one wrong again. That's two. Do you dare go for a third."

"Unfair." He knew she was again referencing his defense of the man that attacked her while pregnant. A man he'd thought to be a friend. A man long gone, who faced frontier justice and got fed to some wild pigs.

"Sorry."

"I thought you didn't lie."

"I can't do this, Thomas. Please, leave me be."

"Nick noticed something in the papers that we think you missed in your very quick perusal in the casino."

"Doubtful."

"Not so much. You looked them over very fast."

"Thomas."

He squeezed her calf. "Sit your ass up."

She expelled a noisy huff of annoyance at his order. After a few minutes she did as asked. "What do you think I could possibly care about?"

"He says to sell the holdings," he reminded her.

"And send the funds to California. He makes no mention of the children. I'm well aware." A bite had returned to her tone. A good sign, he thought.

"No. No mention of the children, we agree on that. There is mention of someone else."

"Who? Alma?"

"No." He leaned across her legs to meet her inexplicable mix of anger and defeat. "No, he mentioned someone else. Someone you know very well."

"Get on with it."

"Annabel Lee."

"What?"

"Apparently she is near Redcliff under the care of a Dr. Tarr."

Life flooded her features in a blink. Her eyes brightened and her cheeks regained color. "Annabel. Redcliff. Dr. Tarr. Are you certain?"

"See for yourself." He pulled the papers from his vest to hand them over. This time she took her time scanning each and every page with intense focus. While she read, he set about cleaning some more of the destruction from the floor.

As predicted, she took a while this time. He didn't know how many times she read it over in the five minutes he spent cleaning. He stopped when the papers lowered to her lap.

"I'm Annabel Lee. That much is certain."

"Painfully obvious," he agreed.

"Redcliff. That could refer to another of Poe's poems, *Alone*." She scooted from the bed to pace the floor. Her finger tapped her lip. "He's obviously alone, we couldn't think of anyone to go out there with him."

Tom perched on the footboard when her pacing brought her close to him. She passed him by, glass crunching under her feet with every step.

"Dr. Tarr. Insanity."

"Perhaps."

"Is he referring to himself being alone? Or is that referring to me? Oh, I wish the man was much cleverer than this."

"Point is, you know he put that in there for you. You were meant to see it and question."

"But why?"

Damned if he knew. It would frustrate her to hear, but he had to admit it. "I haven't the foggiest idea why."

She growled her frustration, the papers slamming onto the dresser. Resuming her pacing, she mumbled under her breath a few minutes. "Why send nothing else? In *The System of Dr. Tarr and Professor Fether* the patients took over the asylum. Oh, this makes no sense."

Her frustration with her husband's puzzle somehow sparked Tom's own guilt back to life again. She was already lost, and when she learned the truth she wouldn't have him, either. If Hammy was going to die, she'd learn the truth sooner rather than later. He should tell her now, but how could he give her more to upset her? The way she ran her hand along her stomach. The stress lining her still-pale features.

She'd already lost one child in this pregnancy, and any further upset could make matters worse. Then again, as he knew, she'd learn this truth soon enough. If he told her now and got it over with maybe it would be better. He'd have to deal with the fallout by telling her now. Better than a rude awakening at an inconvenient time. "Jane."

"Hm?" She'd returned to her dresser. Like her ward out in the apartment was likely doing, Jane scribbled intensely in a notebook.

"I, um." He cleared his throat. "There's something I need to tell you."

"Is it bad news? I want no more of that today."

"Not exactly."

For that she turned on him. Her eyes scanned him intently, once again looking for the tells he tried to keep well-hidden. Silence lingered between them like a thick blanket. Silence he was loathed to break all on his own. After a minute, her lips turned down in a deep frown. "There it is. Guilt again."

"There's something you need to know."

"Oh? You just said there was something you needed to tell me."

"Same thing."

"No. No, it isn't." She crossed her arms. "Which is it? Is it something I need to know? Or is it something you need to tell me?"

"I…" Damn she was too smart for her own good. He was caught in the trap of his own words. How often he'd told Sally words mattered, and he'd tripped on his own.

"I've got enough stress without having to worry about assuaging your guilt. I don't want to hear it. Whatever it is."

"I didn't ask if you wanted to hear it. I told you I needed to tell you."

"Is it worse than you not saving Clara before she wanted to be saved?"

"Depends on your point of view."

She turned her back on him. "Leave."

"Jane."

"Go away." She flung her arm out, the divorce papers in them. "Take these back to James and Nicholas. My previous request stands. Make him bleed."

Tom stared at the papers pointed at him. She wasn't listening. He really needed to get this off his chest. He should have done it sooner, but he couldn't have predicted this avalanche of events that left him worrying for her health as well as the babies. "Lou. I mean it."

"So do I." She shoved the papers into the pocket of his vest. After she'd smoothed the front, she met his gaze. "Thomas, I cannot take *one* more thing right now. Every time I think of that dear sweet man I'm in tears again. I won't deal with your guilty confessions right now. I can't bear it."

He wiped away her tears. As she'd said, the mere mention of Hammy had them coursing down her cheeks. With a deep sigh, he nodded acquiescence. "Just remember when the time comes that you wouldn't let me tell you."

"Go now."

Tom hauled himself to his feet to leave the room. At the door he gave her one last look. Her back was already to him again as she scribbled away.

He carried the papers to Nick's office quick as he could. His brothers would need time to do as Jane asked. He dropped the papers where James sat. "She said her orders remain the same. Make him bleed."

James' eyebrow lifted. "Then that's what we'll do. Are you sure she wants that?"

"Hidden message or not, she's ready for a fight, and it won't be pretty when it happens."

"I'll keep that in mind."

"So will I." Tom exhaled deeply. He cast a dark look to his other brother. Nick was full aware of his secret, as he'd been the man behind all of the paperwork to make it a reality. "She wouldn't let me tell her anything at all."

Nick held his gaze. The damn man didn't let a trick by. Time around Jane might have softened him some, but the man had the best poker face he'd ever seen. Nothing got by. When he spoke, Tom was finally clued in to how he felt. "Then it may not be Cole that receives her wrath first."

"I'm aware."

James leaned forward. He looked between them, a frown forming. "What's going on?"

"One of Thomas's beloved secrets. We all know how he treasures them like a dragon hording gold." Nick's expression remained stoic, his voice calm. A hard light darkened his eyes much as Jane's did in her tempers. "A secret made in good intent, but not something Jane would ever want to know."

James rose slowly. "What did you do, Thomas?"

"A good deed." Tom brushed his hand along his beard. He wasn't lying, it had been a very good deed. Done with another kind soul, the kindest soul he'd ever met. "One that I strongly doubt will go unpunished."

Grief teaches the steadiest minds to waver.
-Sophocles

Jane set aside the book she'd been reading. The words had become blurry anyway. She rubbed her fingers against the burgeoning headache. She released a slow, easy breath to try to relieve some of the tension.

She flexed and opened her hands against the tightness she felt. Unlike her pregnancy with the twins, this time her hands and feet had swelled some. Mostly in the past few days. It was uncomfortable, but yet another thing she had to bear.

She turned her attention to the man on the bed. He lay sleeping as he mostly had for days, in between the occasional seizure and what Charlie suspected were further strokes. She took his hand in hers, rubbing the back of it gently. "I wish I knew if you even enjoyed the story I'm reading."

With a soft sigh, she pulled his hand closer. "I suppose it's best you rest, though. I'll just continue to read the adventure stories Jesse and Alma both love so much and hope you enjoy them as well."

Hammy's eyes blinked open slow as molasses. A crooked smile brightened his features. A few garbled words that made some semblance of his familiar *Lady Jane* crossed his lips.

"Well, hello there, Mr. Hamm." She moved to sit on the side of the bed. "Please don't try to talk too much. From what I've been told it frustrates you to try to talk when we can't understand you. Charles wants you calm."

His hand squeezed hers with a strong grasp before growling lax again. Once again he spoke, but with far less clarity.

"Shhh." Jane used a kerchief to wipe some dribble from his chin. "You're family. You have been from the moment you saved me from Guy."

He smiled again, the right side of his face still not taking part in the action.

"I'm going to be here whenever I can. Don't you worry none. There are many who love you who will continue to stop by. Kat will be here soon. I hear Teddy and Graham are also coming by to spend some time with you today. You have no shortage of folks that care for you."

His hand twitched free of hers. He lifted it to press to her chest right over her heart.

She set her hand over his. "Family. Yes. You've been like family to me for years, and you were family to Cole before me. You're the kindest man I've ever known."

"F-f-foom-el."

"Family." She sniffed against renewed tears. His hand turned to take hold of hers.

Her lip trembled, so she kept her head lowered. It would do him no good to see her so upset.

"Ole."

"Cole?" She dabbed at tears with her free hand. "I—I don't know where he is. I'm sure he'll be along. We told him about you."

If he'd even bothered to read the telegram. It appeared he hadn't read anything she'd sent to him. Or didn't care. The passage bothered her, though. The one that referred to Annabel. To her. What did he want? What was he trying to say?

Jane sighed heavily. "Cole sent me divorce papers."

"NO."

She lifted her head at the first clear word from him. There was anger in the unmarred half of his features. A sad smile was all she could manage. Every time she said aloud a new hole ripped through her heart. "I'm afraid so."

He shook his head, his hand pulling free of hers to pat hers. More garbled words that sounded like he might have been arguing with her.

"According to my brothers the papers appear legitimate, save for one paragraph that makes no sense."

He pushed her. "Go."

"Go? To him? To Cole?" At his nod, she patted his hand. "I plan on it. My tickets are purchased already. I leave next week. We've told him what happened to you. I'm giving him a chance to show up to see you. He adores you, this much I know without a doubt. He told me how you helped him when he first arrived in town."

The next mishmash of words appeared to tire him. She wet a sponge to dab across his forehead in hopes of calming him.

"Shhh. You're pushing too hard, getting too agitated. Charles will have my hide if I let you get too excitable." She used the sponge to push his hair back from his forehead. "Don't worry about me, Mr. Hamm. I will be fine. I'm strong. Remember?"

The smile he cast her was this time was much weaker. His hand clenched hers again.

"Everything will be fine. I must trust that. Get some rest. Kat will be along soon." Jane half stood to press a kiss to his forehead. "Rest, please. You must get well for me."

He cupped her cheek in his hand a moment. Then his hand dropped back to the mattress and his eyes closed.

Jane swallowed her sob so she wouldn't draw him back awake. She forced her shaky legs to take her back to the chair. The headache continued to pulse against her skull like her brain was trying to escape. He wouldn't get better, and she knew it. She couldn't tell him that. Not yet.

Blessedly the door opened a few minutes later, revealing Kat. Jane rose to greet her friend, giving her a warm hug. "He woke for a few minutes. Managed a couple of clear words, but they were simple. No and go."

"You'll let Charlie know?" Kat sniffled, but her eyes were dry.

"Of course."

"And let Bonnie take a look at you? You don't look well."

"I don't feel well, so it's appropriate." Jane hugged her tight again. Once she was situated in the chair, Jane slipped from the room. The steps proved an odd challenge with her headache. There seemed to be twice as many steps to her point of view. She had to clutch the railing to make it down.

Charlie stood when she reached the bottom of the stairs. "How is he?"

"He woke for a few…"

"Jane, why don't you sit down?"

She kept a tight grip on the banister as the room spun. "I'm fine. I just need a moment. How is Archie doing?"

"Better, but his leg still looks bad. I've resorted to using leeches to try to draw some of the blood away before he loses the limb."

"I should go see him." She took a step and the floor swooped ahead of her. Strong arms caught her before she hit the ground. "Oh, dear."

"What you *should* do is sit. Or rather, lie down." Charlie led her to a settee in the waiting room. He got her settled against the pillows. "I'm going to get you some water and find Bonnie. Will you rest here while I do that?"

"I suppose. Can you get me something for this headache, too?"

"Headache? You're still having those?"

"All the time." She rubbed her forehead. "And indigestion. I'm under so much stress, it can't be surprising."

"Let me see your hands." He took them before she could move. His fingers pressed into her flesh for a moment. Her skirts were lifted, and he pressed the stockinged flesh of her legs right above her boots. "Don't move. Promise me, Jane."

"Of course." She draped her arms over her eyes. Trying to breathe through the headache, she closed her eyes.

A hand touched her shoulder. Charlies voice came in soft tones. "Let's get you sitting. I want you to drink this."

Jane did as commanded. The effort of sitting made her groan. She looked into the glass of what appeared to be water. "What's this?"

"Laudanum. It will help you relax."

"It makes me sleep."

"Drink it. I don't want you having a seizure."

"A what?" Jane took the drink at the word 'seizure'. Without another moments hesitation she drank it down. "Charles, what's going on?"

"Eclampsia. According to some doctors, they think it's a toxemia."

"You think different?"

"I believe it's not a toxin, no. There will be no bloodletting for you." Charles sat on the edge of the settee, examining her features quietly. "You haven't had an easy pregnancy, and I don't want it to get worse. You will do what I say."

"Yes. My children are all I have." The grief flooded through her again. Her nose burned with the mixture of tears and fear. "Tell me what to do. Anything. Just please, please don't tell me I can't travel. I must go."

"I prefer you didn't." Charlie held up his hands to ward off her protest. "However, I believe the trip is what you need to ease some of the strain you've put yourself under. If it won't worry you more to leave your children in our mother's hands, of course."

"Charles."

"You must rest as much as possible. When it seems overwhelming, a tincture of laudanum. And please, allow yourself to cry."

"I allow it. Every night and every morning upon waking."

He squeezed her hand. "I'd feel better if I went with you to keep an eye on you while you travel. You managed to keep the twins for nearly nine months. If you keep going as you are, this child will not have such a luxury."

"How can you go? Andrew is still getting his feet wet, and your new doctor hasn't been here long at all. You don't know how they would handle your clinic in your absence."

"Dr. Noe is quite capable. She's fitting in very well. I have another doctor expected in the spring. She's half Cherokee, and has been working toward her degree."

"An Indian doctor?"

"Yes."

"Willow and Jay will like that." Jane sighed as the drink began to take hold of her senses. "I hate laudanum. I have far too much to do."

"You will let others do it as if you had left on tomorrow's train. You'll rest. Take nice warm baths, and take your tincture when you begin to feel like you have been. Now let's get you to a room so Bonnie can examine you properly."

"You're a bully."

"Love you too."

As a well-spent day brings happy sleep,
so a life well used brings happy death.
—Leonardo da Vinci

Jane stood by the balcony doors. The lamplit streets shimmered. People walked the streets despite the late hour. A group gathered on the Inn's porch, singing songs and laughing. She couldn't see much of the saloon, but the few windows she could see were bright with lamplight.

Over the past few days Hammy had gotten progressively worse. While she'd listened to her brother and Bonnie's orders, she'd visited as often as she could. The rest of the time she'd rested and taken laudanum when the symptoms arose again.

Sitting around doing nothing but worrying had done little to help her disposition. Her mind raced over everything that had happened the last six months on repeat until she could hardly think straight. The children and her family had done all they could to provide her with plenty of distraction. She still wasn't anywhere near the calm soul her doctor and midwife would prefer.

On top of the hell her life had become, Hammy's deteriorating condition had done little for her temperament. He'd had an increasing number of seizures and further strokes. He hadn't woken in days except for brief periods. Each of those moments he'd seemed desperately confused and frightened.

For the time being, he slept again. All while the townsfolk prepared to celebrate the new year. The joy for the upcoming year of eighteen hundred and seventy-seven seemed trivial to her now. To that end, she'd taken this shift in the middle of the night to watch over Hammy while most of her family celebrated across the street at the party she'd planned herself weeks before when she'd still had hope.

She knew Charles remained downstairs keeping watch as she did.

A death watch.

One unlike she'd experienced since her own years before. The difference being she'd been alive and fully functioning for hers. Hammy blessedly didn't have that horror. From what she could tell he was little more than a shell now.

Jane returned to Hammy's side to take his hand in hers as she had so often in the past few days. "Fifteen minutes until the new year, Mr. Hamm. There's a party across the street. Beer is flowing, as is every kind of liquor we offer, I imagine. It's likely the same at the saloon, though not a formal party like the one I planned at The Hangman's Inn."

The man remained pale and still. His eyes were open to nothing. His lips moved as though chewing, perhaps trying to speak, but to whom she didn't know. She didn't even know if he even saw anything now.

After minutes of silence his body jerked violently. His eyes rolled back into his head, revealing the whites. Jane tugged on the string to call Charlie. She did her best to turn the man to his side and protect his head from the bed frame with a pillow.

When Charlie burst into the room, she moved to a chair across the way before he could think to order her to sit. Unable to watch the scene while Charlie tended to Hammy, she turned her gaze to the frost-lined windows. Flickers of light from the lamps made the lines dance, tears in her eyes added to the effect. It would have been so beautiful if not for the tragedy unfolding so close.

The first tear slipped through her guards. Charles touched her shoulder. She took a shaky breath. "It's time. Isn't it?"

"I'm afraid so." Charlie knelt in front of her. "Why don't you go to the party? I'll stay here with him. He won't be alone."

"No." She set her hand on his, holding on for dear life. "You're kind to offer, but I can't face a celebration. I'll stay with him. He should have a friendly voice when he leaves."

"I don't know that he can even hear you now."

"It doesn't matter. I can." She attempted to smile, but her trembling lips wouldn't obey the command. "I need to be here. Please."

"All right. Would you like me to stay?"

"No. I'll be fine. I'll ring when it happens."

Charlie rose, kissing her forehead on his way to standing. "I don't know that you should be alone right now."

"I'll be sitting. I won't be strained. I simply wish to talk to him. I want him to know that it's going to be all right."

"He might seize again."

"I'm aware." She pushed herself to her feet. When he guided her back to the bed, she didn't fight his assistance. Rather than take the chair, she sat on the edge of the bed.

Hammy's mouth now hung open. His breath rattled through his lungs like a death knell. She no longer bothered containing her tears as she straightened his hair and limbs best she could.

The door closed quietly, leaving her alone with him again.

"Gilbert." She sniffed against her tears. Her hands shook with every movement. She adjusted the muslin across his chest. "It's going to be fine. Everything will be all right here. You can go now. You'll always be here in spirit, in my heart. I won't ever forget you or all you've done for me. I don't think anyone will."

She pressed a shaking kiss to his forehead. "Take yourself away from this pain, this suffering. Your life was too full of joy and happiness for you to linger in this torment."

She held his hand against her chest, clasped tight in hers. Her eyes closed against the unceasing flow of tears. "Be at peace."

She wasn't certain how long she sat there listening to his ragged breaths. The clock chimed twelve and cheers echoed in from the town, but still he lingered. She held his hand when his body tremored with another seizure. This time she didn't call Charlie.

Once it had passed, she rearranged him again. "It's all right," she repeated her reassurances. Her heart broke with every line. She wondered if they were true, at least for her.

Part of her wondered how long his absence would continue to wound her soul.

"You can go, Gilbert. Mr. Hamm. Lady Jane will be all right. We all will. We know how much you loved us, how much you loved life. I loved you, too. I'll try to live my life with the same joy you did. I will find a way to honor you in a way worthy of you. You don't need to suffer any longer. Rest."

A breath that stung of agony echoed from him, causing Jane to clasp his hand tighter so she wouldn't call Charlie for something he couldn't stop. "That's it. Let go. Be where there is only joy, and no more pain."

After several more desperate breaths, he stilled.

Jane's hands shook when she reached up to draw his lids shut. A sob erupted as she dropped her head to his chest, releasing the tears with no further restraint. When she felt she could contain herself, she straightened again.

Carefully she set his hands on his chest and used the sponge to clean his slack features of the evidence of his seizures. "There. You look handsome. I'll see to it when the ground softens again you're buried in your favorite suit. The one you wore to take me to dinner."

She smoothed down his hair a final time and pulled the bell. Tears still trailed along her face and neck, though she'd managed to slow the rapid flow. When Charlie entered much slower this time, she didn't leave the bedside. "Twelve twenty-two."

Charlie slipped a supportive arm around her waist. "Let's get you in bed. I'll see to his care."

"I gave Graham instructions."

"He won't forget."

She turned into his comfort, another wave of tears bursting free as she clung to his shirt. Through the sobs racking her body she felt his comforting had soothing her, his words mere murmurs. When she'd still enough, she wrapped her arms around his neck and held on, allowing his comfort in place of being alone. "I don't know what to do now."

"You'll sleep. Tomorrow you'll worry about the rest."

"He was the kindest man I've ever known."

"I know. He truly was."

The company of just and righteous men
is better than wealth and a rich estate.
-Euripides

Jane splashed cold water from the basin on her face in hopes it would soothe the heat of her tears. Unable to bear seeing any celebration, she'd ended up sleeping at the clinic under the care of her brother. In the end, her body had caved to exhaustion and she'd managed a few hours of sleep.

Most of her family was out and about in the hotel this morning. The apartment held only herself, Willow and Alma. The quiet was soothing after the turmoil of the past several weeks. It seemed as though her tears would never end. At least for the time being they had eased enough she felt she could function.

They wouldn't be able to bury Hammy until after the melt. She'd found the suit he'd worn the night she'd taken him to dinner to thank him for his kindness her first year there. Right down to the lilac colored gloves he'd been so proud to wear. She'd given the suit to Graham and requested a fine coffin for his burial.

That was all she could do until they were able to give him a proper service. Reverend Greene had visited early that morning to say a prayer with her over him before he left for the ice house. He'd remained to give her words of comfort and support over Cole as well.

She was grateful for the kindness, and her heart had become mostly settled. They'd leave for California soon, and perhaps she'd get some answers to the burning questions. The notepad on her dresser sat with the same notes she'd been poring over for days.

Dr. Tarr. The inmates are running the asylum.

Is that what he meant? It would do her no good to continue on in circles. That morning's dose of laudanum had made her tired, but calm enough to pass Charlie's inspection.

She checked in the mirror to see that the blotchiness of her tears had eased. They had, so she left the bedroom. Right as she settled in on the sofa the door opened with barely a knock. Tom and Nick entered, appearing as grim as ever. Did they have news on Cole?

Tom cleared his throat. "Willow? Do me a favor and take Alma out to play on the piano in the casino while it's still quiet."

Jane eyed her brothers in suspicion. Nick didn't appear much different than his usual stoic self. His shoulders seemed taut, and he kept his gaze on the far wall rather than her. Odd.

Tom's usually jovial features were strained. The man had a strange air about him. She'd call it nervousness if she'd ever seen him nervous.

Jane narrowed her eyes. "Why would they need to leave, Tom?"

"I need to speak with you." Nick didn't care any of the nerves of her brother. Not exactly, anyhow. "It's a conversation we should have before everything comes out in the open."

"Out in the open? Is this about Cole?"

"No." Nick's answer was blunt, to the point. "It doesn't pertain to Cole."

Jane turned to Willow, who still sat with her beads on the opposite end of the sofa. "I'm sorry to interrupt you. You may take your beads with you, if you wish."

Willow shook her head. "It's too much to carry. Do we have to?"

"I'm sorry, Willow. Soon as we're done you can come back to finish." Jane squeezed the girls hand, then pulled her hand back into her lap. In the back of her mind, she imagined she should be nervous, upset, anything. Numbness took over instead. Perhaps it was the laudanum. Besides, what else could happen at this point?

She could perhaps be hopeful or excited if it had to do with Cole. Perhaps they'd received news of what he was doing. Nick had stated plainly it wasn't about Cole. She couldn't conjure up the emotions to match the avenues her mind took. In the silence that swept through the room, the door finally closed, shutting her in with her brothers.

Nick moved to her desk and set his attaché on top. Despite having it right there, he didn't open it. He turned the chair to face her. "Hammy had a will."

"A will?" Jane's brain raced along with this knowledge. "Cole said Mr. Hamm lent him the funds to buy the saloon. I can't imagine those funds sustained him for nearly twenty years. Why would he have a will?"

"He had one, I assure you. I drafted it for him. Before its contents become widely known, I felt it was important to let you know what was included within."

"Why is Thomas here, then?" Jane didn't spare Tom a glance. Her focus remained solely on her hands, which felt safe at the moment.

"You'll find out soon enough, I suppose." Tom remained standing near the front door, just out of sight from the reach of her vision.

She exhaled a deep breath. Something was coming. Something more. "Must we do this now? He's not been dead twelve hours."

"Once the truth trickles out, it will spread like wildfire. It's best to get this over and done with quickly." Nick leaned his forearms on his knees as he held her gaze. "Hammy had far more funds than I believe anyone was aware of. The funds he loaned Cole all those years ago were a drop in the bucket for him."

Jane shook her head over this statement. It went against everything she knew about the man. "No. I don't understand."

"The gold claims he sold to the Daugherty's sold at top dollar, and Hammy was no shirk when it came to handling his money."

"Mr. Hamm?"

"We all know he wanted nothing out of life but some good beer and to work with his hands. Between the way he invested his money, and his income from building, he became immensely wealthy." Nick straightened to open his attaché.

"Immensely?" Surely she was smarter than one word answers, but the news had left her too stunned to be eloquent. "What?"

"The homestead across the valley is his, and he asked Tom to find him someone to watch it and the acres of gold claims above it ripe for mining."

Jane turned to look at Tom. He stood stock still, arms folded across his chest. He didn't look at her.

"He also has quite a few claims north of where the Daugherty's expanded mines are. They actually purchased a handful of claims from him once they opened those so they could continue to expand as need grew." Nick flipped open the folder he'd withdrawn from his case. "There's also the matter of—"

"Wait." Jane turned back to Nick. Her mind caught up with all he was saying. There'd be no reason to tell her this, unless…but it couldn't be. "Why are you telling me all of this?"

"Because he left it all to you, Jane."

Her heart stilled at the words confirming her suspicion. Then it raced forward so fast a sweat broke on her forehead. "I'm sorry. I thought you just said he left it—to me?"

"Yes, I did. He left it to you." Nick met her gaze, not a hint of humor or teasing in the deep blue eyes. "Everything. Right down to the carpentry business."

"Me?"

"Yes, you. Not Cole. Not your children. You alone."

"That's ridiculous."

"Hammy didn't think so." For the first time since the start of the conversation, a hint of a warm smile touched her brothers features. "He said you were always kind to him."

"But I wasn't. There were times he was the brunt of my temper."

"You took him in as family. He was always invited to join you at holidays, you always danced with him. You never once treated him like a fool. People in this town found him little more than a good laugh until you came alone, and he well knew it. He might have only lived to be happy, but he was no fool."

Jane rose, unable to contain the nervous energy that coursed through her. "I was merely repaying an early kindness."

"That kindness was paid over many times." Nick didn't rise with her. His gaze followed her pacing movements. "There is one other matter that needs to be discussed that involves your inheritance before we get into details such as exactly how wealthy you are now."

"There's more?" Jane paused her pacing when she faced Tom. She stared him down even as he continued to avoid her gaze. "This is where you come in, isn't it?"

Tommy nodded once. "It is."

"Nicholas?"

Nick cleared his throat. "Hammy was also partner in an investment company."

"Poor man. Armermann Investment Group." Jane turned to face Nick. Her nerves tightened into a ball closely resembling fury. "Charles told me Armermann translated to poor man. That's what you're talking about, isn't it?"

Nick nodded once.

Jane spun on Tommy. "You're the partner, then?"

Tommy's jaw clenched, but he nodded.

"You *knew* I didn't want money from family. You *knew* I turned down the Daugherty's because I didn't want money from family. And you go and do this?" Jane stared at him until he finally looked at her. "I had made peace with what we had. I was content. You had to do *nothing*."

"It was Hammy's idea. I helped him make it real, with a little help to make it legal." Tom didn't budge from his spot. "It if helps, your hotel has increased my coffers by a considerable amount. It wasn't a loss for either of us."

"Helps? *Helps*? How could that possibly help matters? You knew exactly how I felt and went behind my back to betray me."

"This hotel was what the town needed. I was making a sound investment."

"You were lying right to my face. No wonder Clara hated you."

"Jane." Nick touched her arm.

"What?" Jane spun on him fast, her glare landing on him with equal fire. "You're no better. You helped him."

"You're getting too worked up. Charles will—"

"Don't." She wouldn't deny a headache had bloomed in her ire, but she wasn't near finished enough to go do as ordered. "Thomas, give me your keys and get the hell out of my hotel."

"Lou. Think about this."

"I told you. Get the hell out of here."

Nick's arms went around her waist when she swayed. "Easy. Sit down."

"Get him out—oh." Pain stretched across her abdomen. "Bonnie."

"Tom."

"No. He's leaving." Jane sank down to the sofa. Panic reared to meet her anger. She closed her eyes, running her hands along her stomach to try to soothe the tension. A few minutes later after a murmured conversation a door closed, and a glass pressed into her hands.

"Drink. Bonnie and Charlie will be on their way in short order." Nick settled on the couch beside her, his hand brushing along her hair.

"Ow." Jane rubbed her hand over her stomach as she sipped the laudanum.

"Help is coming. Try to relax. Drink your laudanum."

"Too much is wrong. I can't relax. Not even laudanum can make it better."

"You're being too hard on him. You know I'm the first to hate the secrets he keeps, but Thomas did this with the best of intentions."

"Don't make me punch you." Jane tried to relax as the laudanum kicked in, but another pain stretched across her. "Please, please, please don't let this go wrong too."

"It won't. Just relax."

*Our passions are like convulsion fits, which,
though they make us stronger for a time,
leave us the weaker after.
–Alexander Pope*

Eunice tucked and fluffed the pillows behind Jane. Fussing incessantly enough to drive Jane crazy, but she didn't protest one peep. After the pains she'd had the day before, she knew remaining where she was to be essential until the very last second. Still, when five minutes had passed, she set a hand on Eunice's arm. "Ma. Stop fluffing. I'm comfortable enough."

"You gave us quite a scare." Despite the scolding, Eunice stopped fussing. "I want to be sure you and that baby are safe. You should let Tommy go to California."

"I don't care what Thomas does, but it won't be accompanying me." Jane tried to keep her breathing steady. It was essential she kept her anger in check. Perhaps she was being unreasonable, but after Cole's betrayal she couldn't take any more.

"I meant in your stead."

"No." Jane lifted her head at the knock on the door frame. The distraction was a welcome relief. "Nicholas. Good. Please come in. Mother should be caring for the children, not fussing over me anyhow."

"Did you really think you could prohibit Ma from fussing that easy?" Nick kissed Jane's temple before giving their mother a kiss on the cheek. "She's going to do all she can to make sure that baby stays right where it is, even if her daughter is stubborn."

"That may be true, but she can't accompany me to California. She must take care of the children and hotel. Especially since my orders are to rest as much as possible, and that means the twins will not, in fact, be joining me."

"That's why I'm accompanying you." Nick perched on the bed beside her. "Seeing as you banned Thomas from the trip, you need someone with some common sense along."

Eunice frowned, her arms folded across her chest. "I still do not approve. You might have had that child yesterday and it's far too soon."

"I have my orders and I will follow them to the letter." Tears sparked in her eyes when she'd thought for sure they'd run dry. "The children are everything, mother. I won't do anything to bring them harm intentionally."

"Then allow Thomas to join you." Eunice shook her head. "I don't like it."

"Ma, please. He broke a trust, I won't have him with me."

"A trust." Eunice scoffed. "He did you a kindness."

Jane turned her attention to Nick. "Onto why you actually came by. First matter is the business. I know nothing about construction or carpentry. That should go to Teddy."

Nick pulled a notebook from his pocket. "How about this? You can have Teddy run it, but I'm not certain how good he is at matters of business. We can hire someone to run the paperwork and take care of the monetary aspect. If Teddy proves capable, he can take it over in time. You wouldn't want Hammy's business going under because Teddy was better with a hammer than a ledger, would you?"

"Fair point." Jane took a deep breath, uncertain how to delicately broach the next subject.

"Here." Nick tore a piece of paper out of the notebook. "This number does not include your current status with the hotel, brothel, and assorted ventures. This is only what Hammy's net worth was at the time of his demise. This includes the claims, the businesses, and investments."

Jane fiddled with the paper, relieved she didn't have to ask the question herself. After a few seconds to brace herself, she opened the paper to stare at the number it contained. Her head swam as she crushed the paper in her fist. It was far too much. She already felt too well off with their current stream of income. "It's too much."

"It's yours." Nick tossed the paper she'd handed back toward him into the stove. "Not that anyone will know what that number is. Information will trickle out around town, especially seeing as the Daugherty's had a tendency to buy gold claims from Hammy. Of course, there's the carpentry business and the matter of Armermann Investment Group."

Jane wrinkled her nose at the reminder. "It needs to be dissolved."

"That would be tricky. The Hangman's Inn is not the only business Hammy and Thomas invested in. While you could quite easily buy out the investment in your own business, the others might not have such a luxury."

"Then I'll relinquish my claim on my half of the business. I won't work with someone I can't trust. I won't."

"If you believe Thomas will make it that easy on you, then I'll approach him on the matter."

Jane opened her mouth to retort, but another knock at the door stopped her.

Charlie strode in wearing a bright smile. "I'm very glad to see all the children are still right where they're supposed to be."

Jane did her best to not slap his hand when he set it on the swell of the baby. "I've done as ordered, Dr. Young."

"No you haven't. Not entirely. You're still in a snit of a temper. I can see it." Charlie kissed her forehead, and then their mother's cheek before taking a seat near the end of the bed.

"Your sister has decided to cut off part of her family," Eunice's tone was sharp as a knife. "Rather than allow him to help ensure her safety as well as her husbands, she's kicked him out and is trying to get out of sharing a business with him. Never mind the fact she's had him sharing in all of her business since she met him."

"I'm quite aware she's kicked him out. He's sleeping at my clinic." Charlie turned his attention back to Jane. "As to the matter of her trip out West; if she refuses a Pinkerton, she'll have to accept a spy."

Jane had dared to glare at her mother for her dressing down, but Charlie's words snapped her back to reality. "What? You can't, Charles. The clinic."

"The clinic has two doctors as well as two nurses."

"Millie. George."

"Also have plenty of support. Lee is there daily, or Millie is at Lee's. Ma is right here in town. As are the Daugherty's, Kat, and Leanne." Charles squeezed her leg. "Do you realize how close a call you had yesterday?"

Jane smoothed her hand over her belly. She nodded in resignation. "I am."

"We aren't fool enough to tell you that you aren't making this trip. However, we are making damn sure you and this baby survive it." Charlie smiled weakly. "No matter what we find."

"Thank you." Jane took a shaky breath. "If you're certain you can leave Millie and the clinic."

"Millie is the one who suggested it. As for the clinic, Dr. Cross has proven extremely capable for such a new doctor. Dr. Noe has been a doctor for nearly eight years at her father's side before he passed. She's quite talented. I'm lucky I was able to snag her out of Boston. The clinic will be fine if I'm gone a few days."

"Lucky." Jane snorted. She'd had a chance to speak with Dr. Noe when she'd been in the clinic with Hammy. After her father had died, all of their clientele had gone to other practices, unwilling to trust a female doctor on her own. "More like she came running."

"That's neither here nor there." Charlie chuckled with her.

"Ma?" Jesse stood at the door, eyes wide at the group surrounding her bed.

"Jesse." Jane held out her arm to urge him inside. When he scrambled onto the bed, she drew him close against her and kissed his temple. "It's good to see you."

"Are you really leaving?" Jesse snuggled closer. "Please don't go, Ma."

"I need to go find Cole."

"Then take Tommy."

"I've got two brothers coming with me." Jane sighed as Jesse remained curled against her, gripping her arm tight. "Charles and Nick are coming. I won't be alone."

"Please don't go, Ma." Jesse sat up suddenly, meeting her gaze. "Cole didn't come back. What if you don't?"

"Oh, Jesse." Her own tears rushed forward as she pulled him close. "I'll come back. I promise. There's no scary man this time."

"You don't know that."

"True. But I'm not going by myself. I'll be back. I have too much here to fight for. Don't you worry. I'll be back in just a couple of weeks. I have the sweetheart dance to attend."

Jesse hugged her tight. "Promise."

"I promise." The word hardly made it out before her throat closed with unshed tears. She held Jesse close until she felt more in control. Finally, she let him go. "Why don't you go out into the living room with the others? I'll be out in a little while."

"But—"

"Go on." Jane nodded. "Let me finish with your uncles and I'll come out there and sit with all of you."

As he slumped from the room, Nick squeezed her hand. "They're all worried."

"They should be." Jane close her eyes, slumping down in the covers. "Maybe he's right. I shouldn't go. The two men I've trusted the most betrayed me. That's all there is to it."

"Jane," Charles protested as she pulled the covers over her head. "We have no idea what happened out there. I don't believe Cole really betrayed you."

"Just go away." She closed her eyes. "I'm tired. Go away."

Grief is the agony of an instant,
the indulgence of grief the blunder of life.
-Benjamin Disraeli

Sally climbed the stairs to the second floor, her nose and pencil buried in her notebook as she made some last-minute additions. The past day and a half she'd done little but sit with Archie to keep him company, or spend time with Patrick seeing as he was leaving soon, and with Molly both in pleasure and working on fine tuning her notebook.

A few dates were still missing, and she knew about when things had happened, but needed confirmation. At Tommy's door, she knocked heartily. While she waited, she scribbled another date. Silence met her knock. "Tommy?"

No answer came, which she found odd. She lifted her head, frowning at the silence lingering behind the door. "Tommy."

She pounded again, then tested the door. Strangely, it wasn't locked so she pushed it open.

"What the devil?" The room was completely empty, save for the bed and dresser. The gun racks on the wall hung empty of their usual bevy of weapons.

She spun on her heel and tore down the stairs into the casino. Behind the bar Jane's pa talked with customers and poured drinks. She rushed up to him. "Pops. Where's Tommy? Why are all of his things gone?"

"He's staying at the clinic. Your ma kicked him out." John handed off a drink to a customer, nodding his head along the bar. "Before you go off in a snit, it will get handled."

"But he's supposed to go with her to California. What on earth happened?"

"You miss a lot when you get buried in your friends." John chuckled softly while Sally felt a warm rush of blood bloom along her cheeks. "Never you mind what's happened. If you want to talk to Tommy, you'll find him in room ten over at the clinic."

"But…" Sally glanced around the casino, then back behind the bar. "Where's ma?"

"She's having a lie-down. It's best for the baby right now. Yesterday she had a great several shocks and was in danger of the baby coming early." He patted her hand. "She's fine now, but is resting. Perhaps you'd better go talk to Tommy."

"That's not like ma." Sally shook her head. Suddenly everything felt terribly wrong. Rather than listen to John, she rushed back toward the apartment. Ada was sitting doing a lesson with Jay and Jesse, and Mams was working with Willow. The twins were nowhere to be seen.

Sally ignored the greetings to rush into the bedroom against Mam's protest. "Ma?"

Jane lay sound asleep curled into a pillow. When Sally crawled across the bed, she didn't stir.

"Leave her be, child." Eunice set a hand on Sally's waist. "She needs the sleep. I don't think she's slept since your pa left."

"Ma." Sally shook her heavily. "Ma, wake up."

Jane groaned, her eyelids barely fluttering before she tucked her head under her arm.

Sally lifted her gaze to the bedside table. "Laudanum. Ma, you hate that. Ma, wake up."

One eye blinked open, and Jane all but groaned the name, "Sally. Leave."

"No, Ma. I won't. Wake up."

Jane turned over, her back to Sally and immediately closed her eyes.

"Sally." Eunice pulled Sally off the bed. "Let her rest."

"But she kicked Tommy out? She's taking laudanum? Mams, that isn't ma!"

"She needs to rest and protect that baby. You know she'll do anything for that. Come now, child."

Sally spun on her heel and raced from the apartment, completely forgetting her coat in her rush to get to the clinic. Wind buffeted against her, but she ran on ahead until she'd clamored into the warmth and quiet of the building.

"Sally?" Andrew rose from behind the desk. "Were you here to see Archie? Your uncle is in checking on him now."

"No. Where's Tommy? Is he upstairs?"

"I'm assuming so. I hadn't yet seen him come down today. Is everything all right?"

"No. It's not." Sally stormed up the stairs, headed straight for room ten in the back. She pounded heavily on the door. "Open up, you idiot."

A few seconds later, Tommy opened the door. He leaned on the frame rather than let her in. "Can I help you with something, Sally?"

"You can tell me why you're here and ma is completely doused in laudanum and unresponsive to the world as a whole."

"It's a long story."

"I've got time."

Tom frowned at her. "Maybe I don't."

She folded her arms across her chest. "Clearly you do. It's not like you have a saloon and a hotel to manage any longer. I'm guessing if she kicked you out, she fired you too."

After a heavy sigh, he held open the door. "I'll give you the short version. I broke her trust. Considering what your pa went and did by disappearing and only sending divorce papers, I'm lucky she didn't shoot me. Even if my breach of trust was out of kindness."

"That makes no sense." She dropped into a chair. "Explain better."

He poured himself a whiskey, then offered her the bottle. "You say she's not responding? Should have Charlie check her. Don't want her overdoing it."

"Ma hates what laudanum does to her, why would she do that?"

"I'm guessing to keep the baby right where it's supposed to be."

"Then how's she gonna go after pa?"

"She might not." He tossed back his whiskey. "You kids are all she's got. She won't risk that baby—"

"But we aren't all she's got. She's got pa, I don't care what he sent. He wouldn't do that. It wasn't him. I don't believe it one second, and neither should she."

"Sally." Tom leaned forward and met her eyes. "You keep your nose where it should be, on solving these murders. Let us worry about your ma. If she's sleeping, maybe it's for the best. She hasn't slept right in a long time. It was bound to catch up with her. Betting the laudanum just helped her do that."

"But you didn't see her. How could you just leave?"

"Jane needed some time to calm down." He rubbed his hand over his face with a sigh. "I'll tell you what I can about what happened. Some of it is private, and nothing you need to know unless your ma tells you."

"Then explain." Sally set aside her drink to listen properly as Tom launched into the story of what happened after Hammy died. By his carefully worded story she could tell there were some gaping holes in the story, but true to her word, she didn't question him.

As he finished, he poured himself another drink. "She'll calm down eventually, but often her temper tends to linger so I did as she asked while she tried to deal with the rest."

"All you did was help her open the hotel like it is— which has made her and Cole pretty wealthy."

"What I did was breach her trust and went behind her back to do the opposite of what she wanted, which was to accept help from family."

"Semantics."

"True." He chuckled softly. "She'll get over it."

"Not soon enough. Are you really not going with her to California?"

"Nick and Charlie are taking her, if she decides to go at all. It's best Charlie goes considering how poorly she's been. Nick's got a level head and doesn't trust a soul, so if anyone could go in my stead, it would be him. Your ma will be fine."

"She'd be better if you went with her." Sally leaned back with a deep sigh. "That mean you're going to work at the Inn while she's gone since she won't know?"

"Break her trust again?"

"You've gotta do something."

"Maybe I'll take a job. Get out of your ma's hair a while."

"What?" Sally sat straighter. "You'd leave?"

"I'm thinking on it."

"But…"

"You got no say, Sally."

"What about me?"

"You're doing just fine, and you got Molly helping you out."

Tears filled her eyes. "Why is everything going so wrong?"

"Sometimes, it just does."

For somehow this is tyranny's disease,
to trust no friends.
—Aeschylus

Tom peeked through the window of the apartment. It was late enough for all but the oldest children to be in bed, so he feared Sally might still be about. All he found on his inspection was Eunice lying sacked out on the sofa, her arm dangling off the edge. Caring for the youngest of Jane's children was certainly getting the best of their mother.

Hoping luck was on his side, he twisted the doorknob and opened the door slow as could be. Thankfully the hounds were already out in their run for the night, and he'd swayed them easily with some bones from the butcher. They kept blissfully silent while he slipped into Jane's apartment.

Sally's report from earlier had bothered him more than he dared admit to the young woman. Jane didn't tolerate any use of opium, and even in medicinal form she would normally only take it sparingly, certainly not enough to make her deadened to the world around her.

Creeping quiet enough to keep his mother asleep, Tom made his way to the open door of Jane's room. Once inside, he carefully closed the door all the way shut and locked it for good measure. He turned up the lamps before moving to Jane's side.

She was completely dead to the world, not even the twitch of a dream. The bottle of laudanum that had been full two days before sat near three-quarters empty. He was tempted to throw it out the window, but she did need it for the worst cases.

He was loathed to do it, but there was no other way to wake someone in this state. With a sigh, he yanked the covers back and grabbed a hunk of skin on her thigh, twisting it.

A low groan echoed from her. Her eyes blinked slowly open. "Ow."

"Are you sure you even feel it?" Tom released his grip. He leaned low over her. "Should I throw you out like you do to the whores that indulge?"

"You…go…'way." She made a weak attempt at shoving his face. Her head flopped to the side, once again passed out.

"Not a chance in hell, Lou." This time he shook her hard, but she didn't wake. When it didn't work, he grabbed her skin again and twisted. "Wake up."

"No." She rubbed a hand over her face. When her eyes opened again, they were damp with tears. "Go. Leave me."

"Come on, Lou." He crouched beside the bed to get eye-to-eye with her. "What happened to the woman I liked a fair bit better than my sister?"

"Disappeared." She grunted, her eyes blinking slow as molasses. "With the brother…I trusted."

"You always knew I had secrets. You just don't like knowing any were about you unless you were the one that asked me to keep them."

"Trust. Gone."

"Fine. Don't trust me. I don't care about that." He wondered how muddled her brain had become. One easy way to test. "Solon says to put more trust in nobility of character than an oath."

"'Trust him not'…" Her eyes blinked closed. When he shook her, they opened again. "'That has once broken faith'."

"Shakespeare's not allowed." He kept a hold on her hand. Any time she dared to close her eyes, he squeezed her finger. "And what of the words of Samuel Johnson? 'It is better to suffer a wrong than to do it, and happier to be sometimes cheated than not to trust'."

"'Trust thyself only, and another shall not betray thee'. Thomas Fuller." Her slow blink ended with her eyes closed. A hard pinch made her whole body jerk. "Ow. Stop."

"No. Not stopping." He tried to not be annoyed that even drugged as she was she could still cite as well as ever. He'd love to solve the mystery of her weird brain. "The problem is, you don't even trust yourself right now. You need to. What is it von Goethe said about trusting yourself?"

"'As soon as you trust yourself, you will know how to live'." Her hand jerked away from his when he started to squeeze again. "I thought I kicked you out."

"You did. I have a habit of ignoring such asinine orders. Besides, I heard you'd been hitting the laudanum hard enough to put the whores you've kicked out to shame."

"My doctor ordered me to relax. When I'm awake, I can't relax."

"That's a good way to never wake up again." He kept his gaze level with hers. Though still cloudy, her eyes had sharpened a bit. "You don't have to trust me, Lou. There is something you've got to trust, or rather someone."

"Can't trust myself."

"Then trust your husband."

She snorted, turning her gaze to the ceiling.

"When you were lost, kidnapped by a mad man, what was the only thing I said that made you even begin to trust me."

"Cole would kill you if you broke me more, even if I deserved it."

"That isn't precisely what I meant."

"It killed Cole to leave me in that room, that he told me trust him no matter what happened, then went back and tore up his room, drank three bottles of whiskey trying to keep the image of my looking like I did out of his head."

"Even half in the bag with laudanum, you still remember."

"It stills my mind enough. Just like the opium did. I need some more."

"No. You need that mind, and your trust in Cole."

Tears slipped down her cheek and nose. After a sniff, she wiped at them. "Silence. For weeks and weeks. Then papers. What trust?"

"You know that man better than you know yourself."

"Thought I did."

"You do. You still get surprises from Clara. You know everything about him." Tommy sighed. "I can still come with you."

"No. Not going."

"You really want to live in the limbo of not knowing for the rest of your days, or until he shows up? I doubt that."

She pushed herself to sit upright. Soon as she did, she swayed slightly. Her hand pressed to her head. "Oh. My head."

"Ease off the laudanum."

"Everything is wrong."

"Sally said much the same." He sat on the bed beside her. "I know you don't trust me and don't want me there. What about Sally? She's got a good head."

"Cole…would kill me. He will anyway, with the other two coming."

"I doubt that. Seems to me he's probably in trouble if he's not here."

"If he's not, I'll kill him myself."

"I know you will."

"Thomas?" The weak squeak of his name in question drew his gaze to her. "What if he isn't? What if it was all a lie?"

"That's your addled brain talking. What does your heart say?"

"It's breaking. Every day a little more. I can't breathe."

He pulled her into a hug, rocking her as she cried. "You've got to remember to trust him. If you never trust me again, I'll live. I won't like it, but that doesn't matter. Him, you've got to trust. You've got to trust the life you built here. All these kids, your business, your life together."

"How?"

"Remember how hard you fought to get here. I think he's gotta be fighting just as hard to get back. And then you fight to get it all back."

"What if I have no fight left?"

"The day you've got no fight left is the day you're in the ground, Jane."

What we call our despair is often only
the painful eagerness of unfed hope.
-George Eliot

Jane sat patiently on the bench outside the depot. Her nerves had her wringing her hands around her gloves as she stared at the mountains in the distance. Somewhere up there she would finally find Cole again.

The journey to Fresno hadn't been easy, even though she'd slept for most of it. Stopping the laudanum suddenly after using it non-stop for two days had left her uneasy and unable to sleep deeply, or at all. Of course, much of that could have been the nerves from what they were doing.

Charlie had been annoyingly attentive to every ache and pain she had, but she couldn't be upset. Rather, she found herself infinitely grateful. She didn't know what she'd do if she lost the baby as well. Thankfully, even though her nerves were on edge, she hadn't had any further bad spells. Nick had been kind enough to use the trip to distract her with talk of her newfound fortune.

All the distraction in the world hadn't made the trip any easier. Now faced with a rough and bumpy wagon or stagecoach, she was even less enthusiastic about the last leg of their journey. Making it worse was not knowing what she'd find at the end of the difficult road.

What if the ghosts of Cole's past had proven too strong and he'd stayed for them?

"Jane." Charlie took the seat beside her. His hand settled on her twisting ones. "The next supply wagon doesn't go up for three days."

"Three days?" She turned to face him. "You can't mean it."

"We're securing a wagon and some horses for ourselves. I'm quite certain you can afford the added expense." His lip quirked at her glare. "What?"

"You aren't helping."

"I'm helping a little."

"Fine. You're helping a little. Will it be a smooth wagon?"

"No wagon on that road will be smooth. We'll secure some blankets to ease your aches."

"There are some aches no blanket will aide."

"I know." He pulled her close against him. "Rest for now. Nick will return with a wagon and some supplies for the last leg of our journey. It will pass quicker if you rest."

"Rest is a fool's dream."

"Well, then. Shall we read these letters your family sent on ahead?" He pulled a thick envelope from his jacket. "Ma had the children each send a letter the same day we departed so it would be here in Fresno for you when we arrived."

"Oh, that woman." Jane took the thick envelope, trying not to think of the last envelope she'd received that had been as thick. "I could kiss her and smack her. I don't know if it helps or hurts."

"Both. Open it. See what words your children send you. Perhaps prepare a letter to send back before we leave. We likely have an hour." He kissed her temple. "Sit with your children for a while and remember the strength they give you."

"Right now, they aren't the only ones giving me strength." She squeezed his hand. "Thank you."

"Still hate me, right?"

"With every fiber of my being."

"Good. I'd hate to think I swayed you with loving care."

"Never."

He left another kiss on her temple before he rose.

Jane opened the envelope and read through every letter. To her surprise even Jay and Willow had sent a letter together, likely written by Jay seeing as Willow still resisted learning her letters from Ada. The twins had made drawings in lieu of letters. Jesse and Sally were far more eloquent in their words, and of course both told her to hurry home.

By the time she finished going through them all, her heart swelled with warmth. As Charlie had suggested, she composed a letter that included messages for all the children. By the time she'd finished, a wagon rattled to a stop before her.

Charlie hopped out, slipping the letter she'd written from her fingers before disappearing into the depot to send it off. Nick climbed down, holding out his hand to her. "Let's get you settled in. We've made a sort of bed from some hay and blankets. It's the best we could do in an hour."

"I'm certain it will be fine. Thank you." She accepted his help into the wagon, settling into the makeshift bed. "I do hate being a lie-a-bed."

"You'll suffer it for that baby." Nick got into the front seat, leaning over it to face her. "Right?"

"Only for the baby."

"Of course." He picked up the reins as Charlie got in the front seat with him. "Are we ready to go find your husband, Jane?"

"Let's go."

*I know how men in
exile feed on dreams of hope.
-Aeschylus*

Cole hissed as he poured alcohol over the wound on his leg. The damn thing wouldn't heal, and he worried at this point it would be poisoned enough that he'd lose the limb. "My kingdom for a doctor."

The mutter carried through the empty store for absolutely no one to her. He let out a shaky breath, checking the wound again. He'd cleaned it thoroughly after the earthquake and stitched it up. Still, with the hell he'd been through the damn thing kept ripping open until it now sat infected.

He'd tried to send for medical supplies right after the earthquake, but like everything else he'd tried to send, somehow the message mysteriously didn't get where it was supposed to. He had his suspicions now that like the Poe story Jane liked so much, the inmates were running the asylum.

More specifically, his damn pa. Cole now had a good idea why his pa had stuck around Hell so long, and it had everything to do with the man's hold on the town. He imagined the only thing that had saved James and Ella so long had been Ella's pa, Richard. With his declining health, and subsequent death, it had all gone to hell.

Five times he'd bought a horse in the damned down, intent on riding down to Fresno in the dead of night when he wouldn't be seen. Before he could ever make a trip, the horse would be stolen back and his ass would be thrown in jail for horse theft. Thank the fact that Paul still wanted plenty out of him. It was the only thing that kept his neck out of the noose with those accusations.

Now Ella was missing. Had been for a week. James didn't give a damn, and Paul had the damned smug smile about him all the time. He hoped Jane had gotten his message and sent Tommy, or even brought her own ass to Holle Creek. If not, he'd climb down the mountain on foot, infected leg be damned.

No, he couldn't. If he left, Paul would kill Ella for sure. Cole may not love her anymore, not that she was Ella any longer, but he wouldn't let her suffer whatever fate Paul saw fit to deal her.

Cole wrapped his calf in a length of cotton he'd torn from some old petticoats and cleaned. He dropped the leg of his trousers back down over it and got to his feet. After testing the limb, he limped toward the door. Weak sunlight broke through the clouds, not enough to put any joy in him. "Where the devil are you, Jane?"

He limped down the steps, pondering his next move. Maybe he'd finally do what he'd been accused of five times and steal a horse during the night to ride down the mountain. He had enough skill he could make the trip quick enough, but never quick enough to be back by morning.

A flash of green amid the dank browns of the town caught his eye. In the shade of the porch in front of the telegraph office he could swear he saw a bright green dress. "Jane?"

Two steps forward, and a whistle drew his attention to the left. Paul sat on a horse, Ella in front of him. Without any regard to the woman's frail state, he pushed her off the horse.

"*Ella!*" Cole took several steps toward Paul, but a gun was leveled at his face. Thankfully Ella clamored to her feet. She tore toward him. He caught her, glaring at his father as he disappeared behind a building. He looked down at Ella. "Did he hurt ya?"

"Colton. Colton. Where's Lydia?"

"I told you. I'm not Colton. Let's get you inside and check you out." He guided her up the steps, but paused at the top. While Ella walked into the store calling for Lydia, he turned back toward town. The vision of green he could have sworn he'd seen was no longer there.

He must have imagined it. Wishful thinking. "Damn it, Jane. Where are you?"

"Colton."

"Stop calling me that." Cole went back into the store. Once again Ella was rifling through drawers. "Lydia is asleep, Ella. Sit down. Let me see if he hurt you."

"Colton."

"My name is Cole. I'm not your husband."

"But…"

"No, Ella. I've got a wife. She ain't you."

Her brows knit together and she stared at him long and hard. "Where's Colton?"

"Dead."

To Be

Continued...

In Book 10 of the
Dominion Falls Series

Dead Man's
Switch

About the Author

Sarah Cass, author of over twenty novels in 4 series, is devoted to giving her readers well-crafted, emotional stories, with depth to even her secondary characters—to give readers a full world to explore. Stories that explore not only the labyrinths of the heart, but the nightmares of the soul. A RONE finalist, she is also owner and creator of Redefining Perfect. By day, she's a nurse, a mother, wife and cat-mom to 4 mischievous beasts. By night she crafts stories that take her across centuries. From the old west of Dominion Falls, to the small town of Lake Point for the holidays, and even into the paranormal land of Shifters and Magic in The Tribe. She loves hearing from her readers. Visit her at www.authorsarahcass.com

Other Books in
The Dominion Falls Series

Independent Brake
Changing Tracks
Derailed
Dark Territory
Green Eye
Runaway Train
Home Signal
Red Zone
Dust Raiser
Chasing the Red

Coming Soon in
The Dominion Falls Series

Dead Man's Switch
Bird Cage
A Highball Arrangement
Douse the Glim
Blood
Grave Digger
Bad Order

Books by Sarah Cass
The Tribe Series
The Tribe
The Wolf
The Chief
The Raven
The Lake Point Series
Santa, Maybe
Deep-Fried Sweethearts
Stalled Independence
Witch Way
A Thorough Thanksgiving
Eve's New Year
Heartstrings & Hockey Pucks
Luck of the Cowgirl
Stars, Stripes & Motorbikes
Free Falling
Love for Hire
Haunted Hearts
Stand Alone Novels
Masked Hearts
Leap